Between THE Vines

GRACE ELENA

Edited by Kayla Morton from KMortonServices

Proofread by Jenni Brady from Edits with Jenni

Cover Design by Grace Elena

For a complete list of content warnings, please check out:

www.graceelenaauthor.com

❀ Created with Vellum

TENNESSEE ROOTS UNIVERSE

ALPINE RIDGE

MASON POINTE

NASHVILLE

ALPINE RIDGE

BOOK ONE

For P.
you might not be a cowboy, but you lassoed my heart just the same.

The wildest hearts are the prettiest.

PLAYLIST

Bluebird - Miranda Lambert
easier said - Kacey Musgraves
The Good Ones - Gabby Barrett
Everywhere I'm Goin' - Maddie & Tae
Thinking 'Bout You - Dustin Lynch
Us - Hannah Ellis
Still Fallin - Hunter Hayes
4 EVER 4 ME - Demi Lovato
Steady Heart - Kameron Marlowe
Tennessee Orange - Megan Moroney
Leave You Alone - Kane Brown
Sun to Me - Zach Bryan
Take It Slow (Acoustic) - Connor Smith & Ryan Hurd
LOVE IS A COWBOY - Kelsea Ballerini

CONTENT WARNINGS

Between the Vines is suitable for readers 18+.

Warnings include: explicit sexual scenes with praise kink, mention of war, mental health topics such as anxiety, ptsd, and body dysmorphia, mention of gun use for hunting, age gap by 11 years, drinking, cursing, and mention of divorce.

ONE

CAMILLA

IS this where the road turns? Or is it past the willow tree on my right?

My eyes scurry across the spattered windshield, full of small bugs and leaves from the long drive, until my eyes meet the end of the pavement where there's a sign.

A very tiny, faded green sign. It's a small arrow pointing left where the town is. The town I practically picked out by opening the map on my phone, closing my eyes, and zooming in on a random state.

Okay, to be honest I had the map pulled up for the southern part of the United States... I needed sun if I was going to move out of Chicago. I did not want to pick Wisconsin accidentally.

Alpine Ridge, Tennessee: 15.2 miles.

Alright, I guess I'm going left. I check my rearview mirror to make sure there aren't any cars racing down the abandoned road behind me and make the turn. Instantly, I am hit with a different road surface on my wheels. Gravel and dirt.

Great. I take a deep breath and press my foot on the gas and bring on the slow journey in my small, light-green Volkswagen beetle. Guess this is the start of my life in the country. I'll make the best of it.

My parents swore I would need to trade in my car for something more reliable for the southern town I chose, but I couldn't let her go. Eucy, short for Eucalyptus, was the first car I got when I was in college, and I would be damned to get another car if she was working just fine.

As the gravel and dirt meet the wheels of my Bug, I turn up the music in the car and roll down the windows even more. All that's in front of me are pastures, barn houses, and a few water towers here and there. I have a split second of doubt that the sign wasn't showing me towards town. Maybe a teen hit it with a bat and made it turn in a different direction.

I push down those thoughts, allowing myself to enjoy the view and music. I let my right hand rest on the wheel while my left hangs outside the window, running through the soft wind like waves.

The weather in Tennessee is nothing like Chicago. It's nearing the end of April and I still had a jacket on when I began my drive this morning. There is sunlight scorching through the windshield and I can already feel a tan forming on my hands that are facing the spots of sunlight streaming in the car.

I can't help but smile at the thought of summer being so close because of this weather. The lakes, boats, and even the small town festivities that would start happening. There's supposed to be an amazing cove nearby where a ton of boats, and people, go during the warmer months.

Or at least that's what I read online when I googled *What to do in Alpine Ridge, Tennessee.*

As the car shakes and the music blasts, I let my mind wander into the good things that are to come. Even if there are struggles, I can't wait to persevere through them and come out with learned lessons.

This is something that my best friend back home, Viola,

always admired about me. She says I see good days even if there is a constant storm. I won't let anyone push down my positive personality, even if they try their hardest. I'll be damned if I let them.

By the time the tenth country song comes blasting through the car's speakers, I'm nearing an end to the gravel road and finally see some buildings that I assume are the start of the small town of Alpine Ridge. I can already tell I will need to find some type of car wash to get all the gravel dust and dirt off my car.

As I let my eyes settle into what's in front of me, I hear birds chirping nearby and *no city noise.* I let myself enjoy this silence, settling back in my seat before I press my foot slowly on the gas and enter the town's lines. Everything is greener here, brighter and warmer.

I pull up to the nearest curb in the small street and survey my surroundings and see that there's a sweet shop, legal office, and a salon on one side. On the other side of the street where I parked, there's the realtor business that I have an appointment with to sign papers and pick up my keys.

Next to it is a cute little boutique with ivory French doors and a redheaded woman standing in front wearing a long, baby blue sundress. Her hair cascades down her shoulders and short bangs frame her face perfectly. I can't tell if she's a customer at the shop or the owner.

Getting out of my bug and making sure the windows are up and the doors are locked, I check the streets for any pay-to-park meters, but there are none. I keep a giggle from coming out as I mentally curse myself for thinking a small town would make locals pay for parking.

I place the car keys into my black tote and pull the straps over my shoulder. Checking the watch on my left wrist, I see I am a few minutes early. My sandals hit the sidewalk as I make my way towards the building with *Samson Realty* on the front. The reflection from the windows let me readjust my outfit from the long drive. I settled on some jade green overalls this morning and I don't regret it with the way the sun is beaming down on me. My mom wanted me to wear a hoodie and leggings.

As I grasp the metal handle of the door, I catch the eyes of the redhead who is peering at me with curiosity before giving me a smile and turning back to what she was doing. I attempt to smile, hoping she saw it, but I know seeing someone in town walking into the realty building is not a good sign.

I take a deep breath and pull the handle until the heavy glass door opens and I find myself in a bright lobby where there are a few white cushioned seats to the side and a glass table with a cheery receptionist. There's a marble counter to the right with a glass fridge fully stocked with refreshments and snacks, as well as business cards. I see that there's a cork board on the wall above the marble counter where there are other businesses displaying their cards and photos.

"Hello! How can I help you?" The receptionist's voice is angelic, and her brown eyes meet mine as I step forward and give her a big smile.

"I have an eleven a.m. appointment with Mr. Oliver Samson? I have some paperwork to do."

She nods before she turns her head towards a computer screen and begins typing. "Yes, you're buying out the Stone Vineyard, correct?"

I nod.

"He'll be right with you; he's finishing up a meeting with an investor."

"Okay, thank you so much."

"No problem, darlin'."

I turn on my heel and settle in the cushioned white seat and sigh, letting my body relax in the elegant chair. My car and suitcases were the only things I brought here. I would need to get furniture and more clothes for this weather.

I was told that the house came as is, so I am hoping there is at least a mattress I can put my clean sheets on. My mom wouldn't let me leave for my trip until I packed a whole suitcase full of cleaning products and clean bed sheets. She even took the time to teach me how to clean a mattress in case this one is in worse shape than I'm hoping. She used to work at a hotel when she just moved to the United States, so she was adamant that I knew what to do when I got here.

This thought alone brings a drop to my stomach, making me realize that I really am here in Tennessee. I dropped practically *everything*. I don't know how I'm going to survive living in an enormous house on fifty acres of land without my parents. We've never lived *without* each other.

"Ms. Morales?" I look up to see a well-groomed man in an all-black suit walking towards me.

I get up from the chair and close our distance, and shake hands. His dark brown hand envelopes my tan one. His grip is firm and professional.

"Thank you for meeting with me this early. I know we planned for a later time, but I was already on the road."

"Don't worry about it, ma'am. I assume you're tired from your traveling, so let's get this started."

His voice is deep and calming and his brown eyes are soft as he nods his head towards the door he just came out of. I smile at the receptionist, who gives me a small wave.

"So, I will tell you that this was a surprise when I got your email. Few people requested this place."

We're walking down a brightly lit hallway until he stops in front of a large white door and pushes the handle. The room is vast and there are posters all around the walls of land, homes, and the town. Some of them look like they were from before I was born. It makes me wonder if this is a family business and if these photos have been here for a while.

"Do people not want a vineyard?" I try to joke, but Mr. Samson turns towards me with a pained face. He motions me

5

with his hand towards one of the black leather chairs in front of a glass desk. He takes a seat next to me instead of at the desk.

"I want to let you know something. I couldn't tell you this over the phone—"

My mind instantly goes to the worst, and I let out a shaky breath. Of course, I drove all the way over here for plans to fall through. I knew it. No matter what I do to make things go right, something *would* jinx it.

"Hey, don't look so defeated," Mr. Samson cuts me off and his eyes glide over my face and I can't help but notice how he's even more handsome in person. He seems to be a little older than me. Before I can think more about his appearance, he continues, "The previous owner of the vineyard moved away abruptly."

"Okay," I respond.

"Andrew and Peyton Stone lived on that land for years. Andrew sadly grew deathly ill a few years ago and as much as they tried, he passed. They left everything as is when Peyton decided to sell the land and move with their daughter."

I nod slowly, and I can feel my chest tighten. I didn't think I'd be getting an ownership history lesson with a plate of heartache. There would be some tough shoes to fill.

Mr. Samson waves his hand and laughs as if he's trying to stop himself from getting emotional with the memory of these Stone people. "I'm not trying to get you to back out. I just want you to know what you're getting into. This town of Alpine Ridge is like a family. We stick up for each other and we loved the Stones. I just want you to settle in with that knowledge."

"They don't want me to tear down the vineyard and build apartments," I joke, and Mr. Samson chuckles.

"Exactly."

"I assure you, I just want to continue the tradition and find my place here. I worked at various wine stores towards the end of my college career and then worked at a vineyard up in Chicago for four years. They made me do some of the business side of things until I decided I needed a break from both the city and that place."

"Well, I hope Alpine Ridge treats you well. I can already tell we'll get along," Mr. Samson says with a big grin. He gets up from the leather chair and walks over to the glass table where there are a few papers. He gestures with his fingers for me to follow.

I get up and brush the overalls until they're no longer wrinkled and walk up towards the glass table. There's a sketch of the land on three pages. One of the vineyard, the blueprint of the house, and then a sketched map of the land. I widen my eyes and curse under my breath.

It's a lot of land and one of me. Fifty acres is bigger than I thought now that I have these visuals.

"Don't worry, I had that same face when I signed my land," Mr. Samson chuckles as he hands me a silver pen.

I look up at him and his eyes are observing me. I give him a small smile before leaning over and signing where he's pointing on the papers.

After we're done, he hands me the three papers of sketches before going towards the back wall where there is a safe. He punches in a few numbers and there's a green light. He opens it and rummages through it before he pulls out a keyring full of keys.

He walks back towards me and hands me the keyring. I widen my eyes again at the number of keys. There's at least five.

"Welcome to Alpine Ridge, Ms. Morales."

TWO

BENNETT

"QUIT IT!" I yell, waving my hands in front of me.

The rooster is standing on the henhouse, screeching at the top of its lungs. He woke me up at five a.m. and again two hours later once I fed the animals and attempted to hop back into bed.

He is going to make me go insane if he keeps up with this screeching every couple of hours. My jaw clenches at the thought of him howling into the middle of the night. My shotgun would definitely make him shut up.

I throw a few pieces of pebbled grains at him, causing him to screech at me again, his small head darting back and forth from the front of the pasture next to me. He doesn't even bother getting off the henhouse to eat the grains I threw. Pathetic.

Fuck this rooster, I think as I throw a few more pieces at him and turn my back, sighing. The sun is still beaming hard on the farm, the constant drench of sweat making me annoyed once more. My once light gray shirt is looking more dark gray the longer I stay outside.

It's almost May, so we have more rainy days than sunny in Alpine Ridge, but those sunny days can get up to seventy-five degrees. It might not seem very hot, but when you're not near any shade in the middle of nowhere, the sun has nowhere else to beam besides onto you.

With it almost being dinner time, I have a few more chores to get done. Feed the horses, make sure the chickens are in their coop, and check on the cats in the barn. I could spend hours in that barn playing with those cats, more than I'd like to admit.

Once those chores are completed, I rack my brain for what's left to do before the day is gone. I have to check on the plum trees that are finally blooming and make sure Lushie, the cow, has ointment on her ankle. A few weeks ago, a snapping turtle got a good nibble at her. I was in the pasture when it happened and luckily intervened.

The vet said she's been healing well, but I need to continue to lather some ointment on her wound.

Steve Robinson, my best friend since I can remember, is coming over after he's done at the shop. He should already be here, since it's past six, but he always tends to his Harley after hours. I mean, I don't blame him. He owns the shop and can do whatever the fuck he wants.

As I make my way out of the wired gate that's wrapped around the henhouse, I cast my eyes over the pasture and onto the main road. It's barely visible, but I can see a tiny car to the right of my land drive by. Its headlights are on even though sunset isn't here yet.

With the way it's heading, they're most likely headed out of town or towards the marina. There's nothing else past the left side of my property besides empty land that has yet to be sold. There's even more unsold land to my right—making me the only occupant on this road.

I like it that way.

I have no neighbors—well; I had the Stone family live down the road, but they left years ago. I haven't had time to check on their land in the last few weeks, but I'm sure Oliver or Steve have.

Us locals try to take our turn checking on their land in the event Peyton and their daughter Morgan ever want to come back. It's unlikely, but we still put in the effort for that possibility. I got used to being the only human being on Misty Creek Road. The Stone's land is about three times the size of mine.

I try not to think too much about him or his family. It was so sudden the way he got ill, but it was also a very long departure. We had our time to say goodbye, but we also didn't have time to really process what was happening to one of our local families. I still keep in touch with Peyton and Morgan, but it's hard when they don't visit anymore. I think it's hard for Peyton to come back to a place that holds so many memories of her husband.

The rooster screams again behind me and I blink a few times and try to recenter myself. I try to count to ten and then try to list five things I can see. It happens a lot—getting stuck in my thoughts and staying there for a while, unable to process real life and what's going on around me.

I continue walking down the torn up grassy path that leads from the hen area to the pasture.

This land wasn't something I picked out. My parents left it to me after they passed away, knowing my sister, Riley, wouldn't take it.

Riley left as fast as she could. Once she graduated high school, she picked the furthest college she could drive to and made roots in Washington. I haven't heard from her in months.

Sometimes it's better that way, with how we left things when she moved years ago.

I lift the muddy latch off the black pasture gate and push it open, letting out a grunt as the heavy gate attempts to sway back into place. The pasture is quiet. I usually let the horses out at night, but I like to keep them up in the barn in their stalls during dinner time. I don't need to stress myself out with them in the pasture with the cows. Although I tried not to keep the horses and cows in the same pasture, they seem to not mind. I used to have an electric fence dividing the pasture into two big ones, but I kept finding either a horse or a cow on the other side.

I'm not too sure how they could either jump the electric fence or get through it. It's still a mystery to me, but I took down the fence and nothing bad has happened.

"Lushie!" I call out. I make my way towards a wooden picnic table that's near the right side of the pasture gate where I keep a milk crate full of reins, bits, fly spray bottles, and medicine. Since the forecast said no rain this week, I've been keeping it out here for easier access.

I sigh and grab the white tube and turn towards the rest of the pasture and see an array of cows grazing or napping.

I have ten cows, but I plan to sell two to Steve soon. He finally gave in and bought some land recently instead of staying at those snobby Westland cookie-cutter homes. They're nice, but they're not built for Steve and his lifestyle. I could never see him in those homes, but he tried so hard to fit that mold after graduating college and opening his shop. Turns out he didn't like the marble counters and tiny yard—not to mention the crazy Homeowners Association rules in that small area.

He always asked me to move in right next door, but I'd rather get deployed again than buy a home there.

I'm content with my farm here.

"Lushie!" I call out again and one cow turns its head lazily towards my way and I raise my arm and wave the tube of ointment. She hates this time of day, but I see it as a good bonding moment for us.

"Come on, baby girl!" I shout as I walk faster. She's a bigger build than the other cows, which makes me think that's why she could get away with minor wounds from the snapping turtle.

I had a horse once get its whole shoulder bitten, and the wound was so deep that there was nothing we could really do. It kept getting infected even months after treatment. We had no other option than to put him down.

Within a few more yards, I'm finally closer to Lushie and she continues to graze as I come up to her. Her brown spots are bright and almost look orange. I lay my hand on her hide and she shivers from the touch.

"Hey, it's okay," I calmly tell her. I continue to rub my hand over her and allow her to get used to the feeling of being touched. I do the same thing with my horses when I have to check on them.

I lean down towards her back left leg, assessing the wound. It's looking nice and healing extraordinarily. My free hand brings the ointments closer to my other hand, my thumb pushing the cap open, a clear ooze coming out. I lean over more and steady myself as I smear the ointment on Lushie.

She doesn't move, unlike the first couple of weeks I had to do this. She would continue to whine and adjust her cloven-hooves until I had to yell at her and attempt to hold her in place.

Now, she continues to graze the grass as I smear more oint-ment over the pinkish wound. I can see some hair grow again and I smile.

"Good girl."

Lushie responds with a moo, and I grunt as I get myself back up into a standing position. I close the cap on the bottle and pat her back.

"You did good. Now you can continue to eat."

I glance around the pasture once more, making sure there's nothing conspicuous on the land. Last week, there was a snake that blended well with the grass. A horse stepped on it, thankfully.

"Alright, guys. I'm headed inside. Don't party too late," I joke, turning my back on the cows who continue to nap or graze.

I suddenly remember the plum trees and make my way out of the pasture and towards the back of my house. There's a strip of trees that I started growing once I got ownership of this land.

There are some lemons, oranges, plums, and then some blueberry shrubs.

As I get closer to the trees, they seem to be doing well. I try to keep them a few feet away from each other to not cross-pollinate. I had that issue years ago when I had two apple trees. They became a hybrid of each other. Although I expected extra sweetness, they were pretty bitter. The plum trees look promising and are sprouting small plum bulbs. It will take a week or two for them to reach full size.

I grab my phone from the back pocket of my jeans and see that Steve texted me a couple of minutes ago.

> **STEVE**
> On my way. I got news for you.

> I just finished with Lushie. I'll leave the door open.

> You're not even going to ask what the news is??

> If it's something that will help this rooster shut up, then I'm all ears.

I hit send on that last text just as the rooster screeches again and I clench my fists, almost breaking my phone.

"Fucking rooster."

I HEAR the engine of Steve's bike from a mile away and it becomes louder as he gets closer to the entrance of my property. The crunch of the gravel is loud and I can hear everything. I can pinpoint exactly where he is on the pathway towards my house. That's the downside of living in the middle of nowhere with no neighbors, I can hear every animal and any small sound if I'm not busy. At night, there are coyote screams that I've gotten used to.

It only becomes a real problem for me if I notice any of my chickens missing and I need to take watch overnight near the window that faces the chicken coup. My .22 long rifle is perfect for that job, scaring the coyotes and raccoons.

Sometimes, when I'm really bored and can't sleep from the noises, I'd rub some camouflage paint on my face and dress in all dark green and black attire and find a spot on the ground near the coup. Steve joined me once, but complained that he was too 'one with nature' and ended up ruining the shot I had at a raccoon that was entering the coup.

I was perfectly content there in my face paint and dark clothing. It reminded me of my years out in Colombia. The thrill and excitement of that time in my life was something I've always tried to chase again. It's hard when those years are supposed to be behind me. I'm just left with the nightmares and panic attacks, instead.

"Bennett!" Steve yells as his engine shuts off and I'm opening the screen door. He positions his bike on the kickstand and then jogs over. His white shirt is greasy, and his face still has some stains from the shop. His blonde hair flops in the front as he makes his way across the yard.

"Hey, man," I say as he gets closer and nudges me with his shoulder before pushing me inside. I roll my eyes and turn to pat him on the back as he makes himself at home—literally. He waltzes into the hallway, past the living room and guest room until he's in the kitchen. I trail quickly behind him. It's a small house, but it has what I need. The second floor has a few more rooms, as well as an attic for storage.

"I wasn't too sure what we wanted for dinner, so I was planning to get takeout," I respond.

Steve leans back on the kitchen counter. It's a pretty outdated kitchen that I've yet to renovate. It's next up on my list.

He crosses his arms and sighs. "It's okay, I got caught up cleaning my bike and talking with Oliver."

I nod my head and step towards the fridge, opening the heavy door and pulling out two beer bottles. I hand one to Steve as he nods, and we both pop off the bottle tops with ease.

"How's Harley? And how's Oliver?"

Steve shrugs. "She's good. Just needed a quick oil change. I've been using her too much–I'm changing her oil almost every month."

"Jesus, Steve. How far are you taking her?"

Steve chuckles before taking another sip of his beer. "Apparently too far. You know me, driving wherever the fuck the road goes. I have no destination and Harley knows it."

"And Oliver?" I remind him.

Steve looks at me and then smiles before answering. "Right. He called me around four and by the time we were about to hang up, he threw a curveball at me. He said someone bought out the Stone's land."

There's silence in the room and I grip the bottle tighter in my palm.

"You're kidding," I respond, attempting to calm myself before Steve asks what's wrong with me.

Steve shrugs again. "He won't give me any details. I told him he's just being a pussy and that he's not a doctor with some HIPAA shit to abide by."

I let out a laugh and shake my head. "I'm pretty sure he's still allowed to keep the privacy of new landowners. I wonder if it's some investor wanting to build million-dollar homes."

"I mean, you live near the marina. It wouldn't be such a bad idea."

"It would be horrible," I disagree.

"For you."

"Exactly."

Steve and I stare at each other before busting out in laughter.

"You're never gonna let someone live next to you, huh, buddy?"

15

"Not a chance, unless it was you," I respond, taking a big chug.

"Yeah, I kind of fucked up on that part. I wanted land near my shop. Sue me," Steve responds with another shrug.

I place the bottle on the counter near the fridge and then cross my arms. "Well, where do you want me to order takeout from?"

"I was actually going to suggest that we go out."

"Like a date?" I ask with a raise of my eyebrows.

Steve chuckles and then waves his hand. "I'm flattered, really, Bennett. But your anger issues would make me move to Timbuktu."

I laugh, and Steve does too. Really, we could be brothers with how often we get on each other's nerves yet can continue to be friends.

"Why not go to Nicky's?"

"That dingy old bar you hate?"

"Yes, that one." I roll my eyes and lean my head back in exasperation.

"Alright. But if you get into another bar fight, then I'm dragging you out."

"I can handle myself," I chuckle. Steve looks at me with one raised brow and then barks out a laugh, holding his chest with his right hand.

"Sure, sure. They have mouth watering fried pickle spears."

"And wings. And beer," I add, and Steve nods.

I follow him out near the entrance of my place and grab the keyring off the hook near the front door before locking the door from the inside. We head towards the side of the house where there's some pavement for me to park my vehicles.

Steve heads towards the truck that's on the left of the bike.

"Shotgun!" Steve yells as he opens the door and gets into the shotgun seat.

"You're hilarious, man," I say with a straight face before Steve lets out a howl.

"Alright, let's head to your favorite bar," Steve yells as he rolls down his window and leans his head out, ready for the wind to catch his hair like a dog.

I shake my head and push the key into the ignition and turn it; the truck rumbling to life.

THREE

CAMILLA

THE KEYS RATTLE against each other as I flip the keyring over and over in my hands. It's almost one in the afternoon and I've been sitting in my car on a road near what looks to be the school district.

To the right of me are chain linked fences that go about four feet high and surround the whole stretch of land where three buildings sit. There's an area that I can barely make out that seems to be where the football stadium and other fields for sports are. My guess is that's where schools are.

I barely moved my car, so I knew I had to leave soon before someone started questioning why I was changing my parking spot every hour.

To be honest, I'm nervous. Once I signed the papers and Mr. Samson gave me the keys, my stomach went into flips and I almost hyperventilated back in my car. I drove around the block and got lost on the roundabout roads until I found myself back near the street where I was originally.

The keys stayed clutched in my palm the whole time I was driving until I had to stop again to even my breathing. The indents from the metal are prominent in my palm.

I can do this. I am capable. I am willing to learn new things.

I repeat this mantra in my head three more times before starting the car up again. The engine roars to life and I take the map that Mr. Samson provided me with and begin my journey to the land I now own.

As the roads get less structured and the shops fade in the rearview mirror, I become more at ease. There are cute houses every few blocks and lots of green land. The pastures in this town are bountiful.

I finally find myself on a long stretch of road for about a mile. By the time I roll up to the one-way road, I can see a faint sign.

Misty Creek Road.

My eyes glance at the map where Mr. Samson circled in red the road that I'll be living on. Misty Creek Road.

I silently bless myself for coming here early enough in the day, so I didn't have to drive in this town at night time. I knew how dark the roads could get and there were no streetlights like I'm used to back home littering every twenty feet of road.

I turn right onto Misty Creek Road and keep a lookout for an entrance to my left. Mr. Samson mentioned that there will be two entrances; one closest to the intersecting roads for the vineyard where customers drive through and one further away before the next property line starts.

As I slow my car driving down the road, I see the first entrance and then speed up a little until I can see the next entrance. It's smaller than the first and it looks more private. There are two brick pillars that go about ten feet high and a metal gate in between the two. As I turn left and make it into the small patch of driveway right before the gate, I see a pin pad embedded into a pole that's on the ground.

This is fancy.

I roll down the window and grab the blueprints from the passenger seat and shift through the papers. Mr. Samson mentioned the gate code would still be in use and I could change it once I got settled.

1-9-1-7.

I read the code that's on the paper. I lean over the window and pitifully attempt to punch in the numbers. There's a faint buzz and then there's loud movement as the gate opens in front of me. I trail my car in after the gate completely opens and am met with a gravel road.

The road is long and windy, going up and down the terrain of the land, and I can see in the distance to my left is the vineyard. Along that same area, I can see a barn and another building. It could very well be the main office and where people pay for wine and their food. It looks like there are some benches and tables strewn about the land in front of the trees and buildings.

Looking back towards the road I'm on, I can finally see the outline of the main house. It looks to be about two stories tall, wider than anything I've ever lived in, and a wrap-around porch on the ground level and various balconies on the second floor.

It's gorgeous. White paneling surrounds the whole exterior of the home with black finishings and details. The porch sits higher than the pavement, with a few steps and a wind chime.

To the right of it is an enormous shed, but I'm not sure what might be in there.

Overall, this land is gorgeous, and it seems like the locals have been able to keep it looking more decent than I imagined when I first found the listing. The house still looks as good as new.

A few yards away from the home, I park my car and turn off the engine. I gather the papers and keys from the passenger side and stuff them in the tote. I clutch the keyring in my middle finger and push the car door open.

Suddenly, I'm filled with *silence*. I take a deep breath and close my eyes briefly before I slam the door closed and make my way up the gravelly pavement towards the steps of the house.

There's a faint rooster in the distance screeching, but I smile. It's nice to not have sirens and emergency vehicles blaring down the street constantly. I'd gotten used to the noises, but they were still there.

Now, I'm able to hear my own thoughts and even hear animals.

I walk up the creaky steps of the house and see a few rocker chairs to the right and a bench swing to the left. There was a lot of house and a little me. It would take me all day to tour this home.

I lift the key ring and find the key that is painted red. Apparently, this is the main house key. I unlock and push the heavy door until I'm a foot inside the entryway.

Woah.

The inside is even more beautiful than I imagined. It reminds me of those up-and-coming barn homes that were being built in the suburbs of Chicago.

I walk around the foyer and make myself familiar with the rooms in the house's front—the study, and the sitting room. To the right is a staircase and as I keep walking, there are a few more rooms that have their doors shut. Once I'm past those, the kitchen comes into view and it's spread out miraculously. All the appliances are stainless steel and the counters are marble. There's an island as big as my kitchen back home.

My frozen chicken Alfredo meals do *not* need this big of a kitchen.

I continue walking, finding myself in a day room and a living room, as well as a back den with French doors. It's just as big as the area I was in, but it's screened. There's decadent furniture in here and a TV and a minibar with its own fridge, island, and bar stools.

I step out into it and can see the vineyard a ways away from the screen and see some birds flying around the sky.

Thud.

I turn around towards the French doors and tune my ears into the noise I just heard.

I tip toe, not wanting to make myself known as I get back inside the house and find the nearest weapon.

I chew on my lip as my hands enclose over a metal whisk that was sitting on top of the kitchen island and patiently wait to hear more sounds.

Scratch. Scratch.

I crane my neck, wondering if it's just a squirrel on the roof or if there really is an intruder and they're pretending to be an animal. I lift the whisk towards my chest to protect myself and get closer to the noise.

It continues, getting louder as I near the back of the house where there's one last room I didn't see. The door is closed, and I can see a faint shadow on the floor, indicating *someone...* or *something* is in there.

I continue to tip toe until I'm a few feet away from the door. The scratching stops and I wait for the door to swing open and someone to come out and attack me. But it doesn't happen.

My palms sweat over the whisk and my heart is racing.

I wait a few more seconds and then I finally hear a sound.

A meow.

I sigh and shake my head, laying the whisk down at my side. I grab the handle and push it softly until I see that it's a guest room with no one in it besides an orange cat.

It moves along the door frame as I push the door farther to get a better view.

"Well, hello there. I didn't know this place came with a tour guide," I joke, letting the cat out of the room and watching as it meows again and looks up at me.

"You're a pretty kitty. What's your name?"

I bend down and balance on the balls of my feet as I attempt to see if there's a collar around the cat. There isn't, but the cat comes closer and purrs, pushing its body against my knees and allowing me to pet it.

"You're a silly goose, you know that? Scaring me and thinking you're an intruder."

The cat meows again and jumps on its hind legs to get closer to my face.

"Silly goose... you like that name?"

The cat doesn't make noise at all; its green eyes continue to look at me while its small front paws sit on my knees.

"Silly isn't a good name, is it? What about Goose?"

The cat leans their face closer to mine and makes more noise, and I can feel the vibration of their purr against my knees.

"Goose, it is," I say, caressing the cat's long torso and letting them sniff me before jumping off my knees and walking back to where I originally was.

I've never owned a cat before, but I always liked the idea of it. My parents have two German shepherd/husky mixes and that's all the animal experience I've got. I look around its body to see what gender it might be. It's a girl and I make a mental note to bring her to the vet this week to see if she's up to date on all vaccinations and if she's microchipped. I don't want to steal someone's cat accidentally.

"Are you taking me on the tour now?" I speak up as I follow Goose.

My steps pad against the hardwood floor as I follow Goose around the house and up the stairs, finishing my personal tour of the place I now call home.

IT'S ALMOST six when I finish unloading the suitcases in my car and bring them into the master suite upstairs. I attempted to unpack them, but there were just too many clothes and not enough hands to put them away. There's a beautiful walk-in closet in the master suite, so I just stuffed the suitcases in there for now.

After I followed the cat throughout the house and made sure every room was accounted for, I walked to the shed next to the house and checked inside.

It was dusty, but it was full of machines that seemed necessary for farm living. A big lawn mower sat in the back–the kind where you *sit* on it—and a wrap-around work bench where some tools were laid out that I had never seen before in my life.

The walls are lined with other types of machines, like a leaf blower, grass cutter, machete, chainsaw, and anything else a barn might need.

I would definitely see if there was anyone I could hire to use those machines until I got the hang of it on my own. I didn't want this land to deteriorate a month in of living here.

I'm back at home gathering my tote bag full of my belongings. I wanted to venture out to town to see if I might get some food and anything else before things close for the night.

I say bye to Goose and lock the doors before heading down the steps and back into my car. The sun is still glowing, but I can tell in an hour or two it will fade down.

Once I'm down by the gate, I decide to take the other way quickly to see what else is on Misty Creek Road. My car revs its engine as I change pavements from my driveway to the road. I make sure my headlights are on even with the sun out, just in case.

There's a plot of land right next to my property, but it's vacant and across the road there's just farmland after farmland that I don't even bother looking at.

As I get closer to the end of the property line of my neighbor, I see more land, but this time it's different. There's a few cows out on the pasture and I can see a faint outline of a house up the way.

I wonder who lives there.

I continue driving down the road and make a sharp left before having to make another sharp right. There's a marina to the right and I see some people leaving a restaurant while others are carrying water equipment to their cars after having a day out in the lake.

I'll have to check that out later. I find a place to turn my car as I see a sign stating if I go any further, I'm leaving Alpine Ridge.

I retrace the steps I took from my house and continue back into town. After a few minutes of driving, I find myself back on the same road where I first started. The one with the salon, sweets shop, and legal office. There are a few people walking the streets and I park my car and get out.

I don't see any kind of restaurant on this block, so I head into the sweets store that has a huge banner on its awning, *Bee's Brittle and Sweets*. The doorbell rings as I push the glass door and am greeted with the sweet smell of chocolate, peanuts, apples, and caramel.

"Welcome to Bee's!" A voice greets me.

The shop isn't too big, but it has glass cases of desserts everywhere. The walls are a vibrant white with orange detailing and a big sign in white neon letters on the right side wall displaying the shop's name. There's faint music playing in the background and there's a work table to the left behind some of the glass cases where I can see parchment paper full of caramel drippings.

I look up at the voice and am met with a girl who looks to be my age and is wearing a bright white apron over a plain black shirt. Her strawberry blonde hair is short, just past her jaw, and some strands are pulled back into a clip.

"Hi, thank you," I respond as I walk around. I'm the only customer in here and I take my time looking through the cases until I'm near the one where the worker is standing.

"Can I help you find anything specific? I haven't seen you

around before." Her bright green eyes find mine. Her cheeks are slightly rosy and she has fair skin that compliments her eyes and facial structure perfectly.

"I just moved here! I was just looking around. I'm not really too sure what I want," I chuckle, looking around the store nervously and then finding myself looking back at the worker.

"Welcome to Alpine Ridge! It's nice to hear someone's moved here. We're more popular online and just keep this shop running for the locals."

"It's really nice here and it smells amazing."

"That would be the brand new batch of peanut brittle I made an hour ago. Do you want a sample?"

She moves from behind the case and walks to the back of the shop where there's two big metal doors. She disappears behind them for a minute before returning with a tray of parchment paper and broken pieces of brittle on top.

She finds her way out of the back of the shop and comes closer to where I am. She leans over and pushes the tray toward me. I pick up a piece of brittle and nibble on it.

"Oh! That's sweet, but so good."

She smiles before taking a piece for herself and chewing on it. "It's my grandparents' recipe. It's definitely sweeter than what we usually sell here, but it's a favorite."

I nod and finish the rest of the piece. "I'll probably take a box of that."

She beams and walks towards a glass case where there's the main inventory of peanut brittle. She gets behind it and slides the glass door before putting on gloves and taking a few pieces and wrapping them in parchment paper before putting them in a cute black box with a white bow on top.

"My name's Bernadette, by the way. Bernadette Lowry, but locals call me Birdy and if we're real close, I'll let ya call me Bee," she says as she walks towards the register with the box.

I follow and get my wallet out of my tote. "Camilla Morales."

As Birdy punches the brittle price into the register, I hand her my card.

Once the transaction is done and my wallet is back in the tote, she leans her elbows over the register counter and wiggles her eyebrows. "So, whose property did you buy up?"

I smile and shrug my shoulders. "It used to be owned by the Stone family?"

Her smile fades, but she quickly returns it in an instant. "Wow, so they finally sold it."

"Yeah, I heard they were a big thing in this town. I hope I can keep their place looking just as great as when they lived there."

Birdy can see my hesitancy and gives me a smile before swatting her hand and laughing. "People will jump so quickly to think that the Stone's land can't be bought. It seems like Peyton made that decision and was okay with you being the new owner."

"I guess she is."

"Well, welcome again to the *best* small town on this side of Tennessee. We've got great people here, our high school football team has won state... twice in their lifetime," Birdy laughs and I laugh along with her.

High school football seems like such a minuscule thing to care about coming from such a big city with hundreds of high schools and a professional football team. But I guess in smaller towns, these sports are all they've got for live entertainment.

"Oh, and we've got a great marina that you'll get to enjoy this summer." She looks at me for a moment before continuing. "What are you doing after this?"

"I was going to find somewhere to get dinner and go back to my place and see if I can unpack some."

Birdy shakes her head and claps her hands. "You're coming out with me." She sees my skeptical face and laughs. "I can try to introduce you to some of the town folk! We're all really nice, promise. Alpine Ridge is like a huge family."

"I don't want to impose, but that would be helpful. I don't even know where a gas station is around here. Mr. Samson from Samson Realty gave me a map, but it's just street names."

"Typical Oliver," Birdy chuckles before handing me the box of brittle that I chuck into my tote. She checks around the store and moves her hands behind her apron, untying it.

"Just give me a few minutes to close shop. I was already done with cleaning before you walked in, so I'll be quick."

I nod and tell her I'll put the brittle in my car and wait for her outside.

After a few minutes, I hear the door opening and I see Birdy is out of her uniform. She's now in a thin brown long sleeve, black denim skirt, and chunky black boots.

"We can walk there. It's not too far from here."

I nod and follow Birdy as she makes her way down the block past a salon and then we round the corner. We walk for another block; her asking me about where I'm from and vice versa.

Birdy has lived here her whole life and took over her grandparents' shop after they passed. Her parents have their own legal firm on the other side of the downtown area. The legal office on the street near her sweets shop is apparently up for lease.

Birdy says she moved out from her parents' land and bought her own land close to the marina, a street over from Misty Creek Road. When I asked her why she didn't decide to work with her parents in the legal department, she just shrugged and moved on to the next question.

By the time we're almost done with the basic backstories of ourselves, Birdy points at a lit up sign a few yards away from us.

The sun is setting, and everything here looks so beautiful with the sunset glow.

Nicky's Bar and Grille.

"They have the best wings and pickles. And beer," Birdy claims as she continues walking, pulling me by the arm.

I follow aimlessly behind her and let her open the door before we're met with a cloud of smoke. I briefly cough and then get in.

The dive bar is dark and smokey. There are sounds of people talking, pool balls being hit, and two workers cleaning tables from leaving customers.

"It's small, but it's great. Trust me," Birdy says and I nod, continuing to let her guide me in.

The bar is longer than it is wide, with some booths on the walls and tons of tables in the middle. On the far end is a pool table and a jukebox machine. The walls are black and full of pictures. It feels very homey.

"We'll get a booth over there," Birdy says, pointing near the pool table.

I nod and follow Birdy, taking a seat across from her and set my tote bag down next to me. Birdy looks around the bar, smiling, and then averts her eyes to me. "What do you like to drink?"

I look around the place and see a server walk towards our booth with two menus.

"I'm down for a seltzer," I tell Birdy and she nods.

"Welcome to Nicky's. Hey Birdy," The worker says as she places the menus down on the table and eyes me up and down. She's wearing a tight black tank top and high-waisted black jean shorts, the outfit accentuating her curves. Her skin is sparkling like she put some highlighter powder on her collarbones and shoulders. Her face is beautiful, cheeks rounded. Her blonde hair is wavy and flows down her shoulders.

"Izzy, this is Camilla," Birdy says, taking the menus and passing me one. I give her a smile before turning to the girl eyeing me.

"Hi, nice to meet you. I just moved here."

"Oh!" Izzy smiles, her eyes moving from me to Birdy. "How did you find this town? It's not that famous."

"It's not, really," Birdy agrees.

I shrug. "I kind of closed my eyes and picked a spot. It ended up being here."

"Wow, that is something. Where are you living?"

"Izzy! It's too soon to ask her for her address!" Birdy yells, covering her mouth as she laughs.

I shake my head. "It's okay. Apparently, everyone knows everyone here. I just moved into the Stone's property."

Izzy widens her eyes and smiles. "Nice. Are you—"

"How about you let us order first and then you can sit down and chat with us? I'm sure our newcomer is starving," Birdy interrupts with a smile.

Izzy nudges Birdy on the shoulder before rolling her eyes and smiling. "Fine, fine. What can I get you both?"

"I'll have buffalo wings with fries and those fried pickle spears," Birdy says. "Oh, and a Miller Lite. Cold."

Izzy nods before turning to me, not bothering to write anything on the notepad she brought with her.

I briefly glance at the menu and then look at Izzy. "I'll take lemon pepper wings and fries with some fried pickle spears as well. And a blueberry spiked seltzer."

Izzy nods before tapping the table and then turning on her heel.

"She seems fun," I say to Birdy.

Birdy nods and laughs. "Yeah, she can seem very closed off at first, but she's great. She's been working here for a few years. She used to work with her sister at the ballet studio nearby while it was just starting out."

"It seems like everyone has a business here," I remark.

"Well, when you live here long enough, there's really nothing else to do."

I nod and see Izzy come over with our drinks.

"Alright, Miller Lite for Bee over here and blueberry seltzer for..."

"Camilla," I remind her. She purses her lips before nodding her head.

"I swear I'm better at names. I'll remember you, Camilla. I'll be back once your food is done and then we can all chat!" She gives us both a wave before heading back to the bar.

"I think I like it here already," I tell Birdy as we take the first few sips of our drinks.

There's commotion behind us at the pool table and two men are clinking their glasses of beer with each other before settling down again. I peer over and see there's a tall blonde facing me. He's handsome, and he smiles at whatever is being said near him.

The other man across from him, I can't make out. His back is to me, but even from this angle his shoulders are broad. His long, dark brunette hair touches halfway down his neck. The muscles in his arms flex as he leans over the pool table. There are some faint tattoos on his forearm that I can't quite make out. I lick my lips and hear a noise near me.

I look at Birdy who's smiling widely before I see her lean over her side of the booth to see what I'm staring at.

"Ah, you've spotted the golden boys of our town."

"The what?"

Birdy looks back at me and then settles back in her seat. I move my eyes from her to the pool table as I wait for her explanation.

"The golden boys. Steve and Bennett. They've been here all their lives, and everyone *loves* them."

"Oh, I'm assuming you know them well then," I answer, pulling the seltzer can to my lips and taking a sip.

"Yeah, Steve, for sure. Bennett? It's been a few years. People change, we grow up, ya da ya da."

I want to ask her more, but Izzy comes back with our food.

Without warning, she plops down next to me, causing me to move closer to the wall and no longer able to see the men at the pool table.

Izzy takes a fry from the basket in front of me and pops it in her mouth before turning to me.

"Camilla, where did you move from?"

I look at her and then back at Birdy, who is busy eating her fries. "Chicago, the city. Born and raised."

Izzy nods her head before averting her eyes back to the fry basket and taking another to eat.

"Izzy Pearson, you're supposed to be working!" A voice drifts towards our table and we all look up. Izzy has her half-eaten fry hanging from her mouth before she scowls and chews the rest of it.

A redheaded woman walks up to our table and leans over, slamming her palms on the table, causing our drinks to slosh around the rims of the cans. She's wearing a plain gray long sleeve and her red hair is in a messy braid. She's not the same redhead I saw earlier in front of the boutique.

Birdy stifles back a laugh and continues to eat her fries like nothing is wrong.

The redhead looks at me with scrunched brows and then at Izzy. Her lips turn to a frown and Izzy shrugs, attempting to get another fry from the basket before the redhead swats her hand.

"Hey! I was going to eat that!" Izzy yells before barking out a laugh.

The redhead shakes her head while smiling and then looks at me again. "Who's this?"

"Camilla," Izzy says, leaning her head on my left shoulder before picking it up again. "She bought Andy and Peyton's place. She's going to make everyone mad and hate her."

"Izzy!" Birdy yells, a look of concern plastered on her face. But I just laugh and see that Izzy is smiling through it all. She's harmless.

"I'm Camilla. And I bought the Stone's land." I reach my hand over Izzy's body and attempt to shake the redhead's hand. She hesitates for a moment before closing her palm in mine. "Katherine Pearson. Izzy's older sister."

"Oh, really?" I look between the siblings.

"Unfortunately. She is very hard to deal with," Izzy jokes, before taking more fries and shoving them in her mouth. I unravel the fork in the napkin roll and stab some fries, eating them slowly.

"Oh shut up, you're the most annoying person I've ever had to deal with. And I've dealt with a lot," Katherine fires back.

I try to hold back a laugh, but it comes out and they all join me.

"Well, I just came to pick up some food before I finish my last class tonight," Katherine says, before pointing to Izzy. "Behave yourself."

"Yeah, yeah. I only stop bar fights I know I can win. And I win every single one," Izzy barters back, waving her sister along. I wave too and watch her head back towards the front of the bar.

"She owns the ballet studio and hosts tons of classes and private sessions," Birdy explains, biting into one wing. I bite into some of mine and they're *good.*

"That's amazing. You guys seem to really have it going here. I like this town already." I tell them both. Izzy dances in her seat before leaning over and bumping my shoulder.

"We just met, but I like you already, Camilla. Birdy, you need to bring her over more. No excuses."

Birdy nods and Izzy takes one last fry before she stands and gets back to work.

"Wow, she is a lot but she's so... cool," I tell Birdy.

"Yeah, they're the best. I'm closer with Izzy, for sure."

"Really?"

Birdy nods but before I can ask her to explain, I hear more hollering from the men in the back and Birdy leans over, yelling at them. I sink back in my chair, not wanting everyone in the bar to look at us while she yells.

"Steve! Bennett! Hush it!"

There's laughter around the bar from other patrons and workers as they hear her. Then, there's the shuffling of boots and before I know it, the two golden boys are nearing our table. I gulp and frantically take the napkin to wipe my mouth of any lemon pepper seasoning.

"Is that Bee? What on earth?" A deep, but loud voice comes out of the blonde's mouth as they near our table.

I'm finally able to look up and see the brunette that's next to him, who's focusing more on his empty beer glass than the table. His hair falls over his eyes as he's leaning and he has a faint shadow of a beard growing. I can see the tattoos on his forearms more clearly and they're so many that they make up a sleeve on one arm and a few scattered ones on his other. There's a familiar one I see on his bicep as he lifts his arm to scratch the back of his head.

Semper fi. I've read it once. It's very well known in the military, marine specifically.

"Yeah, it's me, Stevie. Just here trying to enjoy my dinner and not be bombarded by your incessant yelling at the pool table."

Steve shakes his head before patting Birdy's head softly with his big hand. She scowls and rolls her eyes, but I let out a small laugh.

"And who do we have here? You're new," Steve says as he looks at me with a quizzical look.

The guy next to him, who I presume is Bennett, finally looks up after hearing Steve and then locks eyes with me. His blue eyes are the prettiest I've seen. He seems tired, but his eyes look like they have a million stories behind them. I can't help but be curious and stare at him. He shifts in his stance and licks his lips before turning his head towards Birdy.

"This is Camilla. She just moved here. *Be nice.* I'm talking to you, Bennett."

Bennett shakes his head and runs his tattooed hand through his long hair. "Birdy, when am I not nice?"

"Uh, every day?" Steve chimes in and Birdy laughs. I just look at the three of them and give them a chirpy smile, hoping it won't get too heated. I don't like arguments and I hate seeing people fight. Both verbally and physically.

"Fuck you," Bennett spits at Steve and rolls his eyes. I can see his chest moving quickly as he takes deeper breaths.

"You guys can go back to your game of pool. Birdy was just kidding when she yelled at you guys." I try to say, waving my hands innocently.

Bennett stares at me for a second before huffing and looking at Steve. Steve says nothing. He's too busy staring at Birdy as if they're communicating something with their eyes.

"She's from the city, so this small town needs to welcome her," Birdy finally adds, turning back to the conversation. Steve smiles and leans over the tall booth.

"You lucked out finding Birdy. She's probably the best person to be friends with here, especially on your first day."

"Aw, thanks Steve. That's like the first nice thing you've said to me in *years*," Birdy says, taking a huge gulp of her drink.

Bennett huffs again, and I catch his eyes. I pinch my brows and offer him another smile, but he doesn't budge.

"Ben, stop scaring her," Steve finally says.

Bennett shrugs his broad shoulders before chewing on his lip and then running his hands through his hair again.

"I'm going to get another beer. Have fun with Birdy and *bunny* over here."

"Bunny?" I ask, not sure where the quick nickname came from.

Birdy pulls her lips together to keep from laughing and I feel more confused than ever.

Bennett is almost turning on his heels before responding. "You just remind me of the bunnies that pass my farm. Too naïve for their own good. Before they know it, they get snatched up by a hawk... or worse."

My jaw drops at the insult and I can feel the heat rise in my cheeks.

"Bunnies are cute though," Birdy states defensively. Steve nods in agreement.

Bennett registers her comment, looks at me and almost says something, but then shakes his head and huffs again before turning on his heels.

I look at Steve and Birdy for some reassurance, but they both look at each other and shrug.

"Did I say they're the two golden boys? I meant just one," Birdy laughs, pointing at Steve who smiles proudly.

You're not wrong about that, Birdy.

FOUR

BENNETT

BUNNY.

That's the first thought that comes to mind when I wake up the next morning. The rising sun is casting a glow through the sheer curtains in the bedroom as I shift in the bed. The bedsheets are still fluffy and smelling fresh after I came home and washed them.

I couldn't get to sleep after Nicky's. It's not unusual for me, but I just couldn't *stay* asleep even after I tried all my methods. Counting backwards from 100, saying the alphabet backwards, trying to dream of that rooster and killing it... that one almost worked, and then my mind drifted off to the girl from the bar.

Birdy said her name is Camilla. Her dark, brunette hair laid in pretty curls and her bright, brown eyes...

I shake my head and try to wake up and stop thinking about this stranger. Even doing the laundry, cleaning the kitchen, and attempting to fix the leaky sink, I couldn't get her out of my fucking mind.

What the fuck? I barely met her. It wouldn't surprise me if Steve stayed after I left the bar to talk with her and get to know her along with Birdy. I'll just have to swing by his shop later today and try to pry some info from him, but casually, of course.

Steve and Birdy are probably the most talkative bunch I've ever had the audacity to meet. I love Steve, but Birdy knows how to poke my buttons in a way that no one else can.

She used to be my best friend back in grade school and throughout high school. But then I fucked things up and ruined it all. At least she had Steve to be friends with. I don't blame her if she still hates me. I still hate myself too.

Seems to be a recurring theme lately.

I sit up and stretch my arms above my head and look around the brightened room from the sun and groan. The one thing I hate about Tennessee when it gets close to summer is the endless sun.

I contemplated moving to Washington or even Alaska where they have that six-month period of darkness; just to get away from this sunny place.

I lift the sheets off my naked torso and step onto the creaking floorboards. My eyes glance towards the clock and it's almost six a.m. I close my eyes and take in the *silence*.

But that doesn't last long. The walls are too thin in this old house that I immediately hear the rooster begin its early rounds. The screech is ear piercing and I press my lips tightly and shake my head, my hair flinging everywhere.

I head out of the bedroom in just my boxers and make my way down the hallway towards the side door. I whip it open and lean out, making sure I'm in the line of sight of the rooster.

"Hey! Fucker! Shut it!"

The rooster doesn't hear me and continues its round of screeching. I huff, stepping down the few steps that lead to the grass and walk around the side of the house until I'm near the fruit trees. I wrap my hand round a plum and pluck it out of the stem before closing one eye, taking aim, and throwing the plum towards the rooster.

My aim is perfect, and it hits his feet. I don't want him to *actually* get hurt. But I need him to quit screeching this early. Whoever bought the Stone's land will probably begin complaining about the noises and I don't need that right now.

The rooster jumps off the henhouse and begins picking at the plum that fell on the ground after its impact.

I head back inside the house to begin the morning chores. I've been up for five minutes and I'm already annoyed. Great. I head towards the kitchen and find myself in front of the fridge, where there's a whiteboard. I've kept up with my own joke of how many times I'd get annoyed and if there'd ever be a day I woke up on the right side of the bed. Steve insisted I started keeping track.

So, I made a whiteboard tally.

_ days without waking up on the wrong side.

It's blank, of course.

I open the fridge door and grab a water bottle before heading back to the bedroom to get ready for the day.

In the mornings, I rarely shower until I am done with the morning chores. I have to feed the horses and let them roam the pasture, feed the cows and check Lushie's wound, grab any eggs from the chicken coop, and check the fencing around the farm to see if there are any signs of critters sneaking in. There's just no point in showering if I'm going to be out in the beaming sun all morning and get sweaty.

I swear if that god damn raccoon came back last night, I'll actually shoot it. I won't invite Steve like I did last time.

I CHECK my phone and read Steve's text around eleven thirty a.m. after stepping out of the shower.

STEVE

Come to the shop for lunch.

I lay the phone down on the bathroom counter and grab a towel, wrapping it around my waist.

I wipe my hand over the steamed up glass in front of me so I can see myself. My eyes glance towards my chest and torso. It feels like I'm living in someone else's body. Years of war, contract missions gone wrong, and wounds that received shitty medical attention.

Those years are behind me, but I am still in this body where it all happened. It feels like another life I lived whenever I stare at myself in the mirror. I don't like it and it's been like this for a few years now. It just feels weird to be in this body when I no longer feel like I belong in it anymore.

My eyes find the tattoos and scars on my chest. A large, healed gash right under my collarbone, from my left pec up to the center of my chest. That one is always a fun one to tell people about.

So, what did I start doing? Lying. I tell people I was in a freak boat accident.

I can't tell someone I just met that I had a machete knife to my throat for noncompliance in a contract mission that went wrong. They would probably think I'm crazy or feel sorry for me.

The fucker that did that died with that same machete knife. I don't take hostage situations lightly and had to take matters into my own hands. This nasty scar just reminds me of the many lives I saved during that time. It's behind me, but looking at the scar takes me back momentarily.

The other scars littering my chest and torso are just regular old battle wounds from bullets, knives, and shrapnel. I think all the shrapnel has surfaced over the last ten years, so I should be metal free.

I close my eyes for a brief second and take a big, deep breath before exhaling loudly. I grab the phone and text Steve.

> I'll be there soon.

My fingers run through my wet hair and I dry my body off before pulling on boxers and jeans. Before I pull on a navy shirt, I turn my torso to check my back. There's some rash that's formed overnight that I started scratching at this morning. I grab some cream from a nearby drawer and begin applying it to the skin. I'm still unsure how I got it, but I want to make sure it can heal. The placement of it is right where I have a few doves and stars tattooed. Another tattoo that's placed at the top right shoulder blade flashes back at me in the mirror as I try to cover the whole rash.

Fortis Fortuna Adiuvat.

That one I got when I finally left the war life behind. It was the only closure I could get once I returned to Alpine Ridge.

Once I'm done rubbing the cream on the rash, I pull the navy shirt on and make my way throughout the house to gather my wallet and keys. As I get outside and get in my truck, I roll the windows down. If I'm going to have a better day, I might as well start now. It's never too late.

I make my way out of the property and onto Misty Creek Road. As I adjust the radio to a preferred station, I let my hand lay outside the window. The breeze has arrived just in time as the sun beams hard on the town.

As I get closer towards the end of the road, I see someone. It looks like they're walking closer to the property line of the Stone's.

I slow down the truck until I'm closer. The woman is facing away from me, but her brunette curls fall past her shoulders. She doesn't seem to notice me as I slow the truck even more and get closer.

We're side by side now and she's still not noticing the car, so I honk. She finally looks to her left and I curse myself.

It's the girl from the bar last night.

"Oh! Hey! Sorry, am I on the road? There really wasn't any sidewalk around this area." Her voice is chirpy and I stop myself from rolling my eyes.

"Are you breaking into the Stone's home, Bunny?" The nickname rolls off my tongue faster than I intended.

Her brown eyes catch mine and I put the truck to a full stop. I'm the only one who lives down here, so there's zero chance any car would come up behind me.

She shakes her head, her curls falling around her face. She lifts her hand and moves her hair behind her ear. I hold back a smile and clear my throat.

"I-I actually live here."

I huff out a big breath, and she widens her eyes. She gets closer to the passenger door of my truck and I almost want to drive off. She leans her arms over the window ledge and gives me a big smile.

"No, you don't," I counter.

"Yeah, I thought Steve told you? He said you lived on this road too."

"Unfortunately," I grit my teeth. She doesn't seem to see how badly I want to leave this conversation. She gives me another smile and I chew on the inside of my cheek to not say anything snarky.

"I guess we're sorta neighbors. I'll see you around?"

I nod my head slowly before moving my hand out of the window and putting my fingers to the window buttons, rolling them an inch where Camilla's arms are.

"Oh! Sorry!" She exclaims, her cheeks getting red as she lifts her arms and steps back.

I give her one last nod before waiting until she gets far enough from the truck tires. I press my foot to the pedal and kick up dust as I drive away. My eyes glance towards the rearview mirror and I see her wave her hands in front of her to bypass the dust.

I smirk and shake my head before continuing down the road and taking a left. A few more streets and I'm near Steve's shop. *Robinson's Auto.* It's been in his family for decades.

"Bennett, get your ass in here!" Steve calls as he steps out of his shop and watches me park my truck haphazardly.

I don't bother rolling up the windows and get out of the truck. I even leave the keys in there. If someone steals my truck in this small town, then I'll most likely know who they are. And if they're a resident in this town, they know who exactly drives that truck and wouldn't dare to even scratch it without consequences.

"Where's the food?" I joke, walking up to him and giving him a side hug.

He's wearing another white shirt full of new grease stains and pulls a handkerchief out of his pants pocket and wipes his greasy fingers. I'm positive he's got a closet full of brand-new white shirts to wear to work.

Steve nods his head towards the shop. The garage doors are open, and some workers are there under the hood of cars and under suspended cars.

Sometimes visiting Steve makes me miss working with people, but my body isn't cut out for that anymore. I'm retired with how beat up I got during all my years serving. I live comfortably with the money I saved, and that's all I care about.

We make it to the break room where it's empty. The three tables that are in there have a few boxes of food that look to be pizza and fries.

Steve works hard and treats his staff to lunch almost every day. He's too good for this world.

Steve opens a pizza box and starts placing slices on a paper plate. He hands me a plate and I follow along and place three slices on it. I add some fries and then grab a sauce packet of ranch.

We both sit down at the table and begin eating. Steve gives me a big smile as he chows down and I lean back in my chair, spreading my legs comfortably.

"I found out who moved into the Stone's," I exclaim.

Steve finishes his bite and wipes his mouth with a napkin. "You saw her?"

I nod my head. "She needs to be more aware of where the road starts. I almost ran her over."

Steve laughs and shakes his head. "Did you really?"

I smirk and shake my head before taking another bite of the pizza. "Nah, but I wanted to. Is she planning to fix the vineyard and get it running again?"

Steve shrugs. "She didn't really tell us her plans last night. We mainly talked about her hometown and told her the best places to shop at. Well, Birdy did."

I nod my head slowly before finishing the pizza and start on the fries. "She's going to have fun taking care of their land. It was hard for all of us when the Stones were gone. I can't imagine doing it alone."

"She's not going to be doing it alone," Steve states. He looks at me with a serious face and I finish a fry before crossing my arms over my chest.

"What did you do, Steve?"

He looks from the table and then back at me. He is horrible at poker faces. He's always been.

"I told her I'd help her out and—"

"And you said I would too?" I interrupted him.

He purses his lips and nods slowly. I lean my neck back and close my eyes.

"Ben, you're right there in case she needs anyone. She's new and we treat our new residents with respect and all the help they can get."

"She's just another city girl trying to make this *the best vacation home I can get*," I mock in a high-pitched voice.

"She actually worked for a vineyard for a few years and just needed a change of scenery," Steve counters. I can tell he won't budge with my jokes this time.

I roll my tongue over my teeth and raise my brows. "Well, fuck. I guess you made my decision for me." Steve nods and I cluck my tongue against my teeth loudly. "If she gets on my nerves even once when I try to help her... I'm done."

This makes Steve bark out a laugh as he leans against his chair. "I think she already annoyed you. Last night was a shitshow, Bennett. You're horrible with first impressions."

I shrug and roll my eyes. "I'm not here to please people."

"Well, she's really sweet. She was confused and a little hurt last night by your sudden change of demeanor. You won pool and then you act like an ass in front of her and Bee."

"Am I in an intervention? I thought I was just getting free lunch?" I can feel the anger boil inside me. I hate when Steve thinks he can lecture me. We're too old for that shit. I'm nearing my forties and don't need this from my best friend.

"No, but you need to know when you go too far."

"Calling her a bunny was not going too far and you know it."

"I'm talking about the part where you said the bunny dies."

I raise my brow and then huff out a breath. "Well, shit. She moved to Alpine Ridge, which is in the middle of nowhere. Bunnies get eaten by coyotes and get picked up by crows. It's not my fault I'm giving her a reality check."

"Alright, alright. We don't have to discuss it further." Steve coughs and shifts in his seat. "Interesting enough, I heard Oliver was actually meeting with an investor."

I silently thank Steve for switching the conversation. "Is that so? Are they wanting to buy the land near the marina or across from me?"

Steve leans towards the table and shakes his head. His arms fold over the table. "They want the land next to you and Camilla. They want to build apartments or a community of small homes."

There's silence as I register his words and think about what the fuck he just said.

"What?"

"You heard me. They want to develop shit. And they're willing to pay the big bucks."

"Please tell me Oliver didn't approve."

"No... not yet. He wanted to first feel it out and talk to the locals that would be directly affected. He plans to talk to you later this week. And Camilla too."

"Why her?"

Steve looks at me intently. "He has a proposal for you two. He didn't give me any details, but he said since you and her are the neighbors to that land, he's thought of something that might help deter the investors."

"A proposal? I don't know, Steve. Oliver can get these crazy ideas out of fear. Remember when he tried making me buy the land to the left of me just because he thought we needed to own that whole strip of Misty Creek Road?"

"I remember. But I think he's serious about this."

I huff again. "He better meet with me alone. I've had enough of Bunny to last an entire month."

Steve lets out a smile and then chuckles. "She really made a lasting impression on you, huh?"

"Shut up."

I hate when Steve is right... and he's definitely right about this one.

FIVE

CAMILLA

THE VINEYARD IS BEAUTIFUL. It stretches for acres and acres on the first half of the property land, and the rows of vines follow each other. It didn't take long for me to get to the other shed where there were keys to a small golf cart.

There were a few other vehicles in the shed, like a small mountain bike and an ATV. I didn't know very well how to ride those, so I went with the safest option.

It wasn't a far drive out to the vineyard and I've been here all day checking the area out.

There's a cute barn with a huge alcove where a small stage is set up, as well as an area for tables and chairs. It makes me wonder if this was a place where weddings and their receptions took place.

The rest of the outside area surrounding the barn is an open space with a few wooden picnic tables and curved benches. It's a pleasant retreat for people after they get their wine and snacks to just hang out. I'm thinking of either hiring bands to play in the barn for people to sit back and relax or have events hosted here and more. I try to let my imagination run wild with all the possibilities.

As I continued the rest of my day looking around the place, I got holed up at the main building that's just one level with a wrap around a patio with even more seating placements. Right before walking up the steps, though, I found Goose napping on a bed of flowers nearby. I couldn't help but smile at the sight.

The inside of the building has bathrooms, a main office, a seating area, and a gift shop. Customers can purchase cutlery and other necessities from the copious fridges.

There's a wall lined up with various wine bottles. Near the register there's a small handbook of each wine and its origin.

When looking through the office to get more keys for the vineyard, I stumble upon a note from the previous owner.

The best place is always kept secret. - Peyton and Morgan

Alongside the note is a key with no instructions. I look around the room until I see an almost hidden door. I shuffle some boxes away from the ground that's covering it and then fit the key in the lock. My heart pounds as I hear it click open. I turn around and look to see if anyone's in here witnessing this moment.

"Here goes," I whisper as I turn the knob and pull the door open with shaky hands.

The air is chilly as it hits me and I'm met with a dark staircase that descends in a pretty spiral. I look for a switch on the wall inside and once I flip it, all the lights turn on.

It's a wine cellar. I carefully make my way down. It looks to be eight feet by eight feet and every wall is lined with bottles of wine. But these are more decadent and worth way more than anything that's for sale upstairs.

I take in a deep breath before making my way through the room. I can see some bottles from Spain, Greece, and even France.

There's one that is in the center of one wall in a glass box. It's embedded into the wall and I can't seem to find any way to get it out. There's no hole for a key or even a handle to open it.

The bottle is clear with red details, kind of like watercolor overlapping the glass. It's beautiful and I can tell it's a nice white wine. I peer closely and try to read the label and see that it's actually custom made.

Forever my heart, the proof of our love
Made in Alpine Ridge, TN

It must be something that Peyton and Andy made while they were here. But a thought comes to me and I remember Mr. Samson saying that Andy's parents were the ones that established this vineyard. So this bottle might be what they made when they started the vineyard. It's a sweet gesture if what I assume is right.

I step back and move on, looking at the other wines in this hidden collection. There's a table in the far corner that's fixed to be like a bar cart, but there are mainly wine glasses in the small cabinets underneath and bottle openers.

I look over the place one more time before heading back upstairs.

There are more things in the office like an accounting book, ledgers, and whatnot that I'll have to sort through later. It takes everything in me not to sit in the massive leather chair and sigh from the work I'll have to put in to keep this place running.

I'll need to figure out the staffing situation, maybe even put up fliers around town. I've got a great cushion of money saved still, but if I don't get to work, then I'll lose it all.

And I can't have that happen my first month in.

LATER THAT EVENING, I make my way into town to see if I can get more sweets and shop for some real groceries. The fridge needed something in it and I couldn't survive off the leftover wings from the bar from last night.

As I make my way, my mind flashes back to this morning. It was around lunchtime when I was outside and Bennett drove by.

It was strange to see him in daylight and not looking as annoyed as he did last night.

I really wanted to ask him if everything was okay, but he seemed to be busy and not in the mood to talk. The last thing I want to do is push someone to talk if they're not ready. Besides, it looked like he was on a mission on his way into town, seeing how fast he drove away.

When I called my parents earlier to update them on the move, I almost told them about the bar. I kept it to myself, though. I didn't want them to worry about me anymore than they needed to. Being an only child, even at my age of twenty-seven, made my parents worry about me at all hours of the day.

I even called Viola and talked about the house and Goose. It was a brief call, but it warmed my heart and helped me feel more comfortable being alone in the big house this morning.

I park in front of Birdy's shop and grab my sunglasses and tote.

The doorbell chimes as I walk in and I see Birdy helping a customer before she looks up and sees me. She smiles and gives a small wave and I return it.

"That'll be two-fifty," I overhear Birdy as she taps on the register and the customer nods their head and pays for their bag of sweets.

As the customer leaves, Birdy wiggles her eyebrows at me and comes around the counter to be closer.

"How are you? Are you settling in okay?"

I nod. "Yeah, last night was great. Thank you again for showing me that bar. Steve was really nice..." My voice drags and Birdy laughs.

"Yeah, I know. Bennett, on the other hand, is Bennett. Don't be too hard on yourself. It's him, not you."

"Is he okay? He seemed to be in a hurry this morning when I saw him. Seemed like he didn't know I was the one who bought the land near him."

Birdy shrugs. "Not your fault. He tends to be closed off and only brings himself into conversations or situations if necessary."

I look down at my feet and pout. Before I can think of anything, I feel Birdy's arm reach out and her hand pats my shoulder.

"It'll be okay. Just take it one day at a time here. It's hard being the new resident. We're *all* talking about ya," She laughs and I look up at her with horrified eyes.

"What? You are?"

"I'm kidding! Mainly just me. I feel like we're gonna be good friends." Her smile is genuine and contagious.

"Me too. Anyway, I came here for some more sweets. I spent my whole day at the vineyard trying to set it up and it's got me *exhausted*."

"It's a big role to take on! Look around the shop and let me know if there's anything you need help with," Birdy says as she rounds the corner and heads into the back room quickly.

The doorbell chimes again, and I turn to see a young boy enter. He looks around the shop and then catches my eyes. His lips instantly turn into a smile.

"Hey, I haven't seen you around."

I look around the shop and see that he's talking to me. "Me? Yeah, I just moved."

His eyes are light brown and his brown hair is fluffy. He's a few inches taller than me. "My Aunt Rose said there was someone new that Birdy was talking about. She hears everything and tells me all the town gossip, sorry."

I shake my head and laugh. "Oh, it's okay. I'm getting used to the fact that people will instantly recognize me as the new resident."

His eyes shine as he gets closer and reaches his hand out. "I'm Parker, by the way."

"Camilla," I reply, closing my hand in his.

"Parker! Don't bother my new customer!!" Birdy's voice rings as she swings the door open with a tray of chocolates.

Parker instantly retreats his arm and redness creeps onto his fair skinned neck and cheeks.

"It's okay, Birdy," I say as she *tsks* and places the tray on the counter.

"Parker, be nice to her. I already have some people making their impression on her. And it's not good."

"Oh, yes, ma'am. I-I didn't mean to be rude," Parker's words jumble out.

I wave my hands in peace and laugh. "It's okay, Parker. We're just joking."

He looks relieved as he takes a deep breath. "Oh, okay. Thanks."

"What are you doing here anyway, Parker? Does your aunt need more of those caramel chocolates?"

He shakes his head and looks down at his feet. "No, I was actually coming to see if you needed some summer help. She's been wanting me to find work ever since I graduated last week."

"Ahh, no can do. Sorry, bud," Birdy shakes her head.

"Birdy!" I laugh and she sticks her tongue out at me.

"What? This is a family shop. Majority of my sales come from online, anyway. You'd be bored all day until the peak hours hit, Parker."

She makes a good point, but I turn to see Parker and can't help but feel bad for him. He continues to look down at his shoes and moves one, scuffing the tip on the floor.

"Hey," I say to him and he looks up. "I bought the Stone's land and could use some help bringing the vineyard back to life. It won't be a permanent position since I don't know your post-summer plans… but it can work."

He looks at me and Birdy and a huge grin forms on his face. "Do you really mean it? I can work for you?"

I nod my head, and he jumps a little in his place and Birdy laughs.

"If you'd like, you can start helping me organize the main building tonight. It'll just be for maybe two hours. I'll pay you and even get us some food to eat too," I offer.

He nods his head quickly. "Thank you so much, ma'am. I can be there within the next hour if that's okay? I have to go tell my aunt!"

I laugh and nod my head as I see him bolt out of the store and run in the opposite direction. I turn to Birdy, who just huffs and rolls her eyes before giggling.

"Parker James has a lot of energy. Make him do all the heavy lifting and moving, okay?"

"I think that's why my intuition told me to jump at this opportunity. That vineyard is going to be a lot of work," I respond.

Birdy nods before waving me over and handing me a chocolate from the tray.

"You know, if you need me to stop by tonight and help with anything else, please let me know. I get off in two hours and can get to you easily."

"Thanks, Birdy. I really appreciate it and I'll let you know, okay?"

Birdy smiles and nods before we both bite into the chocolate.

BY THE TIME I get home with a trunk full of grocery bags, it's almost seven and I see a pair of headlights turn on my driveway. The car idles near the gate and it's not long before I hear a buzz and walk towards the kitchen where there's a camera and panel of buttons on the wall.

I can see Parker through the black and white camera and I buzz him in, the sound of the gates opening.

I head outside and wait for him to follow the driveway up to the house. He gets out of his car and runs up with a huge smile.

"Thank you again, Miss Camilla. I hope I'm not late."

I shake my head. "You're right on time! Do you know how to drive a golf cart?"

He looks at me with a raised brow before nodding his head. I laugh and toss him the key to the golf cart and let him follow me to the side of the house where I parked it earlier.

Parker turns it on and we make our way towards the vineyard. It's a bumpy ride, but it's visible. The sun shouldn't be setting for another hour and a half, so we should be good for now.

"Wow, I forget how big this vineyard is," Parker speaks up as he parks the golf cart and we both hop out.

"I know. It took me almost a whole day just looking around. Thank you again for helping me. It's been pretty hectic."

He nods. "Of course! My aunt wanted me to tell you she thanks you. She's been so busy with her flower shop she didn't have time to help me find places to apply to. She wants to give you a free bouquet whenever you have time to stop by her shop."

"She owns a flower shop?"

"Yeah, it's called Rose's Flowers... so original," Parker laughs. "But she's the best florist in town."

"I'll definitely try to stop by, then!"

We make our way up the steps. As we enter the building, I make my way towards the switches and turn on all the lights.

Parker and I get to work as we sweep, mop, organize, and dust every corner of the building. We take an hour and a half just to clean the building, so by the time Parker suggests going to the barn to organize it, I shake my head.

"I think we can call it a day. I am beat. We'd need more hands if we continued."

Parker chews on his bottom lip as he leans over the handle of the broom he's holding. "I could call someone to help…"

I shake my head. "No, Parker. It's not even important! We did the biggest thing on my list today: this building."

But before Parker can register my words, he's whipping out his phone and texting someone.

"We're all a big family here. And you're wanting to open this vineyard soon, right?"

I nod my head.

"So, let's get this place looking nice and we can open it up!"

"So, who's coming? I can also let Birdy know to come over." I finally ask.

"Steve. He usually closes his shop around six, so he should be home."

My mouth falls open, and I shake my head. "No, Parker! Don't make him come. He's had a long day at work and I don't need *this* to be added to it."

Parker waves his hand before checking his phone. "Don't worry about it, really. Steve loves helping out, and he's got a soft spot for me. I'm like the little brother he's never had… plus he just said that he'll be here in fifteen."

"Parker…" I start to say, but he shakes his head and smiles.

"Really, Miss Camilla. Don't worry about it! We want you to fit right in Alpine. Plus, it'll be fun, I think. If Birdy comes too, it'll be like a small party helping you clean up."

I finally smile before I point at Parker and the broom in his hand, and he laughs before getting back to work.

By the time Steve's truck rolls onto the property, I get a call from the gate on my phone that Parker showed me how to set up while we waited and click a button for the gates to open.

I'll eventually have to keep the vineyard entrance open

during daylight hours if I want to have people come over with ease and not have to use the private entrance every time.

In a few minutes, I hear the slam of not one, but two doors, and I scrunch my brows at Parker as we make our way outside.

As we get on the patio, I see Steve walk over and there's a figure behind him just as tall. I suck in my breath as I realize who it is.

Bennett presses his lips into a thin line as he walks near us. Steve pats me on the back and ruffles through Parker's hair as he passes us and walks right into the building as if he's used to it.

Bennett walks up the steps and his heavy weight makes the steps creak under it. He looks from Parker over to me and my cheeks get hot.

"Hey, Bennett," I mumble as Parker waves to him before following Steve inside.

We're left outside under the porch light as the sun begins to set. The blue in his eyes are like an ocean, an array of different shades.

"Bunny," He breathes out as he peers down at me and chews on his bottom lip as if he's deep in thought. Before he says anything else, he huffs and then moves past me, brushing his arm with my shoulder.

SIX

BENNETT

STEVE DRAGGED ME HERE.

Parker called Steve, saying Camilla needed some help with organizing and cleaning her vineyard. I'm not too sure why she needed help this late, but Steve immediately agreed... and then dragged me along.

When he told me earlier that I would help Camilla out of my own will, I didn't expect it to be this soon.

I'd rather be home and deal with the damn rooster than be here.

That Parker kid has always been a pain in the butt. He's too cheery and too polite. I just don't want to see him get used to it. He's only got his aunt around, so we've all chipped in with the parenting department where we could.

He has the best relationship with Steve... and surprisingly, Katherine. He took a few classes at her studio, and she seemed to take him under her wing. I guess that just naturally happened after I left for so long.

As soon as my thoughts go to Katherine, I push them away. I don't have the mental capacity for her tonight. She's taken up too much of it during my twelve years married to her.

I deserve one night where she's not taking up every thought in my mind.

When looking at Camilla under the porch light, I couldn't help but notice the small dark freckles that are splattered around her nose and cheekbones. I had to push past her to get inside the building and her skin was soft when I brushed against her arm.

I hear her soft footsteps follow behind me and I make a beeline for Parker and Steve, who are already working on a plan.

"Alright, we can do the actual vineyard maintenance the next few evenings and then this weekend." Steve states as he crosses his arms over his chest.

He's used to taking charge and people let him. The way he's able to assemble a room together in a heartbeat, I'm shocked he didn't run for mayor or something in that realm.

Parker nods his head fast before turning his head towards me and breaking his lips into a smile. "Bennett! Isn't this place going to be so cool once we open it back up?"

I shrug my shoulders and then jump in my place as I feel someone walk and stand next to me. I roll my eyes as I peer down at the top of Camilla's head. Her brunette curls flow wildly and some strands touch my arm, which caused me to feel a tingle and jump.

"Jesus, Bunny. You're quiet."

"Oh, I'm sorry," she replies as she turns and looks up at me with concern. I hear the laughter of Steve and Parker, and I glare at them.

Before I can say anything else to her, Steve clears his throat and motions for us to get closer, as if we're huddling up before facing Mason Pointe in a sports competition. We've always gone against that neighboring town whenever we had tournaments in middle and high school. We even have summer events that bring the two towns together.

"Parker and I will take the outside area around this building, and Bennett and Camilla will finish up inside here. Got it?"

They all nod, and I hold back a groan. Seriously, Steve? I try to hold his eye contact, but he focuses back on Parker and I want to flick him on his head.

"I actually had some boxes that were too high to grab in the office..." Camilla starts as we both back up and watch Steve and Parker goof off with whatever jokes they're making as they head outside. With the sunset lowering, I assume they'll try to clean up around the outside of the house to make sure there aren't any cracks in the foundation or any things out of place.

I nod and motion my hand for her to lead the way. A soft pink blush rises to her cheeks and I try to avert my eyes. Following behind her, we make it into the main office area. It's been a while since I've been here.

I refocus back to where Camilla is standing, where she is looking at me, and then she nibbles on her bottom lip. I watch her, wondering why the hell I'm suddenly... nervous.

We're alone in this room and I can feel my hands getting sweaty and my breathing quickens.

She's not even doing anything except for waiting for me to help her. I haven't felt this rush of... whatever it is for years. Not even the last few years in my marriage with Katherine. That light burned out in year five when I continued my tours and then my contract work in Colombia.

I sigh again, attempting to recenter my mind. I need to stop staying so fixated on the past when it's all gone. It's been said and done and I can't go back and change anything. I don't *want* to. And neither does Katherine. We were no good for each other.

"It's those boxes and manila folders up above that bookcase," Camilla points at the top of the bookshelf. She's probably half the size of the bookcase, and I can't help but smile.

"Alright, Bunny. Watch the tall person and take notes," I joke as I step closer to where she's standing. We're so close that if I leaned to my left, I would bump my shoulder into her head.

She lets out a small laugh before nodding. I get on my tiptoes and reach my arms above my head, and easily grab the big white box and drag it down. She lets out a small groan when I push the box into her arms. I try to ignore that *groan* and clear my throat, continuing to hand her the remaining boxes.

Next to the boxes were some stacks of manila folders, and I handed them to Camilla as well. Once those are down, she pushes a duster in my hand and I give her a look before her face turns into a wide smile and I playfully swat her arm with the duster.

"Hey! It still has dust from when Parker and I were cleaning earlier!"

She takes a step back and I quickly see her back into one of the big white boxes that she placed on the ground. She loses her footing and I drop the duster before leaning over and catching her hands that instinctively reach out to balance herself.

She lets out a small scream before I pull her to a standing position. Her hands are soft and I catch her gaze before I let her hands go.

"Thank you," She lets out breathlessly. I nod my head and lean down to pick up the duster.

"You need to put those boxes somewhere else, Bunny," I say quickly, before turning around and working on dusting the top of the bookcase.

I hear her movements behind me as she moves the boxes and then her shuffling as she comes back to my side. I exhale deeply, knowing she's so close. But I can't help but want her to be close to me in case she trips again.

"That's it for this area. There's still some organizing with those white boxes and folders... I'm not sure where to put those for now. I was going to grab a wine bottle though to give to Steve for coming over. Do you want one too?"

I shake my head. "I just drink beer and some whiskey. Wine is too sweet for me."

Camilla laughs. "There are some bitter ones, too."

I just shake my head again and I see her shrug quickly before heading towards a door in the office's corner and pulling out a set of keys from the desk.

I see her unlock the door and before I know it, I'm following her. To be there if she trips, of course. I can't have her falling again down there where no one will know.

She turns and sees me follow her, and a small smile creeps from the corner of her lips. She continues down the spiral staircase *slowly*. My steps are heavy, and it shakes the staircase which makes Camilla hold on to the railing even more than she previously was.

"I'm just going to grab a Rosé and a Cabernet Sauvignon. The Rosé will, of course, be for me," Camilla says with a laugh.

I just hum in approval as I reach the end of the staircase and look around the room. It's a stockpile of wine, and I wonder where the oldest bottle is. My eyes glance quickly towards the enormous glass case that holds the special wine that Andy's parents made.

There's a label on it. I get closer to it and smile as I read the label. It's a cute quote that Andy's father made for his wife. The bottle that Andy made for Peyton years ago isn't in the case anymore and I have a brief thought that Peyton took it when she left Alpine.

I wouldn't blame her. Andy and Peyton were the staple couple in Alpine, and Andy's passing hurt all of us. It was like a part of Alpine was gone forever. It hurt even more when Peyton packed up and left. What she needed was our support, but she couldn't fathom it.

"You okay?" Camilla's voice cuts through my desolate thoughts and I turn to look at her.

She raises a brow, and I shake my head. "Yeah, just forgot this wine was here," I pointed my thumb towards the glass case.

"Oh, that one. It's really sweet." Her voice drops and I feel my breathing hitch as I wait for her to finish. "They must've had quite a romance. Andy Stone with his wife and then his father with his mother. They've found their person and could create *that*. I think it's beautiful and very sentimental about their proclamation of love."

"Yeah, yeah, Bunny. Don't get all weepy on me. It's just a wine bottle," I mutter, but I can't say that I don't agree. The Stones had a love that I always wanted.

But even their timeline ended.

"Right, sorry. It's a dumb thought." She shakes her head and laughs softly. I curse under my breath and walk towards her, hoping she doesn't get too emotional in this chamber of wine bottles.

I can't handle emotion. It's too much for me. I try to reach my hand up to her shoulder, but she sighs heavily and then shakes her head and smiles.

But before I can do anything else, we hear a crack and then the lights go off in the cellar. Camilla yelps, and I move closer to her and lay my hands on her shaking shoulders.

"It's okay, it was just the lights. Steve and Parker are probably fucking with the breaker box," I say calmly and rub my hands up and down her shoulders.

Her breathing seems to ease up and she sighs. "Sorry, I didn't think it would get this dark without the light. It kind of scares me."

"Try to focus. Look at me and try to make out the outline of my face."

I can see the outline of hers perfectly. Only because I've been training my eyes for years. Adjusting my eyes to see in the dark is like second nature to me now.

"Okay," she replies shakily, and her chest moves up and down.

Her arms raise and touch my forearms and then move up towards my shoulders. I want to push them off me–I'm so used to avoiding touch, but they feel warm and *good.* Her soft touch is somewhat comforting against my hard exterior. Plus, it's seeming to calm her down being able to touch me and know that she's not alone down here in the pitch black.

"Anything?" I ask, and she nods her head.

"I can see the outline of your face. And your body. I can even see the bottles of wine behind you and their shapes."

"Good—" I stop myself before slipping out *good girl.* It would be highly inappropriate. But something in me wants to see how she'd react to those words.

"Thanks, Bennett," Her soft words fill my ears and I nod.

"Alright, now that you've got the room visualized, we can head back upstairs. Okay?"

"Y-yeah, totally."

"Come on, Bunny," I say as I step back and let one of her hands slip from my shoulder. I let her other hand slip down my forearm and down my hand until her index finger wraps around my pinky. I turn and lead us slowly towards the staircase and then up them.

By the time we get up to the top of the stairs, we can hear chatter. Once we're in the office, the lights come back on and Camilla laughs. She releases her finger from mine and I close the door behind her. She locks it up and tosses the keys back on the desk before giving me a small smile.

"Bennett? Camilla?" Steve's voice drifts throughout the building and we walk out of the office and see Steve and Parker leaning against the register podium.

"The lights turned off, Bunny got scared," I tease, and Camilla shakes her head.

"It was so dark down there!" She retorts.

I roll my eyes and Steve belts out a laugh. "That was all Parker. He thought some switches in the breaker box were the wrong way. We didn't notice until we saw the office lights off and you guys were nowhere to be seen."

"Yeah, yeah," I huff and move away from Camilla.

We hear a door open and we all turn our heads to see Birdy walking in. She has two pizza boxes and a bag in her arms.

She stops as she sees all of us staring at her. "What the fuck?"

I groan, and Steve gives me a look.

"Hey Birdy!" Parker waves from his place.

"Everyone's here?" Birdy exclaims as she walks towards a table and drops the pizza boxes. She turns to Steve. "You didn't care to invite me?! We were just together last night, and you didn't utter a word about this get together."

I hold back laughter from the argument that will ensue from Birdy and Steve. I see Camilla from the corner of my eyes looking back and forth between the two. I try to hold her gaze and tell her that this is just who they are, but she doesn't look my way.

Steve raises his hands in defense, "Hey! I didn't know you'd be coming! Parker asked me to help out."

"I asked her to come. I hope that's okay," Camilla says.

Birdy waves her hand away toward Steve, dismissing his words. "Don't be sorry, hun. Steve could've easily told me he was on his way."

Steve widens his mouth before laughing. Birdy smiles and shakes her head before opening the pizza box. Steve's eyes sparkle and he claps his hands together before heading towards the food.

"Thanks for coming again," Camilla says as she heads towards the table of food. I follow her steps.

"Never thank us, we're always here," Steve speaks up as he lifts a slice and immediately takes a bite. Birdy nods and so does Parker as they take their own slice.

Camilla turns to me, and I press my lips together. Her eyes move from mine to my lips and then back. There's a fluttering feeling in my stomach. I clear my throat and lean over her left side before grabbing a slice. My chest is flush with her and I can see the redness creep up her neck and cheeks.

It looks cute on her and I hold her eyes as I bring the slice closer to my mouth and take a bite.

She nibbles on the bottom of her lip and I suddenly register that this movement of hers is her *tell* for being nervous. Like, truly nervous. I want to say something, but to be honest, she's making me nervous too. I contemplate on holding back the rudeness I've been giving her, but then I remember that she just moved here and probably will try to change this town to her liking.

When she sees the change in my face, she widens her eyes and then turns back towards the table to grab a slice for herself.

There's chatter around us as Parker tells Birdy his summer plans besides working at the vineyard. As Parker talks, Camilla puts her right hand on his shoulder, and I see Parker look at her with some kind of look in his eyes.

Great. The James kid is going to crush on the newbie resident her first week.

I want to get in between them and show Parker that he's too young for this kind of shit. But I hold myself back. Camilla doesn't seem to know the effect she's having with her hand on Parker's shoulder, so I let it slide.

"Bennett," Birdy's voice breaks me from my trance focused on Parker and Camilla.

"Yep?" I ask as I take another bite of the pizza.

"You coming with Steve and I to the lake this weekend?"

I look at her and Steve, who's on his second slice chomping down. I shrug my shoulders and then move my gaze back to Camilla and Parker. Maybe Birdy will make Camilla go too… and that I can't miss.

A city girl in the middle of a lake? Count me in.

"Oh yeah, count me in Birdy," I reply as I take one last bite of the pizza in my hand.

SEVEN

CAMILLA

THE WEEKEND COMES by quicker than expected, especially with how much I still have to get done. Birdy invited me to the lake late Friday night and wanted me to join all day Saturday. She mentioned the party cove that I read up on when researching things to do here.

It was just what I needed after spending all Friday covered in dust and dirt after cleaning out the sheds on the land. They were dirtier than they looked and Parker made it seem like it would only take a few *hours*, not a whole day.

His high energy and optimism was something I really liked about him, especially having him work for me now. I don't do well with telling people with an attitude what to do. It gets me really nervous about having to be authoritative.

Thankfully, Parker offers to clean something and then does it. He's independent when he needs to be, and that's what I need while I sort things out and figure out a plan before opening the vineyard.

He even offered to take out the boat that I forgot was hidden in the back of the shed. Parker immediately hopped into it as we cleaned and tested the engine and fixed whatever needed to be fixed that evening to make sure it would work.

Birdy advised me to head to the party cove before eleven a.m. and that she would head there a little earlier with Steve to get things set up and secure a good spot.

Parker insisted he help me drive the boat and the moment I widened my eyes, he laughed and pulled out his boating license to ease any of my worries. Thank God, because when I looked up the age requirement to drive a boat without a boating license, and just using your *driver's* license, you had to be at least thirty. I didn't know the laws regarding driving a boat until moving here.

I spent the rest of the night in bed cuddling with Goose by my arm and called my parents on the phone, and afterwards, my best friend. I tried to convince her to visit soon, but she's been so busy at her job. She works for the federal government, but always complains about how draining it is.

I attempted to persuade her to visit and see if she liked this small town enough to move here, but she immediately rejected the idea. I'll have to work on that. Maybe Birdy can help me. It's not the same here without my best friend. I've known her since grade school and this is the farthest we've ever lived away from each other. My parents are glad I've been able to make myself feel at home so quickly and didn't want to disturb my schedule with a visit as I got the vineyard set up.

Hopefully, all three will visit soon. Whether it's for the vineyard opening or later this summer.

So, this morning I'm a nervous wreck as I got my small beach bag ready with a towel, sunscreen, insulated water bottle, a book, wallet, and keys. I leave some water and food for Goose near the kitchen French doors and then head out, grabbing the sunglasses I left near the front door on a side table.

I opted for a cute, dark blue bikini and a sheer white top with matching sheer skirt. We'd be out in the water all day and I didn't want to wear anything I wouldn't want wet.

Walking outside, my face and body are hit with *heat* and bright sun. It's barely ten! But I read online that the heat only gets worse in Tennessee as the summer months come.

"Hey, Miss Camilla! I borrowed my Aunt's car and attached the boat to the hitch. We're all good to go if you are," Parker yells from a distance as I step down the porch steps and make my way down the gravel road towards Parker and the dark blue SUV that must be his aunt's.

He's wearing red and blue swim shorts and a blue shirt. His brown hair is fluffy, and he smiles brightly from his place.

"Thanks, Parker! I'm sure Eucy is glad she doesn't have to tow that big thing," I laugh as I watch Parker nod and get in the driver's seat. I pull the passenger door open and hop in.

The car is cold with the air conditioner blowing harshly, and I let out a deep breath. I can already imagine the tan I'll be getting today. I lean my head back into the headrest.

"I'm ready. Let's head to the lake!" I squeal, watching Parker shift the car into drive and work slowly to turn the car with the boat attached around the gravel pathway until he's able to drive straight out of the property.

I trusted Parker enough to give him the personal gate code last night, and I watch as he turns to look at me with a smile. I smile back and turn towards the window and watch the trees move by as Parker takes a left and heads down Misty Creek Road. I momentarily glance at Bennett's property as we pass by and I can see the cows and horses out in the pasture.

"Do you think Bennett will be there?" I ask softly, watching Parker turn his head to glance to his left, and then he shrugs.

"He doesn't really go out much unless Steve drags him. He keeps to himself. Mr. Moore is kinda known for that."

I nod my head and purse my lips. The other night was *different*. The way we could be somewhat... *friends* down in the wine cellar. But then once we finished dinner and made our way out of the vineyard, his mood shot down again.

He's a hard one to read, yet there are so many stories I can see through his eyes. He won't budge and I won't make him.

After a few more sharp turns, Parker heads towards an entrance where a huge sign 'ALPINE RIDGE MARINA' is written in big letters. It already looks busy as Parker passes the chain-link fence that surrounds the parking lot of the marina and finds the dock ramp area.

I patiently wait as Parker maneuvers the car into the right position before backing up just enough for the speedboat to get halfway in the water with the boat trailer it's attached to. I chew on my lip in nerves as I feel us get the back tires of the car into deeper water and clutch my bag in my hands tightly.

"It's okay, Miss Camilla. My aunt's car might look small, but it can handle this."

"I believe you, but I just don't want her car to get stuck," I reply through a sharp breath.

Parker puts the car in park and then hops out of the car without saying another word and works on lowering the trailer to get the boat detached from the car. There's a loud thunk and the car wiggles up and down and I yelp.

I turn to look at the back of the car and I see Parker smile and give me a thumbs up as he gets the speedboat lowered into the water. But then I see him look back at the car and then at the boat and that's when I realize he needs to obviously be in the boat and move it back.

I place the beach bag that was in my lap on the ground before hopping out of the car and walking around towards the driver's side and squinting through the harsh sun rays, even through my sunglasses, and find Parker laughing.

"I didn't think this through. Do you mind driving and parking the car? I've got the boat keys in my pocket, and I can meet you here?"

My hair shakes around my face as I laugh and nod. "You got

it, captain! I don't need your aunt knowing we lost the boat *and* her car."

"She would probably kick me out," Parker agrees as he finds his way onto the boat and then waves before turning the engine on and backing the boat up.

I hop into the driver's seat and change the rearview mirror and side mirror to my height, as well as the seat before shifting the car into drive. I drive slowly and make sure to watch all my corners before I find an open spot to pull the car into with the long trailer attached.

I grab my beach bag and turn off the car before plopping the keys into a secure pocket in the bag before making my way towards the dock ramp. My blue sandals clack against the pavement as I make my way. There's more and more people driving into the parking lot getting ready for a nice day out in the water.

I look to the right and see an office attached to a restaurant. The docks where boats are held are in front of the huge porch of the restaurant. There's a long stretch of boardwalk leading to many pontoon boats, speedboats, and kayaks that are most likely for renters. There's a secluded area farther to the right of everything where there are house boats or boats that are held during the season.

I wonder how expensive it is to rent out for a season.

I see Parker in the distance move the boat closer to the dock, where some people are waiting as well for their boat to come closer to hop on. I wave to him and get far out onto the dock as the engine rumbles louder and Parker gets closer.

The boat is pretty, white with silver details, and has huge speakers attached to the top. It looks expensive, but then again I don't know much about boats.

"Get in!" Parker yells as he stops the engine and rushes with a rope, leaning over to tie it to a post near me and I grab his outstretched hand to help him get the boat closer to the dock.

"Alright, I got this," I say, mostly to myself, as I keep my hand in Parker's and throw my beach bag into the boat and then hoist myself up.

Parker backs up to let me find my footing and then he works on untying the rope and heading back to the steering wheel. I sit down slowly, putting the beach bag under the seat and then grip the nearby railing.

"You ready?" Parker asks as he turns the engine on again and the boat roars to life. I yell a yes before he turns the boat around in the harbor and then increases speed as we drift into the wake zone.

I clutch the railing harder as the wind picks up, blowing my hair in every direction. I haven't been on a boat in a long time, so to say I'm a little nervous is an understatement.

Parker looks like he knows what he's doing as I watch him from the corner of my eye. He's focused as his hands stay on the wheel.

Within twenty minutes, we're nearing a cove where there are already a few boats anchored and I can see some people swimming or chilling in floaties.

I squint my eyes as I search for Birdy.

"Miss Camilla, do you see them?" Parker yells over the loud engine and I turn my head around the cove before spotting a small, bright beige pontoon boat that's anchored.

"There!" I scream, a smile forming on my face as I see a familiar head of strawberry blonde hair. But there's a blond and a brunette with her. I attempt to shield my face from the sun with my hand, but we're still pretty far to make out who they are.

"Let's get closer so we can tie up next to them." Parker calls out and I yell out confirmation as I get myself ready with the rope and push the inflatable fenders over the sides of the boat.

"Birdy!" I scream, waving my arm as we get closer and closer.

I see her turn and her eyes go wide, her arms instantly shooting up and waving at me. I see the blond turn as well and it's Steve–he waves at us too. Birdy's wearing a cute, white bikini and Steve's wearing white trunks.

We're now a few yards away from them and I see the brunette turn his head and that's when I feel my chest tighten and my eyes instantly meet his.

Bennett.

"Come on, Camilla and Parker! I knew you'd be here soon. Steve started a bet that you'd get lost," Birdy screams as we finally reach their side of the boat and Steve shakes his head and laughs.

Steve moves towards the front of his boat to roll over the fenders on their boat and grab some rope to tie the bow of our boat with theirs.

As Parker helps Steve, I head towards the back, expecting Birdy to be the one helping towards the back of their boat. As I look up with the rope in my hand, I see Bennett close the distance and push the fender on his side over the side of the boat. His biceps underneath his shirt and his bare forearms flex at this motion.

He huffs loudly and then catches my eyes. His blue eyes cast down towards the rope in my hand and lays his calloused palm out, moving his fingers as if to command me to give the rope over. I gawk and my jaw goes slack with his nonverbal communication.

He sighs and then shakes his head. "Bunny, hand me the rope. I got it."

"It's okay, I know how to tie it," I say confidently, leaning over and wrapping the rope around their metal cleat. But the moment I let go after a few twists, the rope loosens.

"Shoot," I mumble, chewing on my lip as I see Bennett shake his head and a hint of a smile appears in the corner of his lips.

The moment he sees me looking, he returns to his poker face and grabs the rope roughly from my hands, our fingers grazing each other. It feels like a jolt of electricity. The same I felt the night he caught me from falling in the office.

The same feeling when we held fingers walking back upstairs from the wine cellar. Even though that was such a short time of holding fingers, my body felt electrified and my heart wouldn't stop hammering against my chest. Just like now, my heart is picking up and I can feel my cheeks burn—and it's not from the sun glaring down at us in the cove.

"Quit staring, Bunny," He mutters under his breath and I turn around and try to busy myself with something, *anything*.

"Get over here, Camilla!" Birdy's voice drifts between our boats and I breathe a sigh of relief as I find a distraction from Bennett.

I head towards the middle of our attached boats and climb up onto the seating of my boat before crossing my legs over and attempting to find my footing on their boat.

My foot slips and I yelp as I close my eyes, waiting to hit something as I fall, but it doesn't come. I feel strong hands grab my elbow and my waist. I open my eyes and see Birdy running towards me while Bennett holds onto my hand and waist.

There's burning heat underneath his touch where his fingers graze my exposed skin between my skirt and the top that crept up during my slip.

I look up at Bennett slowly as I see him gulp and I feel even more of a burn on my cheeks—and fluttering in my core. *That's new*.

"Be careful, Camilla!" Birdy exclaims as she grabs my other hand.

"I told you guys. She's such a bunny," Bennett shakes his head and Birdy leans over me and slaps his shoulder.

"You be nice to her. She just slipped and almost fell face first," Birdy yells at Bennett.

I shake my head and smile. "It's okay. I'm fine."

Bennett grunts and removes his hands from me and it feels

like a match going out. I can't help but feel a pout form on my lips from the absence of his hands on me.

There's commotion at the front of the boats and Birdy and I turn to see Parker and Steve heading back towards where we all are.

Steve stands near Bennett and looks at him before looking at me. He gives me a big smile and his eyes are a sparkling blue. His chest is starting to get blotches of red from the sun.

"Let's get this party started," he says as he slaps Bennett on his back.

I have a feeling this is going to be a long lake day.

"SO, you're telling me the James kid here drove all the way without getting pulled over by marina police?" Steve asks as he bites into a burger.

Birdy and Steve brought a small grill to cook some food while we were anchored. We've been out in the water for almost two hours and the moment Steve set up the grill, I realized how hungry I was for some hot dogs.

Now, I'm biting into a hotdog, the ketchup moving right onto my top lip. I lick it off and Bennett catches my eyes. I can feel the blush come back as he takes a sip of his beer that he's been babysitting for the last half hour. It's got to be warm by now, I'm sure.

Thank god for the time we've been out under the sun's rays and knowing I had some color to my face from the possible sunburn, so he'd think it was that and not a blush.

Parker is out in the water laying on a floatie that Birdy made him manually blow up. After complaining for ten minutes, he finally inflated it and grabbed a soda before plopping into the floatie and staying there.

I almost laughed at the entire ordeal, but he threw me a side eye before getting in the water and keeping to himself. I would need to make sure he reapplies his sunscreen later. I didn't need his aunt getting angry with me if he came back as red as a tomato. His nose is already as bright as Rudolph the reindeer. I took it upon myself to be his chaperone for today, or like an older sister.

I turn to Steve as he takes another bite of his burger before waiting for my answer. I pinch my brows and shrug, taking another bite.

"Not sure. He drove great. I just made sure to grab onto the railing."

Bennett clears his throat and I catch his eye. "Did you make sure to wear a life jacket?"

I shake my head, taking a final bite into the remaining hot dog in my hand. "No, I forgot. It's no big deal."

Birdy *tsks* under her breath and I snap my head in her direction, wondering what that's about. Steve looks from me to Bennett before shrugging.

"Bunny, you better wear one when you head back home today."

"You're suddenly so cautious," I mumble under my breath as I get up and head towards the makeshift table Birdy set up on a vacant cushion. There's an array of drinks inside of a green cooler that sits atop it.

I grab for a blueberry seltzer and pop the lid open, taking a swig of it and then turn my head back towards Bennett. I'm not usually this mean with my responses back, but it came out. He's been looking at me constantly today and I can't handle that much attention while I'm practically stuck here on these tied boats.

"I'm just watching out for you," Bennett says softly, before getting up with an annoyed look on his face. He passes by me, brushing his shoulder with mine. I hear the cooler open behind me and the movement of cans. He comes back to stand next to me and I hear him crack open another beer. He takes a swig before peering down at me.

I gulp and sidestep to the right a little, feeling like I'm burning right under his stare.

"I'm going to tan up front, Steve... wanna join me?" Birdy speaks up as she gets a drink as well and tosses Steve one. He looks up at her, surprised, as he holds the beer in his hand and then averts his gaze to Bennett and me.

He nods at Birdy and gives us an awkward wave before following Birdy's footsteps to the front of the boat.

There are more cushions up front for laying out under the sun to tan and I turn my head to see Birdy set down a towel on one cushion and lying flat on her back. Steve follows suit on the other side of the boat with his own towel.

I move my gaze to the side of the boat to make sure Parker is doing okay. He's staring out into the cove where the other boats are. I wonder for a moment if his friends are here–he didn't seem to talk much about them. He had just graduated from high school and summer had just begun.

He's a shy boy, but I assumed he'd have some friends to meet up with while we're here. I shake the thought from my head and remember that it's time to reapply some sunscreen on my face and arms. I haven't taken off the shirt or skirt yet, so I am fine in those spots for now.

I set my seltzer down and head back towards the side of the boat where my speed boat connects and lean over, attempting to grab my beach bag I left on one seat. My fingers reach and move as they try to cling to the handle of the strap, but I'm too short. I huff out an exasperated breath before I feel movement on the same cushion I'm kneeling on and see Bennett's big build fill the space to my left.

His large hand seamlessly reaches over and grabs the handle of the beach bag. In one swift movement, he's able to carry the beach bag with one hand and by *one handle*. The veins in his forearms are evident in the movement and I look up at him beneath my lashes, wondering what the hell I'm feeling right now in the pit of my stomach.

"Here," he pushes the beach bag between us and gets up.

My mouth opens and then shuts before I can meep out a thank you. He nods and then grabs his beer. He sits down at the far end of the boat where it curves, his legs spreading wide. His thighs are thick, and I can't help but let my eyes travel from his thighs to his crotch, and then up towards his chest and then face.

The moment my eyes move to his face, his eyes are already staring at me. I look straight down at my bag and let my curls fall past my face to cover up the embarrassment. He definitely saw me looking at him... like, *really* looking at him.

I nonchalantly pull out the sunscreen and unscrew the cap, squeezing the bottle to squirt out some product before dabbing some on my nose, cheeks, and forehead. I place the bottle down and then use my hands to spread the sunscreen around my face, then do the same to my arms and legs that aren't covered by my top and skirt.

I get up from the cushion, feeling Bennett's eyes on me as I head towards the side of the boat where Parker is floating. I lean over the rail and then wave to Parker to get his attention.

"Parker!" I call out and he whips his head and I can't help but bark out a laugh and cover my mouth with one hand.

"What?" He asks, his brows pinched in confusion.

There's a streak of red running across his face from cheek to cheek and then some on his forehead. It's only gotten worse since we anchored. I wave the bottle of sunscreen in my hand towards him, and he shakes his head.

"You need it! I won't let you come back on this boat unless you reapply," I warn him, raising a brow.

"I took too long inflating this thing, Miss Camilla. I'm going to stay here all day," Parker replies, his arms crossing against his chest.

I roll my eyes and laugh before tossing him the sunscreen.

He thankfully catches it and gives me a small grimace before uncapping it and reapplying. He throws the bottle back and I laugh as I miss and the sunscreen bottle hits the floor of the boat. I rush to it and lean down, grabbing the bottle.

When I stand up, I realize I'm in front of Bennett and I look up to see him adjusting his position in the chair and looking right at me. I can see the bright blue in his eyes and his long hair drifts in the wind against his face. He's handsome and I can't take my eyes off him.

My gaze moves from his eyes towards his cheeks and notice he's also getting red. I stand up and walk towards him, leaning towards him. I push the bottle of sunscreen onto his chest and he looks up underneath his lashes. There's silence between us as I stand in between his legs. He doesn't move his legs.

His eyes travel my face slowly until he meets my eyes again. I can feel the thud of my heart increase in beats and weight. Like someone is repeatedly hitting my chest. The weight of it all makes me breathe harder. He's quiet, but I can see some redness creep up to his ears.

We're like this for a few beats before I uncap the sunscreen and squirt some product onto my index finger. I look at him and wait for a protest, but it doesn't come.

I lift my finger slowly before pressing a small dot of sunscreen on his nose *gently* before repeating this process on each cheek and then his forehead.

His eyes bore into mine as I still wait for him to push me away or get up and move. He waits patiently and his Adam's apple bobs as he takes a gulp as I drop the sunscreen bottle to the cushion next to him. I use both hands and gently rub the sunscreen onto his skin.

As I work on his cheek, my fingers rub against the stubble on his face and it's a unique feeling of soft and prickly at the same time. I move my fingers towards his temples and then to his forehead, but the boats move with the waves that suddenly come our way.

With my hands both up on Bennett's face, I'm unable to steady myself on just my feet as the speedboats bump into another and I lean towards my left, almost losing my balance.

I let out a small yelp before Bennett lifts his hands and grabs both sides of my waist to steady my balance. I instinctively hold on to his head, my fingers running through his hair and grabbing strands.

"Sorry," I whisper, releasing the grasp I have on his head before stepping back. His hands drop from my waist, and I see some distance in his eyes as he watches me take a step back.

"It's fine, Bunny," is all he says before he turns to look around the cove and no longer makes eye contact with me.

I stand there awkwardly before I grab the sunscreen and cap it, throwing it in the beach bag. I don't know what else to do after that encounter, so I opt to get in the water instead.

My hands reach for the tie on the skirt and undo it, letting the fabric fall off my body and onto the boat's floor. I then pull the matching top off.

It felt silly climbing down the small set of stairs that attach to the side of the boat, as if I'm trying to ignore this awkward feeling I'm having. He obviously did not like what had just happened. But his large hands on my skin felt nice and even having my hands grasp his hair brought thoughts to my mind that I've never had before.

"Hey, Miss Camilla," Parker's voice breaks my thoughts from behind me as I dip into the cold water and shiver before dropping my body completely in the water to get the hard part over with.

When I resurface, I see Parker smiling and waving me over. I swim a few feet before I grab Parker's outstretched hand and hold on to his floatie. My fingers grasp the plastic inflatable.

"You doing okay?" I ask him, brushing my wet hair off my face as I see him nod and take another sip from his soda.

"It's a great start to my summer," he responds.

"Are your friends here?" I ask, chewing on my lip. I don't want to push him to talk, but it's been at the forefront of my mind.

He looks at me with softness in his face before he looks down at the soda can and shakes his head. "No, a lot of them are on vacation or at home. There are even some that moved to the places where they'll start college to start on summer programs to get ahead."

"Oh," I say, unable to wrap my head around how he must feel.

I reach my free hand out to touch his arm comfortingly. He looks at me and moves his eyes to where we're touching. He gives me a small smile before taking another sip of his soda. Before I can say anything else, I hear movement behind us and look over to see Bennett stand up and stare at Parker and me.

"Come join!" I yell at him as I remove my hand from Parker's arm and turn my body around as best as I can while also holding onto the floatie.

Bennett monitors the scene before him before shrugging. "I can cool off a bit, Bunny."

Parker laughs beside me as I watch Bennett pull off his shirt over his head. I feel my jaw go slack as I see his broad shoulders, defined chest, and even some abs on his big build. His swim shorts run low against his body. I can't help but keep staring, looking over the tattoos that paint his body.

There's a big gash along his collarbone, but the scar is a faint pink, so I know it must be from years ago—but it looks like it was a deep one. There are other knicks and scars along his body, but that's the biggest one that my eyes fall to. He catches my eye and I move my head to look away.

I don't want him to feel uncomfortable with my staring, so I let my eyes study the water. I hear him step down the stairs and then splash into the water.

The water ripples as the impact from his jump pushes waves into the water. I finally look in his area and see him resurface and run his fingers through his wet hair. He slowly swims towards us, and Parker raises his hand for a high five.

Bennett shakes his head and smiles as he completes the high five with Parker. He gets closer to me, and I can't help but let a smile fill my lips.

"Come on, Bunny," he says as he swims backwards, his head bobbing just above the surface of the water.

I check Parker, who continues to sip his soda and not say anything as he watches me make my decision to follow Bennett.

"Eat something, okay?" I instruct Parker, hoping I don't come off too much as a nagging adult. But he hasn't eaten the whole time we've been here, and I don't want to come back to see him passed out on the floatie.

He gives me a nod before I turn around and let my hand go from the floatie. My body instantly sinks from the loss of flotation, and I swim towards Bennett, who is a few feet away, near the back of the boat. I keep sight of a ledge where I can swim to if needed. My swimming skills aren't the best.

"You're an excellent swimmer," I attempt to yell as I close our distance. He treads his feet in the water and reaches his hand out and I gladly take it. The last thing I want to do is drown my first day in this lake.

"I've had years of practice."

I raise a brow. "Really?"

He nods. "There was a time I had to stay just above my chin in the water for five hours. Some dumb training."

His eyes catch my worried one before pulling me closer.

"Well, I had no training. I had to teach myself and I think I'm doing okay," I reply just as the water moves higher than my head and makes me go under for a solid second. I resurface and cough, holding tighter to Bennett's hand.

"It takes time, Bunny. I got you," He states as I wipe the water off my eyes and face with my free hand. I nod and then see how much closer we are.

There are sparkles in his blue eyes from the reflection of the sun hitting the water. His eyes seem like a brighter blue, almost as blue as the surrounding water. We stay like that, staring at each other.

Just as I'm about to let go of his hand to tread on my own, a boat passes in the distance—creating small waves. I instantly move closer and grab Bennett's shoulder, my fingers grasping around it as we fight the wave.

He moves a hand around my waist, and we tread the water until it dies down a little.

I turn my head and we're inches away from touching nose to nose. His eyes move from my eyes to my lips. I feel a flutter in my stomach as we stay in this position for a few seconds.

In that instant, there's something in me that wants to lean in and—

"Maybe we should get back to the ledge," Bennett suggests, and I slip out an 'oh' before nodding my head and letting him lead us towards the back of the boat.

He hauls himself up the ledge where I have a good view of his muscular back and his arm muscles flexing under his weight. He reaches out his hand for me and helps me up easily.

"There you guys are!" Steve yells from just behind the small gate that separates the back of the boat from the seating area.

Birdy is standing next to him, who wiggles her brows at me, and I bite my tongue from saying anything dumb. I know she'll have all the questions. She probably saw Bennett and I in the water.

I can already feel the embarrassment heat my face.

"I was teaching Bunny how to *properly* swim," Bennett calls out before he leans over and pats my wet head. I gawk and then laugh, attempting to push him by the shoulder, but his frame is stiff, and he doesn't move an inch.

"Alright, alright," Birdy says laughing. "No more bullying her, Bennett. It's her first day out here! We need her to like it enough to come back."

I nod and poke his shoulder again and he gives me a side eye, but I can see right through him. He's holding back a smile.

"I'm liking it so far," I respond.

EIGHT

BENNETT

I HATE TO SAY IT, but Steve is starting to be right about Bunny. I'm being *nice* around her even though I try so hard not to be.

Something about her sunny demeanor is slowly picking away at the ice that stands ten feet tall all around me.

Watching her now, in the passenger seat of my truck, makes my chest pull. I'd like to think it's more so a feeling of almost having a panic attack or a heart attack. But I think it's the thawing of the ice around me.

Back at the lake, we spent a few more hours tanning under the scorching sun and hearing Birdy and Steve bicker like an old married couple. Parker stayed in his floatie the whole time and the more he did, the more Bunny got worried for him.

Just seeing her incredibly soft side for the kid made me want to give in to it whenever she turned around and gave it to me. But I pushed the metaphorical wall further out, making sure she couldn't get through with her sweet comments and kind eyes.

But, *damn*, does she make it hard for me to keep this up.

By the time we all headed back to the ramp with our boats, Parker had a long conversation on the phone with his aunt about being out later than he promised. He almost looked like he was on the verge of tears, but Bunny took the phone from him and reassured his aunt that he'd be home and she'd get a ride from someone else.

Birdy and Steve were already packing their things into Steve's truck, with barely any room for a third person. I really didn't want to offer her a ride... but I also wanted to. Like the offer of having some alone time here in my truck was just too good to pass up.

So, here we are, driving towards Misty Creek Road in my truck and her sweet shampoo scent is wafting my way. Like blueberries and honey. I pinch my nose, attempting to not breathe in the sweet scent—not only is she consuming my mind, but now her scent will fill my brain and I won't be able to forget it. I cast a glance quickly toward her and my chest tightens at the sight.

The way her tan skin seemed to still glow even under the setting sun caused me to almost crash when turning a corner. I wonder what she looks like under a rising sun, if this is how she looks under a setting one. I attempt to clear my head from these thoughts and grip the steering wheel even harder than usual.

"So," her pitched voice breaks through the silence and she shifts her body in her seat. I take a quick glance at her before returning my eyes back on the road.

"What?"

"I think Birdy and Steve are quite... close."

I huff out a laugh. "You just figured that out?"

She sighs heavily and I feel a pang of guilt hit my chest at my choice of words. "I just thought they were really good friends. She seems to really care for him... and vice versa."

I shrug. "That's just Birdy and Steve. They'll stick like glue, but never admit they might have feelings for each other. Like I said earlier on the boat, they're like an old married couple without the rings and the title."

"Do you think they'll ever get married?" she asks curiously.

My eyes glance at her and I see her whole body is turned towards me and I take a deep breath at the sight. Her lips are plump and a little dry from the day out in the water and under the sun. Her curls are frizzing around her head, and I imagine just running my hands through—

"I don't know, Bunny. I don't really bother with those kinds of thoughts. You should just ask Birdy yourself," I spit out more harshly than intended.

I see her turn her body back towards the road in my peripherals and I grit my teeth. *Great, she's annoyed with me.*

"Sorry, I just wanted to ask. Seemed like something you'd know with how close you all seem." Her voice is low, and I feel fucking dumb for even responding to her that way.

My brain tries to figure out another topic to discuss as we pull closer to her driveway, but she's the one to speak up.

"Thank you for letting me swim with you all day. I know it wasn't what you were planning on doing today—making sure I didn't drown."

We're finally turning into her driveway right before the gate and I press the button to roll down the window on my side. I press my foot hard on the brake and turn my head towards her.

Her eyes are darting from my eyes to my chest, and I can't quite read her mind. "It wasn't a big deal," I finally let out.

She gives me a small smile that doesn't quite reach her eyes. "The code is 1-9-1-7."

I raise my brows and then realize she just gave me the code to her gate. I nod and then lean my arm out to jab the four digits into the keypad. The static sound of the electric gate fills the air as they open.

The rest of the drive up towards her house is silent. I can see her fiddle with her fingers on her lap every time I sneak a glance.

Once we reach the gravel driveway right in front of her porch steps, I stop the car and put it in park. I wait for a few seconds, but I don't hear her unbuckling her seat belt or opening the door to get out.

I finally turn to look at her and she's looking straight at her house. I furrow my brows before lifting my finger and poking her arm.

She jolts a little before turning her lips into a small smile and looking towards me.

"Sorry, I was just thinking."

"About?"

Suddenly, I can feel the air get thicker. She breathes in deeply and then lets out a long breath. Her brown eyes reach mine and she slowly turns her body towards me again. My heartbeat quickens and my breath is shaky from her stare.

What the fuck is happening to me?

"Bunny—" I start to say, but she shakes her head and runs her hand through her curls.

"Forget it, it was silly. It was about us out in the water."

Again, my brows rise in confusion. Us in the water? What is she talking about?

"Like when we were swimming?"

She nibbles on her lip and I hitch my breath. She lets out a heavy sigh and I clench my fists on my lap for a few seconds before releasing the hold.

"Yeah, when we were swimming... just how close we were..." She catches my staring and clears her throat. "Like I said, it was silly."

"We kind of had to be close when you were gripping my neck that hard to keep from drowning," I joke.

Her eyes widen, and a smile spreads across her face. This time, it hits her eyes. "Hey! That lake was bigger than I thought, and I couldn't feel the bottom!"

She playfully slaps my shoulder and I let my eyes fall to where her hand lays on my shoulder. She doesn't move her hand.

My brain is mush and the next thing I know is my left hand creeping up from my lap to rest on top of her hand.

She lets out a shaky breath as my eyes reach up towards hers and we stay like this for a few moments. Neither of us speaking.

Just existing.

"Are you glad you didn't drown?" I try to joke, but it comes out in a half breath and raspy, my throat becoming dry.

She nods slowly and licks her lips. I can't tell if it's because of nerves or what. But I break eye contact and let my hand slide off hers finally. Her hand stays on my shoulder for a second before falling to her side as well.

"Sorry," she says, unbuckling her seat belt. I turn to her and widen my eyes at her actions.

"Wait," I say, hoping she pulls her hands away from the door handle. She lets them fall at her sides. She turns to look at me and her brows scrunch.

She's trying to read me and I *want* her to, but I don't as well. The ice is still defrosting around me and I don't think it'll ever get completely melted. It's been up for so long.

She looks down at the floorboards before bringing her face up towards me. She takes a deep breath and I can't calculate the next ten seconds for the life of me.

She huffs out an exasperated breath before shifting in her seat and leaning towards me. It's too fast for me to register and throw my hands up. She leans her face close, curls brushing against my temple. Her eyes are shining and darting across my face as if she's second guessing her next step.

But before I can say or *do* anything, she leans in and plants her lips on mine. It's soft and quick. Barely any time for me to blink.

She pulls away fast and then settles back in her seat.

"Wha—" I start to ask but she reaches for the door, pushing it open, and hopping out with her bag.

I lean my body near the passenger window and attempt to

roll it down. But she's quick and already halfway up her porch steps.

What the fuck just happened?

THE WHOLE FIVE minutes of leaving her place and driving up to my own, my mind was a mushy frenzy.

Simply, I was shocked and unsure what to do next.

I couldn't even unbuckle my seat belt until after I sighed, yelled, and punched the buckle until it unclicked and the strap whipped my face as it retracted back into its place.

I let out a muffled shout.

The whole walk up to my door; I was cursing under my breath and breathing heavily.

Why did she kiss me? Why did she think she could just do that?

Thoughts of her soft but slightly chapped lips on mine come back to memory and burn my eyes for a moment. I grunt again and push the key into the front door and push the door harder than I mean to.

I slam it shut and then make my way upstairs towards the bedroom, already lifting my shirt off my body and throwing it on the ground next to the bed. I do the same with my swim trunks and head to the bathroom.

I don't even bother to check if I have any sunburns on my skin. I'm too focused on the memory of her.

My hands reach for the handle in the shower and turn it to hot and lift the lever. It starts sprinkling down and I step in and let the hot water hit me.

Although it's hot as fuck outside, I need something to distract me from what just happened.

But her curly hair, brown eyes, and nibbling lips come into view. I lift my hands towards my face and rub it in harsh motions. I rub my eyes as if I'm trying to scrub off some kind of toxic chemical. But she's still burning through my closed eyelids.

I decide to finally open them and grab the shampoo bottle before squeezing some onto my hand and working it through my hair.

"Fucking Bunny," I grunt out as I harshly lather the shampoo through my hair. Once I rinse it out, I grab a loofah and lather it with bar soap before working it over my body. I wince as I finally feel the sunburn surfacing from the scrubbing.

I clench my teeth as I finish lathering my chest and then work lower. That's when a mental image of her comes back to mind and I can't help but groan and feel my cock harden.

"Jesus Christ," I huff out.

This wasn't something new I've done in my shower, masturbating. But, it's never really been about *anyone*, really. Mostly just the morning release to get on with my day.

But this time I'm fucking hard for... Camilla.

I have two options: ride this out and finish my shower and attempt to think of things that make me forget her that brings my boner down... or *ride* this out and get my release.

I could go with option one... but my mind is already fixated on her lips and her soft smile. And her god damn laugh.

My hand instinctively reaches down and begins to stroke my length, my body shuddering at the contact. I close my eyes and lean to the side of the shower, and bring my other hand out on the wall to steady myself.

The more I stroke myself, the more her image of every encounter we've had comes flooding into my mind. The way we held fingers in the wine cellar, to me holding onto her in the lake.

I wanted to kiss her, but it wasn't right. Not in front of everyone. And I saw Steve stand up from the front of the boat making his way towards the back where he would be in clear view of us in the water. I couldn't risk it. That's why I made us swim back.

But I wanted to kiss her right there and I didn't.

And I couldn't kiss her back in the truck. I freaked out and I couldn't move a muscle.

"Damn it," I grit through my teeth as my thumb and index finger run over the tip of my cock and continue to pump faster over my length.

I just think of her and how her body felt in my hands. The curve of her body and the softness of her chapped lips.

I'm almost there, continuing to pump through this high, and before I know it, I'm coming all over my hand and breathing heavily.

I groan before moving my body back under the water and rinsing off my release. I take deep breaths and shake my head, water splashing everywhere.

If she has that effect on me in my *head*, how am I going to survive any more moments with her alone?

She's going to make me like putty in her hands.

And as much as I hate to think this—I know I'll let her.

NINE

CAMILLA

I DID SOMETHING DUMB.

The walk of shame back to my place was far too much to handle. The moment I got inside, I ran to the kitchen and pulled out the first wine bottle I could get my fingers wrapped around.

Once I finally pulled the bottle out, I turned the label toward me and read the type of wine. It's special, for sure, and isn't in a lot of locations in the world. It's a Viognier where the notes are a deep apricot, peach, and some slight hint of honeysuckle.

I pull out the metal bottle opener from a nearby drawer and unscrew the cork before pouring a hefty amount into a wine glass. I lift the glass to my lips and take a big sip.

Flashes of the kiss run through my memory and I take another sip.

Why did I do that?

I walk around the kitchen in the dark. The automatic lights on the porch that wraps the house are on and they illuminate the inside.

My heart stammers as I suddenly feel fur run across my legs and I look down to see Goose walking all over my feet with her small paws.

"Hey, baby," I say as I reach down and pet her head and then run my hand down her spine. She purrs softly as she curls her body around my legs.

I stand back up and sigh, leaning against the kitchen island and finishing the glass of wine before refilling it. I press the corkscrew back into the bottle and place it in the fridge to keep fresh.

I make my way toward the main bedroom and hear the padding of Goose's feet hit the hardwood floor as she follows close behind. I put the wineglass down on top of the dresser before heading towards the walk-in closet and grabbing a set of silk pajamas.

Once I have the clothes in hand, I head out of the closet and grab the wine glass with my free hand and make my way towards the bathroom. Taking another big sip of wine, I close my eyes before setting the glass down and placing the clothes on the bathroom counter.

I strip slowly out of the cover up and then the bikini before hopping into the shower. I turn the knob to lukewarm water before starting my shower routine. Once I'm out, I dry myself off quickly and pull on the silk pajamas before wrapping my hair up in a towel.

I attempt to finish the rest of the wine in order to carry on with washing my face, my teeth, and then putting on lotion and face cream. I sigh again, looking at myself in the mirror.

My cheeks are flush from either the embarrassment from earlier or the alcohol in the wine. I don't bother to figure out which it is.

Once I'm in the bedroom, I pull the sheets back and hop in, patting the space next to me for Goose to climb in. She does so willingly and cuddles next to me as I wiggle in the bed until I'm comfortable.

"Let's hope he forgets about it tonight," I say to no one as I attempt to close my eyes and forget it ever happened.

. . .

THE NEXT DAY is full of cleaning, organizing the house, and making sure everything is all good. I didn't want to bother Parker and have him come over on a weekend. I had to break some ground rules with him and make sure he wasn't over-worked this summer.

He let me know over text he wasn't in too much trouble with his aunt and that made me relieved. I did not want to get on someone's bad side without even meeting them first.

The day goes by rather quickly as I continue the rest of my time at the vineyard and finish any last touches. I wanted to start the week off right and hopefully open in the next few weeks. There still needed to be lawn maintenance, but I couldn't do it alone and would wait for when Parker could help me.

It was nearing dinner time and Birdy texted me she already had plans and couldn't hang. I've only been to one place so far, so I headed to Nicky's once I locked up the vineyard area.

The drive was short, and it seemed like the streets were busy with locals going out and about on their Sunday night. I park my car and head towards Nicky's, the cloud of smoke welcoming me again.

I look around to see if Izzy was working, but I don't see her. I decide to sit down at a booth and wait for a server to come up. It's a local I've yet to meet, someone I haven't seen before with the name tag of Mabel.

"Hey! Welcome to Nicky's, I hope your night is going well," she says as she slaps down a menu and brings a big smile to her face. She's pretty and she's got some light freckles on her tawny brown skin. She looks to be about Parker's age.

I smile and thank her for the menu. "I think I know what I want to order," I tell her, not even bothering to look at the menu.

"Great! I'm new here, so that definitely helps me. Still trying to learn the menu," She bites her lip and then pulls out her notepad and pen.

"Oh! No wonder I didn't recognize you! Last time I was here I met Izzy."

"She trained me! I just started this weekend. Summer job before college."

I nod, this confirming my thoughts about her age, and then clasped my hands together. "I'd love some lemon pepper wings and fried pickles. With a Coke, please."

She scribbles on the notepad and then nods her head before turning around and heading towards the kitchen to give my order.

I pull out my phone and send a text to my mom, wishing her a good night. I then text Viola, letting her know how much progress I've been able to make today at the vineyard. She immediately texts back.

VIOLA

I'm so proud of you, C! Can't wait for pics.

I hear heels clacking against the hardwood floor and I look up to see a redhead nearing my booth. I sit tall and study her. I can't remember her name, but I remember her the night I was with Izzy and Birdy.

"Hey, you're the new girl, right?"

I nod my head and clear my throat. "Yeah, Camilla. I'm so sorry I can't remember your name. I know you introduced yourself."

She gives me a half smile and shrugs. She looks at the seat across from me and I lift my hand to gesture for her to join me.

"Thanks. I'm just waiting on my takeout order. I saw a familiar face and wanted to say hi."

"Well, it's nice to see you again..." I pause, waiting for her to give me her name again.

She widens her eyes and then lets out a laugh. "Sorry, right. Katherine Pearson."

She lifts her hand for a handshake and I lift my own, closing our hands briefly before we pull away.

My eyes glance around the bar and try to see where the server went. My throat is starting to go dry, and I'd like to drink my soda.

"Are you liking it here?" She asks finally, tapping her fingers on the table.

I look at her and nod, giving her a small smile. "Yeah, I love it so far. I've been able to meet a lot of great people."

"Yeah, you met my sister. She's a nutcase, but she's the best."

Her eyes lock on mine and I smile again and nod. "She definitely made an impression on me. I also met the golden boys, or at least that's what Birdy calls them."

"Steve and Bennett?" She asks, pursing her lips. There's an intonation at her last word.

"Yeah, we went out on the lake yesterday," I say.

She raises a brow. "Bennett... Bennett Moore went out on the lake? How the hell did that go?"

I laugh. "Actually, really well. He seemed to be quite rude the first time I met him. I think he's warming up to me now–"

"That sounds more like the Bennett I know," she cuts me off with a smug look. "He's been like that for years. I'm surprised he's actually leaving his farm and doing things."

"Yeah, but I think he hates me again. I did something really dumb." I bite my lip to stop myself from saying anything else.

Shut up, Camilla.

Why am I confiding in this stranger? I barely know her. But sometimes the best conversations are with strangers. Her face returns to a softer feature as she stares at me.

"I'm sure you did nothing stupid. What did you do?" she asks.

The moment she does, Mabel walks up with my soda and places it on the table along with a basket of fried pickles.

"Here you go!" She says happily before turning back and leaving us.

I pick at a fried pickle spear and take a bite before swallowing and then taking a sip of the coke.

I see Katherine staring at me, waiting for a response.

I clear my throat and see her bright green eyes flicker with curiosity. "Uh, so we were driving back to my place to drop me off since my ride had to get home. And then I kissed him."

Her eyes slightly widen before going back to normal. She presses her lips into a tight line before smirking. "You kissed him, and then what?"

"I ran out of the truck and straight into my house."

She then lets out a small laugh and leans her head back. "How old are you?"

I'm taken aback by her question and furrow my brows.

"Twenty seven. You?"

"Thirty seven. Same age as Bennett. So I wouldn't sweat it."

"I feel like you're silently judging me for my age and thinking I was immature for running away after that."

She eyes me before shrugging. "Not really. It's cute. Besides, I've done worse."

This time I'm the one silently wondering what she's talking about.

"What do you mean?"

She looks down at the table and then at me again. "I lied and made someone hate me enough to leave me."

"Oh, wow. I'm sorry." I take another sip of my coke.

She shrugs. "No biggie. It was time and I'm happier without them. It wasn't even an intentional lie. We were young, and I thought that was the life I wanted until I... didn't. I was trying to be someone I wasn't just to keep them in my life. It wasn't fair to either of us."

"Still, I'm sorry. Does he still live here?"

The question catches her off guard, and she sucks in her cheeks before letting out a deep breath.

"Yeah, it was Bennett."

My eyes widen again and I let my mouth fall in an 'o'.

"Wait, what? I just told you I *kissed* him."

She laughs before shaking her head. "I don't care at all. That's why I asked how old you were."

"I'm not that young," I argue.

"You're not. But don't think too much about it. Our history is long and gone."

"So, you guys just dated and then he broke up with you after you lied?"

She chews on her lip before shaking her head. "I don't know why I'm telling you all of this. I don't really like sharing a lot of stuff in such a small town."

"It's okay, you don't have to."

"No, it's okay." She takes a deep breath before continuing. "We were married for 12 years. He divorced me. It was rough at first, and then we could be amicable and live in the same town."

This new information causes me to sit back in the booth and cross my arms over my chest. "Married? He didn't mention any of that."

Let alone for *twelve* years. That's a long time to be married to someone.

He didn't have to tell me—I just met the guy. But it seemed like maybe something Birdy would've brought up. Something she *should've* brought up. Right?

"Yeah, pro tip. Don't marry your high school sweetheart. It doesn't always end like a fairytale."

I nod my head and then reach for the same fried pickle spear from moments ago and munch on the rest of it as I ruminate on her words.

"I'm not telling you this to back off him and never speak to him again. But I just thought it'd be good to know a little about him. Clearly, people haven't told you everything."

"Clearly." I sigh as I take another sip of my coke.

"Well, it was nice talking with you. If you ever want to get some private dance lessons or do a dance class at my studio, *Releve*, I host them daily."

She stands up, and I nod. "Thanks, I might take you up on that."

"Definitely don't think your kiss was stupid. If you like him, you like him. And if he's closing off because of it, just give him space. That's what he does best—being alone in his own world on his farm."

"Thanks," I finally say as she nods and then heads towards the bar to grab her takeout food and gives me a small wave.

I lean back in the booth again and shake my head, sighing. I take another fried pickle spear and take a big bite before I see Mabel come up with the basket of wings. Suddenly, I feel sick to my stomach, and I ask her for a box and the receipt.

Once she brings both, I put everything in there, throw some cash on the table, and finish my coke. I head out of the bar as fast as I can and into my car.

The drive is short as I speed quickly back home and enter the code to open the gate.

Whatever just happened with Katherine was something I wasn't expecting.

It seems like there is just so much going on in this small town that I've yet to discover, and I don't know how much more I can take.

TEN

BENNETT

IT'S BEEN over a week since the last time I spoke to Bunny.

To be honest, it was a lot of *me* putting space between *us*. I didn't want her to get any mixed signals about the kiss. It felt like I was spiraling, and I locked myself on my property for a few days to just *think*.

I needed to get my fucking urges in check. I didn't need the whole town knowing what I was feeling. Maybe if I just pushed and *pushed* the feelings down, like pushing down the feeling of wanting to throw up, it'll eventually dissipate.

And it worked. For a good few days of tending to my farm, my cattle, the cats in the barn, and fixing my house. I even made a fucking list of what I had to repaint, tear down, or simply move. That took about four days.

By day five, I was driving down Misty Creek Road every couple of hours just to see if she'd have her lights on or be near the vineyard working with Parker. It was getting almost... stalker-ish. It wasn't like me at all.

I stopped myself on the sixth day when I drove by and slowed down just to see her peek out from the gate to get her mail. Her brows were pinched, her nose scrunched, and her eyes narrowed.

She looked confused to see me and I hit the gas before she could think of anything or wave.

Now, it was the tenth day, and I was playing with the barn cats as Steve helped me put some horses in the stalls for dinner.

"You know, Ben," he starts with a huff. I turn to look at him slapping a horse's behind to get it in the stall. It whinnied and ran inside before he glided the gate closed. The horse turns its body to stick its face out through the stall door bars. It whinnies again with a huff and Steve points his finger at it.

The buckets of feed are already in each stall, so we're left with the silence of the horse's chewing.

"What?" I ask, waiting for him to settle down on the bale of hay next to me. He leans over to plant his elbows on his knees.

"You gotta talk to her. You're freaking her out, ignoring her."

"I don't know what you're talking about."

Steve leans to his left and reaches into the small cooler we brought full of ice and beers. He grabs two and passes me one. He opens his and takes a long drink. I do the same as I watch him through narrow slits.

"You know exactly what I'm talking about. I know."

"What could you possibly know?"

"Let's just say, small town means small town talk. Even Katherine–"

I place the beer down on my thigh before glaring at him. "What did you just say?"

It was strange to hear my ex-wife's name come out of my best friend's mouth. We don't really talk about her or have a *reason* to talk about her. What we had was done and what happened has been settled.

He shrugs. "Nothing, man."

"No, you said *her*. What, did she go and talk to you about something?"

Steve knows I fucking hate small town gossip, and that's one of the many reasons I kept leaving. He can sense the anger, but he just rolls his eyes and lets out a low chuckle.

"No, she didn't. Forget I said anything. You just need to talk to Camilla. She thinks you hate her or something. You're her neighbor."

"That means nothing," I bite back.

"It does in this town. You're there for your neighbors and they're there for you."

I let out a heavy breath through my lips and lift the beer can and finish it. I crunch it in one hand before tossing it on the ground.

Steve looks lost in thought as he stares at the drink in his hand. There's a vein prominent in his forehead as he thinks hard, and it won't be long until it pops.

"Jesus, Steve. Just fucking spit it out."

He finally looks up and sighs. "She told Birdy about the kiss. And apparently, Katherine and her had a conversation. She didn't give any details, but she seemed to be worried about you."

"You think Katherine told her shit?" My brows raise.

Steve shakes his head and then shrugs. His eyes seem genuine as he stares back at me. "I don't know, man. Like I said, she said little about their conversation. I don't even know the exact details. Just word of mouth. I doubt she even told Birdy everything."

"She kissed me," I blurted out.

There's silence as Steve shuts his mouth and listens. His lips turn into an 'O' before closing again. His eyes slowly go from normal to wide eyed. And then a small smile slips through his lips.

"Shit, Bennett. You kissed her?"

"*She* kissed *me*," I repeat. I shake my head and get up, striding over to grab another cold beer can and popping it open before returning to my hay bale.

Steve is still silent as he watches me intently. I feel like I'm a bug under a microscope, so I close my eyes briefly as I chug the beer. I hate being under a watchful eye, and Steve is doing a good job at it.

"So, she kissed you, so what?"

"And then she ran out of the truck," I add. There's silence and then a murmur from Steve. An '*oh*' sound.

"Well, you clearly haven't talked to her about it, so she's probably freaking out about what she did. Did you even try to call her or text her?"

I shake my head and take another long sip of the beer. It's starting to make me feel bloated, but I drink through it.

"You have to call her or do… something. You're gonna bump into her, eventually."

"Yeah, yeah. I know. I just don't know what to say. What if she regretted it?"

"You don't?" He questions, raising a brow. There's a glint in his eye and I want to punch him.

"Shut up."

"It was just a question, Ben. I'm not holding you down like a war criminal, interrogating you."

I let out a laugh, but it sounds forced. Yeah, he's not doing that. I'm just making it seem like he is. I tend to do that a lot, especially with Steve. I'm still shocked he hasn't gotten tired of my antics and mentality. Of always thinking someone has it out to get me; that they want to hold me down to get to my deep, dark secrets.

Steve knows them all, well, most of them. He doesn't need to know the dark, *dark* ones that keep me awake most nights. The ones that will haunt me 'til I die–I've only shared them with one other soul and she's not in this barn right now.

"I liked it, okay? Fuck."

Steve laughs. "Atta boy. Now, go talk to her. Or I'll make Birdy talk to her and force her to go to your front door."

"You wouldn't." I look up at him in horror. His eyebrows wiggle as he laughs. "Fucker," I add.

"Stop sulking and talk to her. You seem to really loosen up around her. We haven't seen you like this for a while."

"Not even with Katherine." I joke.

Steve shakes his head. "No, you know why you were never like that with Katherine. I'm still pissed at her about that shit. That's why I'm pushing you towards this. You may seem like a grumpy old veteran to everyone else, but to me, I can see those hidden smiles and secret signs of *happiness*."

Fuck, he was right. Even at the boat, I wanted to keep holding her, but I let my doubts get the best of me. Steve always knew what to say, and he *always* saw through me.

I raise my beer to him slowly before bringing it to my lips and finishing it. "Alright, man. I will."

MY STEPS ARE heavy as I make my way to the front door. The glass is slightly cracked, from what, I don't know, but I look around the outside briefly. There are posters and flyers taped from the inside to show window shoppers what the place offers.

Releve Ballet and Dance Studio is decked out nicely with black and red accents on the outside. It displays a few outlines and shapes of dancers in all sizes painted on the glass. I pull the handle slowly, causing the bell above to make noise. I clench my jaw as I realize what the fuck I'm doing.

It's almost closing time for the place and I wanted to catch her. She's in the middle of the studio as I walk in and I see her red hair swish as she turns to see who walked in. Her eyes narrow and she turns to the little girl she's helping with a ballet move.

The little girl turns to look at me before I see Katherine's lips moving a little to tell her something. The girl nods before continuing to practice the movement they're working on. Katherine stands up and crosses her arms over her chest before she walks over. I head towards the small counter in the front and lean over it.

"What are you doing here?" She asks, planting her feet close to the counter. Her eyes are bright and questioning. She's sizing me up.

"I just came by to say hi," I mumbled. She rolls her eyes before huffing her breath.

"Hi, now I'm busy." She's about to turn on her heels before I grunt and reach for her elbow. That's all I do before I pull my hand back. She stops in her tracks before she turns halfway to give me a stern look.

"I heard you talked to her." I confess.

Her eyebrow shoots up, and she's fully turning to face me again. She steps closer to the counter and her eyes are ablaze. If it weren't for the kid in the studio, I'm sure she'd slap me or worse.

"What about it? And how did you know?" She looks up at the ceiling before shaking her head. "This fucking small town. Can't escape it."

"It doesn't matter. I just want to make sure you guys are on good terms."

She gives me a quizzical look before pursing her lips. "Why wouldn't we be? She's sweet. I spoke to her for maybe five minutes. That was... so long ago. Why are you coming to me now about that? I have a life, Bennett. I don't stick my hands in places it shouldn't be. You know this."

I nod my head. "I know, Kat. Just want to make sure I saw you first to figure out what's going on before I went to see her."

"I don't need to know about you and her. Really," she says before sucking in her cheeks.

"I know, sorry," I mumble, pulling my hand behind my neck to scratch it.

Fuck, why did I even come here? I'm screwing it all up.

Why didn't I just go to Bunny's in the first place?

"Why are you *really* here? You don't come here," Katherine questions, her voice a little deeper.

"I don't know." I admit. I take a deep breath and lean my head towards the counter, slumping my shoulders. I hear her feet shuffle before I feel icy hands touch my arm. I peer through the crevice between my hair and arms to see her hands on me and her eyes sparkling with questions.

"She's really sweet. I mean it."

"I think that's the issue."

Katherine laughs. "Yeah, yeah. We all know. The whole goddamn town knows that, Benny."

I lift my head at my nickname. I haven't heard that name fall from her lips for years. Since... we've been together. Even from other people, it's rare to hear Benny. I've always gone by Bennett, BenBen, or Ben. Or even my last name, Moore.

It felt like a flash to the past where Katherine and I were married and happy. Her eyes continue to study me and I continue to let my breathing come in and out heavily. Her hand smooths over my arm in a calming motion. Just like she used to do when I'd come home tired of the world or wake up from a cruel nightmare. But those nightmares weren't conjured from my head, they were memories of my life. And she was always willing to be there for me during those times until she wasn't. This felt like we were back in our house and it was just *us*.

"Benny," she says my name again and I clear my throat and stretch my arms and stand straight. Her hands slip off my arm and she keeps her eyes on me.

"Sorry I came," I slip out.

She shakes her head. "Don't worry about it. Go see her. But I won't tell you what you know you have to do. I'm not dipping my toes in anything."

"I know you're not, Kat. Thanks."

Before backing up, she smiles. She doesn't turn around, though. She continues to look at me and I can tell she's trying to read me.

"I'm fine, Katherine. Really."

"Mhm. I know. It's just been a while since I've seen my ex act like this for a *tourist*."

My lips instantly curl into a smile. "You're cruel."

She shrugs. "I know you were thinking it the moment you met her."

I roll my eyes. "Yeah, yeah. You're right."

"Usually am. Oh, and Benny?"

I raise a brow and lean closer towards her.

"I heard you went out on the lake. That's ballsy of you. Finally leaving your farm? I'm proud of you." She turns around and heads back to her student, still attempting to twirl and practice the move they were working on.

I tap the counter with my knuckles before I turn around and push the door to exit. The sky has already turned dark, and I knew if I went to Bunny this late, it wouldn't be the best.

Who shows up to someone's home this late? Especially when we haven't spoken in forever.

Steve's words echo in my mind and so do Katherine's. Fuck, I need to see her, don't I?

I head towards my truck and pull the door open before hopping in. It's not like I *have* to go home. Her place is on the way. I can just take a detour.

And before I know it, I'm peeling out of the parking spot and heading back towards our road.

I momentarily remember the gate code she gave me that night. But that would be weird. So, when I pull up to her gate, I buzz in and before I can back out and drive off, the gate... opens.

ELEVEN

CAMILLA

BENNETT IS HERE in my kitchen and it feels like I'm daydreaming or something. He's really here? The moment the gate buzzed, and I could see his face in the camera, I almost spilt my wine.

It's late, but he must've been on his way home and decided to pass by... that's what I try to convince myself. He didn't take any time getting out of his truck and getting inside my home.

The way he came inside and immediately made a beeline for the kitchen made me remember that he probably stopped by the Stone's property all the time and knew this place like the back of his hand.

"You're staring, Bunny."

My eyes gloss over his body again as he leans over the marble countertop. Goose is walking nearby on the floor before jumping up on a stool and then onto the countertop to nuzzle her whiskers and cheek against Bennett's hand. There's a faint smile on his face as he rubs the top of her head.

"Did you want something?" I finally ask in one breath. My hands are resting over the stem of the wine glass I haven't let go of since he arrived. I'll surely have some kind of indentation for holding onto it for so long.

Bennett's eyes avert from Goose to me and there's a cloud of doubt in his eyes, but quickly changes to calm.

"I haven't heard from you in a while, thought I'd check in." His knuckles rap against the marble as if he's nervous or lying. I believe the latter.

My lips purse and I take a deep breath, walking closer to the countertop and leaning on the opposite side of him. My arms glide across the marble and I place the wine glass slowly on top of the counter and then shake my head, curls flying everywhere from the messy braid I attempted to put my hair in not too long ago.

"So, you're here... to just check in? *You're* the one who went AWOL on me, Bennett."

He seems to take my words in for a little and there's a pregnant pause. His lips turn into a curled smile until he's chuckling and shaking his head. And finally he lifts his hand to run it through his growing hair.

"You're getting to me," he says in an almost whisper. I have to lean in closer to make sure I heard right.

My brain racks for what he could *possibly* mean, but no answers come to mind. It's either that I'm too dumb to take a hint, or I'm beyond tired.

I've spent this entire week working with Parker at the vineyard and making sure landscapers knew where to go and how often to come. We also took a day in the wine cellar, taking inventory.

I still have a lot to get done, but I'm hoping the opening date for the vineyard will be sooner than I projected. Parker has been the best worker, and I gave him today off while I took time to continue organizing the big house. There were some things I could live without that I'd sell or donate.

Bennett's sigh brings me back to the kitchen and my brows knit together. I can't read his mind and he's not letting me.

"I've been busy with Parker," I say, rubbing my palm against the counter. Goose gets up from her sitting position and comes over to me, bumping her head against my shoulder until I'm reaching over with my left hand to rub her body.

"That kid is gonna be the death of me."

I look up at Bennett, who is sucking in his cheeks before pouting and shaking his head. This brings a smile to my lips and I can't help but laugh.

"Jealous? You could've come over and helped us out at the vineyard."

Bennett rolls his eyes before leaning further into the counter until he's able to reach out and grab Goose's tail and curl it around his hand. Goose doesn't seem to mind and purrs, continuing to bump her head over my shoulder and arm.

"Not a chance. I think I could win a match, don't you? I could probably name more trivia facts than the kid," Bennett jokes.

I hold back laughter, and he raises his brows. "You make yourself sound so old when you say it like that... Who automatically thinks of trivia? Only old people."

Bennett pauses before smiling and then snickering. "If you need help, I can swing by."

His words fall before he says anything else. I catch his eyes and it's like his nerves are finally catching up to him externally. I see his hand shaking as he pulls it back and away from Goose. He clears his throat and moves his eyes around the kitchen.

"Y-yeah, that could work. I'm thinking I can open it in two weeks?"

Bennett's eyes land on me, and he nods his head. "That would be great. The people are missing the vineyard and would love an opening soon."

I pull my lip in between my teeth and nibble on it as I think of his words.

"They really made the town, huh?" I ask, referencing the Stones.

"Yeah, they were great. Maybe I can let Peyton and Morgan know you're opening soon?"

Before I can answer, he steps back and shakes his head, as if stopping himself from extending the offer further.

I squint my eyes and then nod. "That would actually be really…nice of you, Bennett."

I notice the way his lips turn into a scowl and let a laugh escape my own. "Really, Bennett. I think that would help with the whole transition from their vineyard to mine. Having them here might allow the locals to continue their tradition of coming here."

I don't want to ask for too much from him, but it's a start. Especially if he's offering, which I have a feeling doesn't happen too often.

Flashbacks to a week ago come to the forefront of my mind when I bumped into Katherine at Nicky's. My eyes glance at Bennett and I instinctively grab the wine glass and pull it to my lips, taking a sip.

I haven't been able to get the conversation out of my head and even brought it up to Birdy later. There has been little talk or *revealing* about Bennett's life and past as much as I'd like.

With a town that seems to rely on local gossip, I wasn't getting any of that about Bennett.

Something in me knew if I wanted to get more information about Bennett, I'd have to ask him myself. And that is something I'm not too sure I have the confidence for, especially after I ran away from the kiss.

I clearly don't do well with vulnerability when it comes to myself. Or confrontation. I like to think I'm very open and bring about a calm nature, but in reality, it scares the hell out of me when I have to put myself out there and push past comfort zones.

Slapping a smile on my face is easier than dealing with reality and the repercussions of it.

"I'll call them. Peyton might need some convincing on my part and maybe with Steve and Birdy's help, she'll say yes. Morgan will, without a doubt, say yes. She misses her uncle BenBen too much, I think."

I feel a pang in my chest as I watch his blue eyes cast down at the counter with his last words. He was really close with the Stones and even though I don't know the full story about the family; it seems like they made a very big impact on the town. Even enough to bring out emotion in Bennett. The guy I thought could never crack a smile or talk about something positive around me.

I push myself off the counter and stride towards him, getting close enough to smell his fading cologne and something else. His muscles twitch under his shirt as he turns his body towards me until we're inches apart.

His eyes move from mine to the rest of my face. There's a lighter shade of blue I haven't noticed before and I can feel the increasing rate of my heart thrum against my chest. It's begging to be released and not confined to the restraints of my ribcage. He seems to pick up on my nerves and I'm guessing it's because of my rapid breathing and flushed cheeks.

"Look, Bunny," he starts as he steps closer, lifting his hand to brush against my shoulder. I have to crane my neck to look up at him with how close we are.

"What?" I breathe out.

"I don't know what's going on, but it'll burn. Crash and burn like everything else in my life. There isn't anything I've touched that hasn't been ruined."

My lips part as I take in his words. What does he mean? He's got friends, everyone seems to care about him in this town...

Is this because I talked to Katherine? Does he know? I only told Birdy and I'm positive she didn't tell Bennett. But…now that I think of it? She's been spending more time with Steve and I'm not holding it against her if she spilled the kiss to him. I didn't particularly tell her not to tell anyone and I can only imagine their friendship and *not* talking about an event as big as this.

Well, it's big for me and I know if Viola told me she kissed a boy or hooked up with someone, I'd run home and tell my mom. She's my other best friend and there isn't anything she doesn't know.

I haven't told her about this kiss though…she only knows that I'll be ready to open the vineyard soon. Viola hasn't been able to give me a timeframe of her visit this summer, so I stopped asking.

I'd love to have them all here for the opening, Viola and my parents, but I wouldn't hold it against them. I was the one who moved, so they're not under any obligation to visit me.

"I didn't say or do anything," I finally mumble. I raise my brow, as if to dare him to spill the truth.

His eyes watch me before a sigh escapes his lips. He takes a step back and lets his hand fall from my shoulder.

"I didn't say you did anything. Or do anything. I'm just telling you that this is something that I've known all my life."

When I keep looking at him in confusion, he continues. "Nothing good comes my way. If it does, it'll be running for the hills the moment it gets a peek."

I inhale deeply and cross my arms over my chest. "You're speaking a language I can't quite understand, Bennett. Dumb it down for me, will you?"

I'm feeling an itch of irritation run through my body and I want to walk out of here and go outside or upstairs. Push him out of the door and go about my night.

But he stays put and seems to think hard about his next

words. He takes a deep breath. "The kiss caught me off guard, but you running away didn't surprise me *at all.*"

I loosen the hold my fingers have around my sides. I widen my eyes and stare at the man before me. It feels like we're chipping away slowly at his ice castle and barely getting past his thick fortress.

"I didn't run away, I just—" My mouth falls slack as I think of what to say… I *did* run away, and I have no excuse. He saw it as running away and I saw it as trying to avoid a very awkward confrontation.

Relationships don't come easy to me and this is why. I get too flustered or don't think and do something dumb. Like kiss a man that has no interest in me and who is *clearly* telling me he doesn't think we could be anything.

"You ran away, and that's okay. I just wanted to kind of hash things out before I headed back home."

My brows continue to stay up high. I'm stuck in utter confusion and slight annoyance. He's playing a word game and not telling me what he's thinking directly.

I want to shake him and ask him to tell me the truth, but I don't want to push him.

"Okay," I answer, "I'll let you know when I need you to stop by this week to help."

He nods and then clears his throat before sidestepping to walk around me and head down the hallway that leads to the front of the house.

There's something in my brain telling me to run after him. I hate miscommunication and it feels like we're stuck in this loop.

He says something. I say something. And we both don't understand each other.

"Bennett, wait!" I call out, running after him.

He's pulling the door open and pushing through the screen door before turning back and casting his blue eyes on me. There's a twitch of confusion in his face before I get closer.

"Yeah?"

"I—I," My words are jumbled, and I have to take a deep breath and shake my head to clear my thoughts. It feels like my heart is about to burst out of my chest. My palms feel sweaty, and I don't know what's coming over me right now.

He waits patiently, his body halfway through the screen door and letting in the moonlight into the foyer of the home.

There are crickets chirping in the distance and frogs croaking.

"I didn't run away because I was not interested, or whatever you're probably thinking," I blurt out. "I ran because it was awkward to see you stare at me like some dumbstruck person and not even say anything. I ran because I couldn't face an awkward confrontation."

His eyes run along my face before he looks up at the ceiling between the cracks of the front door and the screen door. He's silent for a while as I watch him, my heartbeat increasing with anxiety and panic. He finally looks down at me and mumbles under his breath, shaking his head.

With the hand that's not resting on the screen door, he uses it to wrap around my waist and pull me closer to him. I can't help but squeal from the sudden movement and before I can think of anything else, I feel his soft lips press against mine, his rough stubble mustache poking at my upper lip.

He relaxes into the kiss and I let myself do the same, letting my arms press against his chest. But not to push him away. My hands ball into fists, grabbing his shirt in the process.

But before anything else can happen or we can continue to kiss, his lips are separating from mine and he's slipping his hand off my waist. My hands loosen their grip on his shirt and fall to my sides.

"I didn't call because I hate confrontation when it comes to things like this—when it comes to a girl I can't get out of my head."

I suck in a breath at his small confession, but before I can reach out for him or reply, he steps further back and lets the screen door close in front of me. He gives me a strained smile before he strides to his truck and gets inside it. The headlights blind me as he turns the truck back and then drives off.

My fingers pull to my lips and brush against the skin, as if touching it would bring the kiss back.

TWELVE

BENNETT

OLIVER IS STAPLING a few packets when I walk into his business. He's wearing a nice red dress shirt with khaki dress pants, looking like he's about to run for Mayor.

Before stepping in, I bumped into Marla Clare, who was opening her boutique next door and I helped her haul in some new shipments. She's been trying to get more summery clothes for the tourists that will for sure crowd this town in a week or two with the rising temperatures.

Daisy, her employee, wasn't there at the shop today, so I let Marla know if she needed any help at all to reach out to me or Steve and we'd help. She seemed more than shocked at my offer and asked me if I fell and hit my head.

I definitely woke up feeling less... annoyed. I almost changed the whiteboard tally, but decided against it.

"Ben! What brings you here?" Oliver's brows pinch together before he throws a smile my way.

I smile at the receptionist, Gina, who I've known since forever. She grew up with my sister and they were practically inseparable.

"You doing okay, Ben?" She asks as I head towards Oliver across the room. I turn to her and give her a curt nod.

"Yeah, I just wanted to ask Oliver something." I don't mean to be brash, but small talk isn't really something I want to do with my sister's friend. Riley hasn't called me still and has left my last call and email unanswered.

I don't blame her though for all the times I left her unanswered.

"You good?" Oliver asks through the sounds of stapling. He puts the stapler down when I'm near him and I nod my head.

"I was heading towards Steve's when I remembered you mentioned something to him about meeting an investor?"

Oliver presses his lips into a thin line and looks up in thought. "Yeah, that was a while ago and it's been at the back of my mind. I guess I just didn't get around to it with other things going on."

I look around the space and see that it's empty. Beside Gina and Oliver, I'm the only other occupant here.

Oliver laughs and waves the stack of papers he's stapling. "Just creating more agreements for any future homeowners. I was running out and my computer was bugging the other day. I'd rather have printed copies than have to rely on that old thing."

I nod my head as if I know exactly what he's talking about. He's always kept busy, whether it's selling land to locals, meeting with outside investors to build more farms, apartments, or homes on the outskirts of Alpine Ridge. There really aren't any small towns near us, besides Mason Pointe, to deal with the real estate outside the city limits, so he takes care of all of that.

We're about three hours away from Nashville and that's the biggest city we'll get around here. Nothing but farmlands, pastures, and the occasional hiking trails between the two places.

"Well, I know Steve mentioned you wanted to talk to Bun-" I

stop myself and realize that Oliver doesn't know who Bunny is unless I say her real name. "Camilla and I." I clear my throat.

Oliver nods, "Oh! Right, that was it. So, when the investor met with me, he wasn't very *specific* about what he wanted to do with the land."

"The one between us?"

"That one," Oliver confirms. "He just wanted to get some conversation going around the idea of possibly building a few homes, an apartment, or even a business."

I gawk at him and furrow my brows. "He would consider a business being built there? In between two big plots of land? That doesn't seem logical."

Oliver shrugs. "He sees that there's a vineyard where Ms. Morales lives. So, really, it wouldn't be an out of the box kind of idea. He'd be just creating more options for people to go to."

"Absolutely not," I bark out. My hands form into fists and my breathing grows rapidly.

"Bennett, I didn't even say yes yet. I wanted to ask the locals first and then go from there."

I look at Oliver and shake my head. "Tell him it's never going to happen."

"And that's why I had an idea…" Oliver perks up. He sets the papers down on the table next to him and beckons me to follow him down the hall to his office.

Once we're in there, he closes the door and heads to his desk. He takes a seat and I follow suit in the chair across from him.

"Would you and Ms. Morales be opposed to making that land worth keeping to just locals?"

"She's not a local," I quip. Oliver's eyes narrow and he shakes his head.

"Bennett, you know what I mean. As far as I'm concerned, she bought the Stone's land and hasn't changed a thing. She hasn't even swapped out the name of the vineyard sign."

He has a point. The Stone's land is exactly the way they left it. She has changed nothing except cleaning up the place.

I hate when Oliver or Steve are right. But I won't call her a local. I refuse.

"How would we be able to make the land sustainable between the two of us?" I ask incredulously.

My mind is racking for answers that would make sense, but I can't find any. What could he be thinking?

Oliver leans back in his chair and shrugs as he makes eye contact with me. He's totally trying to not give me a grin, but his lips curl into a smile, regardless. "Why don't you both buy the land? You can split it for your farm, and she can take the other half and extend her property either for herself or the vineyard."

I stare at my friend for a few seconds and wait for him to say more, but he doesn't. He stays silent, waiting for my response.

"I don't know… I don't know if I even want to bother with this. I don't need more land; I've got enough as it is. Plus, she's got acres on acres."

"So, you want me to give it to another local or the investor?" He inquires.

I raise a brow and shake my head. "No, I just don't think Camilla and I can come to a solution."

Now he's the one raising a brow. "Ben, what's going on?"

I shrug and this time I'm the one being silent. "Her and I are still trying to *get along*." I think back to the kiss *again* and try to push it away. Push the memory, the feeling, and *her* away. She's messing up my thought process.

With that, Oliver chuckles and shakes his head. He learns forward and plants his elbows on the desk and stares at me.

"Steve mentioned you were having issues with the new girl. I didn't think it was this bad."

He doesn't know half of it. I want to tell him everything, but he's at work and I'd rather tell him either at the barn over beers or at Nicky's with a pool game.

I press my lips into a firm line and shrug my shoulders. "She's just annoying. You know how tourists are when they come to a cute little town."

"I'm aware, but she's staying for a few years, at least. She won't be a tourist for that much longer."

I know he wants to say more, but he doesn't. And I don't bite back. I'm getting tired already of talking with him and it's not even ten in the morning. I stand up and smooth my hands over my white shirt and give him a curt nod before walking to the door.

"I'll talk to Ms. Morales when I have time later this week. I'm sure I'll get some kind of response so I can move forward with an answer for the investor. I really don't care who gets it, but I know Alpine Ridge is like family and I want to keep it that way if I can."

I turn my head slightly to look at him, letting him catch my eye before opening the door and leaving.

It's rude, but I don't care right now. I just need to get out of his office. I breeze through the hallway and pass by Gina, not even answering her when she tells me goodbye.

Once I'm out onto the street, I look up at the sky, close my eyes, and take a deep breath.

Alpine Ridge has always been a small town where everyone knows everyone and we're like a family. This investor hasn't been the first person to come around and want to change this town.

I'll be damned if this isn't the last.

IT'S quiet in the shop when I enter. There isn't anyone around when I peruse around the front of the place and then find myself checking the break room. There, I find Steve staring at his phone, leaning back in his chair.

His eyes are focused on whatever is on the screen, his lips being pulled back between his teeth. He finally looks up as he hears my boots scuff the floor near the entrance.

His blue eyes brighten, and he gives me a half smile.

"Hey, Steve," I call out, making my way into the break room and finding a chair across from him. He settles his chair back to the floor and raises a brow.

"What's up, man? Everything okay?"

I nod.

"Yeah, just saw Oliver. We talked for a little."

This brings Steve's raised brow even further up his face. "Oh?"

"He told me about the investor he met with weeks ago." I cross my arms over my chest and lean back in my chair.

"What did he say?" Steve asks. "He hasn't told me yet what your part is in his idea, really."

I shrug. "He said that he has an idea for the land that is between Bunny and I. He wants us to work together and buy it and split it."

There's a pause as Steve listens. His raised brow finally settles, and he takes a deep breath. "You said no."

I wince. "You make that sound like a bad thing."

He shrugs and leans towards the table. "Ben, as much as you try to make everyone believe you hate Camilla... I see right through you. She's getting to you."

I want to immediately deny it, but the way he's looking at me... He knows. He really knows. And that's why I hate having a long-time best friend and living in a small fucking town.

"Maybe she is," I breathe out.

There's a hint of a smile growing on Steve's face, and there's even a glimmer in his eyes.

"There's something you're not telling me. I can sense it."

I roll my eyes and shake my head. "I don't know what you're talking about."

Flashbacks to last night come to my mind and how I pulled Bunny in for a kiss. I try to push the memory away, but it won't budge. If I don't tell Steve now, it'll haunt me. And I know he'll just continue to ask.

I finally sigh, bringing myself to tell him the truth. "Okay, okay. You got me."

"Ah!" Steve exclaims, slamming his palms on the table. His small smile has grown into a full one, with white teeth glistening and dimples showing.

"Fuck you," I mutter.

"Tell me or I'll make Birdy get it out of you," he warns.

"Get what out of him?" A voice calls from behind me and Steve's eyes avert from mine to whomever is at the door.

I cringe at the voice and roll my eyes, turning my head. "Birdy, what the hell are you doing here?"

Birdy smirks and walks into the break room. Her short hair moves around her face as she carries a carry out bag and another bag from her shop. "I brought lunch, duh."

I don't answer as I watch her plop down in the seat next to Steve and pass him the carry out bag. Steve claps his hands in excitement and starts pulling the boxes out like it's a Christmas present.

"Now what was I getting out of you?" Birdy asks again as she pulls out some peanut brittle from her shop bag. The smell is heavenly, and she breaks off a piece and leans it towards me.

I extend my hand and let her drop it in my palm. I lift the candy to my lips and take a bite, relishing in the sweet, yet salty taste.

"He's keeping a secret about Camilla. He won't spill," Steve says as he pulls out utensils from the bag and begins eating a prepped salad and then digging his fingers into some wings. It looks and smells like food from Nicky's.

"Oh? Did you see her?" Birdy asks, biting into her own

broken piece of brittle. Her eyes glisten with wonder as she stares at me for an answer.

I roll my eyes again and chuckle. "Okay, you're both going to annoy the hell out of me if I don't say it. I kissed her. Last night."

Steve stops his chewing and stares at me before glancing at Birdy, who is keeping her eye glued to me. She's watching my every move, and I feel like an ant under a microscope. It makes my skin crawl and I want to bolt out of here.

"You did?" Birdy asks, her lips curling into a smile.

Steve finishes chewing. "That's great, Bennett."

I furrow my brows. "What? What do you mean, 'That's great, Bennett'?"

"We were just talking about how Camilla is getting to you..." Steve reminds me. He looks to Birdy, who nods her head. I give her a scowl.

"What?" Birdy shrugs. "I see the way you try so hard to push yourself away from her. She's really sweet. And you know she is. Why fight it?"

Even though Birdy and I have had our ups and downs, I know her words are solid. And I hate it when she's right. Damn it.

"I'm too old for this," I finally tell them. I scoot my chair back and stand. They both look at me with puppy eyes, as if they are begging me to stay and spill the details of the kiss.

The hell I will.

"Well, did you want to go to the lake again this weekend? We'll be paddle boarding this time," Birdy asks as I walk to the door.

I turn and give her a shake of my head. Steve is back to eating the salad and working on the wings to even bother tuning back into the conversation. Birdy has pleading eyes, but I don't care.

"I'm actually going to contact Peyton and Morgan. See if

they want to visit for the opening of the vineyard next week. And then fix some things at the barn. I heard a storm is coming later this weekend. I don't need another power line falling on the property."

"That'll be sweet for Peyton and Morgan to come. I've missed them," Birdy replies with a nod.

"Me too. I think we all do," I answer before I give her a smile and wave to Steve, who is still too busy digging into the food.

I make my way out of the shop and back into my truck. My hands tighten around the steering wheel and I hold back from slamming my fist against it.

I didn't necessarily lie to Birdy. I planned to call Peyton and invite her and Morgan out to the vineyard, but I also didn't have any fixing to do at the barn.

I just can't find myself going out this weekend and being with people. My social meter is down and I'm finding myself isolating and wanting to shut everyone out. It's not because of the kiss, per se.

It's how the kiss made me feel.

THIRTEEN

CAMILLA

"ARE YOU OKAY, MISS CAMILLA?" Parker calls out in the distance. I look up from the red wine bottle I'm placing into a basket.

"Yeah, Parker, why?"

He walks a little closer towards the table I'm leaning against, my bottom half on the stool, half standing up. We've been working on getting some pre-made baskets to buy in the shop when we open.

These baskets help a lot when people don't know what to buy; they'll be able to see these and have some kind of encouragement to buy them. I've paired each wine with some wine glasses, cheese knife, tiny cutting board/charcuterie board, and then a voucher for a cheese and meat of their choice to add to their platter from the fridges in the back.

We offered these a lot in the vineyard I worked at in Chicago and they were big hits for people who lacked knowledge of wines; knowing what foods pairs well with what wine.

I'm adding some frilled paper to the basket for added volume when Parker finally gets to the table and leans his elbows on it. His brown eyes glimmer with curiosity.

"What?" I ask again, trying to focus on the basket. My tongue juts out in concentration.

"You've been quiet the whole time I started my shift. Is everything okay?"

I sigh and plant my ass on the stool before looking up at Parker. His face is full of concern and his brows raise in question. I don't want to be mean and tell him to stop asking questions, but I also need to talk to someone.

I'm itching to talk about the kiss. And Birdy is busy at work or else I'd call her.

"Nothing. I've just had something on my mind. Don't worry about it," I attempt to assure him. But he's not buying it.

He shakes his head, and a smile turns at his lips. "What if we trade our worries?" I knit my brows together and give him a look to continue. "I'll tell you what's on my mind and you tell me what's on yours…"

A laugh escapes my lips, and I shake my head. "You've been chatty all morning, Parker. I can't imagine what else is in that mind of yours."

He smiles wider at that and he shrugs his shoulders slowly. "I have a… kind of date next weekend."

My eyes widen at this and he lifts his hand to wave the air, seamlessly waving me off.

"Who is it?" I ask, wiggling my eyebrows in a teasing manner.

There's a rush of redness creeping into his cheeks. His hand lifts and his fingers run through his mass of brown curls on his head as he breathes out heavily.

"Just this girl that graduated with me. I didn't know she stayed in town this summer. Like me."

"That's not so unusual," I tried to affirm him.

His eyes dance from me to the basket, and he shrugs again. "I thought I was the only one staying here. Her name is Mabel… but I think her friends call her MJ, short for Mabel Jones."

I try hard to dredge up any recollection of her name, and I finally filter through the memory and halt. I look at Parker and smile. "She works at Nicky's? Timid girl, right?"

Parker nods and his face becomes even more crimson from the blushing. Is this how I look to him when I talk about Bennett? God, I need to learn to stop blushing.

"Yeah, she was our waitress when my aunt took me out for dinner the other night. She's really sweet and Aunt Rose kind of pushed me to ask for her number."

"Oh?"

"Yeah," Parker pulls his hand behind his neck and starts rubbing it. "She's always been kind of like that whenever she sees me look at a girl for more than one second."

"Well, hey, it worked, didn't it?" I wink. His cheeks turn even more scarlet, and I laugh.

He's smitten.

"Now," Parker taps the table again. My teeth pull my bottom lip and start nibbling on it. "Your turn."

"I'm not sure if I should, Parker. You know, a boss and their employee talking about their issues isn't something I'd consider as productive."

Parker looks around the vineyard building and then casts his brown eyes on mine before lifting a brow.

"I think there aren't any cameras in here. Corporate wouldn't know."

I bark out a laugh and shake my head, moving my hands back on the basket and redoing the ribbon that was perfectly tied around it.

"Come *oooonnnnnnnn*," Parker sings as he leans past the table and grabs the basket, pulling it towards him.

"Hey, I was working on that!"

He gives me a raised brow and shakes his head. I huff out a loud breath and roll my eyes.

"Okay, fine. Bennett came over."

Parker gasps and smiles. I want to slap that grin off his face, but I stay put.

"And?" Parker is leaning even further into the table and I swear he's going to make the table flip with how much force he's putting into it.

"*And*," I continue, "he was... well, he was Bennett. We talked a little bit."

He knows that I'm keeping out valuable information. I try to reach for the basket that's now sitting next to him on the table, but he rears back and grabs it, cradling it against his chest.

"No! I told you the details. I deserve the details."

I raise a brow, and Parker's cheeks go back to a crimson red. He opens his mouth and then closes it again. "No, not that kind of detail! I mean, what did you guys *talk* about?!"

I wave my hand in the air and he huffs out a breath before settling the basket back on the table. The curls on his head are rampant and he runs his hands through them again.

"Well," I start again, "He kind of told me how anything he touches, he ruins." My mind replays the memory and my heart strings pull at Bennett's harsh words.

They weren't harsh towards me. They were a confession to me about what he *truly* believed to be his ultimate destiny in life. To always turn whatever he gets into stone. To live a life that doesn't end in happiness, because they get ruined. But it doesn't feel like that with him.

Sure, he's grumpy and seems to have a lot of resentment and hurt bottled up in him, but he's not what he thinks he is. His eyes tell me so, and I know there is more that he could tell me—when he's ready.

"That's typical Bennett, Miss Camilla."

I look up at Parker and there's genuineness in his voice. I shrug and continue.

"We kind of admitted that we hate confrontation when it comes to the hard things. But then we were able to understand *why* we both felt like we were needing a confrontation."

Parker is leaning again, as if he's at the edge of his seat watching a movie. It's comical. I laugh and scoot the bar stool back and stand up.

"Wait! You can't just leave it at that!!" Parker begs.

I sigh and cross my arms over my chest. "Parker, you're a kid. I shouldn't be telling you my adult problems."

He shakes his head. "I'm about to go to college! I'm old enough! Please, Miss Camilla."

His eyes hold a plea that I can't let go, so I sigh and shake my head, lifting my hands to run through my own curls.

"He kind of told me how he feels about me. That he can't get me out of his head."

There's a long pause as Parker takes in my words and then his brows shoot up and a *huge* smile spreads across his face.

"BENNETT IS IN LOVE!"

"What?!" I exclaim, waving my hands in the air and shaking my head. I can feel the heat rise to my neck and face. Why does he think *that*?!

"He totally is!" Parker shouts, jumping in place and smacking the table.

I stomp over to him and grab him by the shoulders and gently shake him, hoping to shake this audacity out of him.

"*Parker*, he's not in love with me! He just told me one thing," I pause before adding, "and then kissed me."

Parker gasps and then squeals like we're middle schoolers in a bathroom confessing secrets.

"Miss Camilla, we have to tell someone!" He steps back out of my grasp and starts walking towards the front counter, where the register is and where his wallet and keys are.

I watch him with wide eyes. "What? Tell who? Why?"

Parker shrugs before laughing and jumping again in place. "You don't know how *monumental*... how *historic* this is to hear about Bennett."

"We don't need to tell anyone!" I yell at him, slowly feeling the annoyance and anger build up in me. But he doesn't see that, yet.

He's still smiling and even grabbing my tote bag. I left it on the counter next to his belongings.

"We're going to Birdy's. Now, Miss Camilla."

I want to protest, but he heads towards the front of the building and pulls the door open. Sunlight continues to stream in through the windows, but I can feel the instant heat from outside fill the room.

Before we lose any more cold air from the open door, I walk fast to where Parker is, and he passes me my tote. I roll my eyes as I dig for my set of keys and shut the door, locking it.

Parker runs down the steps before bending down to where Goose sits on a slab of concrete near the steps. Goose lifts her head up and hisses at Parker, causing Parker to step back and pointing his finger at her. I chuckle under my breath, watching them continue their rivalry ever since they met.

Goose seems to love Parker when he's not looking and then will hiss or swat her paw at him if he tries to get closer.

There was a time I asked him to bring Goose closer to the vineyard when we were working on tying some stalks to be more straight with a plastic rod and some twine. I had turned and saw Parker was carrying a metal bucket and Goose's head poking out. As if Parker was scared to physically carry her.

"Let's go!" Parker calls out, heading to Eucy and tapping the roof, waiting by the passenger door.

"Okay, okay!" I call out as I pat Goose's head before unlocking Eucy.

"BIRDY! BIRDY! BIRDY!" Parker yells once we enter the sweets shop, causing the customers that are inside to whip their head at his entrance.

I follow behind, feeling the embarrassment build. Birdy throws daggers at Parker once she sees us and lifts her finger to her lips to shush him.

Parker purses his lips to shut himself up, and I giggle. I wave at Birdy and she gives me a smile before finishing helping the older couple.

"That'll be thirteen dollars, please."

I grab Parker by the elbow and drag him further into the shop, hoping to not cause any more distractions or embarrassment.

"I think I'll have some brittle," Parker whispers as we lean towards a window display. He's playing it cool, and I let go of his elbow before using *my own* to jut into his side. He yelps softly, turning his head and sticking his tongue out.

We hear the bells jingle at the front of the store and then a loud sigh. Parker and I lift our heads and see Birdy crossing her arms, heading towards the other side of the window display we're standing near.

"Now, Parker. Don't make me tell your aunt how disruptive you were," She warns.

Parker gulps and shakes his head. "It was a joke," he answers. He looks at me and there's a gleam in his eye. "Miss Camilla dared me to."

"I did not!" I elbow him again and he yelps, shifting a little further from me.

Good. I'll keep elbowing him until he hushes.

"Darlin', I know she didn't dare you," Birdy winks and leans over the counter, watching us.

"How are you?" She asks me once we lock eyes. We haven't had time to catch up all that much.

The last time I could update her on Bennett was when I met Katherine at the bar and spoke with her. Birdy seemed to be surprised by that, but didn't go into further detail about Katherine and Bennett's history.

It wasn't hers to tell, anyway, but it would've been nice to at least get *some* information before I tried to speak to Bennett about it. Or, honestly, try to *pry* it out of him. That seemed to be something I had to do with him to get any ounce of information from him.

"I'm okay. Bennett stopped by, and we talked a little."

Parker laughs beside me, and I glare at him before looking back at Birdy, who raises a brow.

"Oh? And what did Mr. Moore say?"

"HE LOVES HER!" Parker yells, slamming his palms against the window display, causing it to rattle.

"PARKER BENJAMIN JAMES!" Birdy scolds, raising her hand and pointing her index finger at him.

There's fear in his eyes as he lifts his palms from the glass and up towards his chest in a surrendering position.

"He did *not* say that, Birdy," I quickly say, correcting Parker. I give him another glare and he sticks his tongue out again.

God, he's going to spill the beans that aren't even *beans to spill* to the whole damn town.

I sigh and look up at the ceiling and wonder how the hell the universe chose this specific town to come to. I should've tapped my finger on that map on my phone *twice*.

"So, what did he say?" Birdy asks, turning to grab a rag and leans over the glass and cleaning where the imprints of Parker's palms are.

I shrug. "Said he couldn't get me out of his head."

Birdy stops mid-wipe and looks up at me before looking at Parker.

"Oh, shit."

Parker nods. "Yep, that's what I said."

He didn't, but I didn't bother to correct him. I roll my eyes at them both and shake my head. "What?"

"Bennett Moore... said that?" Birdy questions, raising her brows again and watching me slowly.

I nod and turn to see Parker, who is now pulling his hand to his mouth and biting his nails.

I feel like I'm in court and Parker is the audience watching Birdy question me to figure out if I'm guilty or not.

I'm not guilty of anything, but it feels like it with the way she's staring.

"He did," I breathe out. "And then he kissed me," I confess.

"See!" Parker chimes in, smiling. "He's totally in love with Miss Camilla."

Birdy laughs and raises her hand with the rag in it and tries to swat him with it.

"I don't think Bennett would appreciate you spreading a rumor like that," she states. Parker laughs again and I nudge him with my hand on his shoulder.

"I feel like an animal at the zoo. Stop staring," I tell them, feeling their eyes and the increasing heat form in my cheeks and neck.

I regret telling Parker anything, but I know I had to tell someone. Someone who knew Bennett. Because it feels like the next time I see him, he will take back everything he said. He'll tell me he regrets the kiss and wants nothing to do with me.

He'll make what he said about what happens in his life true. That he can never get happiness because it all gets ruined.

Did he ever think that maybe it's because he stops himself from getting there? From getting what he truly deserves in life? Happiness and peace? I don't know his full story, but I know that no one in life deserves the condemnation he's set for himself.

I nibble on my lips and watch my friends continue to study

me and think of their own reasonings why Bennett said and did that.

"Okay," Birdy says finally. But her lips press into a thin line and I feel defeated. Parker stays quiet too, finally seeing Birdy's response.

What does she know?

FOURTEEN

BENNETT

THE SUN IS bright as I finish checking on the cows out on the pasture and wiping sweat off my forehead. There are birds chirping above and a slight breeze as I make my way back to the house.

The horses are fed and Lushie is healing up nicely. She's been a fighter throughout her healing process, and she's been such a good girl anytime I went to check on her.

There has been no mishap on the farm for a few weeks now and it's been... *great*. The rooster still wakes me up at the crack of dawn, but that's what I'm used to.

My eyes glance towards the far out land that connects the back of my land to Camilla's. It's never used and what Oliver told me yesterday comes to mind—how an investor wants the land in between us, but Camilla and I can find a way to use it instead.

As if.

I don't think that would do any good for the town, but I don't want an investor to take it. I mentally take note to look at my finances later to see if I have enough to just buy the land on my own or if I'd have to take out a loan. I contemplate even reaching out to my sister to see what she might think, but something stops me.

I still haven't heard from her. I'm not even sure if she's still in Washington anymore. I hate to admit it, but I miss her and it's also been my fault as well. I haven't reached out in a while, so she didn't either.

As I enter the house, I grab a glass from the kitchen cabinet and fill it up quickly with sink water before gulping it down. Birdy and Steve will be out on the lake paddle boarding today and invited me out, but I had one thing to do before I joined them.

I know I told Birdy that I probably wouldn't come, but I woke up feeling less like I was on the wrong side of the bed. Not enough to change the whiteboard tally. Yet.

I pull out my phone as I set down the glass with my other hand and click the screen open before pulling up my contacts list. As I scroll to find the contact, I make my way around the kitchen to pull out some breakfast ingredients to make quickly.

I find the contact and click on it, pressing the call button and lifting it up to my ear.

She picks up after five rings.

"Bennett? Is that you?"

"Hey Peyton, how's it going?"

There's laughter on Peyton's end, and I can hear a small squeal. My heart strings pull for the voice it belongs to. Morgan.

"What a surprise! How are you?" Peyton pauses before laughing. "Morgan, baby, it's BenBen! Do you want to say hi?"

There's more laughter on Peyton's end before there's shuffling and then heavy breathing.

"Morgan! How's my favorite girl?" I shout. A smile creeps on my lips and she giggles.

"Uncle BenBen! Are you coming to visit mommy and me?"

"No, Sweetpea, sorry. But I want to talk to your mommy if that's okay?"

She fake gags at the nickname I call her, Peyton finally taking the phone and laughing. "What's up?"

"I met the new owner of the vineyard."

Peyton is silent for a second before exhaling loudly. "Are you being nice to her, Bennett Moore?"

I wince at the full name. It doesn't make me cringe as much as when other people say it, but there's more of a motherly tone to it with Peyton's voice.

"Why are you pestering me about that?"

Peyton laughs on the other line. "Oh, quit. You know exactly why."

I roll my eyes and puff out a harsh breath. "Yeah, yeah. Anyway, the reason I called..."

"Oh, yes, please continue. I hope it isn't anything bad. Morgan keeps asking me when Aunt Kat and Uncle BenBen will get back together."

I wince and sigh. "Never gonna happen, you know that."

"I know," she answers softly. "But she's a kid. I can't exactly tell her what divorce is and why you guys separated. Remember how close you three got?"

I do remember, that's the problem. And one of the main reasons for the divorce. Not Morgan, per se, but kids in general. I try to shake off the feeling that is overcoming me, that is making me angry and wanting to hang up.

My breathing falters as I grip the counter with one hand. "Peyton."

"Sorry," she whispers.

I clear my throat. "Her name is Camilla. She's having a grand opening soon, and I thought it'd be nice for you and Morgan to come down and see it."

"You think so?"

I nod. "Yeah, she didn't really change much. She's actually keeping the name of it and left everything as is."

"Wow, that's surprising. I haven't spoken to her yet or even got involved with the selling process. I just handed it over to Oliver and let him do everything."

I don't tell her that I already know that. I was there with Oliver helping him. It was a shock of the century for the town to hear that the last bloodline of the Stones would leave Alpine Ridge. But we knew they needed to leave and find something different.

My mind briefly goes back to Andy, and the last few times we could hang out. He was very sick, but he pushed through. I can feel my heart tug and weigh heavier in my chest, so I bring myself back to the present.

Dwelling on the past won't change what happened.

"Camilla said she'd like to meet you. I think it would be nice. Birdy and Steve miss you as well."

"Are they finally dating?"

Now *I'm* the one laughing. God, even Peyton and Andy knew about their years-long friendship that is obviously more.

"Not yet. Maybe you can get Morgan to beg Steve to ask her out soon. She always has a way to get what she wants."

"She really tends to get what she wants." I can hear the smile in Peyton's voice.

There's muffling on her end, and before I know it Morgan is back on the line. "BenBen! Tell Auntie Kat I said hiiiiii!"

"Will do, Sweetpea," I murmur before Peyton takes the phone back and laughs.

"Alright, just text me the information and I'll book us flights."

"Yes, ma'am," I respond.

"Oh, and Bennett?" She pauses. I wait and hold my breath for what she'll say next. "Thanks for calling me. We miss you."

"Of course, Peyton. Miss you more. Bye."

And with that I end the call and sigh, leaning over the sink and letting the feeling of whatever the fuck I'm feeling leave my body.

IT'S a couple of hours later and I'm finding a beer in the cooler that's strapped onto Steve's paddle board. We're on the lake and found a quieter spot where there isn't much boat traffic.

Although we love the party cove area with our boats, it's not a place for people on paddle boards to go to.

Birdy bumps her board into mine and laughs as I flick an ice cube at her. She screams and Steve turns to look at the commotion behind him.

"Hey!"

"What?! She started it," I groan as I give Steve my best apology smirk and then turn to give Birdy the finger. She gasps and leans her hand in the water before lifting it and splashing me with a ton of water.

"Ay! I almost opened my beer!"

"So? You know what you did, Moore!"

Steve laughs as he finally turns his body around to watch us bicker. "You guys really can't go a day without being at each other's throats, huh?"

Birdy and I look at each other for a few seconds and at first I see something flicker in her face change before she slaps on a smile and laughs. I bring a smile to my lips, but I know it doesn't reach all the way.

"Yeah, Steve. You know it," she finally says as she leans over and grabs a drink from the cooler as well. She shuts it closed before leaning back on her board.

She's wearing a yellow bikini while Steve is wearing... you guessed it, a matching pair of yellow swim trunks. I roll my eyes at the sight and keep myself from gagging.

"So, Ben, you never told us why you were late today."

I look at Steve, who is cracking open a beer as well. There's a group of people in kayaks passing by and I wait for them to go further from us before paying attention to my best friend. I crack open my beer can and take a long sip.

"I called Peyton."

Birdy sits straight up and whips her head towards us. "What?!"

I nod.

"I invited her and Morgan to come to the opening of the vineyard."

Steve leans closer to pat my shoulder before smiling. "That's great. Look at you."

I cringe at his words and take another sip of the beer. Birdy makes a weird face before laughing.

"What, Bee?"

She presses her lips firmly into a thin line before shrugging. "We can see right through you, but you just won't admit it."

This makes me sit back onto my board, and I huff out a loud breath. "And what is that?" I turn to look at Steve, but he's ignoring my eye contact.

"We already told you back at Steve's shop! You totally have the hots for my new friend."

"She's my friend too," Steve mumbles, laughing.

Birdy gasps before shaking her head. "Steve, you only met her because of me."

"Why are you guys competing in figuring out who she's friends with?" I ask, watching them two give each other stern looks as if they're mentally arguing.

"Nothing." Birdy rolls her eyes and then smiles. "Parker James has been telling everyone that they're really good friends too. I have to keep reminding him she's his boss."

I sit up at this. "He's what, now? I thought he had a date with that waitress, Mabel?"

"Oh, yeah!! They'd be so cute. I love young love," Steve pipes up from his place.

I give him a look and shake my head before turning my

attention back to Birdy, who quirks a brow and sips her drink. "He is, but he's young. He likes the attention Camilla gives him. It's just like a schoolboy crush. Nothing to come from it and she clearly knows that too. We all do. Plus, she's—" Birdy stops herself mid-sentence.

"What?" I ask, pinching my brows together.

"Nothing, forget it."

Steve lets out a low whistle.

"What, Steve?"

"Nothing, man."

I look at them both and can feel annoyance rise in me. "What are you guys not telling me?"

Birdy groans and then sits closer on her board towards us. "Bennett, you need to really date more and *learn* how to say the right things to women."

I knit my brows together again and try to think back to what I might've said to *anyone* to show that I was a bad flirt or I said something offensive. There were many times I was rude, sure, but I never outright offended a woman the way some guys would. I take pride in being a gentleman. Mama Moore didn't raise a misogynistic asshole.

Well, I take back my offensive sayings. I told Camilla that she reminded me of a bunny that would get picked up by a bird. That was quite rude of me, but I just couldn't hold back.

Tourists do that to me.

"Well, we talked to Camilla," Birdy finally spits out.

I look at her and then at Steve, who shrugs.

"You both talked to her? About what?"

"No, not me and Steve," Birdy laughs. "Me and Parker."

"You're seriously talking about adult shit with Parker? Birdy, he's barely in college."

"Woah, Bennett. He's just as invested in this as we are."

I sigh and press my free hand to my temple. "Invested in what, exactly?"

"You and Camilla," Steve and Birdy say in sync. I look at them with crazed eyes and they smile.

"What?"

"You know," Birdy shrugs again. "She told us you guys kissed. *Again.*"

"Does everyone in this town know my fucking business?" I seethe.

Steve sucks in his cheeks and Birdy looks down at the water before looking at me again with remorse on her face. Her green eyes dance all over my face.

"It's good for you to put yourself out there, you know," Birdy starts. She takes a deep breath and looks at Steve, who gives her a reassuring nod. "We just want the best for you and we're thrilled to see you like this. You haven't been like this in forever. Even with Katherine and we all know the reasons for it, but still. You didn't seem like this with your own *wife*."

"Yeah, we all know why. But her and I moved past that. The divorce kind of set us free in that department. So what's the other issue?" I push.

Birdy nibbles on her lip, setting her eyes on the water once more. "Even though Camilla is new... She's not the typical tourist. She cares about this town. You know it. You even convinced Peyton and Morgan to come back! That's *huge*. You wouldn't have done that for a tourist who is ruining our town."

She's not wrong. I definitely would've made Morgan and Peyton stay where they're at if Camilla was different. I think my cold exterior infiltrated my brain too and couldn't see past my own judgements against the woman.

"You also confided in something with Camilla that I won't repeat, because that's not my business," Birdy says. I furrow my brow and Steve does the same.

"What? Tell me!" Steve pleads, inching closer on his board.

Birdy laughs before shaking her head. "It's about how Bennett *feels* about Camilla, dummy."

"Oh," Steve says before shutting his lips.

"Are you trying to be my therapist right now?" I ask her.

She shakes her head. "No, but I want you to be happy. You deserve it. Despite you thinking that whatever you touch, you ruin. You have touched nothing that got ruined. That's just in your head."

I distinctly stare at the water now, in between our boards, and shake my head. There is a lot of stuff that went on in the years during my tours and time in Colombia. Things I can't take back and that will always stain my memory. *Those* are the things that I refer to when I tell someone that whatever I touch, I ruin. My hands are killing machines and they've done more awful than right.

Sure, whatever I did in the past during tours and my time in contracted missions were things they paid me to do, or had no choice but to partake in to survive, but I still have to bear the weight of it even years later.

The people in my life knew I came back differently, and it almost became a skin to wear back in Alpine Ridge to get people to stop pitying me for what happened or what they heard on the news.

Katherine took the brunt of it, and so did Steve and Birdy. They didn't deserve the Bennett that came back wounded and scarred.

"Hey, you there?" Steve asks softly, tapping my shoulder. I look up and realize that they've been staring at me for a while.

A tear falls down my cheek. I sniffle and quickly wipe it away, focusing back on the beer can in my hand and putting it to my lips and finishing it. I crush the can in my hand before nodding.

"Yeah, I'm fine."

"You still do that thing," Birdy says with worry in her voice.

"What thing?"

"Zone out as if you're reliving painful memories."

I finally look up at her and sigh. "It's because I am, Bee. You guys might think this is all in my head, but I went through some tough shit. I know you guys know that, but it's different from actually being the person who went through it. I don't mean to be a hardass or even a dick, but it's been so ingrained into me since the war and my contracts that it's become second nature."

"Your scars seem to be fading well," Steve pipes up. I give him a small smile but don't bother looking where their eyes are fixed at.

Like after taking a shower in my bathroom, I still can't fathom the nerve to look at my body. It's not who I am and not who I want to be. It's a body I no longer claim to. The scars are a daunting reminder of it, and sometimes I wish I could go back in time and change things. Never pursue Katherine, never join the army, never marry my high school sweetheart with a foundation built on lies, and never come back to Alpine Ridge.

Riley had the right idea of moving when she had the chance.

I finally look up at them, and Steve reaches for another beer and passes it to me. "Here, take this. We can finish up and head back to the shop to talk… or go to Nicky's for wings. I heard they're gonna do karaoke."

"Ooh! Sing Josh Turner!" Birdy squeals.

Steve laughs. "I will *not* be doing that. You got so drunk last time I did that you almost pulled me off stage in excitement!"

Birdy groans and leans her head back, "Okay, fine. How about we both sing a song? A sad duet."

"Absolutely not. We want a live crowd, not a dead one," Steve counters.

Birdy huffs her breath and I can't help but laugh at their bickering. Peyton is right. They do need to start dating.

MY FEET HIT the gravel pathway as I get out of my truck and head towards Bunny's door. Even though I protested the whole time, Steve and Birdy said they'd only invite me to karaoke night if I invited her.

So, here I am. Because I'm tired of constantly letting down my best friends and today was a nice and unexpected heart to heart that all three of us really needed.

I told them I'd pop over to talk about the investor that Oliver told me about, but they immediately shut down the idea and said to just go to her door, ask her out, and then get to Nicky's as soon as possible.

There's a faint meow to my right as I continue up the pathway and see Goose slowly stretch before walking up to me. She purrs as she wraps her body around my leg. I lean down and scratch her head before carefully picking her up.

"You're so pretty, yeah you are," I coo as she nuzzles her face to my cheek. I hold her tightly against my chest as I walk us up towards the steps.

I see a bed of wildflowers and decide quickly to snap a few from the roots and hold them in my fist like a bouquet.

My feet make it to her front step and I take a deep breath. Goose purrs again and I look down at her, giving her a smile and a small smooch on her head as a thanks for the calming reassurance.

My hand with the bouquet reaches up to the door and knocks on it. Bunny swings the door open, and she smiles softly. Since I called the gate, despite knowing the code, she knew I was coming up but didn't know why.

"Bennett, what are you doing here?" She asks, staring at me before looking down and seeing Goose snuggled up underneath my chin. "Goose?"

"The ladies love me," I joke.

She holds back a laugh before shaking her head. I slightly cringe at my bad joke and lift my hand up with the flowers.

"For you," I blurt.

She widens her eyes and takes the flowers, forming a fist around them as well to keep them intact. "Wow, I love them. Where did you get them?"

There's a hint of sarcasm in her voice, and I step aside and point to her garden bed. "The finest in Alpine."

She laughs and I can feel my chest swell. I can feel my hand sweat and I clear my throat.

"I—I uh, wanted to see if you'd like to go to Nicky's with me? It's karaoke night and Birdy and Steve will debut their first song."

She widens her eyes again. "Oh? I'd love to see that."

"And I thought we could go together and sit... together."

She furrows her brows, a hint of a smile escaping her lips. "Like a date?"

I groan and lean my head back before shaking it and looking back at her. Goose purrs again and I silently thank her for being the supportive third wheel.

"Yes, like a date, Bunny."

"Are you still really only calling me by that?"

I shrug. "It's cute. I like it."

She laughs and shakes her head, her hair whipping around her face. "Didn't seem like it the many times you called me it when we first met."

I shrug again and look down at Goose. "I guess I changed."

There's silence as she takes in my words before I look from Goose to her. She has a sparkle in her eyes before she nods. "Yeah, I guess so. Let me go grab my purse and I'll be right there."

And with that, she turns on her heels and leaves the door open. I watch her turn a corner and disappear. Goose meows again and moves, wanting to be put down. I gently bend down and let her jump off before I see her dash into the home.

Camilla comes back with her hair now back in a clip and a

few pieces of hair framing her face. She pulls her purse over her shoulder before shutting the door behind her.

After opening the passenger door for her, I take a deep breath and settle inside the truck, turning the engine on and feeling the patter of my heart start to *really* increase as I turn to see her smile beautifully.

"Alright, let's go," I say quickly before backing up the truck and driving it out of her driveway.

FIFTEEN
CAMILLA

THE CAR RIDE is fast as we make our way to Nicky's. After he finds a parking spot on the street where the bar is at, he gets out of the truck and heads towards my side to open the door for me. I give him a smile, not wanting to cause too much of a scene with how nice he's being tonight.

It was quite shocking to see Bennett in the gate camera, and it was *really* shocking to hear the word 'date' come out of his mouth after I asked him if that's what this is.

He didn't seem to notice my fidgeting in the car—he looked too focused on the road, which helped me calm down a little before we made it to Nicky's. He seemed nervous, but also like he's been thinking about me as much as he told me the other night.

I smooth my lilac sundress before hopping out. As we walk closer to the bar, he walks close to me, positioning himself closer to the side of the road. He opens the door for me as we reach the bar, loud music emanating from the inside. I briefly forgot amid my nervousness that it's karaoke night.

I thank Bennett quietly as I walk past the entrance and wait for him to reach my side. It's crowded tonight, more than the other nights I've been here. I see Izzy working hard, passing drinks around as well as taking orders from customers.

I see Birdy and Steve in the middle of the bar at a huge rounded table where Parker and Mabel are sitting near them. I widen my eyes and smile, making a beeline for them. Bennett follows close behind as I near the table.

Birdy smiles brightly and waves before standing up and reaching for a hug. Steve is drinking his beer before he raises it with a smile towards me. Parker and Mabel are deep in a conversation but the seats next to them are empty.

"Here," Bennett says before pulling out the chair next to Mabel and nodding for me to sit down.

"Oh, thanks," I sit down before he pushes my chair closer to the table, like a true gentleman. He nods before taking his own seat and sitting close to me, our thighs almost touching.

The sundress is riding up a little, so when he rubs his hands over his thigh, it glides along my bare skin for a moment. My body stills, feeling that flutter in my stomach.

"I'm glad you guys made it!" Birdy interrupts my thoughts and I look up and give her a big smile.

"I'm excited to see the hype around karaoke night!"

"It's kind of our thing." Steve says with a shrug.

There's another worker assisting Izzy that I don't recognize. She talks to them quickly before heading to our table with her mouth open wide.

"Birdy! You brought a whole crew!"

"It's karaoke night!" Birdy yells back over the music. Izzy laughs before she finds me and squeals, running towards me and instantly pulling me in for a side hug.

"Oh! Hi to you too!" I giggle, wrapping my arm around her waist. She squeezes me tightly and pats Bennett's head before pulling out her notepad.

"What can I get for you, Camilla?"

"Hmm…" I think slowly before remembering the fried pickles I usually order. "Fried pickle spears and cider, please."

Izzy nods as she writes my order. She then looks at Bennett and raises a brow. "Bennett? What can I get you?"

Bennett leans forward before lifting his arm and laying it over the back of my chair. His cologne wafts in my direction. Izzy's eyes slowly go to where his arm is at before looking back at Bennett.

"I'll have a burger and… a beer."

Izzy nods and writes his order before asking the rest of the table if they need refills or anything else. Then she turns on her heels and heads to the back of the bar.

I lean back and jump a little when I remember his arm is still on the back of my chair. I look at him and bite on my lip before he gives me a small smile.

"So, how's the vineyard? When's the opening?" Steve asks, sipping on his beer as Birdy pulls out her phone.

"It's really great! I'm almost ready to open. I was thinking of next weekend?"

"We've done so much. It's really looking good," Parker pipes up from his place. I finally turn towards him and flash him a grin.

"Parker has been such a big help, really. And I was hoping everyone could come for the opening?"

Birdy looks up with brightness in her eyes. "Of course! I think Bennett said he invited Peyton and Morgan?"

Bennett shifts in his chair, but keeps his arm over the back of my chair. "Yeah, she just asked to let her know when." He then looks at me. "I'll let her know it's next weekend."

"Thanks, Bennett."

"No problem, Bu—" He stops himself before he calls me Bunny and I pinch my brows, wondering why he stopped.

But the conversation continues around the table. Mabel tells us about her plans to attend the University of Tennessee in

Knoxville and Parker ends up telling us he chose the nearby community college to be closer to his aunt.

"Well, if you ever want to make your job a permanent one, let me know," I end up telling Parker.

He seemed almost relieved at my proposition and thanked me before Bennett, and I's food arrived. As we ate, conversation flowed about other plans for the summer. Birdy brings up plans to go to Nashville for a weekend. As Bennett and I finish our plates, Birdy and Steve get called on stage for a song they requested.

I clap and whistle as they sing and that's when I realize the song they chose is Jason Mraz's *Lucky*... the one about falling in love with your best friend.

Bennett and I stare at each other, and he slips out a smile before chuckling and shaking his head. They're so in love and don't even know it yet. Mabel and Parker watch closely, Parker copying Bennett's movement of leaning his arm behind Mabel's chair. I catch them looking at each other and I squeal under my breath, leaning close to Bennett until my head rests against his chest. I feel him tense underneath, but then feel the arm that's around the back of my chair move to caress my bare shoulder.

By the time Birdy and Steve are done singing, Izzy comes over to get our empty plates and I order another cider.

"So... how did we do?" Birdy asks with a wide smile before plopping back down in her chair.

"So good!" Parker claps and Steve waves him off.

"You guys were great!" I cheer, winking at Bird.

"We usually do that song, so why not?"

"Well, you guys killed it!" Mabel affirms, and we all nod.

The next person goes on stage and begins singing and Izzy brings over my new drink. I look at Parker and Mabel as they exchange glances before giggling.

I overhear her complimenting him. "You look nice with that button down."

There's a slight redness that creeps into his cheeks. "Yeah, I haven't been on a date in a while and forgot how fun it can be dressing up and stuff."

Steve nods and raises his beer. "Cheers to that. I love that part."

I smile and raise my own drink, and so does everyone else at the table. As we clink glasses, Parker laughs.

"What's your favorite part?" Parker asks Steve.

Steve looks up at the ceiling before looking around the table. "Being able to know there are plans for my evenings. Being able to dress up and kind of forget about work for a little."

"Is that where you go off to all the time? Whenever I drive by your shop, you're always jetting off to go somewhere," Mabel pipes up from her chair.

Steve smiles and nods, but Birdy gasps next to him. "What? You're seeing someone?"

Steve's lips press into a tight line and stays silent for a second. Birdy looks around the table for an answer, but we're all silent. What *just* happened.

I want to ask Steve if what he was talking about had anything to do with Birdy, but now I'm more confused. Is he really seeing someone and we're all just blinded by the possibility of him and Birdy being a thing? They sure act like it… but now, I'm not so sure. Instantly, Birdy turns to look at Bennett and pats his shoulder.

"Bennett, did you know he's dating someone?"

Bennett tenses on my side and I lift myself up from leaning against him. I can tell he doesn't want to be caught up in the middle of this.

"Birdy, stop being dumb, you're better than this."

Birdy snaps her mouth closed and scrapes her chair back, standing up and walking away.

I almost stand up to follow her, but Bennett shakes his head and presses his hand firmly on my shoulder and pushes me to sit back down.

"What was that about?" Steve asks the table.

We all look at him before we look at Bennett, who just sighs and runs his other hand through his hair.

"Come on, buddy. We all know you and Birdy are closer than most friends. And I know she's the person you usually go out with after work."

Steve looks at us incredulously with widened eyes.

"Me and Birdy? What? She's my best friend! Yeah, sure, I was talking about that, but I was talking *generally* about what I like about dating. Not that I'm dating anyone *right now.*"

I bite back a laugh as Bennett chuckles and shakes his head. "Do we really have to spell it out for you?"

Before Steve could say anything, Birdy returns with two beers and she plops down in her chair. Her hair has a tousled look to it and I can only imagine she was running her hands through her hair with anxiety and annoyance at the bar.

"Bee?" Steve asks, turning his body towards her. She says nothing, just takes a sip of her beer. Her eyes catch mine and I can *kind* of read her mind. She doesn't want to explain herself.

So I don't make her.

"Who wants to dance?" I ask.

"I'm going to get another beer. Bennett?" Steve asks, scraping his chair back. Bennett clears his throat before moving his hand to tap my thigh as he gets up as well.

I look up at him as he gives me a wink and follows Steve to the bar.

"Come on," I urged Birdy, getting up and reaching my hand out. Mabel and Parker stand up as well, giggling in their own conversation and make it to the small makeshift dance floor right in front of the karaoke stage.

"He's such a jerk," Birdy mutters as she takes my hand and lets me pull her to the dance floor.

"You didn't let him explain, Birdy. He was talking about the times he went to see *you*."

Birdy stops at the edge of the dance floor and shakes her head. "We're not dating though."

"You guys act like you do," I counter, laughing.

"God, I hate small towns sometimes," She mutters before pulling me into the dance floor and dancing to the beat.

I roll my eyes and laugh, attempting to follow her dance moves but failing badly at it.

As the song ends, a nice country song comes on and that's when Birdy and I notice a handsome stranger walk up to us. Nicky's is busier than usual tonight, so I'm not surprised we didn't see him before. He's decked out in white cowboy boots and a matching cowboy hat. He grins at us both and his stark green eyes make Birdy squeeze my arm.

"Can I ask a lovely woman to dance?"

I turn to Birdy and nod towards her, pinching her back. "She'd love to."

"What?!"

The guy laughs before turning his attention towards me. "I think your friend is beautiful, but I was asking *you*."

I turn to Birdy, who is smirking and pushing me towards the man. I look at the bar quickly, but Steve and Bennett's backs are facing us. They're still ordering their drinks and focused on their own conversation.

"I—uh… sure," I squeak out as the man reaches his hand out and I take it.

Birdy whoops before running towards Mabel and Parker, who are about to leave the dance floor.

"You new in town?" He asks as he wraps his hand around my waist and I put both hands on his shoulders.

The song is slow and so I try to follow his movements. His green eyes look down at me and I smile.

"How'd you know?"

He chuckles before pulling away and twirling me around him. My sundress sways with the movement.

"Because I've never seen such a gorgeous woman on this side of town."

"And you're from here?"

"I'm from outside Nashville, but travel here to visit my family. They live in the town next door. We come to Alpine Ridge all the time." He winks at his last words before spinning me around again.

"Well, I'm loving it so far. It's a sweet town," I respond, as he pulls in closer. His cologne is a little too strong, but I try not to think too much of it. His hat looks stiff, like brand new, the closer our bodies get.

As the song gets closer to the end, he twirls me one last time. The people on the dance floor depart and another song starts with less of a slow-dancing vibe. He pulls me off the dance floor and before I know it, he's smiling and reaching over his head.

He pulls his cowboy hat off himself and places it on top of mine. "Catch you at the next slow dance, partner?"

"Sure," I reply. He gives me a smile before heading to the back of the bar, where there's a small table with other men.

I cast my eyes towards the other side of the bar where Steve and Bennett are, but it's just Steve shaking his head and staring at the front of the bar, near the front doors. I raise a brow and turn to look at what he's staring at and that's when I see Bennett slip out.

My feet move quickly to get to Steve and I falter with my smile the moment I see him frown.

"What happened? Where's Bennett going?"

"Whose hat is that?" Steve asks, pointing at the hat on my head.

"The guy who danced with me. What's the big deal?"

Before I know it, Steve is pulling the hat off me and throwing it on the bar top. I hear hollering at the back of the bar and see the guy I was dancing with stand up and march over to us.

I widen my eyes as I see the change in his demeanor. Steve stands tall as the guy closes in on us. Steve beats him in height as he sizes the guy down.

"What the fuck, man? That's my new hat!"

"Clearly," Steve scoffs. "She's with someone." He nods his head towards me.

"Didn't seem like it to me," the guy says, lifting his hands and cracking his knuckles.

"Hey!" Birdy screams from behind us, making her way towards Steve and the guy who is just getting angrier.

Before I can hear anymore of the argument, I decide to slip away and find Bennett. If I can get any answers, it's from him, not two men about to fist fight. I'll thank Steve later for having my back since the guy clearly had different intentions with that dance.

I push through the front doors and look up and down the street. I see Bennett walking fast towards his truck, so I bolt out of the bar and try to catch up to him.

"Bennett! Wait up!"

He doesn't stop, so I try to speed up. I reach him and tug his shoulder back. He looks *pissed* and I raise a brow.

He huffs before shaking my hand off his shoulder. I see him get close to the car and almost get to his side of the truck before he backtracks and heads for the passenger side, pulling the door open.

He doesn't say anything, but I know exactly what he wants to say. *Get in the truck.* I keep quiet as I hop in the truck. He closes the door as I slip my seat belt on. I try to rack my brain with what the hell just happened as he slips in the driver's side and starts the car.

By the time we make it to Misty Creek Road, his knuckles are almost white with how hard he's gripping the steering wheel.

"Bennett..." I start. He sighs. "What happened?"

He's silent for a moment before finally looking at me. "Did you forget you were my date?"

I shake my head. "No, of course not. We went there together."

"So, why did you let that man give you his hat?"

I laugh. "Is that why you're mad? Why does that matter? It was one dance and then he gave me his hat. I didn't want to say no, that would've been rude."

He huffs again and exhales sharply. "You don't get it. Around here, when a man gives a woman his hat, that means she's his. He's claiming her."

My mouth falls open, and I stare at Bennett before shaking my head. "What?! I'm not something to claim."

"Fuck, that's not what I meant..." He presses his lips into a thin line before shaking his head. "What I *mean* is that when a guy gives a woman his hat, she goes home with him."

I gasp and shake my head. "What?! I didn't know that! How could I?"

That's when Bennett finally smiles and laughs. Full on *laughs*. I cross my arms over my chest and before either of us can register where he turns, he's already up the driveway to *his* house.

I sigh and look around me before peeking behind Bennett's seat. I see *his* faded and dusty cowboy hat and get an idea.

He seems to be fine now, but I know he's still fuming inside with what happened. With what *I had no idea* was going on. But it seems to be a big deal in this town, so I want to show Bennett that he has nothing to worry about.

Bennett pulls the car next to his house and gets out, walking around the front of the truck to get to my door. Before I can do anything else, I grab the hat and pull it over my head.

When Bennett reaches my door and pulls it open, I remove my seat belt and hop down.

"Is that—"

"Yep," I smile. "Well, you said that whoever's hat I'm wearing, I'm going home with."

A smile spreads across his face as he registers my words and looks from me to his hat before shutting the door behind me and grabbing my hand.

He pulls me towards the front of the house before I can say anything else.

SIXTEEN

BENNETT

THE MOMENT I saw her in my hat and hearing those words...
all the anger and annoyance dissipated.

There was just one thing I had in my mind so I grabbed her
hand, pulled her closer to me, and dragged her toward the house.
She willingly followed and let me pull her along. The moment
we got through the front door, I slammed it and pinned her up
against it.

Her eyes widened as she watched me, her breathing
increasing as her chest moved in bigger motions.

The house is quiet and not even the wildlife can be heard
from here besides our heavy breathing. Not even the rooster or
that damn raccoon could disrupt us.

She continues to stare at me, a smile edging at the corners of
her lips.

I lean my arm and press my palm against the door, right by
her ear, and lean in close. We're nose to nose and she closes her
eyes briefly, breathing in sharply.

"You look better in that than me," I finally break the silence.

"Really?" She whispers. And before I can respond, she pulls

the hat off her head and I take it with my free hand, tossing it to a nearby chair before turning to look at her again.

"You can wear it anytime you want," I breathe out.

Her eyes dance all over my face before she bites her lip and moves her face closer to mine. I can tell she's thinking of something else, but she rushes to close the space.

"Kiss me," she whispers.

My eyes glance at hers to make sure I heard her right. But she doesn't falter.

"Yes, ma'am," I say happily, leaning closer and closing our distance. Our lips connect and she smiles through the kiss.

Her lips are soft and I nibble on her bottom lip, causing her to slip a moan out. With that sound, I groan and remove my arm from the wall, sliding it down her arms and then around her waist. Her hands find their way to my shoulders, wrapping themselves around my neck.

I take no time to bend down and move my hands from her waist to under her thighs, my bare hands touching her skin. This lights a fire in me and she giggles as we continue to kiss.

My hands gently lift her up to press her against my core, and she wraps her legs around my waist. She deepens the kiss and I open my eyes just enough to see our surroundings and lead us out of the front hallway and near the living room.

The couch is closer than I thought as the backs of my knees bump into it, causing me to fall back into the cushions. She stifles out a scream as we go down on the couch; her legs still wrapped around my sides.

As my left hand reaches up to clasp her cheek, my right goes back to her side, rubbing in up and down motions along her bare thigh, her sundress riding up the more I do it. Just the feeling of her soft skin under mine causes me to push out a moan through my lips as we kiss.

She pulls her lips away, watching me closely. We're both

breathing deeply, but I narrow my eyes to wait for her to say what she's thinking.

She nibbles on her lip then, averting her gaze from my face to my chest.

"What is it? We don't have to continue," I assure her.

She shakes her head and removes her hands from around the back of my neck. My brows knit together in confusion.

"It's not that. I just—it's been a while." She bites her lip and looks up at me from underneath her lashes.

There's a hint of pinkness that I can see settle into her cheeks.

My hand continues to rub her bare thigh, but not as high anymore, so she knows I'm listening to her and not wanting to pressure her into anything.

"We can take it slow," I comfort her. "You're not the only one that hasn't done this recently. You just tell me how far you want to go and that's how far we'll go."

"Yeah?" She whispers. She hangs her head down, but I remove my hand from her thigh and press it under her chin, lifting it up for her to maintain eye contact.

"Yes."

She closes her eyes and takes a deep breath before exhaling and opening her eyes. Some of her dark curls fall to her face, so I push them behind her ear. She continues to look at me before leaning in, closing our distance. Our lips connect and there's an instant spark between us. The flutter in my core brings me back to moving my hand along her thigh and she groans in response, deepening the kiss.

She opens her mouth slowly, allowing me to kiss her deeper and swipe my tongue against hers. She whimpers in my mouth, which causes me to grip her thigh harder.

"Jesus," I whisper, before continuing the kiss.

Her hands are back behind my neck, wrapping around me tightly. Her core is flush with mine and she rolls her hips. I know the only thing separating us from the *real* skin to skin contact would be her underwear and my jeans.

This thought alone brings my mind to a frenzy as my cock gets harder and I grab her hips with both of my hands, applying more pressure on her skin.

With this, she moans in my mouth again and keeps moving her hips against me in circles.

"Fuck, don't—" I moan, separating our kiss. She looks at me with mischief in her eyes.

"Bennett, we can stop," she whispers. But I shake my head.

"It's n-not that," I breathe out. She raises a brow and I take a deep breath. "If you keep moving your hips like *that,* it's going to make me want to do other things."

She chews on her lip before there's a hint of a smile on her lips. She holds tighter onto my neck before moving her hips again in slow motion, taunting me. I grunt through my teeth and I close my eyes, leaning my head back. The grip I have on her hips tightens.

"What kind of things?" She whispers.

This catches me off guard. I pull my head back and stare at her with widened eyes. My cock twitches at her question and a list of *things* flash in big bold letters in my mind.

I move my hand from her hip to grasp her thigh, rubbing slowly from her knee up to where the fabric of her dress is bunched up near her hip. She closes her eyes and breathes out a shaky breath.

"Bennett—"

I lean my body closer to hers while simultaneously pulling her closer with my other hand. My hand continues to travel further up her thigh, slipping underneath the bunched up fabric.

"I'd do this," I finally say, dipping my hand further underneath the fabric to rest my fingers on her bare hip. Her skin jumps underneath my touch, and I move my fingers to hook around the waistband of her underwear.

She circles her hips again, pressing up against me more. I shut my eyes briefly, breathing steadily to control myself.

I can't help but press my hand behind her back to press her deeper into my core. She gasps at the contact, and I instantly feel her grind against me. The fabric of my jeans and her underwear are so close that I can feel *everything*.

I groan and lean close, pressing my lips to the side of her neck, biting. She giggles and continues to grind against my cock. My fingers are still playing with the waistband of her underwear, teetering on the edge of slipping a finger underneath the fabric and—

"Lay me down," she whispers, causing me to halt my hands and nod. I shift our bodies until she's plopping on her back and I hover over her, my thighs in between her legs, stretching her wider and her dress continuing to ride up past her thighs. It's on the edge of spilling over her hips and giving me a full view of her clothed pussy.

I lean my head back into her neck, leaving kisses along her skin and her legs wrap tightly around my sides. My hand moves back to her thigh, slipping underneath her dress again. I lift my head to find her eyes.

Her soft brown eyes watch me as I continue to slip my hands underneath the fabric of her underwear. I wait for a moment to see if she'll ask me to stop, but she nods quickly.

"Use your words," I murmur.

Her brown eyes light up and she nods again, cheeks turning even more rosy. "I want this. I'm clean, if that's something you're worried about. Always try to stay up to date with those kinds of things and besides, I haven't been with—"

"Me too," I cut her rambling off with a smile. Her brows raise and her eyes light up like fireworks. With both of our consent given and knowing that we're being as safe as we can, even if it is just oral, I focus back on my hands.

My fingers dip into her mound and I'm instantly met with wetness in between her folds. I let out a shaky breath, as does she, as we continued to maintain eye contact. Her eyes flutter closed for a moment as I slide my index and pointer finger down along her wet folds. They tease her entrance, and she lets out a deep breath.

"Oh," She murmurs and I lean down to kiss her before I slowly insert one finger into her slickness. She's very tight, and it's driving me *insane.*

"Fuck, Bunny," I moan.

She falters and moans, her pussy clenching around my finger.

"Bennett, please," she whines. My finger moves slowly in and out of her, attempting to stretch her more.

"S-sorry, you're just so *tight,*" I shudder as my finger continues to thrust into her.

"Oh, God," She moans, clutching the fabric of my shirt with her hands, pulling me closer to kiss me.

Her tongue is quickly in my mouth as I move my thumb to her clit and start rubbing it in slow motions. She tightens around my finger again, causing me to moan through our kiss.

"More," She moans and I nod, shifting my hand to add my middle finger, causing a whine to escape her lips and into my mouth.

My heart rate is increasing, and beads of sweat are forming at the base of my neck. She pulls me closer into the kiss, which causes my body to press further into her, making my fingers go *deeper* into her.

Fuck, I could come just from this. My cock twitches at the thought of how tight she is, and I thrust my fingers at a faster rate.

She lets out a few wanton cries, lifting her hips to bring my fingers at a deeper angle. Her hands clutch my shirt as if she's willing to tear the fabric apart. I don't care. She could tear every piece of clothing I have if I can get her to cry out like this every time.

It's like a symphony in my ears and I can't stop my rhythm now. Her slickness only provides more lubrication as I continue to finger her and we make out. Our teeth clack together, our tongues are sloppily gliding over another.

We're feral and we've yet to go that further step.

"Bennett, I'm *so close*," she whines as she separates our lips and pulls her head back. I catch her eyes and she flutters them as I thrust my fingers in her and curl them at an angle. "Oh, just like that."

"Yeah?" I whisper, grinding my erection against her bare thigh.

She nods and presses her lips into a thin line. There's sweat forming on her forehead and it only adds a glow to her golden, sun-kissed skin.

"I'm about to—"

"Do it," I murmur, and she squeezes her eyes shut as I rapidly finger her. Her wetness coats my fingers and travels down my wrist. It's all too much and I dry hump her even more.

She jolts under my touch, her pussy clenching around my fingers as I feel her cum. My cock twitches and I moan as I cum inside my jeans. Fuck.

I thrust my fingers for a few more strides before she cries out and pulls her hand down between us and grabs my wrist to stop me. I pull my fingers out of her gently and she whimpers. I lift my fingers to my lips, slowly, and lick her release off them. Her eyes widen for a moment before she beams. I lean into her, resting my forehead against hers, and we stay there, our breathing in sync.

"That was—incredible," she whispers.

We stay like this for a few beats, allowing ourselves to catch our breath. I swear I can hear her heart beating with how close we are and it causes a smile to form on my lips knowing *I* did that to her.

I finally groan as I lift myself off. She pulls the fabric of her dress back down over her hips. There's redness creeping into her cheeks and I can't help but lean down and kiss her nose. She giggles and wraps her arms around my shoulders again, pulling me in for a deep kiss.

"Bunny—" I try to warn her, but she pulls back and laughs.

"What?" She smirks.

"You're trouble," I mutter, shaking my head. She watches me for a second before she bursts out in laughter. I try to shush her, but she continues to laugh, so I reach my hands down and tickle her sides.

"No! Bennett!" She squeals, attempting to push me away with her palms on my chest.

I move my fingers from her sides to hold her wrists in my hands. She hitches her breath before looking up and catching my eyes.

"Don't rile me up again, or I'll have to do more of those things I had in mind," I warn.

There's a gleam in her eyes as she listens. She nods slowly before pulling her hands back to her chest and I release her wrists.

"You're not so bad, Bennett Moore," she mutters under her breath.

A smile forms at my lips, and I shake my head. *You're not so bad, Bennett Moore.* Her words repeat in my mind and I laugh, staring at her incredulously.

Those are words I haven't really heard in a while.

I like it.

SEVENTEEN

CAMILLA

"LAST NIGHT WAS..." I can't even finish my sentence when Birdy nudges me with her elbow.

She wiggles her brows and widens her eyes. "What?!"

I lift my hands to cover my face as I shake my head. I can already feel the blush coming from what I'm about to tell her.

After Bennett and I hung out at his place last night, we did nothing more. It felt perfect as is and I wanted to make sure I could get home with a straight mind.

He makes my mind go into a frenzy and I knew we'd get ourselves in trouble if we continued anything... not that I *didn't* want to do anything more with him. But I wanted to wait and not go too far in one night.

He just started being nice to me and he's warming up to the *idea* of dating me. I want to take as much of it as I can get before it gets ruined or something.

So, I went home, and he even offered to give me a ride. Goose was waiting right by the door when I opened it. Bennett *insisted* on walking me up to my door, but I assured him I was completely capable. In response, he kissed my forehead and said goodnight. I felt like a lovesick teenager all over again.

I woke up early and couldn't stop thinking about Bennett, so I cleaned the entire house and was about to resort to cleaning the vineyard's main building when Birdy called. She wanted to check in after the whole dance with the random stranger last night, so I invited her over.

We got a random red wine from the cellar, popped it open, and poured it into large wine glasses. Then we pulled chairs from the porch of the vineyard office and brought them closer to the vines of the vineyard. We even laid out a blanket to place our belongings on them and a few snacks on a tray.

I turn to look at Birdy before averting my gaze and watching Goose nuzzle against her ankle, sleeping peacefully.

"We did things, okay? And it was amazing," I reply sheepishly.

She squeals and raises her glass, to which I raise my own and click it with hers.

"Wow, that's wild to hear," She jokes.

I shake my head and lift the glass to my lips, taking in a long sip of the red liquid.

"We didn't really do *that*, but it was close. And he did all the work…" I murmur.

"That's Bennett Moore for you. Will try to please everyone first before he can even please himself," Birdy eyes me before adding, "In every sense. I wouldn't know the bedroom stuff… and I never want to." She shudders and I laugh.

"Right. You mentioned you've known him forever?"

She nods, eyeing me. "We were best friends all throughout middle school and so on. We were like two peas in a pod. But then he got with Katherine sophomore year because of a science project."

I nod my head, taking another sip of wine.

Birdy sighs and shrugs. "It felt like they just left the rest of us when they got together. I wasn't even that close to Steve. We only became close because we didn't get to hang out with Bennett anymore."

"Because of Katherine?" I ask slowly.

She eyes me again before shaking her head. "No, it was both of them, actually. They instantly clicked and were inseparable. God, they even talked about running away once they graduated high school to get married. But her parents never allowed it. So, they both went to the same college."

"The community college nearby? The one Parker will attend?"

She nods, taking another sip of her own wine. "That one. Steve and I decided to just say fuck it to Alpine and go to college in Chattanooga. Then it was *us* against the world. He was my new Bennett. When we finally moved back after graduating college, we came back to a fucked up Bennett. He was miserable. He kept leaving for his tours. I didn't even *know* he joined the Marines. Let alone began contracting on these horrific missions; I can't even imagine the headspace he was in to go to that extreme. I even googled it because it was so uncalled for, coming from Bennett."

"What did you find out?" I ask slowly. She stares down at the wine glass in her hands and shrugs.

"That people who go that route usually have nothing else to lose in their life… and don't care what the outcome is."

I suck in a breath and watch Birdy as her eyes get glassy. She must be hurting, to know the lengths Bennett went to. To not have anything worth coming back home to, in his eyes. Not Birdy. Not even Katherine, his then wife.

Birdy clears her throat before continuing.

"Katherine was a wreck and lashed out at everyone. Including Steve and I, which, by the way, we were fucking clueless about everything. The only times we visited Alpine were for the holidays, but I spent most of it with my grandparents and figuring out my next steps after college. They wanted me to take over their shop, so that was my focus whenever I could visit."

I nod and lean back in my chair. "Did you ever figure out what Katherine got mad about with you and Steve?"

She shakes her head. "It wasn't really because of something we did, or she did to us. She just needed an outlet when Bennett was gone."

"An outlet for what?"

Birdy stops and presses her lips into a thin line. "Now that is just something I can't tell you. I'm sorry, Camilla. It's not my business, and it tore Bennett and Katherine's relationship —*marriage*—apart. I love town gossip, trust me, but this is not gossip."

I nod my head. I don't want to push her to tell me more. Besides, I don't even know how Bennett would take it if I told him all that Birdy has told me so far. It seems like I am still in the dark about a lot of things here in Alpine Ridge. Including Birdy and her history here.

"Well, thanks for sharing as much as you could. Really."

She finally smiles and lifts her glass, and I clink mine against hers. "Of course. If you make Bennett happy... like *really* happy. Then I'm all for it. I'm your number one cheerleader."

"Thanks, Birdy," I laugh.

She stares at me for a second before looking down at Goose at her ankle. She reaches her hand down to pet Goose's head, who continues to purr in her sleep.

"You know," she starts, catching my attention. "You really are making him happy. As grumpy as he is, we all see it. I might've lost him for a few years, but I still know Bennett like the back of my hand."

Heat creeps up my neck to my cheeks, and I nibble on my lip.

"And he may be really stubborn, but he's amazing. Once you have him in your corner, you want no one else there."

"Yeah, well, remember last night..." I murmur, thinking about the random guy who danced with me and gave me his cowboy hat.

She waves her hand, dismissing me. "Oh, *pfft*, that? You didn't know! I honestly thought you'd be better off dancing with that guy instead of forcing Bennett to get on the dance floor. I thought it was harmless."

"Really?"

She nods.

"I've never seen Bennett dance. Not even at senior prom."

Now this makes me laugh. Just picturing Bennett attempting to dance. I make a mental note to get him to dance with me next time.

"What happened when I left to chase after Bennett?"

"I was hoping you'd ask that," she grins. "Steve took care of it. The guy is a major douche, thinking he could just swoop in and take a woman like that. Steve let him know you did not know what his plan was. That you were with someone and actually left with him."

The blush grows in my cheeks, making it harder to smile. "I mean it's true."

"Yeah," she nods. "He seemed to let up once we explained it all. But he got super offended by Steve throwing his brand new hat on the bar counter."

I laugh and take another swig of the wine.

"Just a hint, never accept a cowboy hat that looks brand new."

I place my wine glass on my thigh and lean in between our chairs to grab the bottle we've been working on. It's almost empty, but I packed another just in case. I start to work on opening the other bottle as Birdy watches.

"Yeah, Bennett's one in the back of his truck was pretty worn out," I mention.

Birdy laughs, "Yeah, he's a real cowboy. Got the cows and

all."

I finish pulling the cork out and fill up my glass. I lean the bottle towards hers and she thankfully moves her glass to be near the bottle. I refill her glass before setting the bottle down in the grass.

"I haven't really seen the farm yet. Besides, it was dark last night, and we practically ran into his place."

Birdy nods before taking a sip of the new wine. She turns to stare at the vineyard and the wind picks up, brushing through the vines and even our little picnic area. Goose's fur moves with the wind and she wakes up, yawning and stretching, but staying put at Birdy's ankle.

"I'm sure he'd love to show you!"

"Maybe I'll go over there... or—"

Birdy whips her head back towards me and wiggles her brows. "Oh, make that man come over here!"

I look down at my outfit and realize I'm wearing another simple sundress but this time it's a nice jade green. Birdy is wearing a flowy yellow maxi dress. We didn't mean to dress up for our outing, we just happened to be wearing these. Flashbacks to last night in that lilac sundress make my stomach flutter and I clear my throat.

"You don't think I'll be too buzzed or dressed up for him to stop by?"

Birdy shakes her head. "I think you're just helping yourself by looking like that. He'd do whatever you'd ask of him."

I laugh and shake my head. "Oh, stop!"

"I'm serious! But let's finish this bottle before you call him over... plus, we need to plan the opening. Do you want me to cater for the desserts? We can ask Parker to give you Rose's contact info for the flowers."

I nod my head, smiling. "That would be amazing! I know I'll have a lot of work to do the following days, so please stop by whenever. And thanks for even offering."

"Of course!" Birdy smiles. "You're a resident of Alpine now. We help each other like family."

Her statement warms my heart and I lift the glass to my lips and drink more, feeling the liquid warm my body even more.

She's not wrong. Alpine Ridge is like a family and I'm glad I'm able to be a part of it.

THERE'S a knock at the front door an hour later as I slide along the hardwood floor in socks and *feeling* the copious glasses of wine I had with Birdy. It feels like I'm a kid again, pretending to skate along the floors of my childhood home. Minus my mom waving her chancla at me, screaming that I'll hurt myself. It always happened after she mopped the floors, so they were *extra* slippery.

"Ah!" I scream, as I almost slip and fall on my ass. I giggle and grab the marble counter to steady myself.

Control yourself, Camilla. I try to tell myself as I slide along the hardwood to the front door. I didn't mean to put on socks, but I didn't want to wear my slippers once I got back to the house, and I did not want to keep wearing the sandals I wore at the vineyard.

Birdy kept refilling my wine glass and although my thoughts were coherent, the wine was craving other things.

Bennett things.

It wasn't unusual for me to drink wine and have an increased sex drive. It always happened, but I never really had anyone around to play around with. But I texted Bennett to come over and I might have sent a few promiscuous emojis to entice him.

And it worked. He's standing on the porch with a real bouquet wrapped in plastic as I throw the front door open.

The sun is still shining brightly behind him, casting a golden glow outline around him.

"You're like an angel," I mumble out as I lick my lips and watch him smirk.

"I'm guessing you and Birdy drank more wine than planned?"

"How'd you know we drank wine?"

He looks down at his feet, shaking his head and chuckling. "Bunny, you texted me you were drinking wine with Birdy and needed to see me."

"Oh," I squeak out.

"And then the other texts," he clears his throat, finally bringing his head back up and there's a gleam in his eyes that I recognize from last night. I can feel my core tighten and the butterflies in my stomach fly around more.

Before I can respond, he reaches his hand outwards to hand me the bouquet. I take it gingerly in my hands before I step back and let him enter my place. I continue to slide on my socks along the floor as I follow him to the kitchen.

"Vase?" He asks, turning back around to see me slide up to the counter. He laughs at the sight.

"Uh, the top right cabinet. Near the fridge."

He nods before turning around and heading towards the fridge, getting on his tiptoes and leaning over to open the cabinet and fish out a vase. My mouth drops as I see the tattoos and faint scars on his back appear as his shirt rides up.

My throat goes dry and I gulp, attempting to calm myself from the sight.

I'm just tipsy. Not horny. At all.

He finally pulls out a vase and heads to the sink to fill it with water. He then plants the vase on the counter and reaches his hand out. I look at him before lifting my hand and placing it in his. His palm is soft.

"The flowers," he chuckles. I widen my eyes and pull my hand back before giving him the flowers.

He watches me for a moment with a smile before he rips the

plastic from the flowers, but I'm more so watching the way his biceps flex at the motion before he places the flowers into the vase. He fluffs up a few leaves and petals to make it look nicer before he pushes the vase onto the center of the island.

"There," he murmurs, nodding at his craftsmanship. I giggle, and he turns to look at me, widening his grin. "What's so funny?"

I press my lips into a line firmly before shaking my head and holding back another giggle.

"You're in a goofy mood," he laughs, moving closer to where I'm leaning on the counter. His cologne is faint, but I can still smell the woodsy, musky scent that is Bennett Moore.

"You smell good," I whisper, glancing up at him. He cranes his neck down and reaches his hand out to touch my chin.

"You're drunk," he chuckles before releasing his hand from my chin and stepping back to sift through the cabinets before he finds the glasses for water. He heads to the fridge to fill it up from the automatic water station.

He walks back towards me and lifts the glass to my lips. "Drink," he orders.

I open my mouth and grab the glass before drinking it. He watches me the whole time before I finish the glass, and he moves it to the sink.

"Come to the couch," I say abruptly, taking his hand and pulling him towards the living room. Goose is nestled into her own chair near the sectional that wraps around the living room.

"Okay," Bennett laughs behind me as we get closer to the couch. I turn around and my chest touches his torso with how tall he is.

"Sit."

His eyes cast down at me before he grins and nods. "Yes, ma'am."

He looks behind him before he sits on the couch comfortably. His thighs are spread out and I lick my lips.

The wine is giving me the confidence to do what I'm about to do, and I'm thankful for that. I'm such a wimp when it comes to flirting and asking guys to do what I prefer.

And right now I want to make out with this man. And possibly more if he'd let me.

His hands run smoothly along his thighs and I bite my lip. He watches me and there's like a switch being flipped in his eyes as he continues to stare. His eyes travel down my face to my chest and then my dress. It feels like we're back on the boat when we kept looking at each other.

I move to stand between his spread legs. "May I?" I ask, pointing my chin towards his waist.

He nods, watching me as I lift my legs and hold my dress to my thighs as I sit on top of him, adjusting myself so our cores are against another.

He sucks in a deep breath, and I gasp, closing my eyes. His growing erection brings more flutters to my core and I bite my lip, accidentally letting out a moan.

"*Oh?*" Bennett whispers, placing his hands on my thighs and rubbing them up and down.

I open my eyes quickly and watch his blue ones turn to a darker shade. There's mischief in them and *hunger*. I wrap my arms around his shoulders and wiggle my hips to bring some friction to his core.

He tightens his hold on my thighs, and I want him to sink his fingers into my skin.

Bruise me.

Ruin me.

His brows raise, but I don't wait for him to warn me about anything. I lean in and close the distance between us, collapsing my lips onto his. His lips melt into mine, and we're kissing feverishly, just like last night. Our breaths are heavy and we go at it until we have to finally separate.

"Are you sure? You've been drinking wine," he murmurs

close to my lips. His hand on my left thigh travels up my side, up my neck, and then clasps my cheek.

I nod. "I know you're really respectful and all, Bennett. But I'm giving you consent for whatever happens next."

He chuckles deeply, and it vibrates throughout his body and into mine, causing me to shiver and bite my lip.

"You're dangerous, Bunny," he warns.

I look at him before I lean over to whisper in his ear, circling my hips again at a slow pace. "Do more of what you had planned last night. I'm ready."

"Fuck," he mutters under his breath as his hand goes back to my thighs and rides up further until his fingers hook underneath the waistband of my thong.

It's lace, and I subconsciously wore it with the thought that *maybe* he'd take it off.

"Yeah?" I murmur softly in his ear, increasing the speed of my circling hips. I'm grinding right over his erection and it's making me wetter.

I won't last if I keep doing this and I know he won't either.

"Yes. God, *yes*," he groans as he stills my hips and I lift my head from his ear. His eyes are observing me before he grabs my hips tighter and shifts me to the cushion next to him. He moves to hover half his body over me. I squeal and giggle as my head hits the pillows.

His hands run along my bare thigh and hooks under the waistband of the thong again, but this time he pulls it down until he can slip it off me. He tosses it to the ground next to us and returns to his position, where he's hovering over me.

He leans in and starts kissing me softly on the neck and I moan, closing my eyes. His hand moves underneath my hip under my dress and his other pushes the other side of the dress until it's bunched up over my stomach. His hand glides slowly to my core, rubbing along my inner thigh. I try to clench my thighs, but he's in the way.

"*Hmm*," he murmurs before his lips reach my cheek and then my lips. Once our mouths connect, his hand moves to slip two fingers through my wet folds and I moan in his mouth.

It feels so good and he's barely touched me. He chuckles before diving his tongue in my mouth *as* he dives a finger into my entrance. My body accepts him willingly, and he moans.

"So tight still," he whispers before continuing our sloppy kiss.

His thumb moves to my clit and my body jolts up.

"You like that, baby?" He whispers, lifting his lips from mine. I nod and whimper as he inserts another finger into me.

I bite my lip, and he grins.

"Fuck—I need more," I whimper.

"Oh?" He raises a brow.

I nod. I bring my hand down between us, and I cup my palm over his clothed erection. He jolts from the touch, and he inhales sharply.

"Fuck, Bunny. Don't do that."

"Do what?" I ask, moving my hands to rub against his clothed cock. I giggle and his jaw twitches.

"You want more? Fine then," he murmurs before he pulls his fingers out of me. I cry out from the absence before he grabs my wrist with the same fingers, spreading my juices around my skin. He pulls my wrist to the side, and he pushes himself back.

I raise a brow and think he's going to leave, and I'm about to apologize for going too far. But then I watch as he leans his head down and pushes the dress even further up my stomach. His stubble glides along my inner thigh.

"*Oh*," I squeal as his lips press against my thigh and continue to travel closer to my pussy.

Before I can say or do anything, he's placing his tongue on my wet folds and licking from bottom to top, sucking on my clit.

My whole body shudders and my hands move to grip his hair tightly. He moans before he continues to lick me.

But he doesn't stop there. He inserts his fingers again and continues to go at a rapid pace, thrusting his fingers in and out of me as well as eating me out with his tongue.

It's so many senses at once that my mind doesn't know *what* to do. I'm lying there unable to speak, just enough strength to moan when he curls his fingers inside of me.

He's getting me to my orgasm faster than last night and he knows it. He chuckles against me and I shudder again at the vibrations.

"So, close," I finally moan. I clasp my eyes shut and tighten my hold on his scalp. He doesn't give me any indication that it's hurting him, so I don't release it.

He continues thrusting his fingers and swirling his tongue on my clit, causing stars to form in my vision. My heels are pressed deeply into the couch cushions and I cry louder as I feel the coil in me tighten, begging to snap.

"Bennett," I moan and without notice, my body snaps and I cum all over his fingers.

But he doesn't stop. He continues to lap up my orgasm and his fingers continue to thrust into me.

I cry out from the sensitivity and move my hand from his hair to grasp his hand.

"Stop," I whine, attempting to push my body up to get his fingers out of me. If he continues, I'll orgasm a second time and it will be *way* more. I've never squirted before with a partner, so I'm not sure if I'm ready for that or how he'd react.

He moans before slowly pulling his finger out and swirling his tongue one last time over my clit and between my folds. My body shakes from the sensation and a cry escapes from my lips again. He laughs before he lifts his head up and pulls the dress back over my core.

He leans over and maintains eye contact as he lifts his fingers to his mouth and *licks every single one* that was in me. I hitch my breath and attempt to steady my breathing from the orgasm and how he's making me feel.

"Come here," I whisper breathlessly. He nods and moves closer to me. I wrap my arm around his neck and kiss him, tasting myself on his lips.

He moans into the kiss and rubs his erection on my inner thigh. I close my eyes and bite my lip, causing him to lift his head.

"Do you want me to?" I whisper. He furrows his brow, so I continue. "Do you want me to make you come too?"

There's a redness that creeps into his cheeks, but he shakes his head.

"No, I want you to get all the pleasure for now. Don't worry about me, Bunny."

"Are you sure?" I raise a brow, but he grins.

"How about a deal?"

I look at him with wonder and curiosity. A deal?

"What kind of deal?"

He bites his lip before laughing and kissing my lips again. "If I can make you come five more times, then you can make me come."

I gasp and laugh. "How is that fair to you?"

"Because that means I get to hear you scream my name relentlessly all those five times."

"Bennett Moore!" I scream, pushing his chest with my palms. He laughs, and he winks before kissing my nose.

"I'm not usually like this, but I really like how you make me feel, Bunny. As cheesy as that sounds."

I shake my head. "That's not cheesy at all."

He stays silent as he registers my words. He's contemplating if I'm telling the truth, so I pull him in for another kiss.

"We've got a deal, Mr. Moore," I finally say as we pull away from the kiss.

EIGHTEEN

BENNETT

THE SOUND of both the rooster and gravel crunching outside my window causes me to whip my eyes open and groan.

Fuck that rooster.

The last few mornings I've been able to sleep through his screams, but this morning I'm wide awake.

The sunlight is streaming into the bedroom, and I curse under my breath for forgetting to close the blinds last night.

Today is the day the vineyard opens and I know exactly who is here outside my house. I groan as I pull the sheets off my body and quickly hop out of bed and head to the bathroom to take a shower and be as presentable as I can be before I open that door.

I give myself ten minutes. Shower, wash my face, and brush my teeth. By the time it's minute eleven, I'm stepping out of the bathroom and pulling over a clean shirt and tugging it down my chest and then tightening the strings on the waistband of my pajama pants.

There's a knock at the door and then high-pitched giggling as I get closer and run my hands through my hair before pulling it open.

A small body rushes towards me and wraps their arms around my thighs.

"Oof!" I yell, pretending to take a step back and almost fall down.

"I'm not *that* strong!" Morgan giggles as she takes a step back. Peyton follows right behind her, taking off her black sunglasses and placing it in her purse that's draped over her shoulder.

"You're early," I groan at Peyton while leaning over to pick up Morgan under her arms and lifting her. She wraps her arms around my neck, and we hug for a moment before I drop her back down. Her brunette hair swishes this way and that.

"I'm surprised you're *clean*, thought you'd be up at the farm or with the horses in the pasture," Peyton laughs as she gets closer and reaches her arms out.

I close the distance and hug her, wrapping my arms around her small body and swinging us slowly.

She sighs and we stay like this for a few seconds before Morgan's feet shuffle down the hallway. Peyton lets go and stares at me, her blue eyes moving all over my face. Her fair skin has some color to it, but not much. She usually gets a reddish hue to her skin by now with tons of freckles when she lived in Alpine.

"What?" I ask, raising a brow.

"You don't have those deep frown lines anymore," she murmurs, while lifting a hand and running her fingers alongside my cheek and then my forehead.

I roll my eyes and huff out a breath, but she gently slaps my cheek and smiles. "That's a good thing, Ben. Don't look so offended."

"They gave me character," I argue.

She shakes her head and laughs, pulling her hand away from my face. She looks around the front of the house before looking behind my shoulder to where Morgan must've ran off to. We hear clanging in the kitchen and we both laugh.

"Marshmallow sandwich," we say in unison.

I reach my hand out to grab her purse and she thanks me as I put it gently on a chair in the hallway. We walk towards the kitchen and sure enough, Morgan is whipping out ingredients to make the sweetest sandwich ever.

On two slabs of bread, she's spreading peanut butter, marshmallow fluff, and then some honey before slapping the two pieces together.

There's three plates in front of her and she's preparing a sandwich for each of us.

"I'm surprised you still have the ingredients," Peyton whispers as we get closer to Morgan, who is in deep concentration. Her tongue is sticking out and her eyebrows are furrowed.

I shrug, "Kinda had the feeling you'd be over, eventually."

I head over to Morgan and lean over her head and plant a kiss on the top. She giggles and I momentarily grab the knife in her hand and back up, walking where I have the rest of my utensils.

"Uncle BenBen! I wasn't done!" She whines. But I grab a plastic butter knife from a drawer before returning to her and handing the utensil over.

"No sharp objects, Sweetpea," I warn her, making sure she understands. Her eyes widen and then she nods, taking the plastic butter knife in her hands and resuming her work.

I head back to where Peyton is and lift the knife to my mouth, licking the opposite side of it to not cut my tongue, cleaning it from the marshmallow fluff.

"You baby her too much," Peyton jokes. She pulls out her phone and I toss the knife in the sink.

"I will not take her to the hospital because of a marshmallow sandwich, Pey. Not today."

She finally looks up from her phone and smiles widely. "Right. You've got big plans today."

I roll my eyes again and sigh. "Not really big plans, just an event to go to."

"The vineyard opening *is* a big event."

Peyton seems to want to say something, but Morgan speaks up. "Where's Aunt Kat? Is she here?"

Peyton and I look at each other before I run my hand through my hair and shake my head. "Sorry, Sweetpea, she's not coming. Remember how your mommy and I told you that Kat no longer lives with me? She lives in her own house."

Morgan looks up from the third sandwich she's spreading peanut butter on and she frowns. "Can I see her?"

Peyton presses her lips into a thin line before nodding her head. "Of course, baby. But not today, okay? We've got to go to the vineyard."

"You mean our old home? Are we moving back? I can stay with Uncle BenBen while you move us, mommy."

Peyton laughs and I smile. "No, baby. We're just visiting. And I'm sure Uncle Bennett likes his privacy."

I shake my head. "You're always welcome, Sweetpea. Always."

Morgan beams at us before she slaps the slices of bread together on the last plate and claps her hands. "Breakfast is ready!"

Peyton and I thank her as she hands us each a plate. She even goes back to the fridge to get us a glass of milk.

It's way too sweet of a sandwich, but Peyton and I eat every bite.

The vineyard opening is at noon, so we had a few hours to prepare. Birdy texted me early yesterday morning, wanting me to help her with some kind of plan for after the opening to congratulate Bunny on opening the vineyard so fast. It'd be an intimate dinner outside, in an area where there are wooden tables. We set it up without Bunny noticing.

We wanted it to be perfect for her. *I* wanted it to be perfect for her. We've been busy the last few days that we haven't done anything since that night at her place. We got lunch and dinner a few times, but that night was the last time we did anything intimate.

I can't lie–I miss her. It'll be good to see her. Plus, I can't wait to see her reaction tonight.

By the time we finish breakfast, I change into jeans and help Peyton bring in their suitcases into the guest room. Morgan dressed herself up in cute sparkly barn boots and a small cowboy hat. She must've found them in a closet somewhere. It's the ones she used to wear when I'd have her over.

"What's this?!" I laugh, walking into the living room.

"I want to see the cows and horses," she giggles before running out the back door.

Peyton is in the guest room laying out their attire for the vineyard, and I pass by the room, knocking on the door. She turns to look at me and I catch her glassy eyes. I pinch my brows and frown.

"What's up, Pey?"

"Nothing!" She waves her hand and then wipes her eyes quickly. Her cheeks are rosy and she attempts to smile as I enter the room.

"Are you sure? We can talk about it."

"It's nothing, really," she reassures me, but I can see through her. She shrugs before laughing. "I just didn't think I'd come back here so soon. It hasn't been that long, and I don't know how Morgan will act."

I shrug my shoulders and stuff my hands in my jean pockets. "Everyone misses you guys and I think just seeing the way Bu— Camilla has kept everything looking the same, but in her own way will help you see that and not feel you're coming back into the past."

She nods her head before sniffling. "Yeah, and it's time. It's *been* time for us to visit Alpine. I can't thank you guys enough for even keeping the land maintained. I wouldn't have blamed anyone if it became an inhabitable mess."

"Never, ever." I shake my head and close our distance, pulling her into a bear hug. She breathes deeply after I hold her head to my chest. I rub the top of her head. "We'd never let it get that way and you know it. We love you guys and knew how hard it was. You and Andy would've done the same thing for any of us."

She nods her head and sniffles on my chest. She finally shifts her head to stare up at me. Her eyes are sparkling and red from crying. "I miss him, Ben. So much."

I can feel my chest swell and tears brim my eyes. I sniffle and laugh, shaking my head.

"Damn it, Peyton. Don't."

She laughs and sniffles as well. "Sorry. I know you don't like people seeing you be emotional, or whatever."

"No, it's not that. I'm not afraid of showing my genuine emotions to you. I'd cry a damn river with you if you'd like to right now. We can even lay out in the pasture and stare at the sky. Anything you'd like, I'd do."

"Then what is it?"

I bite my lip and sigh. "I'm worried that Morgan hasn't been adjusting well to the change. She still thinks Katherine and I are together. She wants to move back here."

Peyton nods and takes a step back, separating our bodies, but she lets me keep my arms on her shoulders.

"She's fine, really. She doesn't really get the whole divorce thing and I think being here helps her see that you're perfectly fine without Katherine. And about the whole moving thing... I think she just misses Alpine and the people. She was too young to remember that house and the vineyard."

I nod my head, attempting to understand. She's not wrong. Morgan was only two years old when Andy started getting sick.

She was barely turning three when he passed. She really didn't know the property like we all did.

She just knew the people that always visited her. She only remembered the times Katherine, and I took her under our wings when Peyton and Andy got really busy with business.

We were like her second parents, taking her on weekend trips, letting her work the farm life with me whenever she had the time. Staying all day with Katherine at the ballet studio if Andy and Peyton had events at the vineyard with businesses from out of town.

I know she really misses Kat and I together, but she just saw the mask that we showed everyone, making them *think* we were the perfect married couple.

Peyton seemed to be the only one who saw through it all. The masks, the lying, the heartbreaking nights. Fights and yelling. The fucking screaming until Katherine and I would take weekends off from each other, when she'd stay with either Peyton or in a hotel to get away from it all.

Morgan saw none of that. *No one* saw any of that except for Peyton. Not even Birdy or Steve. They got the brunt of it all when it all crashed and burned. They didn't *see* or *hear* a lot of what happened until it was too late and I had to come clean— Katherine and I had to come clean.

"Bennett?" Peyton snaps me back to the room and I shake my head, sighing.

"Sorry, I got stuck in my mind again."

"It's okay. It's getting better though?" Her eyes are full of worry now and she pinches her brows.

I nod my head. "Yeah, it is."

"Good," she smiles. She then presses her palms on my chest and pushes me until I take a step back. "Now, go get your cute little helper and show her how to feed the horses."

I laugh and nod my head. "She knows how to handle the

farm on her own. She's probably hunting down that raccoon in full camo gear right now."

Peyton squints her eyes and shakes her head. "She better not be! She will *not* be a replica of you, Bennett Moore! I don't need two of you hunting down raccoons and coyotes while I'm here!"

I shrug and fake tipping an invisible hat before I turn around and head to where Morgan is outside.

BEING out on the pasture with Morgan was comforting and felt like hours, even though we were out for maybe an hour at most.

She helped me feed the horses, tend to the cows, and then play with the barn kittens. There was a moment when I turned around and she had three kittens squeezed in her arms, attempting to run past me and back to the house. I had to remind her they were barn kitties and not for the house. They had a roof and food and didn't need an actual house. A wild cat is hard to tame and these barn cats and kittens love their life here.

Once we got back into the house, Peyton ordered us both to shower and start getting ready for the event. She reminded me it was a black-tie event, so we had to dress up. I didn't mind, but I groaned as Peyton shuffled me towards the stairs to my bedroom to shower. Morgan kept giggling and started screaming and running once Peyton turned around to get her in the bath.

I was out in eight minutes this time, attempting to shave my beard into a more suitable look before trudging into my closet and staring at my wardrobe. I had nothing, really, except for *one* tuxedo. When I was married to Katherine, I didn't really dress up.

I have a few ties to select from, but even then I was stumped. I slipped on the pieces for the tuxedo before grabbing all the ties and marching downstairs and over to the guest room. I stop when I see Peyton in a stunning blue sparkly dress that falls to her ankles. Her ginger hair is pinned back in an updo and she turns, flashing me a grin.

"Bennett Moore, you are too handsome for your own good." She waves me over while she turns back to where Morgan is sitting, pouting and crossing her arms over her chest.

I head towards her, kneeling in front of her. "What's wrong, Sweetpea?"

She sighs before looking up at Peyton, who is fastening a cute pink bow on her curled hair. She's wearing a matching light pink dress.

"Mommy knows I don't like pink anymore."

I chuckle and look up at Peyton, who rolls her eyes from where she's standing, shaking her head. "You agreed to this dress when we were packing, Morgan! Don't turn this on me."

Morgan's lips tremble and my heart swells. "Hey, it's okay."

I pull my hands up where the stack of ties are in multiple colors. "Why don't you pick my tie? I think there's a pink one in there... You know, I hate the color pink too. We can hate it together."

Her eyes widen for a little bit before her small fingers roam my palm and pick up the pink tie that is almost an exact color match to her dress. She lifts it up and wiggles it in front of me.

"This one," She smiles.

"You got it," I nod before standing up. I pull the tie around my neck and look in the mirror in the room as I loop it around and tie it up.

"Alright, we're all ready," Peyton says from behind me. I crane my neck to see Morgan jump off the chair she's sitting on and running to me, hugging my thighs.

"Oh! Sweetpea," I laugh.

"Thanks, Uncle BenBen," she says before letting me go.

Peyton gathers a smaller purse and stuffs her wallet and phone in it before she catches my eyes.

"Let's go," I tell them. Morgan follows me and slips her hand in mine as we walk out into the hallway and then to the front door. Peyton's heels clack behind us and I make sure to hold the door open for her as we step out.

I lock the doors and let go of Morgan's hand as we near the truck so I can open her door and get her inside. I then do the same for Peyton, making sure her dress doesn't get caught in the door.

I momentarily whip my head around and remember that my hair is still down. When I get inside the truck, I turn to Peyton. "Do you have a hair tie?"

She nods and shifts through her purse before she pulls one out. "Here."

I take it and quickly fasten my long hair into a small bun. That'll do.

"Alright, Sweetpea. We're about to head back to the vineyard and see all your favorite people!" I yell behind me as I turn the engine on and head out of the property.

Morgan hums a song and I look in the rearview mirror and see her staring out the window in her car seat. I had it saved in a closet since they left and I remembered to take it out and put it in the truck last night before I knocked out.

Peyton is silent as we near the vineyard entrance. There's already a few cars lined up in parking spots near the entrance and I can see some folks walking up the pathway that leads to the vineyard. To the left there's all the grapevines and then to the left is the parking. Up the driveway and walking path is the vineyard building. Behind that is where the other barn is for big events where we'll have the intimate dinner.

I can feel my heart rate increase as we near the driveway. I grip the steering wheel a little harder and Peyton finally turns to look at me.

"You okay?"

I nod. "Yeah, just a little nervous."

"About her?"

I turn and nod at Peyton. She can always read my mind and through my expressions. "Yeah, we finally went on a date the other night."

She widens her eyes and smiles. "I never thought I'd hear those words come from your lips, Bennett."

I shrug and drive up the pathway and signal right as I wait to park. "I'm excited for you to meet her..."

"I'm *very* excited to meet her. Especially now." She turns her head back to where Morgan is sitting. "You're going to be excited too, baby. Okay?"

I watch Morgan from the mirror, and she shakes her head. I pinch my brows. "Hey! You'll be nice, young lady. Camilla is kind and you'll like her."

Morgan crosses her arms over her chest. "I want Auntie Kat."

Peyton sighs and shakes her head before I sigh. "Morgan Stone!"

She finally giggles, and I huff out a loud breath. "I got you, Uncle BenBen!"

"She's gonna give me a heart attack," I tell Peyton. She presses her lips into a thin line and I frown.

"Shit, sorry, Pey." I bite my tongue and wish I never said that, especially with how Andy suffered so many heart complications. It was the reason he passed.

She shakes her head and takes a deep breath. "It's good to crack some jokes. I'm just overwhelmed with everything. Especially now pulling up to the land."

"Well, I'm here for you. I won't leave your side."

I turn the car to get into the parking lot, which is just a grassy area with some gravel to help keep cars from sinking into the dirt. I pull into a spot and turn the engine off. We unbuckle our seat belts and my eyes glance at Peyton. She pulls the visor down and flips the mirror open to fix her makeup.

"You ready?" I ask Morgan, craning my neck back to look at

her. She nods and smiles. I push my door open and hop out, grabbing Morgan's door and opening it. I help her from her seat and pick her up before settling her onto the gravel. After shutting her door, I head to Peyton's door next. I pull it open and move to reach my hand out to help her out.

Peyton slowly steps out and slips the chain of her purse over her shoulder. She's a little taller now in her heels. She grabs Morgan's hand before letting mine go so I can shut her door. I place my keys in my pocket and we all turn to walk up the pathway to the vineyard. There are balloons at the entrance and there's some more lining every few feet tied to trees and grapevines to the left of us.

Morgan skips along the gravel as Peyton and I hold her hands. It's not a far walk, but I let Peyton take her time with her heels.

I look around the vineyard and notice that there are tons of locals, as well as out of towners here. It makes me happy seeing how many people are showing up for this opening. No one knows except for the ones who set this all up that Peyton and Morgan are here.

"It's gorgeous. The same, but even better," Peyton breathes out as we finally reach the building and head to the wrap-around porch. There are people sitting and chatting, laughing, and even popping champagne bottles already. Everyone is dressed so nicely.

There's a huge banner at the top of the building that states *Grand Opening*.

"Let's head inside and we can grab a bottle and some snacks. Birdy catered."

Peyton widens her eyes and nods her head. She looks down at Morgan between us. "You hear that? Birdy brought dessert!"

"Peanut brittle!" Morgan squeals before releasing our hands and running fast up the porch steps. She swings the door open as much as she can and slips inside the building. Peyton and I laugh, watching her body disappear.

"God, if it was that easy, I'd ask Birdy for that damn recipe," Peyton jokes.

"It's pretty good. Even I would run like that," I laugh. I lift my elbow for Peyton to slip her arm around it so we can head inside.

Once we're in, I can smell the sweet desserts that line one enormous table on the right side of the building. There are other tables with drinks and sodas, finger foods, and wine samples. There's even more clear fridges placed around the room to store wine and snacks. Birdy is cutting a piece of brittle for Morgan in the far corner and placing it on a plate before handing it to her.

She looks up and waves at me before she sees Peyton, and a smile spreads across her face. She talks to Morgan for a moment before she heads to us, wrapping an arm around me and I hug her back before she pulls Peyton into a hug.

"Peyton! I'm so glad Bennett called you."

"Me too," she murmurs as she hugs Birdy back. Birdy is in a nice black floral dress that swirls around her thighs as she moves.

"Where's Steve?" I ask Birdy. Morgan comes running back to us and she is munching on the brittle.

"Uh, I think he's with Oliver? They went out to the other barn where tonight will happen." Birdy lowers her voice.

"How are you and Steve?" Peyton asks, leaning in close. Birdy's cheeks grow rosy as she looks from me to Peyton.

"We're—uh, we're good!"

"Hmm," Peyton hums before she turns to look at me with a gleam in her eyes.

I raise my hands in a surrendering motion. "Don't look at me, Peyton."

I look at Birdy. "Where's Bunny?"

"Who?" Peyton asks.

Birdy laughs. "Camilla, Peyton. The *new* owner of this beautiful place."

"Why do you call her a bunny?" Peyton laughs. I shrug and shoot daggers at Birdy with my eyes.

"It's a long story," I finally let out.

"She had to grab more wine from the office. She got a huge shipment this week and kept them in the boxes. She didn't expect this many people to show up!"

"Is she alone?" I ask slowly.

"Parker's with her," Birdy eyes me. She watches as my jaw twitches. She laughs before adding, "Kidding! God, the look on your face. She's alone. Go see her dummy."

I attempt to laugh, but I'm embarrassed at how I reacted. God, Parker and his dumb crush on Bunny is still getting to me.

I turn to Peyton. "You okay with me going to see her?"

Peyton nods and leans down to grab Morgan's hand. "Birdy, show me around the place. Tell me what's new! And tell me how you and Steve *really* are."

Birdy blushes again before nodding. I take this as my cue to head to the back office. The door is ajar and I push it slowly and see Bunny on her tiptoes, reaching for a box that's higher than she is.

She's wearing a pretty pink floral dress and I smile, noting how we're basically matching with my tie. She doesn't hear me and I head to her, crouching to wrap my arms around her waist and bury my head in her neck.

"Excuse me!" She yelps before she whips her head around and sees my face. "Bennett?"

"Mhm, you look pretty, Bunny."

She giggles and places her hands around my arms that are wrapped around her. She relaxes back on her heels and leans her head back, giving me more access to her neck. I take this time to lay soft kisses along her skin and she shudders, hitching her breath.

"*Bennett Moore*, not here!" She giggles before turning around and wrapping her arms around my neck, and I stand taller. She gets on her tiptoes again before planting a kiss on my lips.

I wrap my hands over her hips; her dress a silky material against my skin. I moan as I kiss her. I want to close that office door to continue making out with her and maybe do a little *more*, but she places her palms flat on my chest and pushes me.

"I've got an opening to attend to, sir!"

My dress pants tighten near my crotch at her word and I raise a brow. "Sir?"

She bites her lip before nodding. "You're dressed the part in this handsome suit."

My hands run down to her ass and squeeze firmly. She squeals and attempts to step to the side to get out of my hold, but I pull her closer to kiss her again.

God, I can kiss her forever.

"Looks like we're matching," I murmur.

She nods and smiles. "I guess so. Unintentionally, of course. Unlike Steve and Birdy."

"Maybe we're turning into them."

She laughs and shakes her head. "As much as I'd like to deny it, you're right. You and her are almost the same. And I guess that means Steve and I are almost the same."

"Don't make me see you like Steve. He's like a brother to me," I groan.

"Not what I meant!" She giggles.

I step back and shift my hand to grab hers. Her touch is warm and her cheeks turn red as I pull her closer to the office door.

"Wait! The wine!"

"It can wait. I've got two people I really want you to meet."

She looks at me before nodding and letting me pull her out of the office to find Peyton and Morgan.

NINETEEN

CAMILLA

THERE ARE SO many people at the opening of the vineyard that it makes me want to fall to the floor and sob happy tears. Full on, clutch my chest with both hands and let any sob that is building up in my body escape.

I never thought this amount of people from Alpine Ridge would be interested in *my* grand opening. Yes, I know that a lot of the locals probably missed having the vineyard since the Stones left, but it's still heartwarming to see the town come together to celebrate the grand opening.

Bennett brought Peyton and Morgan, and I was more than excited to meet them. To finally meet the people that *changed* my life here in Alpine Ridge in just the short amount of weeks I've been here. It feels like I've lived here for months, but it's barely the start of summer. This place is just magical like that and I love it.

Bennett pulls my hand that's entwined in his as we walk through the office door. Suddenly, my ears are filled with the sounds of people chattering around the building. Everyone has either a clear cup of wine or a plate of Birdy's catered desserts and snacks.

I look around the room and can't help but smile. Bennett squeezes my hand and I look up to see him staring before he winks and pulls me towards a gorgeous woman who is decked out in the prettiest blue dress. Next to her is a mini-her, but wearing a pink dress and her brunette hair has cute pink bows.

"Peyton," Bennett calls as we reach them. The redhead turns around and beams at us, her blue eyes softening as they find mine.

"You must be Camilla!" She reaches over and pulls me in for a hug. I let out a small gasp and laugh as my hand releases from Bennett to complete the hug.

She holds me for a few seconds before pulling away. Her eyes search my face before she casts her eyes onto Bennett.

"She's pretty."

"She's my Bunny," Bennett smiles before reaching his hand back towards mine. The little girl near Peyton is still munching on a piece of brittle.

"Morgan! Don't be rude. This is Camilla. Remember Bennett said she was the owner of this place?"

Morgan turns around as her mother scolds her and a smile spreads across her small face. "We're matching!"

I look at our outfits and notice that we *are* matching. We're both wearing dresses with pink on it. I laugh and nod my head. "We are! I think your dress is better than mine, though."

She's absolutely beautiful in her dress, and her smile fills her face. It makes my heart warm at the sight.

She looks from me to Bennett and squeals. "Uncle BenBen! We're *all* matching!"

Bennett shakes his head and chuckles under his breath. "You're right, Sweetpea."

Peyton laughs as she leans over to fix the bow on her daughter's head. I watch as Morgan continues to squeal and smile before returning to munching on the brittle on her plate. Peyton looks up at me and smiles.

"You really kept it the same. I was definitely surprised. But I love it, nonetheless."

"I hope that's okay," I rush. Her eyes widen, and she shakes her head, waving a hand to dismiss me.

"No, no, please don't take that badly. I think the town needed this after we left. The vineyard wasn't just special to Andy and I —it was almost a landmark for Alpine."

Her words are heavy, and I nod. It's clear with how much the town loved the Stones, with how many people showed up today. And even more continue to roll in. I can see Birdy in my peripheral, continuing to set out more and more batches of sweets and snacks as she brought in prepared trays.

"Well, please, if you'd like to stay over at the house, you're more than welcome," I tell Peyton.

She shakes her head. "I don't want to impose. Bennett is already letting us stay over in his guest room. Morgan loves that farm. She never really liked the vineyard part of our land."

I turn to look at Bennett, and he smiles. "She's my cowgirl. Got her a hat and boots and everything. She could round up the cows and horses if I really needed her to."

I laugh and lean down to talk to Morgan. "Wow, you sure are amazing. I'm kind of jealous! I'm from a city, so I don't know how to handle a horse or a cow."

She sways in her place, the brittle on her plate sliding a little. Her pink dress sways, with her movements around her legs. "Uncle BenBen is a *real* cowboy! We're going to ride the horses tomorrow!"

"Hey, that was a secret!" Bennett calls out behind me. Peyton sighs and laughs.

"I guess I wasn't supposed to know?"

I stand back up next to Bennett and he wraps his arm around my waist so nonchalantly it catches me off guard. My breath quickens and the heat in my face continues to grow. I'm sure if he paid enough attention, he'd feel the increase of my heartbeat all throughout my body.

"You'd most likely be sleeping by the time we got the horses in the morning. So, yes, it was a secret we'd thought you'd never find out... until now."

I can't help but laugh. Peyton doesn't have an angered expression on her face, but she shakes her head.

"Like I said earlier, Ben. Don't make my daughter a replica of you. We don't have the same access to horses and land back home."

Bennett chuckles, "Well, then. She'll have to visit more often."

Morgan perks up at his invitation and she nods her head rapidly. "I want to stay with Uncle BenBen, momma! *Pleassssseeee!*"

"You have school! Only for the summer," Peyton replies.

Morgan smiles, and Bennett reaches his other hand towards her and forms it into a fist. Morgan laughs as she forms her own hand into a fist and bumps it with him.

I watch them continue to mingle as Bennett returns to a standing position and tightens his hand over my hip. I step a little closer to bring my body flush to his, almost tempted to lean my head on his shoulder.

But I know if I do that, I'd want to close my eyes and just revel in this moment of being here at the grand opening with people I've come to really like.

"BENNETT! WHERE ARE WE GOING?!" I squeal as I almost trip over a step.

Bennett laughs behind me, his lips right at my ear, and it sends shivers down my spine. His hand is tight on my hip and his other continues to hold the blindfold that's over my eyes.

It's a few hours after the grand opening. It wasn't meant to be open all night long since it was the first day opening. I wanted to get a feel for things and then adjust my hours as needed. So far, I've gotten such good feedback from the customers I had today.

I met so many people that live in town or came from the town over, Mason Pointe. It was nice to know that people from all around were willing to come around for the grand opening and I had my friends to thank. I knew Birdy talked to her friends and family. Bennett probably did too, as well as Steve.

It was such a success that all of Birdy's catered food ran out two hours before we closed! And I had to finally break into the boxes in the office to restock the fridges after they ran empty as well.

"Just one more step, Bunny," Bennett reassures me as he leads us with his hands, and I slowly step down and then feel the change of the wooden steps to the grassy texture. The late summer breeze is starting to come into the vineyard and the wind ruffles through my dress. I squeal and try to lift my arms to my blindfold, but Bennett tightens his hold on me.

"Not yet!" He laughs.

"Okay, okay," I giggle.

There are sounds that I can't decipher as we continue to walk along the grass. That's until I smell amazing food and stop in my tracks. With Bennett being right behind me, he stumbles right into me.

"*Oof*, why'd you stop?"

"What's going on, Bennett?"

"You'll see when we get there! We're so close."

I sigh and nod my head, letting him continue to steer me. It's not until a few minutes later that the commotion of people talking and laughing are within earshot. If I take off this blindfold, I'll be able to see the owners of the voices.

"Alright," Bennett whispers as he brushes his chest to my back. Goosebumps run along my arms as he runs his hand that was on my waist up my arm and then on the other side of the blindfold. He *slowly* unties it and I tap my feet.

"Hurry!" I laugh. He finally lets the blindfold fall and I blink a few times to let my sight adjust to the night.

I gasp and feel the tears fill my eyes. The commotion stops and everyone that I've met in Alpine Ridge is standing around a makeshift wooden table.

Birdy is leaning against Steve's chest as they each hold a glass of wine and have the brightest smiles on their faces. Peyton and Morgan are to their right and Parker and Mabel are to the left. Across the table are Oliver and Izzy. Izzy winks at me and smiles.

"What is this?" I ask, pulling my hands to my mouth.

Birdy laughs and pushes herself off Steve's chest and walks around the table before she reaches me. She's holding an extra wine glass that I didn't notice before and pushes it into my torso before I take it.

"It was all Bennett. I just helped a little."

I turn to look at Bennett, who sheepishly smiles and nods. "Just wanted to throw a little party to congratulate you on the successful grand opening."

"Oh? I'm glad you thought it would be successful," I joke, leaning close towards him and before I even think of what I'm doing, I get on my tiptoes and plant a kiss on his lips. He freezes for a moment before he wraps an arm around my waist and pulls me into his body. I move the hand that's holding the wine glass quickly before it gets crushed between us. He took off his suit jacket and has his shirt sleeves rolled up, the muscles in his arms evident. His hair is still pulled back into a small bun, but some strands are starting to fall around his face. He kisses me one more time.

Birdy laughs and I hear small clapping behind us.

"Thank you," I whisper, pulling my face back.

He smiles and clears his throat. His blue eyes are soft and it feels like I can read what he's thinking—which is a rare occurrence I've come to find. He's not very good at expressing his emotions and always keeps up a wall.

"Anything for my Bunny," he whispers back.

I smile and bite my lip. He's said that *twice* now.

My Bunny.

Before I can respond, Birdy claps her hands and yells, "Alright, make out time is over and it's time to eat. Because ya girl cooked it all and I refuse for it to go to waste!"

We all laugh and I nod, releasing myself from Bennett's hold and finding a spot around the table. There aren't any real chairs, but big fluffy pillows to lounge on. It's a more relaxed setting, and it makes my heart warm.

There are tons of string lights lined around this side of the vineyard. We're next to the huge barn that is used for events. It's far enough from the main spaces of the land to be really intimate. It makes me wonder where Bennett and Birdy knew how to find this place. But with how close he is with the Stone's it doesn't surprise me if he knows every hidden part of this land.

As we sit down, Birdy beckons for everyone else to sit. I see some kicking off their heels to get more comfortable and I follow suit. It feels nice to have my bare feet on the cool grass.

Birdy lifts her wine glass and pulls a fork from the table and starts clinking it to draw everyone's attention.

"I just want to say that this wouldn't be possible without Bennett... or Peyton. Thank you for letting my new friend Camilla buy your land. And Camilla, I'm so proud of how much you've worked on this renovation, yet kept the same feeling we've had with the Stone Vineyard. You really outshined yourself and I am so proud of you. I think I can speak for everyone else in saying this—you were destined for our small town and I'm so fucking glad you chose us."

Everyone claps around the table, and I feel the tears flood my face. I blink and they fall past my cheeks. I smile and attempt to keep the sobs in, but they still escape. Bennett leans over and wraps his arm around my shoulders.

"I'm fine, really," I laugh, lifting a hand to wipe the tears from my face.

Birdy sits down and Peyton stands up. I widen my eyes and she looks around the table before smiling. "I just wanted to give a little speech. Camilla, I know we just met, but I see the love you poured into my husband's favorite place. And I can't thank you enough for making it seem like he's still with us."

She sniffles, and Morgan reaches over and hugs her legs. We all make an audible *aww* sound as Peyton continues.

"I never planned to return to Alpine... but I'm glad Bennett talked me into it. It's like I never left, but in an even better way."

I bring my hand to my chest and I mouth out a *thank you* before more tears fall from my eyes. She smiles and tears brim her eyes as well.

"Alright, enough sappy speeches," Birdy exclaims from her end of the table. We all laugh. "We've got some amazing chicken breast with lemon, garlic, herbs, and a side of parmesan asparagus. There's also some homemade mashed potatoes and then, for dessert, peanut brittle."

She points to our plates that are covered with tinfoil to keep the heat in the dish as well as the bugs out. My mouth waters at the descriptions, and we all eat our dinner. Conversation flows around the table and I see the big smiles on everyone's faces. It warms my heart and I reach over, resting my hand on Bennett's thigh before squeezing slightly. He turns to look at me and smiles, leaning over and kissing my cheek.

By the time we're ready for dessert, Birdy has to get it from the building and recruits Steve to come with her. We all stand from the table to stretch and I fall into conversation with Izzy.

I see Parker run back to the building. I pay no mind to it and focus back on Izzy.

"So, Camilla, are you and Bennett together?" Izzy nudges my elbow with hers as she sips her wine and gives me a wink.

My cheeks heat as I turn to look at Bennett a little past the table, in deep conversation with Peyton. He's holding Morgan, who is slowly sleeping on his shoulder. He sways in his place and rubs his hand over her back.

I turn back to Izzy and nod. "I think so. We went on a casual date the other night."

She beams before taking another sip of her wine. "You guys are super cute. You need to let me know the next time you're at Nicky's. I will make sure your fried pickles are free."

I laugh and shake my head. "No! You don't have to do that. Seriously!"

She rolls her eyes and laughs. "You guys are so cute. I know you probably don't want to hear this from me, but he looks really happy. And it's because of you."

I widen my eyes and turn to steal a look at Bennett, who is leaning his head back and laughing at whatever Peyton said. He *does* look happy, regardless of how grumpy he originally was when we met.

I think people just needed to crack open his shell and remind him of his roots.

"Yeah, he does, thank you." I grin.

Izzy smiles and nods as she watches me and sips more of her wine. Before I can change the subject, I hear footsteps running towards us and then a hand wrapping around my elbow, pulling me from Izzy.

"Oh!" I gasp as I stumble in my steps and find Parker being the one pulling me away. I glance around the area and catch eyes with Bennett, who starts to raise a brow. I throw him a confused expression before I let Parker pull me further from the area and closer to the event barn.

"Parker!" I laugh as he finally stops in his tracks and runs his hands through his brunette waves.

205

"I-I saw something, and I had to run to tell you…"

"What did you see?" I push, starting to get concerned with how wild his eyes look. He continues to run his hands through his hair and I have to lift my own to grab his wrists before he pulls his hair out.

"Parker! Focus!" I shake his wrists. This calms him down and he takes deep breaths before locking his brown eyes with mine.

"I saw—uh… I saw Birdy and Steve."

I stare at him and take a deep breath. "And? What did you see?" I want to laugh, but there's still worry all over his face.

"I saw them…"

I shake him again, and he exhales loudly. "I saw them kiss!"

"What?" I laugh.

He shakes his hands in my hold, and I finally let go. He walks in circles before landing his hands on his hips. I can't help but crack a smile at his distress.

"This isn't funny, Miss Camilla!"

"They kissed, so what?" I laugh.

"That means they're dating!"

I roll my eyes and shake my head. "No, it does not! Plus, you know Steve and Birdy. They're super close and if they want to date, then they can date!"

"Yeah, but I saw them kiss! ON THE LIPS!" He runs his hands through his hair again and I reach out and grab his wrists again and pull them at his sides.

I look at him, and his eyes settle. He takes a deep breath.

"I don't know why you're freaking out about them kissing, but maybe they finally realized what we all saw."

"Y-yeah… I guess so, Miss Camilla."

"Let's just keep taking deep breaths, okay? I know this is monumental for you to witness and I kind of knew this would eventually happen… but it's nothing to get riled up over."

I continue to hold his wrists, and he closes his eyes and takes a few deep breaths. I finally release my hold on him and pat his shoulders.

"There you go!"

"Thanks, Miss Camilla. I just get so excited when I see people who secretly like each other finally make a move."

"Yeah, you freaked out when I told you about Bennett and I kissing," I remind him.

He laughs, "Yeah, well, that was really surprising. He's a big grump, and I *never* thought I'd hear that in my whole life. Not even on my deathbed."

I laugh and shake my head. I rub his shoulders again before there's a voice clearing near us. We both snap our heads to the noise and Bennett stands there with his arms crossed over his chest.

"Bennett! What's up?" Parker chirps from his place.

Bennett's eyes peer at us before I see them lower at where my hands are on Parker's shoulders. I immediately drop my arms from Parker and I can feel the tension grow in the air. Thick like molasses.

"What are you doing here?" I ask.

"Birdy and Steve are back and ready to serve dessert," His tone is clipped and I can see his jaw clench from here.

"Yum! I wondered when they'd come back," Parker jokes as he steps back from our bubble and I breathe a sigh of relief as he heads towards Bennett.

"Parker, behave yourself," I remind him, hoping he doesn't make a huge commotion back at the table about the kiss he witnessed.

"Oh, of course. My lips are sealed," He laughs before passing Bennett and patting his shoulder. Bennett's whole body tenses. I watch as his eyes follow Parker, who walks back towards the area with the table. I slowly walk towards Bennett, and he turns his head. His lips are pressed into a tight line and his eyes are darker, almost a cloudy blue.

"What?" I ask, reaching to touch his crossed arms.

He takes a step back and bewilderment consumes me. I cock my head to the side, waiting for him to answer.

"You know he likes you, right?" He blurts out.

My eyes search his face as I take in his question. "Parker?" I laugh.

He nods his head and his jaw clenches again.

"You can't be serious, Bennett…"

"He's got like a middle school crush and then he goes and pulls you away to this secluded area…"

I throw my head back and laugh before shaking my head. "Are you jealous, Bennett Moore?" I step closer to him and wrap my arms around his neck and his tense body loosens a fragment.

"Of course not."

"Mhm, sure."

"I'm not."

I look at him and his face breaks as he rolls his eyes and huffs out a heavy breath. "Okay, fine, maybe a little."

"You know he's dating Mabel… and he's a teenager, right?" I remind him with a smile.

He finally lets his arms fall from his chest and they land on my hips, pulling me closer to him. His cologne is still strong enough to fill my head as he leans closer. Our lips are almost touching and I hitch my breath.

"I've just never had this kind of trouble before," He breathes slowly.

I raise a brow. "What do you mean?"

He takes another deep breath. "I've never had this kind of trouble with seeing how enamored other people are over someone I'd like to call *mine*."

I chew on my lip. He leans in, his lips touching my neck and I flinch at the sudden touch. He kisses my neck before moving up to my chin and then my lips.

I melt into it and pull him closer with my hands that slowly wrap around his neck. His hands on my hips fall lower until they cup my ass and he squeezes.

He groans and I pull us apart to breathe.

"Is this you officially asking me out?" I question.

We're both breathing deeply before he nods his head.

Before he leans in for another kiss, I take the moment to finally tell him my answer. The one I knew he was waiting for this whole time.

"I'm yours."

TWENTY

BENNETT

THE REST of the weekend flies by as I spend time with Peyton and Morgan before they leave. It was a bittersweet goodbye, but Peyton promised to visit more often.

I reminded her Morgan is more than welcome to spend the summers with me if she'd like and Peyton got misty eyed from that proposal. We even had a civil dinner with Katherine at her place.

Morgan really missed her aunt and I couldn't force her to *not* see Kat. Even Peyton mentioned it was healthy for her to see the people that meant a lot to her in Alpine—and that included Katherine.

It went better than expected, and it was nice to see Kat smile and laugh with Peyton and Morgan. It was especially nice to see her happy around Morgan and really mean it. I could tell she wanted to talk to Morgan more about things of the past, but I had to remind her it simply wouldn't help right now. Maybe when Morgan is older.

Bunny was busy with the aftermath of the grand opening, and she's had a packed vineyard all weekend. It made me happy to see everyone in town supporting Bunny in her new business while still maintaining the atmosphere of the Stone Vineyard that was once there.

It seems like she's even increasing her staffing, which is always a good sign. Landscapers are also constantly at the vineyard when it's not open to guests. I see them driving to her property in the early mornings while I'm out on the pasture fixing a fence or feeding the horses.

Flashbacks of that evening when we were at the event barn fills my thoughts. When we finally made it official.

It was what just felt *right* at that moment and I honestly never thought that'd happen. Something about her makes me feel differently about things that I used to feel bitter about.

I'm about to head to the vineyard to hopefully sneak Bunny out of her work.

Once I got back to Alpine after dropping Peyton and Morgan off last night, it was too late to swing by Bunny's and I didn't want to keep her up. She's been working so hard and I'm so proud of her.

I hop in and buckle my seat belt before turning my truck around and heading out of my property. It's nice and sunny and I wanted to grab her before it became sweltering outside. I even brought a small bottle of sunscreen to put not just on *me* but to offer to her as well, in case she forgot it at her house.

I can't help but smile as I head onto Misty Creek Road and take a turn, heading towards the entrance of the vineyard.

It's barely eleven in the morning and there are a few cars lined up in the grass parking lot and some people getting chairs, coolers, and anything else they might need out of their car. I can see Parker running further up the hill towards the building and waving to a group of people already at the vineyard with their hands full of wine bottles and whatnot. There are some other workers milling about the property with their wide smiles and welcoming hands.

I continue driving up the gravel road until I'm close to the building and see Bunny on her tiptoes outside on the wrap around patio fixing a string light that seemed to fall on its own.

I park my truck before unlatching the seat belt and getting out. I shut the door before heading up the stairs and wave to Parker, who is ushering another family now towards the back of the vineyard where the event barn is. He looks up and gives me a small wave and a big smile.

My feet are heavy as I finally make my way around the patio and see Bunny back on her heels and looking down as she fidgets with the remaining string lights in her hands.

"Need help?" I ask, watching her jump in her place before she turns towards my voice and a big smile spreads across her lips. I can't help but smile back at her.

She's wearing a pretty merlot colored sundress that hits above the knees and has matching red earrings with her hair pinned up by a black clip. There are some strands of her curly hair that frame her face and the freckles on her face are even more prominent than I remember against her sun kissed skin.

"Yeah," she laughs before she watches me step closer to her and wrap my arms around her waist. I don't think before I lean in and kiss her, pulling her closer and catching a squeak out of her.

"Hi," I breathe out finally once our lips separate. She smiles before her brown eyes catch mine.

"Hi," she giggles. Her arms are still holding the string of lights and now we're kind of tangled. I have to maneuver my hands out from behind around her before we're free.

She steps back and looks up at the corner of the building's porch that has the rest of the lights hanging. "I tried to put them back up on the nail that's sticking out, but I can't reach it."

It's the cutest thing as she purses her lips and then chews them in frustration. I reach my hand out for the lights and she finds my eyes before smiling and handing the bundle to me.

They're basic string lights with black wire and then a normal looking light bulb. I've got a few sets of these around the barn, so it's not rocket science to me. I take a step in front of her where the nail is up ahead. I see it and get on my tip toes before lifting the string light's wire and placing it over the jutted nail that allows it to hang freely.

"Ah! Thank you!" She squeals as I make sure it's a tight fit before I get back on my heels and step back. She rubs her hand on my right shoulder. I look her way and see her eyes shining at the work done above us. "It's perfect."

"Yeah," I whisper, taking a deep breath.

She finally turns her gaze back to me and smiles more. "What are you doing here, by the way? I thought you were gonna have a day with Steve?"

I shake my head. "He's got plans, apparently. I wanted to see if I could whisk you away for a little?"

She widens her eyes before looking around us at the vineyard. "I-uh, I'm not sure how packed we'll get. The day's just started."

I try to give her my best puppy dog eyes, and she laughs as she shakes her head. "I swear it'll be for like two hours max... Please?"

My arms are wrapping around her waist again, rubbing my thumbs around her hips, and she takes a deep breath before laughing. "Okay, fine!"

I bite my lip and smile before stepping away and grabbing her hand, pulling her along until we're running down the stairs. Parker is heading back our way and looks confused as he watches his boss run away from the building.

"She's taking her lunch break early!" I yell behind me as Bunny giggles next to me.

"I promise, I'll be back!" She screams at Parker as I pull her closer to the truck.

Parker laughs before waving us off. "We got this, Miss Camilla!"

We make it to the passenger side and I open the door for her, letting her get comfortable before shutting the door. I walk around the front of the truck before hopping into the driver's seat and starting the engine.

She clicks her seat belt on before clapping her hands on her thighs. I watch for a second, gulping before I clear my throat and click my seat belt in. I lean back and reach for the floorboards of the back seats and find the bottle of sunscreen, grab it, and place it on her lap.

"Put this on. You'll be needing it," I tell her.

She nods before twisting the top open and squeezing some lotion onto her fingers and dabbing it on her face and neck. I turn the truck around and head out of the vineyard. We're on the main road when she makes a noise and I glance at her.

"Can I take a guess? Of where we might be going?"

I shake my head. "You can, but I don't think you'll get it."

She hums as she continues to place sunscreen on her face. "A car show? A festival? The woods to murder me?"

I bark out a laugh. "Definitely the last one."

"At least I'll be protected from the sun before I die," she jokes, closing the cap of the sunscreen bottle and placing it back behind her seat.

"You can have one more guess," I tell her.

There's a moment of silence as she contemplates her next guess and I take this time to adjust my hands on the wheel where my left is on the top in control and my right hand moves to comfortably lay on her left thigh. Her dress is pulled up from her sitting down, so my fingers brush against her bare thigh.

I peek over to her side and she's looking out the window. The sun's getting really bright, casting into the window and making a bright aura around her. My breath hitches for a moment as I watch the sight before me.

Like an angel in the sunlight, meant just for me.

She finally turns around and I bring my eyes back to the road so we don't crash. It wouldn't be fun making our date change into one where people are pulling us out of a ditch.

"A diner you want me to try?"

I shake my head. "No, but that's close. I was planning to take you to the town's cafe for some coffee one day. They've got killer scones… don't tell Birdy I just said that."

"I've passed it many times! Haven't been there yet. I'd love to go." She giggles before adding, "Your secret's safe with me."

We're entering town now, and I squeeze her thigh momentarily as I take a turn. There's a small squeak that escapes her lips and I glance quickly at her, seeing her bite her lip. I want to stop the car and lean over and kiss her and more, but I attempt to guide my gaze back to the road.

We pass by the shops, restaurants, and town hall before we enter the other side of downtown Alpine. There are fewer restaurants and shops here, mainly businesses that people don't need all the time. A laundromat, a small cinema, another cafe that isn't as great as the main one near the more touristy side of town, and then a huge parking lot space for events.

Bunny wasn't wrong about an event we'd go to. We usually have flea markets and farmers markets in the summer. Since it's getting closer to summer, we're opening up the farmers market a weekend early. I usually go in the early morning to miss the crowds, but I wanted this year to be different.

Going with Bunny seemed to be the difference I needed.

I scan the lot where there's the farmers market and parking spots. I find an empty one and pull my truck into the spot. Shutting the engine off, I take my hand off her thigh. I turn to her and she has doe eyes and pinkness on her cheeks.

"What?" I ask, hoping it's okay we're still in town. I didn't want to take her *too* far. I still wanted her to go back to work and not leave Parker all alone. But I had to keep reminding myself that he's not alone. He'll be fine.

She shakes her head before pulling away her seat belt and

leaning over, wrapping her arm around my neck, and pulling me close towards her. I let go of the wheel with my left hand and find her jaw. I brush my thumb over her lips and she shudders before kissing me.

I melt into the kiss like never before and I close my eyes, shifting my body to move my right hand over hers and pull her closer by her neck. She breathes through her nose deeply and I do too as we continue to kiss. It takes everything in me to not pull her off her seat and onto my lap. But I remember that we're in a public parking spot with another truck pulling in next to us.

I part our lips and we continue to pant, her eyes finding mine. She smiles and I kiss her nose before kissing her forehead.

"If we don't go now, we might never leave," I warn her.

She bites her lips before pulling herself away from me. She reaches for the door handle. "Next time," she murmurs before pushing her door open and hopping out. I adjust my jeans quickly to hide my growing boner.

I groan before getting out of the truck and lacing my fingers in hers. We head towards the noise of the lot where the farmers market is.

I see the truck I came for and pull her along, causing a giggle to leave her lips as she follows behind. There are people walking around and I wave to a few I've seen here and there. We're a small town, so it's mainly locals here. The food trucks are an array of restaurants from all over Tennessee.

Rudy's Nashville Hot Chicken truck is one of my favorites. He makes the best hot chicken in Tennessee, and I scan my eyes for his truck.

"Oh! Peaches!" Bunny exclaims beside me as we continue to walk past many vendors. I turn to see where she's pointing at and it's a peach cobbler truck. It's from a nearby town that I don't really venture out to, but I heard this truck is fantastic. I get my own peaches from my land and then give them to Birdy to make into a cobbler or anything else that I might want with peaches in it.

"Do you want some?" I laugh, feeling her drag me towards the truck. I follow blindly as she makes her way towards the truck and scans the small menu on the chalkboard standing outside on the ground.

She looks up at the person in the truck waiting for her order.

"I'll take the peaches and cream cobbler, please," she asks before she reaches for her purse, but her hands run along her dress. She turns to me with wide eyes.

I forgot to let her get her purse. It's still at the vineyard. I laugh and reach into my back pocket, pulling out my weathered wallet to get my card. I lean over and hand it to the guy who's punching in her order and yelling at the guy in the back who's making the cobbler. He swipes my card and then hands it back to me with the receipt and a pen. I scribble a nice tip before stuffing the card back in the front of my jeans and then my wallet in the back pocket. I know I'll be using it for the other trucks I had in mind and didn't want to keep digging it out.

"Thank you, Bennett, really," Bunny says, coming up to me with a look of concern on her face. I pull her hands close to me and I brush her jawline before I rub my thumb over her bottom lip.

"Don't be. I didn't really think when I pulled you away from your job. Kinda happens whenever I'm with you. I tend to not think logically."

She laughs as she closes her eyes, and a blush creeps up her cheeks and nose. I kiss her nose before her order gets called, and she turns around to the small cup of the cobbler with two spoons stuck in it. She spins back towards me with a big smile on her face.

"Yay! It smells so good," she says before getting closer to me and pulling out her spoon with a big glob of the cobbler on it. I take my spoon and nod, pulling it out and tapping her spoon in a 'cheers' before we take our bite. We're silent for a moment and I widen my eyes at the soft, but crunchy texture and how warm and sweet it is.

Fuck, I can't tell Birdy how good this is. I gulp down the cobbler, and Bunny swings her hips as she finishes her bite and smiles. "That was so good. I might eat this whole thing."

I push the cup towards her and hope to the gods that Birdy isn't at the market to see me gush over this cup of goodness.

"Please, take it. Too sweet for me," I lie.

She nods before gladly taking the cup and eating another bite. I lick my lips clean before I toss my spoon into a nearby trash can. I let my eyes scan the parking lot again before I eye the truck I wanted.

Amelia's Flowers. It's a Nashville staple flower truck, and they so happened to announce that they'd be in Alpine Ridge this summer. They've been to Leiper's Fork, Ashland City, Franklin, and of course Nashville. But they've never ventured out this far to Alpine, and I wanted nothing but the best for my girl.

I turn towards Bunny, who is finishing the last bite of the cup before I take the spoon and cup and toss it. She thanks me before I take her hand and pull her towards the truck. The flowers are arranged beautifully in their own bucket on the truck and there's a woman helping a customer that's picking out the flowers they want in their bouquet. It's a pretty cool truck. For a set amount you get to pick as many flowers as you'd like as long as it didn't overflow the bouquet when they wrapped it.

The colors are super pretty too, and I see Bunny studying all the various colors and types of flowers that are in front of us. There are some cards out in front of the flowers on little silver stands to let people passing by know the names of each. Once the woman is done with the customer and rings them up, she turns towards us and smiles brightly.

"Welcome to Amelia's! We're so excited to be here in Alpine Ridge."

"Are you not from here?" Bunny asks, stepping closer. She adjusts the clip in her hair and a few more strands fall in front of her face.

"Nope! We originated in Nashville and got pretty big! Ever been there?"

Bunny shakes her head as she gestures her head towards me. "Not yet. I just moved here!"

I smile before lifting my hand for a small wave at the lady. She gives me a big smile before nodding and waving her hand towards the many flower options. "Well, then! You can just pick as many flowers as you'd like for the bouquet. Or if you'd like me to make one for you, I can totally do that."

Bunny turns towards me and gives me a smile. "How about you pick the flowers?"

"Me?" I ask, laughing.

"How sweet!" The lady exclaims before waiting for my response.

"I-uh, I don't know much about flowers or what goes with what."

Bunny laughs and so does the lady before she waves at the flowers again. "How about you pick flowers that remind you of your girlfriend?"

We both stare at each other after the lady says that word. *Girlfriend.* We've yet to say it out loud since that night, even though we made it official. Feels odd hearing it from a complete stranger. But I can't help but crack a smile before Bunny does too, stepping closer to me and wrapping one arm around mine. Her head leans towards my shoulder, and I lace my fingers with hers.

"Okay," I mumble out before I point at a few flowers and the lady plucks them out of the buckets and lays them on a brown paper before letting me know to stop.

I picked all the ones that I imagined myself finding on the

side of the road and picking them up for Bunny. Pretty like her and wild like her heart.

The lady wraps the bouquet tightly before tying it at the bottom half, handing it over. Bunny grabs it softly with her free hand and I pull out my card and hand it to the lady.

"Thank you for shopping at Amelia's!"

We smile and thank her before we step away and shift our positions so we're still holding hands, but she's able to hold the bouquet. She leans her nose into the pile of flowers and inhales.

"Wow, these smell amazing," She looks up at me with a sparkle in her eyes and I feel my heart quicken its pace.

"Let me." I clear my throat and lean over to smell the flowers. They smell like... flowers and I can't help but laugh. "Yeah, they smell great. I just picked out the ones that reminded me of you, like the worker asked. Kind of like the wildflowers I picked at your property or what I'd pick on the side of the road."

"Wildflowers?" She repeats. I nod.

"Because they're pretty like you and wild like your heart. The wildest hearts are the prettiest, Bunny."

That was a saying my mom always told me growing up. She wanted me to learn all the things about tending to our land that didn't involve animals since my dad was the one to teach me that stuff. That meant getting down and dirty with the wildflowers around the property. I wanted to pluck them all, but she stopped me and told me they reminded her of me and my wild spirit. So we kept them all and some are still thriving even today.

The wildest hearts are the prettiest, Bennett. Never forget that.

And I never did.

Bunny smiles before she leans her head on my arm, and we continue to walk around the farmers market. It's getting busier by the second and there are other vendors I'd like for her to see before I bring her back to work.

We find Rudy's Hot Nashville Chicken truck and he waves

and hollers out of his truck as if it's an emergency. His black hair is falling over his face and his fair skin is getting red and burnt from the sun already, from where the light is beaming into the truck. "Is that Bennett?! Get over here!"

Bunny giggles beside me as I pull her along and Rudy widens his eyes at me. Jesse, his business partner, pops his head out of the truck and gives us the biggest smile. His eyes bug out of their sockets as he takes me in. He's the chief cook out of the two and even helps his family with their taco truck.

"Who is this beauty?!" Jesse shouts as Rudy attempts to push him out of the window they're both squeezed into.

"My girlfriend, B-Camilla," I say, biting my lip while almost saying her nickname.

Bunny smiles and removes her hands from mine and waves at them. "Nice to meet you."

"Wow, Ben. You finally found a girlfriend."

I roll my eyes at him and Bunny just laughs before Jesse eyes her and points at her. "Where you from? There aren't many people with that kind of name around this town or nearby."

"Jesse! That is so rude!" Rudy yells, slapping his friend on the arm. Jesse yelps and eyes Rudy before shrugging.

"It's okay!" Bunny laughs. "From Chicago. If you're asking where my parents are from... Mexico."

"*Ay,* I knew I liked you!" Jesse yells with a smile.

"You just met her," Rudy shakes his head.

I smile at the odd encounter before Rudy ushers Jesse back to prep more food and we order something small. We choose a spicy level that isn't too much, and Bunny requests extra pickles on the side. I could tell she was looking for fried pickles on the menu, but I had to let her know that Jesse and Rudy make their own yummy pickle brine that is ten times better than Nicky's.

Once Rudy gets the food for us and a water bottle, we find a vacant plastic table with two chairs in the middle of the farmers market. It's an area with other chairs nearby and some people flock to those vacant tables as we dig in.

"How'd you meet them?" She asks, biting into a chicken tender and then shoving a pickle in her mouth.

"They're from the next town over in Mason Pointe, but they run their food truck in Alpine every time we have the free spot. They've been here every summer for the past... ten years?"

"Wow! And this food is *amazing*," She takes another bite and I join her, dipping my tender in the side of ranch.

"Rudy is good people, so is Jesse. But Jesse says things without thinking. If you ever were alone with him, he'd go off into so many tangents and then forget what you guys were originally talking about. He comes from a big family too."

"Sounds like fun—all of it," Bunny laughs.

I've been to Rudy's location in Mason Pointe and the Nashville location years ago with Katherine before we got divorced. It's a great spot with live music and such, even at the location next to us. I haven't been since the divorce, but I always got the food when they were here at our farmers markets.

"We can always go to Nashville, if you'd like," I blurt out finally as I finish one of the tenders.

She looks up from underneath her lashes as she's mid bite and smiles before nodding. She finishes the bite in her mouth and then opens the water bottle on the table and takes a long sip.

"I've never been, so I'd love that. I heard it's a lot of country music?"

I shake my head and laugh. "That's just downtown. There's all kinds of music there. There's even a karaoke pub I love going to whenever I go with Steve and Oliver."

"Only if we can go to the flower shop and Rudy's chicken place," she counters.

I nod my head. "Of course. What's a Nashville trip without visiting those places?"

We smile before we finish our plate of chicken and pickles,

and then we head back to the truck to take her back to work. We hold hands all the way there and it makes my heart patter against my chest like a drum.

We're back in the positions where my hand is on her thigh and it feels comfortable. Super comfortable, and that's something I never thought I'd feel again with someone.

But with her, it seems like anything is possible.

TWENTY-ONE

CAMILLA

IT'S BEEN a few weeks since our farmer's market date and we're into the swing of things at the vineyard. We're into the last week of June, stumbling into the weekend for the Fourth, and things have been hectic.

It's been nice to get into a steady routine of opening the vineyard, having a few more hands working with me, and then having some days off. It's been a whirlwind that these past few weeks doesn't even feel like that long.

The time has gone by so fast, I'm surprised it's almost the Fourth of July. Parker has helped me with anything that I might need for the vineyard, and I am grateful for his decision to keep working here while registering for courses for the fall. I'll miss him once he starts college, but it's comforting to know that he'll still be in town.

This morning has been nothing but crazy attempting to fulfill online orders for people from out of town that heard the vineyard is open again. My office is full of paper receipts and boxes with the wines almost ready to be shipped to the prospective buyers. I had to contact a financial advisor the other day to make sure the finances were steady. The last thing I wanted to do was crash and burn before I even got a summer under my belt with the vineyard.

Now, it's almost lunchtime and I see Parker swinging into the doorway, peeking his head in. I'm putting the last shipping label on a box when I look up towards the noise.

"It's time to eat! What are you doing?"

I shrug and laugh. "Just trying to keep this business alive, Parker. You know."

He shakes his head and heads over to the table where I'm at and takes the box from me, pulling it off the table and placing it with the rest of the 'ready to ship' boxes.

"I know, I know. But eating is just as important. I was actually gonna swing by Nicky's quickly to get some wings and fries if you wanted some? There are some landscapers here to clean up the area around the event barn."

I chew my lip before he adds, "And we're not that busy. I just saw the last car leave for the morning. According to my projections, we shouldn't have more traffic for another hour."

I can't help but smile and roll my eyes. "Okay, fine. You've convinced me! I planned to get an outfit for the Fourth weekend anyway and I can swing by while we wait for the food."

"Oh, at Marla's shop?"

"Yep! That cute storefront caught my eye. I just haven't had time to stop by."

He nods and smiles before waving his hand for me to follow him out of the ransacked office. I grab my purse from the hook I added to the wall right by the door and grab my keys as well, locking the office behind me. Parker has a set of keys for everything on the property, but we'll both be leaving and don't want to risk anything.

I have a few other employees that are at the event barn and keeping an eye out on the vineyard in case other visitors come, so we should be good, anyway.

"I can drive!" Parker exclaims as we walk out of the building and head towards Rose's car. I laugh, shaking my head as he opens the passenger door for me.

As he gets to the driver's side, I see a cute black cardigan on the dashboard and I pick it up gingerly, looking at Parker. "I wonder who this belongs to?" I say in a teasing tone, wiggling my brows.

Parker's cheeks grow a deep red as he takes the cardigan from me and tosses it to the back of the car. "No one's, Miss Camilla!"

"How are you guys?" I laugh, watching him shake his head and turn the car around and start heading out of the property and into town.

He lowers both windows, and I enjoy the wind blowing through, ruffling through my hair that I left down. The wind is hot, but not too much to get annoyed. They weren't joking when they said it would get super hot here with humidity.

A lake day sounds so good right now. Maybe I can convince Bennett to go paddle boarding with me... amongst other things.

"We're really good," Parker answers. "She's excited to go to school at the end of August, so we're trying to enjoy everything while we can. It sucks that we both work a lot."

"I can cut down your hours, Parker!"

He shakes his head as he keeps his gaze in front of him. "No, I need the money for school. I plan to keep working and then save enough for both community college tuition and then eventually transfer to where she's going."

"That's really sweet. I bet you'll be able to visit each other a ton. She'll be back for all the holidays."

He nods his head and smiles. "She's pretty great, Miss Camilla. I will miss her though when she's gone, but it's only temporary."

We're entering town and he takes a right and then a left, finding an open street spot to park on. He shuts off the engine and I can feel the heat of everything hit me again. The more we sit in the car, the more I sweat. Thankfully, I wore a tank top and flowy shorts, or else I'd be melting even more.

"Well, I'm proud of you two for working so hard on your relationship and your future. I'm sure you can apply for some scholarships if you plan to transfer to where she's going."

He nods. "I already started looking into them. I know my aunt wanted me to apply and see if I could transfer my first year, but I want to save as much as I can. Hopefully she understands."

His brows scrunch and I lay my hand on his shoulder. "You'll figure it out. Things always end up working out like they're meant to. Don't stress."

He smiles. "Alright, let's get out of this hot car. I'm feeling sweat on my back and I hate that."

I laugh and nod as we both exit the car. He locks it, and we head to Nicky's to put in an order for takeout. Izzy isn't working today, and neither is Mabel, so Parker joins me as we walk to the sweet shop to say hello to Birdy.

It's decorated with some window paintings and signs all ready for the Fourth. As we enter, I'm engulfed in the sweet smell of peanut brittle and everything else she has in store. The bell dings above the door and we hear a squeal.

Birdy runs around the counter and pushes past Steve, who is biting into a fresh batch of peanut brittle before wrapping her arms around me. I steady myself, laughing, before I wrap my arms around her.

"It's been too long! I swear if Bennett is keeping you away from us and your job, I will have a firm word with him."

"No, it's just work. He's been great," I tell her truthfully. We've been able to go on more dates recently and even tried out that cafe he told me about. We've yet to travel outside of Alpine Ridge, but I'm hoping we can do that soon.

"Well, then!" Birdy exclaims as she pulls away from me and gives Parker a side hug. Steve is still near the counter finishing his brittle as he gives us a wave. Birdy rolls her eyes playfully at him and I give her a side eye.

It's no secret that they've been hanging out more than ever since Parker told me about the kiss, but I've yet to hear it from Birdy herself.

To be fair, I've been super busy myself. I haven't found the time to tell her that Bennett and I are officially together. I really wanted it to be in person and not something over the phone or in a text message.

She widens her eyes slowly, raising her brows before smiling. "What?"

I pull her by her elbow to the side while Parker watches us and then walks over to Steve to talk to him. I see Steve give us a confused look before smiling at Parker and immediately getting immersed in whatever Parker is saying. Birdy wipes her hands on the apron that's tied around her waist. Her green eyes are bright and asking a million questions.

But I have some questions of my own. I clear my throat and watch the redness creep into her cheeks. "You've been spending tons of time with Steve lately..."

She shrugs before smiling again. "Yeah, he's helping me plan the Fourth. I'm going to have a cookout! I wanted to tell you it's a huge thing here."

"What exactly goes on during the Fourth here in Alpine Ridge?" I ask slowly, letting her think she's changing the topic. Sure I'm interested in the Fourth weekend activities... But I'm more interested in Birdy and Steve gossip.

God, I sound like a local already. Pulling at any strings I can to get to the gossip.

She peers at the ceiling before looking back at me. "A rodeo in Mason Pointe, so try to find something *really* cute. And then a fair slash carnival. And then the cookout at my place to end the weekend."

"Well, good thing I was going to stop by the boutique around the corner," I tell her.

She hums and bites her lip and I laugh, knowing she is leaving out some other details about what she wanted to talk to me about.

"And?" I ask, tapping my foot before crossing my arms over my chest.

She blinks a few times before turning her head back to where Parker and Steve are. They're eating more of the brittle and clueless to our spying eyes.

"And what?" She asks softly.

"Oh, come on!" I playfully slap her arm before returning to my arms crossed position. More redness creeps into her face. "Parker saw you guys at the vineyard a couple weeks ago... I didn't wanna mention it until we saw each other again in person."

"Oh? And who's fault is that?" Birdy laughs and I raise a brow before she zips her mouth and a blush creeps up to her ears.

"Why didn't you tell me?!" I ask her, attempting to get closer to her and lowering my voice a smidge.

Her green eyes are wild as she glances all around the store before landing back on my eyes. "I-I don't know. It felt too good to be true. I kind of thought if we were stuck in that small bubble that we'd be there forever and things wouldn't go wrong."

I widen my eyes and reach my arms out to hold her shoulders. "Why would you *ever* think that?"

She shrugs. "Like I said, Steve and I kind of became friends because of Bennett drifting off and leaving us to fend for ourselves. I think because we became such good friends, I didn't want my emotions to ruin anything. Or his emotions..."

I think back to our conversation weeks ago about her and Steve and how they became really close because of Bennett's distance. It's a fragile thing relying on one another and then finding out you have feelings for them. You never know if admitting your feelings will ruin what you worked so hard to build.

"The way he looks at you and acts around you is not how a friend would," I reassure her. She nods her head before nibbling on her bottom lip.

She takes a deep breath before making eye contact again. "Okay, fine. You already saw through me. Through us. And if Parker didn't find us there, then someone else would've. So, yes. We're slowly becoming something. We haven't made it official yet."

I smile and nod, rubbing her shoulders before bringing my arms back to my sides. She takes a deep breath and exhales a long one as if she just admitted an enormous secret. Which, technically, this is a big secret for such a small town.

"And you? I haven't heard about you and Bennett and all that," she wiggles her eyebrows.

Now I'm the one blushing and looking anywhere but at her. She clears her throat before I lean my head back and sigh.

"Okay, you got me. I meant to tell you earlier, but we've been so busy. It honestly doesn't feel like weeks have passed since the vineyard opening."

"Tell me about it!"

I take a deep breath and continue, "It actually happened that same night at the event barn."

"What did?" She widens her eyes.

I nibble on my bottom lip before I finally spill the beans. "He asked me to be his girlfriend."

Birdy is silent for a moment before she squeals and jumps on her feet, reaching over to grab my arms. Her momentum swings me this way and that, and I can't help but giggle.

"Hey! What's going on?" Parker asks, as he and Steve head over to us.

"Tell them!" Birdy urges me as she pulls Steve over by the elbow. He's still munching on peanut brittle and gives me a goofy smile.

"Tell us what, Miss Camilla?" Parker asks softly.

I wait patiently as I rack my brain on whether I should tell them. But I don't know why I *wouldn't*. Parker would find out eventually with how often Bennett comes to the vineyard.

"Bennett and I are officially dating," I blurt out.

Steve's smile spreads even more on his face and Parker's eyes bug out of his face before he smiles and laughs. "Took him long enough!"

"I knew he'd eventually grow a pair," Steve chimes in.

"This is monumental and I think we need to celebrate!" Birdy squeals, clapping her hands.

"No! Don't make it a big thing, please! It's been weeks, and it's nice for us to just tell people and then continue with our lives." I confess.

"Are you sure?" Birdy asks with a raised brow.

"We need a party," Parker chimes in with a nod. I shake my head again and give him a look that makes him seal his lips shut.

"I'll take him shooting or something," Steve says with a shrug.

"How is that celebrating?" I ask with a laugh.

Birdy rolls her eyes and pats Steve's chest. "They like to hunt and shoot whenever they have big things to talk about. They almost got a raccoon the last time they did that. Didn't you honey?"

Parker and I lock eyes at the word Birdy calls Steve, and I know we'll be talking about it once we're back at the vineyard. I look at Birdy, who is looking at Steve with adoration on her face. Steve is like a puppy and just nods, lost in her trance.

"Okay, I'm going before I puke," Parker whines as he steps away and heads for the door.

"Wait! I'm coming with!" I yell, attempting to squeeze past

Birdy and Steve, but she catches my elbow. I get yanked back, and she gives me a side hug.

She leans into my ear before whispering, "I always knew you were something special when you first came into this shop. I'm glad that 'special' was meant for Bennett."

Tears brim my eyes. She leans back to lay her head on Steve's chest. I give one last smile before I follow Parker out of the shop. My feet are fast as I try to catch up with him as he nears the end of the block where Samson Realty is.

There's a shop right next to it and I remember walking near it the first time I came to Alpine RIdge. Marla must've been the woman I saw with a long dress and the most beautiful red hair.

"Come on!" Parker rushes as he waits near the door of the shop. There's a mannequin displayed in the windows showcasing the summer clothes that are in stock. Some jeans on the mannequin catch my eye.

"I'm coming! Then we can get our food, okay?" I tell him before we walk into the shop. Once we're inside, we see Marla with a bright smile on her face.

"Welcome! Parker, are you here for your aunt?" She walks over and I watch her green eyes find mine. She's wearing a pretty white dress with lace detailing that falls past her knees. Her long, red hair flows in curls and her curtain bangs are perfectly framing her face.

"No, my boss, Miss Camilla, needed some things," Parker answers before pointing towards me.

I give her a small wave. She widens her eyes and ushers me further into the store. "Come in! You moved here, right? Word travels fast around here."

I nod before I look around the shop and see tons of designs that I would love to try on. My initial plan was to find a new wardrobe, but now I want to find an outfit for the rodeo. I don't even know what they wear there. I've never gone to one.

"I heard there's a rodeo that opens up for the Fourth?" I ask her, and Parker gasps and nods his head.

"Yes! It's the best time. I forgot to tell you! We have to close the vineyard; everyone goes to the rodeo!"

I nod my head, "Noted, thanks Parker!" I turn my attention back to the redhead and she scrunches her nose and smiles before gesturing towards the rack that has clothes that were on the mannequin up front by the window. The pair of jeans I was eyeing have various sizes on the rack.

I immediately walk near it and pull out a pair in my size and lift it to study it.

"It's perfect," Marla says as she shifts through the rack and pulls out a cute white cropped tank top. The straps are thin like spaghetti straps and the fabric is ribbed.

The jeans in my hands are a light wash but they're tight at the top to accentuate curves and then fan out into bell bottoms at the bottom. There are red sequins in the shape of a star on the back pockets.

"Do you want to try them together?" Marla asks as she leans over a rack and studies me.

Parker is off looking at accessories as I turn my gaze back to Marla. I shake my head and clutch both items in my hands. "I'll take them."

She smiles and nods her head. "Great choice. These will look amazing on you. I'll be there, so I'll keep my eye out to say hi."

"I'm sure I'll be back here too, to find more dresses. Chicago and Tennessee have such different temperatures I don't really have a summer closet."

Marla laughs as we walk towards the register, and she scans the items. I see some cute, thick gold hoops the size of a quarter and put them on the counter as well to be rung up.

"Well, you're just in luck. I'm getting a new shipment on Monday with tons of new dresses for summer!" She exclaims as she puts the ringed up items into a bag.

I shift through my purse and pull out my wallet, paying for the items. Once my transaction is done, I turn to see Parker walking up with a cute, dainty necklace in his hands.

"What'd you find?" I ask him, eyeing the jewelry.

He brings it closer to me and I see that it's a cute black flower pendant necklace.

"It's a dahlia. Mabel said it's one of her favorite flowers. I didn't know there were necklaces of it."

Marla squeals and nods. "They just got in! I was wondering who would buy the first one. I haven't sold one yet."

"You think she'll like it?" Parker asks us. We both nod and I decide to hand Marla my card again.

"I'll buy it for you!"

"No, you can't!" Parker shakes his head, but Marla thankfully takes my card and swipes it. She hands me the card back and reaches for the necklace in his hand and he gives it up. She carefully wraps it in thin paper before putting it in a bag and handing him it.

"It's all done and now we can go back to the vineyard and you can think of all the ways you'll present it to her." I say, already picturing Parker practicing a thousand lines in the mirror.

"Thanks, Miss Camilla. Really."

"I like you already and we just met," Marla smiles.

"Thanks. I keep thinking this town is amazing and then even better things happen." I confess.

"That's Alpine for you," Marla states.

"Alright, let's get our food and then head back to work," Parker speaks up. I nod and we both wave to Marla before we walk out of the boutique.

As we head back to Nicky's, Parker walks closer to me and nudges me with his elbow. I turn to look at him and he has a creeping blush on his cheeks.

"What?" I laugh.

"Thanks for the necklace. I really hope she likes it."

"Oh, she will!" I assure him. "I know we've only known each other for a little, but I want you to know that you deserve the happiness we're all finding here."

He nods and chuckles under his breath. He reaches up to scratch his head before he holds onto the bag tightly to his chest.

"Thanks, Miss Camilla. I can't wait to show my aunt later."

"She'll love it. I do hope I can meet her eventually, you know."

He laughs and nods. "I'll have her come by the vineyard later. She's been wanting to meet you too and thank you for giving me a job at the beginning of my summer break."

"Well, tell her she's welcome to come to the vineyard and even my house anytime," I let him know. His smile grows wider.

We finally make it to Nicky's and he runs inside to grab our food. I look around the block and see the bustle of people walking towards shops or to get lunch. I look to the distance and see the sun shining brightly over Alpine Ridge.

I take a deep breath and let my eyes close for a second as I take a mental picture of what I'm witnessing.

The town that is really starting to feel like home.

TWENTY-TWO

BENNETT

BUNNY SENDS me a photo attachment in the evening. I hold my finger up to Steve as he's mid bite into a burger. I get up from my spot and walk a little further from his prying eyes.

We're in my backyard where I got a small wooden table and a few camp chairs to place around it. I started building a makeshift fire pit next to it and even hung up some string lights around the area to make it look more lively. Steve was definitely impressed and even more shocked that I asked him to come over so we could grill some burgers for dinner. I didn't plan to see Bunny today, but we've been texting back and forth.

She asked me about the Fourth weekend and if I'd be joining her and Birdy in any of the events. I told her about the rodeo, but I knew nothing regarding the carnival. I wanted to first talk to Steve and get some info out of him. The info that Parker told Bunny and I when we were in the event barn weeks ago. About him and Birdy kissing. We haven't gotten to talking yet. We grilled the burgers and then popped open some beers before I got the text from Bunny.

At first I have to squint my eyes with the sun still shining brightly over us with the summer sun blazing, even though it's almost seven. I click on the attachment and I widen my eyes at the sight.

She's wearing tight jeans that flare out at the bottom and she's posing with her leg lifted and twisted enough so I can see how the jeans mold perfectly around her ass. There's bright red stars on the back pockets. The heat in my body rises and I clear my throat before I respond.

> Where on God's Earth did you get those pants?

I cringe at how bad the text is, but my thumb sends it, anyway.

"What's up?" Steve calls from behind me. I turn and see him raise a brow in curiosity before taking another bite from his burger.

"Bunny sent a picture."

His eyes widen. "Like a *picture* picture?"

I shake my head and laugh. "No, Steve. Not *that* kind of photo. But it's still amazing. I just sent a really poor response though. I'm not cut out for this dating stuff."

He chuckles and picks up his beer, taking a sip. "You only had Katherine your whole life. Of course, you don't know how to date. We're in a different decade, hell a different century, from when you guys started dating in high school. It's different now."

I give him a look and he lifts his other hand into a surrendering motion before I roll my eyes and get back to my chair. My phone pings and I see a text from Bunny.

BUNNY 🩶
Marla's. You like? 😊

I grunt before shaking my head and typing out a response. Steve whistles, and I look up at him.

"What?"

"What are you about to text her? Better not be one of your cheesy lines."

"I am not!" I argue, leaning over and punching his shoulder. He fakes leaning back from the hit.

"Well, what are you gonna say?"

I raise a brow. "You really want to know what I'm about to text her after getting a picture from her?"

"You're right. I don't need to know. If it was anyone else but Camilla, I'd help."

"Exactly," I respond.

I look back at my phone and there's another text I didn't notice she sent.

> If you come over tonight, you can see it in person.

My eyes bug out, and I take a deep breath. I let my thumbs do the typing and hit send.

> You're dangerous, Bunny.

She 'heart reacts' the message and I click my phone off before flipping it over on the table. I pick up my burger and take a bite out of it as Steve watches me.

"What now?" I ask, my annoyance gradually growing.

He shrugs and laughs. "Nothing, Ben. Nothing at all."

We stay like this for a while, eating our food and drinking our beers. When we're done, I finally decide to ask about the kiss.

He's throwing some sticks and chopped up wood into the fire pit and starting it again after it died out as I carry a few sticks and hand it to him.

"So, Parker saw something at the vineyard opening," I start.

He raises a brow before throwing the sticks into the pile and leaning down to blow into the bottom of the pit to make the fire grow.

"Yeah? What did he see?"

"You and Birdy kissing," I blurt out.

Steve stands up, placing his hands on his hips before he looks up at the sky and then back at me. "Shit."

I begin to laugh and lean over to pat my hand on his shoulder. "What? It's not like we all weren't expecting it. It's about damn time."

"Yeah? You're not mad?"

I furrow my brows and shake my head. "Why would I be mad?"

He shrugs. "I don't want you to think I'll start spending so much time with her and not as much with you anymore."

"You're really worried about that? We're adults Steve. We can have relationships and then have time for our friendships."

"I know, Ben… I just didn't want to disappoint you, too."

"Why on Earth would you disappoint me by dating Birdy? You guys are head over heels for each other."

He shrugs again and stares down at the flames licking the wood in the fire pit. I can see the reflection of the flames dance in the pupil of his eyes. "I think putting a label on it freaks me out. We're so good at being friends, I don't want to ruin it."

I shake my head. "Trust me when I say that you and Birdy have been acting like a couple for months now, even years, to be honest. I don't think you guys have to change anything for it to *feel* official."

"I guess you're right, Ben. I just get so lost in my head sometimes." He shakes his head and continues to look down at the fire. I squeeze his shoulder and he laughs, giving me a smile.

"So, you gonna go over to Camilla's tonight?"

I shrug my shoulders. "I think so. She's amazing."

"I can see it, man. You haven't really been this open and *happy* in a while. It's nice to see after everything."

He waits for a moment to gauge my reaction and I give him a smile. I don't want to think about the past, but he's right. It's been a monumental shift lately, ever since Bunny moved to Alpine. It's like my entire world got turned upside down.

"She makes me really happy. As cheesy as it sounds, she's the sun to most of my mornings. Just thinking about her when I wake up makes me have a better day."

Steve laughs before bringing his own hand to my shoulder and pats it. "Look at you, Ben. Never thought you'd be like this. And for an outsider?"

I roll my eyes. "I know, so shocking. I guess I should give them more credit and more of a chance."

"Well, now you know what happens. By the way, did you ever talk to Oliver with Camilla?"

I shake my head. I completely forgot about the proposal Oliver had for us about the land that's for sale in between Camilla and I. I didn't really want to deal with it and planned to tell her she could have it to add to her vineyard if she wanted.

"Not yet, I plan to."

"Better hurry. I think Oliver has a meeting with the investor again after the holiday."

I nod. "I'll talk to her about it soon. I've just been enjoying this time with her."

Steve nods in agreement. "Me too."

We stare at the fire before we get our beers from the table and finish them. Steve helps me clean the grill and the table. He lets me know he can stay on the property and kill the fire while I go over to Bunny's. I thank him and leave him with the rest of the beers before I head inside to wash up and get my car keys.

Once I'm in the truck, I make my way to Bunny's place. Her property is quiet and dark, except for some string lights on her porch and the porch light near the door.

I park quickly and get out, almost running towards her porch and up the steps. I'm a little too eager to be honest as I press the doorbell and wait for her to come to the door. It's not even ten seconds before she pulls the door open and I feel a hand reach out and clasp my shirt, pulling me inside.

"Woah, hello to you too," I laugh.

She giggles as she shuts the door and gets close to me, wrapping her arms around my neck. She smells like honey and faint blueberries, a scent I've come to love. I lean my forehead to hers and take in a deep breath, inhaling her sweet scent.

"Hi," she giggles again before locking her lips with mine. I wrap my hands around her waist and pull her closer. The fabric of her dress is soft and I moan into the kiss as I feel her pull me closer to her.

"What are you doing to me?" I whisper once our lips separate. Her brown eyes lock with mine before she smiles.

"I don't know, but you're doing it to me, too."

"Am I really?" I ask, leaning my head back to get a good look at her. She chews on her bottom lip and nods.

"Yeah, always. Since the day I met you."

I laugh. "But I was horrible to you."

She cranes her neck and takes a pause before answering. "You were, but you were going through things. You just needed patience."

My eyes search through hers and I know there's more that she wants to say but she holds back. I rub my hands over her hips again and she sucks in her breath. I can't help but smile and know that I'm bringing these kinds of responses out of her.

That someone is capable of feeling *this* feeling with me. The same way I am with them.

There's a word at the tip of my tongue that I want to tell her, but I don't want it to be too soon. I don't want to ruin the good that we have right now.

"What are you thinking about?" She asks softly, lifting a hand to run her fingers through my hair. She then rests her hand under my jaw.

"That I'm the luckiest man in the world," I confess. I can't say the word, it's begging to escape my lips, but I hold back.

"Mm, I can say the same for myself."

"You're the luckiest man in the world?" I joke. She shakes her head and giggles. I lean in and kiss her.

I kiss her with passion and hope the 'Love' word can escape through my lips and into hers. That she can *feel* the word. That I don't have to say it right now, but that she'll still know.

She leans into the kiss and a groan escapes through her mouth before she wraps her hand again around my neck. I clutch her close and walk us towards the back of the house where the main living room is.

I take the time to bend my knees and move my hands from her hips to under her thighs and lift her up to wrap her legs around my waist. She giggles and we continue to kiss as I walk us down the hall and to the couch, plopping her down. Her head hits the pillow softly and we separate from kissing. I lean on the couch, attempting to position my left knee in between her legs and then my right knee right by her hip. She breathes heavily and I watch her brown eyes watch me slowly, licking her lips.

"What?" I ask slowly.

She smiles before answering, "Remember what you said weeks ago?"

I pinch my brows together and shake my head. Sometimes, I have terrible memory and hope I didn't promise her anything and forgot about it. She makes me forget the simplest things when I'm around her. I really hope something important didn't slip past me.

"About how you wanted to… make me scream your name a few times before I got to pleasure you."

I raise a brow and lean in, laying kisses on her neck. Her breathing quickens and a pant escapes her lips. Her legs raise a little and I take this moment to glide my hand along her exposed thigh.

"You're not wearing the pants," I blurt out, finally remembering the text she sent me.

She laughs before grabbing my cheeks and pulling me off her neck.

"I kind of did that on purpose. I needed a reason for you to come running here."

I stare at her. "You missed me?"

She looks up above us before she makes eye contact again. "I did. I really did."

"I did too," I confess.

My mind takes me back to what I told Steve before I came over here. She's my sun and my mornings really are better with just the thought of her.

The way the sunlight brings some golden color to her brown eyes, the way she tends to get more freckles on her cheeks and nose when she's outside for longer than necessary, and how her hair is even starting to get lighter.

It's like the sun has enveloped itself onto her and *into* her. And now she's transferring that to *me* with just the thought of her. Just being here with her, it's like I'm warmed by the sun's rays.

I never want to leave.

"Good," She finally breathes out as she pulls me by her hands that are still on my cheeks and kisses me.

As we continue to make out, my core fires up, and my cock tightens against my jeans. I don't want to pressure her into anything and I made a promise to her that she can't reciprocate oral sex until she's gotten enough orgasms from me.

To be honest, I don't even care about getting the same pleasure. I just want her to get it all and be happy. We've all got our preference for what we like to do intimately. I'd rather just do this and then, eventually, sex. But I push that thought aside for now.

My hands go back to her hips and run down the length of her

body as she moans again and pulls me in for more kisses, soon moving her lips to my neck.

I let my head fall to the crook of her neck and I rub my boner against her thigh. She sucks in her breath and squeezes her legs around me as much as she can. I chuckle underneath my breath in her ear, and she moans again.

"I need you Bennett," she breathes out, kissing my neck some more before finding my lips again.

I shake my head. "I'd like to wait."

Her brows knit together and I can see her eyes search my face and the questions running through her mind.

"Trust me, I want to," I tell her. "But I want us to wait a little longer. I don't want our first time to be on this couch. As nice as it is."

She nods and smiles, taking in my request. I kiss her, hoping she can take it as a thanks for respecting my decision to wait.

What I don't tell her is that I want to wait until I have my slate clean. I want to tell her everything about me before she decides to sleep with me. I don't want her to regret it after hearing what I need to tell her.

About my life, Katherine, Morgan, my time in the military and in Colombia. I want her to know everything and give her the decision to continue a relationship with me.

I want to give her a chance to run.

"I'll wait. I like this," She breathes out, breaking me out of my thoughts. She closes her eyes and takes a few deep breaths. It seems to calm me as I synchronize to her breathing.

"I like this too," I confess as well. She purses her lips as she opens her eyes.

"I like you a lot," she whispers.

I lift my hand and brush her chin before caressing her jaw. "I like you more."

She smiles, and there's a glimmer in her eyes before she blinks it away.

"Can we maybe just lay here? We can watch a movie or something."

I nod and adjust my body so I'm flush to the couch cushions and she's cuddling me. She looks into my eyes before taking another deep breath.

"What are you thinking about?" I ask her after a few moments.

She's silent as she stares at me and studies my face. I usually cave into myself if I have someone looking at me this much, but with her it's different.

"I've never really been with someone who's as patient as you are. In this regard."

I rack my brain to figure out what she means and it finally clicks. I pull her in closer and kiss her nose softly.

"I'll always wait for you, Camilla."

TWENTY-THREE

CAMILLA

BENNETT DIDN'T STAY the night, but that was okay with me. We cuddled some more before he left and I was able to get some sleep. The next few days flew by with small events at the barn for birthday parties and people having work luncheons.

Business has been booming, and I had to make sure we'd get everything done in time for the weekend. We were planning to still be open all weekend long except for the actual Fourth of July.

I didn't want anyone thinking they couldn't either hang out at the vineyard or not be able to get some wine for their parties. And that's what made the week go by faster—there were hundreds of orders for wine that I almost ran out of stock.

It's Friday now and Bennett and I have been to lunch twice at Nicky's as well as making small trips to the nearby Tractor Supply. He needed to get more feed for his animals and anything else for his farm. We also helped get some simple hay stacks as seating options for Birdy's place.

I didn't have time to drop them off with Bennett, but I can't wait to see her place. I remember her telling me she lives right across from the marina and down the road from me.

My phone vibrates from a message and I pull it out as I sign off on another boxed order for this weekend.

BENNETT 👑

Pick a color: White or Red.

I hesitate for a moment before typing out a response and hit send.

> Are you talking about wine? Because white.

Almost immediately, my phone buzzes again.

No, but I already knew that. Just pick a color.

I sigh and shake my head, unable to contain a smile forming at my lips as I type out my answer.

> Red 🔥

He likes the message before I stuff my phone back in my pocket and resume my day of packing orders for people that will pick up their wine boxes later this evening before we close. We'll be open tomorrow as well if they need to pick them up then.

A few more hours go by and I check my phone to see a few texts from Birdy sending me some pictures of outfit choices for tonight. It's the night of the rodeo and I've never been to one. I'm a city girl and haven't even seen a bull with my own eyes unless it was on tv. Same thing goes for horses.

I help her pick out the one I think Steve would love the best and what compliments her skin tone and hair before I make my way to the front of the vineyard building. The boxes of orders are stacked neatly near the door and Parker is finishing restocking one fridge with more wine.

"Are you going to the rodeo tonight?" I ask him, leaning against the counter nearby. He pops his head up and shakes his head.

"No, not this year. My aunt actually wanted to have dinner with Mabel."

I widen my eyes. "Really? Just the three of you?"

He nods his head. "Yeah, I'm kind of nervous."

I dismiss him with the wave of my hand. "Nervous about what? Mabel is great. I know your aunt will love her."

There's a pinkness that creeps up to his cheeks as he listens.

"Seriously, Parker! Do you know what you'll wear?"

He nods his head. "Yeah, a blue button down and then some black slacks. I want it to be a really nice dinner. Aunt Rose is cooking some steak and veggies."

"Wow, I'm sure Mabel will love it."

"You think so?" He asks, pushing the last wine bottle into the fridge before closing the door. He grabs the box and starts breaking it down, throwing it near a pile of other broken down boxes.

We usually go to the recycling center just right outside of Alpine Ridge's town lines every Friday night, so he'll be bringing them over once we close.

"I know so," I assure him.

He gives me a smile before he rubs his hands together and then heads towards the register on the other side of the building. There's no one left on the property but us. The sun is still shining brightly down into the surrounding windows.

"Are you excited about tonight? It's gonna be loud and lots of drinking," Parker states as he works on closing the register.

I nod my head, but pull my lip through my teeth in nervousness. "Yeah, I've just never been to one before. What do they do?"

"Bull riding, barrel racing, saddle or bareback riding horses, and steer wrestling."

I look at him with a puzzled face before we both bust out in laughter.

"I have no idea what any of that means."

Parker looks at me before shrugging. "I don't either. It's a lot of words just to say they go on horses and play around the arena. And then you have the bulls that they just hop on and attempt to get the longest riding score before falling."

"Sounds so fun," I joke.

"The townies love it," Parker shrugs again.

"It's between Alpine Ridge and Mason Pointe, right?" I finally ask as I see him finish closing the register. I planned to help, but he counts everything so fast that I would just slow him down.

He nods as he opens a few draws and throws things in it before grabbing the cash envelope for the draw and making his way to me. He hands it to me and I grasp it with two hands.

"Yeah, it's like the only time we come together as neighboring towns. Our high school teams are rivals with them and people get pretty intense about it. Fourth of July is like our white flag weekend where we just have fun together."

"I've never had to deal with that in a big city," I counter.

"Yeah, but it's actually fun and brings us purpose sometimes as a small town. Especially with the high school sports. Those games can get crazy."

Since I moved here once school was out for the summer, I haven't been able to see what he's talking about whenever I drive by the school district. It's pretty empty except for the occasional jogger. I assume there will be sport tryouts and practices in August, though.

"Well, I can't wait to see what it's all about."

Parker nods before I head back to the office to put the cash envelope into the safe that's inside before I head out with my things and close the office door, locking it. Parker has the broken down boxes in his hands by the time I reach the front door and we work together to get into his car.

Once they're all in the trunk, I give him a once over before holding his shoulders. "You're going to do great tonight and I can't wait to hear all about it tomorrow."

He laughs before nodding. "Yes, Miss Camilla. I'll be at the fair tomorrow too, so hopefully we can all hang out."

"Of course," I promise him. I let his shoulders go, and he heads for his car and I do the same. The vineyard is quiet, but I can hear some birds chirping nearby. Once I get into my small bug, I turn on the engine and immediately turn up the AC.

It's sweltering outside and I'm hoping for the best tonight. If it continues to be this humid, then I might forgo makeup and just do my hair. I don't need to be sweating off my makeup.

I wait for Parker to head out of the vineyard entrance while I follow with him. I rarely use the shortcut path that leads to the house, in case my car gets stuck in the grass.

Once we're through the gates, I see Parker turn and head back to town where his place is. I stop my car for a moment and get out to press the button to close the electric gate and hear it whir as it closes.

I get back in my car and head to the house where Birdy is meeting me to get ready. My car trudges along the gravel pathway as I near the house and see her car parked already. She's sitting on the porch with a duffel bag plopped on the porch steps next to her.

I park and shut off the car before getting out with my things. "What's with the bag? You bring your entire closet?"

Birdy shakes her head as she stands up and joins me as I walk up the steps to the door. "I brought the one outfit we decided on... but then I had to bring all my makeup and hair stuff. I didn't know what to do about that situation."

I stick my keys in the door and twist it open, pushing the door and letting her go in first. Goose is napping on a nearby chair in the hallway, and I rub her head after closing the door behind us.

"We can get ready in my room. I'll go find an outfit and shower," I tell her as we make our way through the house. I pause momentarily to fill up Goose's bowl for dinner and some water before we resume.

"How's everything going? It feels like it's been weeks even though I saw you a few days ago," Birdy asks behind me as we enter the master suite.

She heads for the bed and plops on it before heaving her bag up and plopping it next to her. She unzips it and starts pulling out an array of accessories and products. I make my way to the walk-in closet and start looking through the many hangers of clothing I have. There are a few options I was thinking of throughout the day that I wanted Birdy's opinion on.

I pull clothes off hangers and pile them on the chaise that's in the middle of the closet.

"Camilla?" Birdy's voice breaks me out of my trance and I crane my neck towards the open door that leads out of the closet and into the bedroom.

"Sorry, kind of got distracted. Everything has been so busy. I'm glad I can have some breathing time tonight and then tomorrow after work. How's the shop?"

I hear noises on the other side of the wall before Birdy answers. "It's good. Got tons of online orders and I'm thinking of closing tomorrow, so I can have enough time to prepare for Sunday."

"Oh, right! Did Bennett drop off everything you needed from the tractor supply?" I ask as I finally lay the last piece of clothing on the chaise and lean down to gather the pile in my arms. I walk out of the closet and into the bedroom and plop the pile on the bed.

Birdy is standing up now near the full-length mirror near the corner of the room and starting on her makeup. She's lifting a brush to her cheeks before turning around and looking at me. "Yeah. I knew he'd be able to come through with that help. I'm sad you couldn't join."

I pout, "I know, but we have Sunday. I can't wait to see your place."

"You're going to love the way I set it up."

I pull some high waisted denim shorts from the pile and show it to Birdy as she turns back towards the mirror to keep doing her makeup. She looks at the shorts through the mirror and nods her head.

"These?" I ask, and she nods again. "Also, I think I'll love it. The way you set up the vineyard opening night felt like a fairy-tale. I can't imagine how your place will look like for the cookout."

"Big thanks to Bennett too. He helped a ton," Birdy says as she puts down the makeup brush and picks up an eyeshadow palette. She begins working on her eyes while I sift through the pile for the best top to go with the shorts.

My hands find the perfect top. It's a black bandeau top I can easily wear underneath a jacket or cover up. I pull the hanger and show it to Birdy. She nods again.

"That will look super cute. Plus, it's gonna be hot there, so you don't want to sweat under tons of layers."

"My thoughts exactly," I tell her as I find a matching black belt. I look through the pile to see if I can find some kind of shirt I can wear over it. "Do you think I'll need a cover up?"

Birdy finally cranes her neck back and studies the outfit on the bed that I sectioned off from the pile and shakes her head. "No, you should be fine. I'm not bringing any cover up and I'm sure Bennett will have a jacket of some sort with him you can use."

I nod before gathering the clothes and making my way to the connected bathroom. I shut the door and lay the clothes on the bathroom counter before heading to the shower.

I take about fifteen minutes to shower before I pull on the clothes. Once I have it all on, I quickly work on my hair with the dryer and mousse before heading back to the bedroom to do my makeup. I have a small vanity in there that I head straight to.

"You look cute!" Birdy exclaims as she works on the last bits of her hair. She's already changed into her outfit and she looks amazing.

Her hair is slightly curled and her makeup compliments her complexion and green eyes. She's wearing black jean shorts with sequins on the back pockets and then a silver ribbed tank top to match the sequins. She put on some combat boots to finish the look.

"I love your outfit!" I say back to her.

She sighs and laughs. "Yeah, I tried on like fifteen different outfits to see what I thought would be the best. Is it bad that I really want Steve to say something?"

I finally turn to look at her, setting down the eyelash curler that's in my hand. "Doesn't he always say something?"

She shrugs, finding my eyes. "Yeah, but that's just him. The friendly Steve we all know. I want him to notice me like a boyfriend would. God, that sounds so stupid."

"You said you've yet to make it official, right?"

She nods and sighs again. "Something in me is telling me that if *I'm* not the one to ask him to be official, then it's never gonna happen."

I rack my brain for a response, but I'm stumped. For the time that I've known the people in this town, I can say that she's telling the truth about Steve. He's a very happy-go-lucky guy and goes with the flow. He sometimes acts like a lost puppy and needs some guidance.

"And you'd be fine with that?" I ask her honestly.

She cranes her neck and looks off into the distance as she thinks of a response. "Yeah, I think so…"

"Well," I say, "if you want to make the move, then do it.

What's holding you back? But don't make it a habit where you're the only one making the first move, okay?"

She nods slowly. "Yes, ma'am."

I laugh and turn back to the mirror and grab the eyelash curler again. I see Birdy in the mirror turning back around and finishing her hair.

Before we know it, we hear the honking of a horn and the doorbell ringing, letting us know our boys are here to pick us up for the rodeo.

BENNETT KEEPS his hand on the lower part of my back as we enter the rodeo area. It's loud and *crowded*. I take my time observing the place.

It's an outside event, and it took almost an hour to drive here with Birdy and Steve sitting in the backseat of Bennett's truck. We mainly listened to music during the drive while Bennett kept his hand on my thigh while he drove. He let me steal his cowboy hat to add to my outfit tonight.

I'm feeling like a hundred bucks with his hat on as we enter the arena. It's a big oval arena with tons of bleachers for seating and gates lining the inside of the arena. There's a portion of the arena where the horses enter and then where they keep the bulls stationed. There's some people on their horses taking some laps around the arena as we find our seats.

Birdy was determined to find seats pretty close to the ground so I can get the full experience. I didn't expect us to get *front row seats* to the show. Bennett and Steve make their way to the concession stand to get us some snacks and beer.

"How you feeling?" Birdy asks, nudging my elbow to make me look her way. I adjust the hat as I turn to look at her. She's wiggling her brows, and a smile spreads across her face.

"I'm excited but also nervous. I've never been to one of these!"

"You might get muddy as the horses ride by. But don't worry, I packed some baby wipes if it gets on your face or arms."

"Always prepared," I tease.

She shrugs and laughs again. "Always. I'm also predicting that Steve will get a hotdog and spill the condiments all over his chin and possibly his shirt."

As if on cue, we turn to hear the sounds of their footsteps as they approach our bleacher and get closer. Their hands are full of beer and... hot dogs. I reach my hands out to help Bennett, who is attempting to juggle four beer cans in his hands.

"Here, I got it," I tell him, taking two. He gives me a smile before letting Steve get past him to sit by Birdy. She helps him with the hotdogs he's holding, making sure he sits down before she distributes the food to the rest of us. I let her put my hotdog on my lap before I give her the two beers I'm holding.

I take Bennett's hot dog and replace it with a beer that's in his hand that's mine. His blue eyes find mine throughout the exchange and even here, of all places, I feel my stomach flip.

"What, Bunny?" He asks slowly as he takes a sip of his beer and sets it on the bench next to him.

"Nothing," I murmur before lifting the beer to my own lips and taking a sip. I follow his motion and place my beer can on the bench in between Birdy and me before I lift the hotdog from the paper holder and take a bite.

Bennett watches me for a moment before he averts his eyes to the arena, smiling. I try to take a mental picture of what I'm witnessing before Birdy pulls me into the conversation she's having with Steve.

"Look, Camilla! He totally did it!" Birdy screams as I crane my neck and burst out laughing.

Steve, sure enough, has some ketchup dribbling down his chin. Birdy quickly reaches for a napkin and wipes it off. He smiles sheepishly before thanking her. I watch their exchange and nudge her with my elbow.

They need to make it official before I go crazy watching them fall for each other like this.

I turn my head enough to see if Bennett is looking too, but he's looking at me and my face grows hot as I watch his blue eyes travel down my face. The butterflies in my stomach swarm immensely.

"What?" I ask him, laughing. I mindlessly bring the hotdog up to my mouth and take a big bite. A dollop of ketchup ends up in the corner of my mouth. He reaches over with his thumb and gently wipes it away.

"You and Steve are the same," He jokes. I roll my eyes playfully before attempting to finish my hotdog.

The people around us shake the bleachers, slamming their feet on the floors and screaming. I look up towards the arena and see a man on a horse enter the area, taking a few gallops around the pen. Birdy joins the crowd with a scream and Steve joins in. I look at Bennett, who shrugs and starts hollering as well. The hyped up energy around me causes me to smile and want to picture this moment forever.

The man on the horse gallops near us and he takes a moment to pause and lock eyes with Birdy and I, before winking at us and then riding off. Birdy squeals and takes her free hand to shake my shoulder.

"He winked at us! Courtland Hayes... the *best* bull rider in the state, if not the country... WINKED AT US!"

"Birdy!" I exclaim, lifting my hand to cover my mouth as I giggle. I look at Steve, who shrugs and continues to eat his hot dog. I turn to look at Bennett and he seems to not care either. He stares at the arena before I lean close to him, near his cheek.

"What's going on in that head of yours, cowboy?"

He smiles and shakes his head, lifting his beer to his lips

before whispering, "I don't care if that man is winking at you *or* tries to flirt with you."

"Oh?" I ask, laughing. He nods before turning his head to peer down at me. My heart skips a beat as I watch his blue eyes blaze into mine.

"Yeah. Cause I know you'll come home with me. He's got no chance."

I laugh before he leans in and gives me a soft kiss. I melt into it and close my eyes, wishing we could do more. But we're front row at a rodeo and everyone can see us. I separate our lips and Bennett exhales deeply. I do the same and smile.

"I'll always go home with you," I whisper.

A smirk spreads along his lips before we lean in for one more kiss. Once we separate, the crowd goes wild again as the cowboy leaves the pen and they announce what's going on tonight. There's an entire list of events and the bull ride will be the last thing. I finish my hotdog and some more of my beer in case mud gets sprayed in our direction.

When I check on my friends next to me, I see Steve casually drape his arm over Birdy's shoulders and she smiles brightly. We make eye contact briefly, and I wink at her.

The event goes for two more hours before the bull ride finally starts. My legs and jean shorts are already full of mud from the pen, but I don't care. Birdy kept handing me her little container of baby wipes, but after the first hour I gave up in trying to clean myself from the mud.

Bennett gave me a rundown of every event and so far, I loved barrel racing. They even had a girl get on her horse, run around the pen with a bow and arrow, *stand* upright on her horse's saddle, and shoot targets. She got every single one.

So far it's been incredible and Birdy and I squeal as the same cowboy that winked at us positions himself on top of the bull. He has tons of helpers around him and the bull is getting more and more antsy.

"So what happens?" I ask again, leaning into Bennett. He laughs and rubs his hands over my muddy thigh. But even just that action alone sucks the breath out of me and I almost forget what I just asked him.

"So, your pretty boy will attempt to stay on the bull for as long as he can until he gets thrown off."

"Hey!" I giggle at his choice of words.

"What?" Bennett laughs. "At least I called him pretty."

I laugh again. "He's got nothing on you. Besides I've got *your* cowboy hat on."

This brings a smirk to his lips before he squeezes my thigh. The announcer starts a countdown. A loud siren blares above us and Birdy hollers alongside the rest of the crowd. Once the announcer counts down and screams "One", the gate opens and the cowboy drops onto the bull and the bull bursts into the pen. There's a gigantic screen with a stopwatch on it. The seconds go by *slowly* as we see the cowboy attempt to hold on for his dear life.

But he's good. He seems to have a good hold on the bull. His balance is perfect, and it looks like it's a breeze for him. No wonder he's as famous as Birdy claims he is.

Five seconds pass by and I keep my breath held. It's intense and the rest of the crowd continues to holler and cheer him on.

There's a moment on second seven where it seems like the world stops. The cowboy keeps his free arm in the air and even *waves* to the crowd toward where Birdy and I are. Birdy jumps in her seat and shakes me.

Eight seconds go by and the alarm sounds indicating that he won. But he *stays* on the bull. The timer doesn't stop, and the crowd goes nuts as he continues on past ten seconds.

The announcer is even yelling, "This is insane, ladies and gentlemen! We've never seen Courtland go past his national record of ten seconds until tonight!"

The timer hits twelve seconds before he lets the bull fling

him off. There's enough people to help him out of the pen and get the bull. But, of course, he lands seamlessly to the ground and gets up in time to run. The bull is taken out of the pen and we all cheer. I stand up with Birdy and we're jumping in place, clapping and screaming. My throat is already feeling hoarse from the screaming.

Before we know it, there are fireworks going off to end the rodeo. It's all too much, and I feel like I'm in a euphoric state. I never want to leave and I pull Birdy into a hug as we continue to jump up and down.

"Okay, okay! We get it, he's the best," Steve yells with a laugh.

"Let them enjoy the pretty boy, Steve," Bennett argues from behind me. Once Birdy and I are done jumping, Bennett takes the opportunity to slap my ass and I squeal, turning around.

I step closer to him to slap his shoulder, but he's quicker and pulls me in with his hands on my waist until I'm sitting on his lap.

I laugh, and he smiles.

"Have fun tonight, Bunny?" He leans in and brushes his nose with mine.

It feels like it's just us, and the screaming from around the arena fades.

I nod. "I had the best time."

"Good, now you can go tell your pretty boy bull rider you're coming home with me," he smiles.

"Yes, sir," I tease, leaning in to kiss him.

TWENTY-FOUR

BENNETT

I KNOW I told Bunny that I'd wait for her, but the way she's staring at me from across the bar in Mason Pointe makes me want to drag her away and fuck the living daylights out of her.

She and Birdy are dancing to the music and making friends while Steve and I are drinking away at the bar. I'm taking it slow though, since I'm the driver. I've been sipping on water ever since we made it to the bar.

The beer at the rodeo was enough for me. Just the sight of Bunny in her outfit and the way her eyes kept lingering on me tonight, make me drunk off that. I didn't need anymore drinks to feel what I'm feeling with her.

Steve nudges my elbow as we lean against the bar's counter, and we watch our girls. I crane my neck towards him and he gives me a small smile before nodding towards the girls out on the dance floor.

"What?" I ask, lifting the plastic water cup to my lips and taking a refreshing sip.

He smiles even brighter. "Look at us. Who knew?"

I finish drinking before responding. "I know, man. If you ever asked me…"

"I know." Steve shakes his head and leans closer, patting me on the shoulder. "Especially you. Wow."

I let out a heavy grunt. "Okay, Steve. I know I'm so grumpy and miserable. This is such a big deal for me."

"Because it is! And you know it."

I nod, but don't want to admit it. Because I'm still the grumpy Bennett, everyone knows. I've just been able to turn on my 'nice' switch and haven't turned it off since. But in reality, I'm terrified that there will be a time that it'll get switched off... for good.

I don't want that to happen. I deserve this.

"You okay?" Steve breaks my thoughts and I nod my head, lifting my water cup and clinking it with his beer bottle.

We both turn again towards the girls that are dancing now to a line dance song that Bunny clearly doesn't know, but she's trying. Her legs are flying everywhere, her hands are placed on her hip, and *my* hat is nestled on top of her curls. She's smiling brightly and catches my eyes, blowing me a kiss quickly before going back to focusing on the dance.

"Wow, Birdy is so absorbed in that dance she won't even blow me a kiss," Steve jokes and I laugh.

"Get your girl, then!" I urge him, nudging him with my elbow this time. He shakes his head before setting his beer down and mustering up the courage.

Steve has always been the shy one in relationships or even simply asking a girl out. That's why I think he and Birdy have been so good together. They don't need to *try,* they just hang out and the rest comes.

I momentarily remember that he's yet to tell me if he and Birdy are official. I hope they are by now. If not, I know Birdy would probably be the one to take the lead and ask him out.

"I'm going in. The next song is starting," Steve exclaims as he gives me a nod and heads to the dance floor as people break off or stay and beckon their partners to join them.

I look out for Bunny, but I don't see her anymore in the crowd. I take another sip of my water before I feel soft hands grab my wrist that's at my side. I turn to see Bunny and her bright brown eyes.

"Hey," she giggles, leaning closer. Her perfume is still going strong after the rodeo and I put the cup down on the counter before pulling her in by the waist.

"Where on earth did you get that hat?" I joke, watching her eyes light up as she lets me position her right between my legs as I stay put on the stool.

"Some really attractive cowboy... he might snatch me up tonight," she replies, huffing out a breath and rolling her eyes.

"Pity, I thought you might come home with me?" I tease, leaning down and bringing my lips to her ear. She stiffens and wraps her arms around my neck.

The music is pulsing around us and there's a nice romantic country song playing over the speakers.

She breathes harder as she pulls me closer with her hands. I nibble on her earlobe before moving my lips down to kiss her neck and litter her cheek and nose with kisses. She giggles and I barely catch it with the loud music around us.

"I have to get up early, but maybe tomorrow?" She says just loud enough for me to hear.

I nod my head and kiss her lips. We both melt into it and our tongues clash almost instantly. We're breathing heavier and I can feel the strain in my pants grow even more. I try to not think of any more dirty thoughts with her being the center of them, but it's fucking hard.

"Okay, no more," she moans into my mouth before pulling apart. I lean back and smile, watching her eyes roam my face. Her cheeks are blazing red and her lips bite into one another.

"Did I tell you how amazing you look tonight?" I remark.

She shakes her head. "No, I don't think you did. I can go find someone else to tell me..."

I squint my eyes and shake my head, pulling her into me again. She laughs and kisses me once more.

"You're trouble, Bunny," I whisper.

"Just wait until the fair… I'll be wearing *the* pants…"

My ears perk up and I lean my lips to her neck, nibbling on her skin. She squirms underneath my touch, but I hold on to her tightly.

"Bennett!" She laughs.

"Don't say those kinds of things. I'm about to throw you over my shoulder and take you to the truck. *Right now.*" I tell her before I lean back and watch her reaction.

Her pupils grow and her lips quiver. She looks around the bar before turning back to me and nodding. "I won't talk about *the pants* anymore," she says before lifting her finger to her lips in a *shushing* motion.

"Good, because you drive me crazy already. I can't imagine seeing those in person," I confess.

She laughs before we kiss again. She finally turns and nestles her head back towards my shoulder. We both watch the people in the bar as they dance the night away.

THE NEXT MORNING goes by too slowly for me and I almost run over to the vineyard to help Bunny and Parker to make the people leave quicker. But it wouldn't matter because the fair doesn't start until the evening time.

I'm finishing up cleaning up the horse stables before I get a text from Steve asking me to come over. I clean up inside before I head over to his shop. The workers are too focused on their job to see me walk in and head to Steve's small office. It's not really an office, it's just a table and a few chairs around it. He's got some filing cabinets along the wall and some photos. Some of our high school days, his college days, and then some of me and him, as well as him and Birdy.

I've tried to tell him he needs to decorate it some more and maybe organize it, but he'd just waved his hands. Steve isn't complicated and won't want to waste time on that kind of stuff if what he currently has works good.

Once I'm in the office, I see him flipping through an old manual for a Ford truck. His eyebrows are furrowed, and he's nibbling on his pinky nail before he looks up and sees me.

"Hey! You doing okay?" He asks, flipping the manual closed before he pats the table for me to sit.

I take a seat and lean back, crossing my arms. "Hungover?" I ask.

He shakes his head and laughs, "Surprisingly? No. But thanks for asking. I drank tons of water last night."

"Because you were sober enough to remember or because Birdy had to remind you?" I joke.

He gives me a look before scoffing. "Come on, Ben. You know I was perfectly capable last night."

We both burst out into laughter. Because Steve definitely was not capable of even going into his house. Birdy had to take his keys and get him inside. He kept drinking more and more and I think it was because he was nervous.

He knew he had to ask Birdy to be official, yet he was taking his damn time. Bunny and I even talked about it during the drive back to her place so I could drop her off.

"Sure, but I got your text. Everything okay?"

He looks up at the ceiling before settling back to me and shakes his head. "My car isn't working. The engine is slowly dying and now it's got some issues with the brakes. I was thinking we could check it out."

I nod, "Of course. Do you know how long it'd take? We have the fair to go to later today."

"It won't be right now. I want to finish working on the cars we have scheduled today at the shop. Don't want to keep the workers here after closing time."

I widen my eyes and take a deep breath. I let it out slowly. "Yeah, of course. Did you tell Birdy?"

He shakes his head. "Not yet. I'm going to after lunch."

I get up from the chair and scrape the chair back into the table. "Alright, just keep me updated."

He nods and thanks me before I walk out of his office. I head out of the shop and back into my truck as I take out my phone. I text Bunny that plans changed and I might not make it tonight to the fair.

I don't get an immediate response, but I don't hold her to it. She's busy and hopefully she can see it in time before tonight. I don't want her to wait for me when she and Birdy can figure out their transportation on their own.

I try to make the rest of the day go by quicker as I clean the house and feed the cows and horses out in the pasture. Time goes slower as the clock ticks down towards the evening time. Bunny did text me back though and let me know she'll figure out tonight with Birdy and for me to not worry.

I let her know I expect to get more pictures with her in those damn pants and she, of course, agreed. With a few emojis after her response.

It's not until five that I make my way to Steve's shop. He's already driving his car into the shop and getting ready to inspect it when I arrive. I park my truck and get out, heading into the shop.

It takes longer than expected, but we get his brake pads fixed and even make sure all other areas of his car are good to go. It's a little past eight when we're done and the sun is already setting. By the time we get home and change, it's nearing nine.

The fair is open late and usually closes around two in the morning. It's a big thing here and people still have to work, so it stays open for them to catch it at night.

Tomorrow is the holiday, so it's the perfect way to ring it in and stay up all night. There's gonna be fireworks at the fair as well and I couldn't wait to go.

We don't tell Birdy and Bunny that we're on the way. We want to surprise them. I'm wearing some dark blue jeans, my regular work boots, and a nice jade button-down short-sleeve shirt. Steve is wearing light faded jeans with a Hawaiian shirt and his work shoes as well.

We make it to the fair in time to get good parking that's not too far from the entrance. While we're walking towards the entrance, we see Bunny's green beetle.

Steve wanted to pull a prank and leave a note telling them to park better, but we had no paper and marker to write on. The parking here is free rein, and no one parked correctly, so it would've been funny for them to find that note.

Steve and I pay for our entrance fee and then head into the fair. We plan to find the girls and then go on some rides. I was craving a lemonade too and hoped Bunny would want one.

"Alright, where are they?!" Steve yells as he looks around the crowded fair. There's too many people to find them, so we continued walking. We're near the games area where people are tossing rings onto bottle caps and winning small prizes.

That's when I see *the pants*.

I slap Steve's chest as I look ahead and point towards the pants that are bright and like a neon sign beckoning me over.

"Woah," Steve murmurs.

"Yeah," I bite my lip. I know he's talking about Birdy who's wearing cute clothes as well, but my eyes are straight to the source and the owner of the pants.

She's leaning back laughing and her curly hair is cascading over her shoulders and back perfectly. She's wearing a tight white tank top. But the jeans… they're perfect on her body. They are tight enough to accentuate her curves around her ass but then flare out at the bottom.

Once we get closer to the girls, I finally look up to see who they're talking to. I furrow my brows and feel my chest tighten. Steve nudges my arm quickly and I give him a shake of my head.

Lance King is chatting it up with Birdy and Bunny. Birdy is shaking her head while Bunny continues to laugh. She's holding a small stuffed animal, attempting to give it back to Lance, who is waving his hands and trying to make her keep it.

Lance went to our high school and was always a trouble-maker. He grew out of it, but his womanizing ways didn't. And it's clear now that he's attempting to work his charm on our girls.

There's someone else there, and that's when I feel the anger rise in my body. The same guy who tried to give Bunny his cowboy hat weeks ago at the bar. The one who came into *my* town and tried taking *my* girl.

"Ben—" Steve starts, but then he stops in his tracks too when we see Lance lift his hand and place it on Birdy's shoulder.

"Not today," I breathe out as I attempt to keep my cool as we near the girls.

I don't want to cause a scene, so when we are a few feet away, I reach over to Bunny and wrap my arms around her waist. She yelps, grabbing my forearms and attempting to pull me away before she hears my laughter fill her ears.

She cranes her neck up and catches my eyes. "Bennett! What are you doing here?"

"Wanted to surprise my girl," I mutter as I give her a long kiss. Her lips form into a smile before we pull apart.

"You scared me! I thought you were some random stranger trying to kidnap me."

Birdy laughs beside us as Steve wraps his arm around her shoulders and stares Lance down. But, of course, Lance doesn't flinch.

His blue eyes settle on the four of us. He runs his long, pale fingers through his unruly black hair and smiles at us. "Nice for you guys to finally show up. Your women were getting lonely."

I grit my teeth and try to not grab Lance by the neck and punch him. Bunny laughs and shakes her head underneath me. "We weren't lonely. Birdy and I were perfectly capable on our own."

I don't even bother to ask Lance what he's doing with them. I turn to see the other guy slowly widen his eyes and take a step back.

"Hey, I thought they were alone. I swear. I just remembered them from that night."

Steve laughs. "Yeah, and you remember how that ended?"

Bunny turns to look at Steve. I squeeze her waist with my hands and she squeaks, looking up at me.

"Whatever, let's go, Lance," he scoffs before Lance gives Birdy and Bunny a wave before blowing kisses to them.

"What a tool," Birdy finally breathes out as we all watch them leave.

"That's Lance for you," I tell her. Steve looks at me before looking at Birdy, who gives him a smile.

"What's this?" I ask, lifting my hand to take the stuffed animal that's in Bunny's hand. She pulls it away and hands it to Birdy.

"Lance was trying to impress us. So, we told him if he could win at ring toss then we'd hang out with him for an hour. He's really desperate these days," Birdy says, taking the stuffed animal and placing it on a nearby counter where there's another game going on.

"Want me to win you a really big one?" I lean down and ask Bunny.

She exhales loudly before leaning her head back. "How big?"

I can feel the strain in my pants grow and I pull her closer to me, causing her to let out a breathless laugh.

"The biggest," I whisper in her ear. She stiffens, and she doesn't move.

"We're going to get some funnel cakes," Birdy calls out, breaking us from the small bubble we're in.

"Oh-Okay!" Bunny mumbles as I litter her neck with kisses. When Birdy and Steve finally leave our vicinity, she turns and gives me a look.

"What?" I raise a brow.

"You know what you're doing, Bennett Moore!" She points her finger and pushes it into my chest. I laugh and grab it, letting my other hand snake around her waist and pull her in tightly. She gasps as she feels my growing boner and she bites her lip.

"Want to go find something to ride?" I ask, kissing her forehead before kissing her nose. Her cheeks redden and I know it's from the filthy innuendo. I'm doing it on purpose though, I want to see her reaction.

Her eyes flutter before she nods. "Y-yeah, sure," she shakily answers.

I smile and take her hand, encasing our fingers together as I walk us towards the rides.

It's getting even busier and most of the rides have long lines. And I can't wait.

I pull Bunny towards the vacant areas between the rides. There's a ton of room in the back of the rides where there's darkness and no one idling. There are some people sitting on benches and tables that workers put out while they were prepping the fair, but they're near the other rides. Not behind the one we're at.

Once we're far enough for the screams and music to fade a little, I pull her near a wall. The ride's motions jolt through the wall and shake Bunny as I pin her against it.

She groans before looking up through her lashes. I place both hands near her head and lean in. She takes her own hands and loops them around my neck.

"I thought we were going to ride something," she murmurs.

I laugh and shake my head. "The lines are too long. Plus, I wanted you alone."

"Oh? You could've taken me to the house of mirrors or the fun house."

I shake my head. "It's too bright in those houses. Trust me. I thought this through."

Her eyes widen, and I can see those hints of golden hues fill her iris. She's even more beautiful under the moon that's shining above us.

I couldn't believe it. With how gorgeous she is under the rising and setting of the sun, *this* is even more mesmerizing.

"What?" She asks, searching my eyes.

"I'm just admiring you," I breathe out.

She smiles before pulling me by my neck and smashing her lips against mine. I moan into the kiss and she does the same. I let my hands drop from her waist to roam her body. She moves with me as we continue to make out. Her hands move from my neck to grasp my hair and pull on it.

I groan and move my lips to her shoulder and bite down hard. She yelps before giggling. Her hips push against mine and she feels my boner, hitching her breath.

"Fuck, Bennett," she whispers before we kiss again.

I briefly lift my head to see if the people that were at the back of the other rides are gone and they're nowhere to be seen. It's just us. Screams grow louder from the ride we're behind. I take that opportunity to move my hand right by her waist, hooking my fingers in the loops of her jeans.

"Please," she whines softly.

"Yes, ma'am," I reply, running my fingers towards the button and then the zipper of her pants. I keep my body pinned to her so if anyone walks nearby they'd just see our bodies really close.

Besides, if anyone came close by, I'd make sure they didn't see any part of her.

She breathes heavily, latching her lips to mine as I let my

fingers roam and unbutton her pants before pulling down the zipper. My hand slips inside and I have to maneuver a bit with how tight the pants are on her.

She giggles through a kiss, but I grunt. "I'm making this work," I breathe out in frustration.

"If you have to break the pants, do it," she responds. And although I'd love to do that, she needs pants to walk out of this place. I shake my head and dig my hand deeper past the high-waisted fabric until I feel the lining of her panties. I slip my hands through it and immediately feel her pussy flinch at my bare fingers.

I chuckle under my breath as we continue to kiss and I move my fingers to slide through her wet folds. She's so wet for me and I moan, feeling my cock grow harder against my jeans.

Without a moment's notice, she moves one of her hands to cup my jeans and moves her fingers along the length of my cock that's attempting to break through the jeans. I push her body closer to the wall and she squeals.

"Fuck, keep doing that," I moan. I slip another finger into her folds and maneuver them until I'm slipping them inside her.

I pump my fingers in and out of her as best as I can with her jeans in the way. I move my thumb to rub against her clit and she whimpers in my ear, causing me to go feral.

I move my lips to her ear and bite on her earlobe. She whines again, and this time *she's* playing with the button on my jeans. I tsk under my breath and pull my face back to see her. She widens her eyes and bites her lip.

"What did I say?" I tell her.

"You don't want me to–?" She whispers. I shake my head and lean in, giving her a kiss.

"Oh, I want it. But I want you to come first before you do anything for me."

She presses her lips into a thin line before nodding. I kiss her and she smiles again before I flick my fingers inside of her and she flutters her eyes closed, slipping out a moan.

"Like that?" I murmur, and she nods, biting her lip.

"More," she begs.

I smile and slip in a third finger, stretching her out and thrusting into her in a quicker motion. She clenches her eyes shut and grabs onto my shoulder tightly. I quicken my pace and rub her clit in circles, and watch her fall apart in my arms. And in my hand. Her orgasm is strong and I keep fingering her through the high, causing her to squeal and attempt to push my shoulder with her hand.

"One more for me, baby. Ride these fingers like a good girl." I whisper, causing her to throw her head back against the wall and bite her lip, keeping her eyes shut tight.

Her hips move through the motions of my fingers that are still fucking her. My hand is wet, but I don't care. I continue to rub her clit and she squirms underneath my touch and within seconds, she's coming again in my hand.

"Please, no more," she begs, and I nod my head.

I drag my fingers out of her and then out of the pants. She yelps from the sudden loss of my fingers inside her. She pants before opening her eyes. Her chest is heaving up and down and her eyes are blown with ecstasy and riding off the two orgasms.

I lift my hand to my mouth and lick all my fingers. She watches slowly, looking dazed and confused. But it's cute on her and the fact that *I'm* the one that's making her act like this.

"You okay?" I ask once I rub the rest of my hand against my jeans and adjust my jeans where my boner is. I try to not think of her giving me a blowjob or letting me turn her around and sinking deep into her—

"Yeah, that was amazing," She breathes out before zipping her pants back up and folding the button closed with shaky hands.

I watch her take another deep breath and run her fingers

through her hair. It's a mess from our movements, but she still looks beautiful. I push some strands behind her ear.

"What?" She giggles, watching me.

"I'm starving," I tell her.

"For food? Or…"

"Food, definitely food," I smile before I step back and let her get some breathing space.

She smoothes her hands over her outfit before she takes a step forward and catches my clean hand with hers. There are a few porta potties near the rides that we can go to quickly.

"And a lemonade," she tells me as we head out of the back of the rides and into the blinding lights of the fair. The screams are echoing everywhere and the music comes back at full sound.

"Let's go get some," I wink at her before pulling her further into the fair.

TWENTY-FIVE

CAMILLA

THE FAIR WAS SO fun and Bennett not only won me two big stuffed animals from the games; he won tickets to a baseball game in Nashville. I didn't even know they had games where you could win those kinds of prizes and he almost threw them away, but I pulled them out of his hands and threw them in my pants pockets.

I definitely wanted to make that an excuse for us to go to the big city. I knew we'd already planned to go sometime this summer, but having these tickets with a date to use them would push us to go.

It's the next morning and I'm already at Birdy's helping her bake some last-minute things. Steve and Bennett are in the back setting up decorations as well as creating a platform to set the fireworks off from.

Birdy told me it'll be a big party that almost everyone in Alpine Ridge comes to if they don't already have their own party. And then at night while there are fireworks on the beach, people leave for those while she and her family and friends have their own fireworks and a bonfire. I couldn't wait.

She's rolling some dough as I work on filling a cupcake tin

274

with cake batter. She said the best cakes are fresh from the morning instead of overnight. I didn't think twice or bother to ask and got to work the moment I got there this morning.

Bennett and I drove over together after a much heated make-out session in the living room. He wanted to come check my dripping faucet when I noticed it this morning and then it led to me seeing his muscles work against his shirt... and then we found ourselves on the couch.

It wasn't until Steve called him we forgot we had somewhere to go. It felt like we were getting closer and closer to finally having sex, but things kept stopping us. Either our own hesitation or outside forces. But I didn't mind. I knew the moment we'd finally have sex it would be mind blowing.

If all the times we had fun led to me being breathless and in a euphoric state, I couldn't wait to know how he'd leave me after having sex.

But I try to push that thought away as I plop the last glob of cake batter in the cupcake tin. I head over to the already prepped oven and slide the tin inside before setting the timer for the cupcakes. I lean against the counter and admire the kitchen.

It's very homey in her place, and the kitchen looks like it's been decorated before I was born. But it still has Birdy touches here and there. She mentioned it was her grandparents' land before they passed and she took over their shop.

She rolls the last piece of dough and looks up, her green eyes brightening as they find mine. "What? You look dazed."

I shake my head. "Just admiring your place. I wish I came over sooner."

She laughs as she works on mixing brownie batter into another bowl. She cracks an egg into the bowl and whisks it. "You're always invited, darlin'."

"Thanks, Bee," I tell her, pushing myself off the counter and heading towards the sink where there's a massive window that pans out to the backyard of the property. It's a huge plot of land with not a ton of things on it.

It's not like mine or Bennett's, where we have *things* on it to use. It's just a lot of land surrounding a house. But that's all she needs since she has her shop in the center of downtown Alpine Ridge.

I see Steve chopping wood for the bonfire and Bennett is grabbing the chopped pieces and throwing them into an enormous pile. I sigh and lean over the sink counter, placing my elbows on it and lifting my arms so my chin rests on my knuckles.

"You admiring the boys?" Birdy asks behind me.

"Yeah," I hum. Bennett's wearing a tight white shirt and the way his muscles are bulging are making me weak in the knees.

He throws another piece of chopped wood onto the pile and turns his head towards the house. I'm not sure if he can see me from this distance, but he raises his hand and waves. I lift my land from under my chin and wave before putting it back.

"How are you guys? I didn't get to see you guys after we separated at the fair," Birdy asks.

I turn to glance at her, but she's focused on the batter in front of her. She's now lining a pan with butter and flour before pouring the batter in. She then adds some more chocolate chips and pieces of caramel into the batter. I turn back to the boys and watch Bennett some more.

"We're good. Really good."

"Mm," Birdy hums. "Have you guys… You know?"

I gasp and look back at my friend who widens her eyes before wiggling her brows. "What? I'm a curious creature! I need to know these kinds of things."

"You really want to know the details of your childhood friends' sex life? I don't care about sharing, but you've known Bennett all your life."

Birdy laughs and shakes her head. "Okay, now you're

making it weird. I do not care about that and whenever I'm with you and talking about your relationship, my mind blocks off the part where I know Bennett. So please, continue."

I take a deep breath before lifting myself off the kitchen sink and turning around, leaning my back on the counter. "We kind of snuck off behind the rides and did stuff, but not all the way."

She raises a brow. "And why not?"

I shrug. "He's still hesitant about it all. I know we've talked about it a few times, but something seems to stop us. Either it's me one day or him the next. I think we just need to really talk about it."

"And in 'it', are you talking about you guys or something else?"

I watch her green eyes study me before her brow raises. My cheeks heat quicker than I'd like. I huff out a deep breath.

"Okay, yeah. He didn't mention it. But he wanted to wait. He wanted to be sure it was the right time. I don't blame him."

"And what do *you* want to talk about? You still haven't answered that part."

I nibble on my lip before sighing. "I want to know the whole truth about his marriage with Katherine. That is holding him back, I think."

Birdy looks at me before nodding and pressing her lips tightly. She turns her head back towards the batter tin and lifts it, smacking it down on the counter to level it. The noise is loud and I jump at the sound.

"I don't know if he'll ever tell you," she finally says.

I cross my arms before giving her a look. She shrugs when she makes eye contact with me.

"Why?" I ask. I don't want to push her like this, but when it's keeping Bennett from going to the next step with me, then I want to know.

"It was a lot. And it's definitely not some scandalous thing that either of them did. They were really healthy until they weren't. Things were promised, things were broken, and they both were left to build themselves back together. Katherine had herself and her family, but Bennett chose to leave. To run."

"Yeah, but he came back," I counter.

"And then we all found out what happened. He filed for divorce shortly after."

"I think I remember Katherine mentioning that to me when we talked at Nicky's."

Birdy nods. "I don't want to say too much. It's not my business. But, yeah, he was the one. I know people change their minds about things in life, but this wasn't what Bennett was expecting when he came back."

I furrow my brows. "What do you mean by that?"

She sucks in her lips before shaking her head. "Shit, I said too much. I have a bad habit of that. I swore I was going to change that. Don't get me wrong, Camilla, I really want to tell you, but it's not my place. It's something *he* has to tell you. It won't be as huge as you think or make it out to be. But it has to come from him. Not me. Not anyone else."

I nod, letting her words sink in. I really want to push her to tell me, but she's right. Regardless of how big of a deal it is, I need to hear it from Bennett and no one else.

"Okay," I finally breathe out. She gives me a smile before pointing to the fridge.

"Can you hand me another egg? I want to start on breakfast. I'm starving."

I nod before heading to the fridge and pulling out a few eggs. I don't hand them to her, but instead head to the stove and help her cook. We make enough for us and the boys. We're hard at work for the next fifteen minutes before the boys come back inside, dripping sweat.

Bennett runs towards me, wrapping me in a sweaty hug and I scream before Birdy lifts a spatula and points it towards Steve to make him stop.

"I'm already encased in flour, Steve! If you come any closer to me, you will get the spatula."

Steve laughs before running towards her and lifting her up into a hug, spinning her around. She squeals from the movement and giggles as he sets her down. She softly slaps his cheek, causing flour to stick to his already sweaty face.

"Alright, lovebirds," Bennett starts. "We're hungry and heard you call us for breakfast. If I don't get any, I'm taking Camilla back into a ro—"

I swat at Bennett's arm and widen my eyes in horror. "Bennett!"

"Gross!" Steve yells, lifting his hands to his ears and making a fake gagging sound. Birdy laughs and shakes her head before waving her hand towards the kitchen table where we set up breakfast.

Bennett groans before dragging me by the waist to one of the chairs. But before I can separate and sit in my own chair, he pulls me onto his lap and drags my plate next to his. He wraps his arm around my waist to keep me from running.

"Bennett," I laugh, turning to watch him smile before lifting a fork and eating his eggs. I roll my eyes before lifting my own and taking a bite of the eggs and then the bacon.

Birdy and Steve take a seat and begin munching before we're all falling into silence. The only sounds are chewing and drinking noises. The freshly squeezed orange juice is perfect. It's nice having everything fresh. I expect nothing less though from Birdy. She refused to let me buy a carton of orange juice and said I'd have to manually squeeze the oranges she had.

I almost yelled at her before she laughed and pulled out a juicer.

I look around the table and smile, admiring my small friend group. Birdy and Steve keep making eyes at each other and Bennett's hand keeps sliding down my waist and onto my bare thigh where my dress hitches up.

For the party, I decided on a blue dress with tiny red flowers on it and then wore white sandals. I wanted to keep on theme with the Fourth, but wanted to make it my own way without having clothing with the flag on it. Birdy is wearing a white bandana in her hair to keep it back from baking and a red dress with blue flats.

Steve is matching her with a blue button-up shirt and some khaki slacks. Bennett's hand travels even further up my thigh underneath my dress and I hitch my breath, attempting to focus on the food in front of me. His fingers hook around the waist-band of my thong and I shift my thighs on his lap. This causes him to make a sound as I feel his boner growing underneath me.

I've never felt this much *attraction* to someone before. We've been like this for the past few days, where we get so close to almost doing it. We keep teasing each other like this and then he'll either finger me or eat me out until I see stars. But I want more.

With Steve and Birdy this close by, I focus on finishing my plate before I tap his arm and he slides his hand from under my dress and snickers. I push off from his lap and take my plate and glass of juice. I finish the juice and place everything in the sink. I turn back and see Bennett watching me with darkened eyes. I smile innocently.

"You done?" I ask, pointing to his plate. He nods and hands it to me when I near the table again. Birdy and Steve are deep in a conversation about some ducks they found roaming his property the other day.

I take this time to walk to the sink and place Bennett's things in there. I lean over the counter, letting my dress hike up my thighs and leave little to no imagination for Bennett as I play with the curtain that's high above me near the window. I finally get it completely open before I stand back on my heels. I turn around and see Bennett clutching his thigh with his fingers and I look at his knuckles, they're almost white. Birdy and Steve finally look up from their spot and Birdy laughs.

"You okay, Bennett?"

He nods and breathes out heavily. "Yeah, I just felt a kink in my back from throwing the wood."

I watch him avert his eyes from me to his friends. Steve shakes his head. "I told you, you gotta lift them by your *legs,* not your back. You're gonna break something."

I throw my hand in front of my mouth and can't help but giggle. Bennett turns his gaze back towards me and shakes his head, a smile turning up at the corners of his lips.

He's totally going to get me back for that.

I hope.

IT'S a few hours later and Birdy and I have all the desserts and baked goods ready to pick and eat. We decorated the entire kitchen with food and outside tables that have the grilled items for Steve. He brought his own grill since Birdy didn't have one.

He and Bennett were busy the rest of the morning as they prepped the grill. They were still wearing the same clothes they wore from this morning and Steve's face still had some flour from when Birdy playfully slapped his cheek.

Birdy let me know the first group of people would arrive soon as we set up the inside of the place for people in case they get too hot and need to cool down. It's about two in the afternoon when the guys come inside to change to get ready for the party.

Parker and Mabel are already here with his aunt, and I was able to meet her. She's the sweetest woman, and I was able to let her know how helpful her nephew has been this spring and the start of summer with the vineyard.

I'm in the kitchen washing some leftover dishes from our baking chaos this morning, looking out the window. Steve's in Birdy's bathroom, showering while Bennett is still outside. He's talking up a storm with Birdy, who is laughing like I've never seen her before.

She nudges Bennett with her elbow before heading towards the many coolers we set up outside. She grabs a few beers and pops one open before handing him one. He raises his and clinks it with hers. I smile and resume cleaning the dishes until I hear the door that faces the backyard open a few minutes later. I shut the water off before I feel hands wrap around my waist.

I shiver and gasp before I feel Bennett's lips press along my neck.

"I thought you were outside tending to the grill?" I laugh.

He shakes his head and waits for me to dry my hands before he turns me around. His blue eyes are bright and I can see different shades in his iris. I run my hands up his arms, and he bites his lip, closing his eyes momentarily.

"What?" I chuckle.

He curses under his breath before he steps back and takes me by the hand, rushing us through Birdy's house. She didn't have time to give me a grand tour of the place yet, but I have a feeling I'm about to see a room really soon with Bennett.

I let a few laughs escape my lips as he continues down the long hallway before opening a door to our right and pulling me along. Once we're inside, I notice it's the laundry room. There's a washer and dryer to our right and then a folding table to the left. The walls are lined with shelves with laundry necessities and pictures. Some of Birdy when she was younger and some of just random places and things she must've taken and printed out to frame.

"You were such a tease this morning," he finally breathes out as he pulls me close and twists me enough so my back is hitting the folding table's edge. I gasp before he closes his lips on mine.

I moan into the kiss and lift my arms, sliding my fingers through his long locks as he runs his hands all over me. My heart races and my core tightens, wanting him more than ever.

"*Bennett,*" I whine, gliding my tongue along his. He moans before pressing his hips against mine, caging me even more into the table.

"What's wrong?" He teases.

"You know," I breathe out, pulling his hair tightly against his scalp. He hisses before letting my lips go and leaning his head back to look at me.

"Say it then," he challenges.

His eyes search mine, and I pause for a moment, watching him. I want to say *You turn me on and you brought me here to give me my punishment,* but I don't.

Because what I'm seeing in his face at this moment is something else. He's wanting me to tell him something else entirely, and he *hopes* I can read his mind to say just that. His eyes are no longer darkened or devouring me. They're light, wanting to know the actual answer.

Why I'm here with him and how I really feel. He wants to know that I *want* him. Not just sexually, but on every level.

But I want to know him fully before I tell him those three words. Because I deserve to get the Bennett from all stages, and even if that's selfish of me, I won't go on if I don't get that.

I want his past, present, and future. Only if he's willing to give it to me. And it takes both of us to get to that place. I can't ask for it if he's not ready to give it to me. And I'll wait for fucking ever if he makes me. I'll do anything for this man right here in front of me.

His eyes spark up as he watches a smile creep into the corners of my mouth. Until it's plastered wide and I laugh.

"You know what exactly, Bennett. I want you. In every way," I tell him.

I'm on the precipice of telling him I love him, but I want to wait until he's ready to hear those words. He deserves them, but I want his *soul* to be ready to hear those words and *believe* them.

Because I know right now, with how we've been lately and

still talking about his past marriage and getting nowhere with the information, he won't believe me when I tell him I love him.

He needs to believe it in the way I touch him, hold him, and talk to him. Then I can physically say those words where he'll believe them.

A smile surfaces to his lips, and he leans closer, rubbing his nose against mine. He breathes out deeply before kissing my lips. His whole body relaxes against mine and although we're still very horny, I can tell he feels more comfortable and not as high-strung as he was moments ago.

He's starting to believe my words and believe that he deserves the kind of love that can wait for him to be ready to hear those words. And I can't wait to say them to him.

He kisses me again with even more force and I have to push him back a little to take a deep breath before we go at it again.

His hands are still on my waist, but they roam lower until they're under my dress and caressing my thighs. Until his fingers loop around the waistband of my thong and he pulls slightly, causing a whimper to leave my lips.

"Can I?" He asks softly against my lips.

I nod before whispering *yes*.

He moves his fingers to roll the thong down until they're at my knees. He moves one hand to go back over the dress to caress my clothed breasts. He squeezes one nipple against the fabric and I let out a sharp moan before his hand that's at my core lowers until he's cupping my mound and slipping his fingers along my wet folds.

I hiss my breath through my teeth as his thumb finds my clit and begins to draw circles against it. His fingers glide along my folds before one inserts itself. I suck in my breath at the intrusion and he begins to pump his thick finger in and out in slow motions, causing my mind to go into a frenzy.

"Please, faster," I beg in his ear. He drags his tongue along my cheek, down my neck, and then to my collarbone.

He grunts before pumping his finger faster. He then inserts another finger without a moment's notice and I gasp loudly from the feeling. "Oh, fuck," I whine.

My hands are everywhere on him. His hair, his broad shoulders, his large biceps, his toned chest. I need him closer to me and I lift my leg, causing him to leave my nipple with his other hand to grab my thigh and lift it higher, pushing his hip even more against me so I feel the length of his cock.

My eyes roll to the back of my head as he enters a *third* finger and continues the fast pace of thrusting his fingers. It's all so much, and I want to scream out as my core tightens.

"You'll have to be quiet," he murmurs. And before I can do anything, his other hand moves the thong down my ankles and lifts it to my mouth.

"*Open*," he commands and without arguing, I part my lips. He pushes the fabric inside and I'm silenced as he continues thrusting his fingers into me.

Within seconds, the coil snaps and I'm coming all over his finger. But his thumb is relentless, and he's not stopping. My jaw goes slack as an animalistic muffle comes out of my mouth.

I whine through shaky breaths as he leans his head back to watch me carefully with his blue eyes.

"You gonna come for me again? Come on, baby," he coos before I roll my eyes again to the back of my head and then shut them tightly as I feel the orgasm build up again with the way he's thrusting his fingers with even more force.

His fingers are curling inside of me, hitting all the right spots. He lifts my thigh even more to get the right angle, and I'm a mess in his hands. My jaw is sore from how tight I'm clenching my teeth around the fabric. I finally lift my hand to take the thong out and drop it.

"Bennett, please," I beg breathlessly, attempting to push his defined shoulders. I move my hand to his arm that's still controlling my orgasm. He's looking at me as if he's waiting for something else. For me to say something else.

Is this why he's been making me come more than once in one session lately? He wants me to the point where I can't think and my thoughts aren't coherent? Where he can really see that I want him beyond desire. Beyond sexual attraction. Beyond his past mistakes and future ones?

I finally find my voice and try to repeat what I said moments ago, but this time with more passion and power. "Bennett, you have me. You have all of me. And I want all of you. Please."

His eyes finally widen and his blue irises are full of words that I don't need for him to verbalize. He leans in, bringing his lips to mine. I don't last as he circles his thumb along my clit one more time and curls his fingers *one more time* and I'm done for. I'm coming all over his fingers again.

Both of my thighs are shaking uncontrollably and he finally slips his thick fingers out of me, lifting them from under my dress and licking them slowly, making it a show for me. I feel dazed and almost *hypnotized* by the feeling of two orgasms that just ripped through me. I can't focus on anything and my breathing is erratic. My body doesn't know what to do and my legs won't stop shaking. He finally lets my leg fall down and he leans down, wrapping his arms under my knees before picking me up and sitting me on the folding table. He's tall enough where our heads are at the same height as we stare at each other.

He leans his forehead to mine, and we control our breathing, almost making them in sync. He breathes out sharply before lifting his head and I lift mine.

"Bennett," I whisper.

He smiles and shakes his head. "Bunny, I know."

And we stay like that for a few more minutes before we join the party outside.

IT'S MORE people than I imagined. Almost as many people that were at the grand opening of the vineyard. Birdy ushers me around meeting a ton of people before we get to a family.

There's a man with the sides of his hair buzzed and the hair at the top of his head almost like a mohawk. There's a pretty brunette next to him while their three kids are waving to Birdy and she pulls them into a hug before they run off.

"This is my cousin, Lorelai, and her husband, Archie," Birdy says once the kids are gone.

I lift my hand to a wave, but Lorelai laughs and pulls me in for a hug.

"Birdy has told us the sweetest things about you! I'm so happy she's been able to find such a good friend this summer," Lorelai says as we break off from the hug.

Birdy waves her hand and laughs. "Stop, Lorelai. Don't make me sound like a loner. I've been very busy with Gram and Gramp's shop."

"You didn't need to take it over, you know this," Lorelai teases.

"Well, it's the best place in town," I speak up, hoping there won't be any family disagreements today.

But they just laugh it off, so I assume it's something they bicker about constantly. Birdy gives me a smile before Archie raises his hand and shakes it with mine.

"They always forget I'm here. I'm the sheriff of the town, so welcome... but I'm a few months late on that."

I shake my head and laugh, "That's alright! Thank you. This is such a lovely town and I'm so glad I picked it."

"Yeah, it's a funny story," Birdy says before Lorelai gives me a raised brow and I explain to her and her husband how I picked Alpine Ridge out of all places.

They seem to love it, and Lorelai pulls her hand to her chest. "Like it's meant to be." She leans back and places her head against her husband's chest, who kisses the top of her head.

They're cute together and I wonder why I've yet to see them around town.

"Well, that's my family. All three of us, that's what's left of us in Alpine," Birdy says before she pulls me by the elbow and I quickly wave the couple goodbye.

"They're really sweet!" I tell her. She nods before we head to the guys who are throwing a football with Oliver and his family.

Bennett catches the football that Oliver threw before he runs a circle around Steve, laughing before he takes position and throws the perfect spiral back to Oliver.

We watch them for a few more throws before we head to the food table and start piling on our plates. We make it to a farther part of the property where there are hay bales for sitting space and we take a seat, munching on the food and admiring the party.

"You did such a good job. I'm glad I'm here," I tell Birdy as we continue to eat.

She beams from her hay bale and gives me a smile. "Thanks, Camilla. I love doing this every year. It's the best time, honestly. We all wait for it like Christmas."

"Oh, I can't imagine Christmas, though. Or any other holiday! If it's just as amazing as this one…"

She wiggles her brows. "Guess you'll have to see, huh?"

I nod. "You know I'm here for good."

She takes my words and smiles in response. She finishes her burger and takes a sip of her beer before she nods her head towards Steve and Bennett.

"You gotta watch them tonight when they do the fireworks. They go crazy."

I laugh and see the guys continue to play football. "I'll try to stay closer to the house," I tell her.

She nods. "Definitely do that. They say they know how to set up fireworks and Bennett has all this 'experience' and 'knowledge' with pyrotechnics, but he just really just likes things that blow up. He doesn't really care where it lands."

"Maybe I'll go inside the kitchen and watch from a window," I joke. She nods her head, giving me a look that tells me I should do just that.

By the time we finish conversing and hanging out with more people that are there, it's getting late. People who were here from the start of the party are starting to say their goodbyes and letting us know they're heading to the marina to watch the fireworks with their families. That leaves us with just our small group. Mabel, Parker, Birdy, Bennett, Steve, and me.

Izzy stopped by earlier to say hi before she went over to her sister's. It was quick, but it was nice to see her again. I really like Izzy and hope we can still be friends despite my relationship with her ex-brother-in-law.

The guys all start a fire at a different spot on the property and the girls help set up chairs that aren't flammable like the hay bales. They even started to set up the fireworks platform a few yards away and set up the fireworks on top of it.

We're making s'mores while we watch the guys head back. Parker is laughing at something Bennett said and Bennett slaps Parker's shoulder before they head back to us. I pat the chair next to me for Bennett and he takes it, leaning in to kiss my cheek.

"Aww, so cute," Birdy exclaims from across the fire and I shake my head and stick my tongue out to her.

"Marshmallow?" I ask Bennett, pulling my stick from the fire and showing him an almost burnt marshmallow. His kiss distracted me.

"Mm, burnt, my favorite," He jokes as he pulls my hand with the stick and bites the marshmallow off. He chews and I watch slowly, feeling my core tighten at the sight of him. I lick my lips and he winks before I hear screaming.

Steve has a marshmallow on fire and is waving it towards Birdy, who is attempting to get up from her chair to run away.

"Blow the fire! I swear to God, Steve!" She screams. Steve

finally pulls the stick towards him and blows on the completely burnt marshmallow before taking a bite.

I fake a gag and Mabel and Parker yell out, *Ewwww* in unison.

"Maybe we should start the fireworks," I whisper to Bennett and he nods. He gets up and reaches his hand out to Steve.

"Come on buddy, before she throws you into the fire," he tells Steve. Steve laughs it off before he gets up and heads to the fireworks area and they start lighting it. I get my hands over my ears just in time as some start screeching and sparking insanely, shooting up to the sky and exploding in a million different colors.

My eyes are blinded by the colors, but I don't care. It's such a pretty sight with the stars up above us in the sky. I don't get to see as many stars in the city and I love this.

"More!" Mabel calls out and Steve gives her a thumbs up before grabbing some Roman candles that shoot out fireballs wherever it's pointed at. He lights it and starts running around the area, pointing it towards the sky in different directions.

We all scream and clap before he accidentally shoots one too close to Birdy's house. She screams for him to stop, but he doesn't hear it. Another fireball comes out of the roman candle and hits something on the side of the house. It looks like it was a homemade wind chime that is almost three feet tall and hangs at the side of the house. It's all glass with mosaic patterns that were once reflecting the pretty colors of the fireworks, but now shattering all over into millions of pieces.

"Steve Robinson!" Birdy screams, her face full of horror. She stands up from her seat and Parker throws his head back and laughs. But once we see her reaction, he immediately zips his mouth.

"Birdy," I call out, but she's not listening. She runs to assess the damage and I see Bennett still working on some of the fireworks, not hearing the ruckus. Before I know it, another couple of fireworks are blasting into the air and exploding.

"Bennett!" I call out, hoping he can stop so we can console Birdy.

Steve runs to her as she leans over the corner of her house. She pushes him off her and I widen my eyes. She shakes her head at something he says before she heads back to the fire.

Bennett finally heads back to the circle before he sees Birdy's teary, red eyes and he looks at Steve, who is slowly walking back to the circle. Bennett takes his seat next to me and gives me a look, but I just shake my head.

"I'm sorry, Bee," Steve calls out as he finally makes it closer to us. She throws her hand up to stop him as she gathers her things from the chair.

"You knew how important that was for me!"

"Birdy, come on, calm down. I'm sure he didn't mean it," Bennett says, defending his best friend. But Birdy shakes her head and scoffs, throwing her head back.

"Really? You're defending him?"

I look from her and Bennett and he clenches his jaw. "What's your issue?"

"It was her grandparents, I forgot," Steve finally breathes out. Mabel, Parker, and I are quiet as we take in the scene.

Birdy's eyes fill with tears again and the fire in the pit dances across her face, casting an orange glow against her fair skin. Her green eyes lick the flames in the reflection and she furrows her brows.

"He's my best friend," Bennett shrugs next to me. "He didn't mean it."

Birdy laughs again and looks from Steve to Bennett. "You guys just forget that I was here first, huh?" There's silence before she continues with anger in her voice. "Bennett, you knew *me* first before you fucking left me. Before you ran off with Katherine and left me with *him*."

I know she doesn't mean her tone to be condescending, but Steve's shoulders roll back as he takes in her harsh words. I feel for her at the moment, knowing that it's not fair for Bennett to be defending Steve almost immediately after he destroyed one of her grandparents' decorations. Accident or not.

"Maybe we can—" I start, but Bennett stands up from his chair.

He crosses his arms over his chest, and I crane my neck to look up at him. He's staring daggers at Birdy, who is staring daggers right back. It's like two wild animals ready to fight to the death and I don't want to be in the middle of it. Mabel and Parker continue to stay silent and I peer over at them briefly and see Parker pulling a marshmallow off of Mabel's stick and chewing on it slowly, watching them.

"I'm not taking your shit, Birdy, not tonight," Bennett spits out. He moves his hands again and they're running through his hair before I see his muscles flex and he goes back to having arms crossed over his chest.

"Well, deal with it," Birdy spits out harshly. "You made me tiptoe around your life for long enough. Making me feel like the second best to Steve. *I* was your best friend. And I was always there to talk to you about shit that you couldn't even tell Steve. I was always there despite *all* the shit you put us through."

Steve looks at Bennett then, his brows pinching together. I have no idea what she might be referring to, but then it clicks.

Did Bennett tell Birdy the *whole* truth about his reason for leaving Alpine Ridge and divorcing Katherine meanwhile, he told Steve a different story?

"Fuck off," Bennett finally spits out, shaking his head. He turns on his heel and starts walking away. He stops in his tracks before he turns around and lifts a finger, pointing at Birdy. "Fuck you, Birdy. That was between us."

My jaw goes slack as I watch Bennett's eyes go from anger to *hurt*. There's a slight glaze over his eyes and I can tell it's tears forming. He turns back on his heels and walks faster around the house before he disappears.

The air is thick and quiet as we stay like this. The crackling of the fire is the only thing making noise. Birdy and Steve are still standing while the rest of us are sitting. Mabel and Parker finally stand up, grabbing their chairs.

"Thanks Birdy, for the party. I think it's getting pretty late," Parker says.

She sighs and shakes her head. "You can leave them; I'll grab them in the morning."

Mabel shakes her head. "No, please let us." They fold their chairs before they head to Birdy and give her a small hug. She sniffles and I see some tears fall from her eyes as she hugs Parker.

They head to me and I stand to give them both a long hug. I whisper to Parker to let me know when they're both home safely and he nods before they walk to the side of Birdy's house and place the chairs along the brick siding.

I turn back to Birdy and Steve, but they're both quiet. My feet are dragging me closer to my friend and I lift my arms up and wrap them around Birdy. Despite her not hugging me back, she breathes deeply into the crevice of my neck and her body shudders for a moment.

I rub her back for a moment, my eyes glancing to Steve, who is looking at the ground. He doesn't dare to look at me and that's fine. I don't think it's my place to console him right now. He needs to talk to Birdy and they really need to figure this out.

Birdy and I separate from the hug, and she lifts her fingers to wipe her tears quickly.

"Want me to put the rest of the chairs away?" I ask her, but she shakes her head.

"No, it's okay."

Birdy then gives me a smile before turning and walking away

from Steve and I. She heads to the backdoor and pulls it open, walking inside her house. Steve and I are left here.

"Well, I don't hear Bennett's truck, so he's still here or else I'd offer you a ride home," Steve finally speaks up.

I nod my head. "Want to go find her and I clean up?" I offer.

He shakes his head. "No, she needs time. I think it's best if I do that. I fucked up, but that was just… *wow*."

I nod my head again and pat his shoulder before I turn on my heel and head to the house and round the corner to the front where the cars are parked.

Bennett's car isn't on, but he's inside it. I can see the outline of his head through the back window and I head towards the passenger side. I knock on the glass and he jumps in his seat before he turns to find me.

He gives me a small smile before unlocking the door and leaning over, pushing the door open for me. I pull it and hop inside. The air feels even more thick in here and I know he's been lost in his thoughts.

We're silent for a while. I know nothing I say will help him right now. Silence is sometimes the best thing to give someone after a blow up like that.

Bennett finally takes a deep breath before leaning his head back on the headrest and exhaling sharply.

He bangs his hands against the steering wheel. His hands grip it, knuckles turning white. The moon casts its light over us brightly and I can see every feature of Bennett. His eyes are blazing as he turns his head to look at me. Peering down at me, full of sorrow and emotion. I turn my body to face him, bringing my knees up to the seat and holding it with my hand.

He finally breathes out again and closes his eyes. "Sorry, that was just out of my control."

"It's—" I stop myself. It wasn't okay for him to say those things, but it wasn't okay for Birdy either. They seemed to hold in those feelings for a while and finally found the time to say them. Bad timing, but they were able to express themselves.

Bennett chuckles slowly before sliding his hands over the steering wheel, his grip loosening. "Birdy and I were the best of friends. Childhood friends. Everyone thought we'd get together or something. But we were like brother and sister."

I take a deep breath, not wanting to say anything and cause Bennett to shut down and not continue. I'm finally getting to hear his side of things.

He looks off into the distance in front of him.

"We both grew up in Alpine. Our parents were best friends. We all went to the same school as Steve, but we had different classes. Then high school hit. We were still super tight knit, but then Steve and I were on the football team. We became best buds. We were all in the same chemistry class when I got paired up with Katherine. Birdy and I were *never* not together for projects or sitting next to each other in classes. Or it would be me and Steve. But this one class had a seating chart. I got close with Katherine and felt things I never did with Birdy. Infatuation and that high school boy hormone shit they tell you about. I distanced myself from her and Steve. They got closer because I pushed them away. Katherine was jealous that I was so close with Birdy and gave me an ultimatum."

He looks at me finally, and I stay quiet. He continues as he moves his eyes over my face before going back to what's in front of him.

"I left for college and chose the school Katherine would go to instead of the one Birdy and I dreamed of since we were kids. I knew that was a low blow, but I was so in love. Katherine and I didn't care about *anyone*. We were in our own bubble. Just us. Then we graduated from college and got married at 21. We stayed in Alpine and bought a house. I forgot about Birdy and Steve for a while until we kept bumping into them in town. They tried to hang out with me, but Katherine's jealousy was still pretty present. I knew it had faded for a little while since we were in college and I had to convince her she married *me*. I didn't choose Birdy over her. But she still didn't care.

"That's when I couldn't stand Alpine and the people in it. Steve told me about army recruits coming to Alpine to talk to the high schoolers, so I looked them up. I decided that this was my way out. So I took it. I enlisted in the Army first before deciding that the Marines were better for me. I loved the time away because I didn't have to think about the people I left. Katherine and I planned to have kids before I enlisted, but she kept pushing me to wait. So I went off on my tours and every time I came back, she'd find another excuse why we couldn't start a family. It got to a point where I enjoyed being *away* from her. I finally told her that and that's when she told me she was ready, but only if I came home and left the military entirely. It had become a part of me. But I wanted to please her. So I left and then…"

His words falter and his voice cracks. I suck in my breath and lean over, lifting my hand to rest it gently on his arm. He looks at me with tears in his eyes before he looks away.

"I did all of that for her to just tell me she never wanted kids. This was after we met Morgan and spent time with her, as Andy and Peyton took care of the vineyard. We were like her second parents. I thought she wanted kids because she was so good with Morgan. But it was all a lie. She made me go along with things based on her own timeline because she was selfish. The moment I heard her say those words, *I never wanted kids. I just wanted you*, I had to get out. I packed my shit, found a private contract that would take me, and was on the next plane to South America.

"I didn't let her explain herself anymore. She tried calling me for weeks and then it turned to months where I ended up staying in another country. Birdy and Steve would try to call too, but our friendships weren't the same anymore. I didn't even know what they were up to. I finally came back a year later and Katherine begged me to stay with her and work it out. She begged me and said she was finally ready for kids. But I wasn't the same *me* anymore. All of that hatred she brought out of me just made me resent her and the idea of making a family with her. I didn't want kids anymore, and I had Morgan. She was the next best thing to a kid I'd ever have. This time it was me who gave Katherine an ultimatum. A divorce or move out of Alpine. It was harsh, I know. But I was so angry. *Pissed.* She, of course, didn't want to leave the town she grew up in and I couldn't force someone to leave their hometown. So I left. I left her with divorce papers and took another contract. This continued for a while before she finally signed the papers and we sold the house. I came back different that last time.

"Steve and Birdy found out about the divorce and tried for five years to piece me back together, but I wasn't the same. Birdy knew I was a different man than she grew up with. I gave her all my shit, and she still stayed despite it all. She heard the truth from me first before I gave Steve pieces of it. I didn't know what to do. When my parents passed, I took over the farm. I had plenty of money from those contracts to retire and not think about finding a job, so it was perfect. I could stay on the farm for the rest of my days. My sister, Riley, wanted nothing to do with this town after she saw it tear me apart. I wanted her out, too. I didn't want her to have to see me like that. People you love shouldn't endure you at your worst when that's all you give them. And that's all I gave Birdy and Steve for years."

Tears are streaming down his cheeks, and he wipes them quickly, sniffling and taking a deep breath. I furrow my brows and my heart pulls for him. I rub my hand on his arms and he finally drops his hands from the wheel. He turns his body to face me and he closes his eyes. I inch my body closer until my hip is pressed against the center console.

"It's not your fault," I breathe out.

He shakes his head. "It was. Everything was my fault."

"*No*, it wasn't," I say firmly. He opens his eyes and studies me. "You did your best and what your heart wanted. Until you gave too much of it away and couldn't get enough of it back."

His brows pinch, and he takes a deep breath, exhaling a shaky one. "I don't think they ever forgave me. I think they just put up with me for the sake of it."

I know he's referring to Birdy and Steve and probably the rest of the town that knew Bennett before he came back scarred and broken. But being broken doesn't mean you're worthless. It just means you've endured what life threw at you and still survived, despite it all.

"It wasn't your fault," I repeat. "Especially when it came to your marriage. You were given cards you couldn't deal with. It was unfair of her to do that to you. But you guys are okay now, right? I see you guys acting civil."

He shrugs. "Doesn't make it okay, what we had for twelve years. And that was just the married part. A chunk of my life was devoted to her and then another chunk was devoted to resenting her."

"I think that was completely justified, don't you?"

He looks at me again, and his eyes are shining. He nods slowly.

"You thought you were living a life with a woman who promised you the world. Someone who promised you the dreams you had for your life. And when she twisted her words, they hurt you. Badly. It wasn't fair of her to do that to you. Making you wait for years until she was ready and then basically pulling the rug from under you and telling you she didn't want that. And then to come back and say she was ready for it? That wasn't right. It was manipulative and I can't imagine the pain you went through when you heard that from someone you deeply loved."

"Everyone thinks I ran away," he blurts out.

I lean over and lift my hands to cup his face. I stare at him. "You didn't run away, Bennett Moore. You were put in a position that no person should be in. There are ultimatums that shouldn't have been given in a marriage. *You* were promised a life with a woman that should have been honest with you from the beginning. Because that's all you gave her. Honesty and your entire world. She didn't return it and you had to get out. You didn't *run*, you did what you had to do to survive the circumstances."

"And what about you?" He sniffles, tears forming at his eyes again.

"What about me?" I knit my brows together and cock my head.

"Why haven't *you* run from me yet? I would've if I were you."

I let out a small laugh and lean my head closer to his face. "You've been pretty honest with me the moment we met. Even if it was harsh honesty."

This makes him laugh, and it vibrates through his throat up to where my hands are cupping him. I brush my thumb along his lip.

"I didn't run away, because *I want you*." I take a deep breath and prepare myself for what I've been wanting to tell him for what felt like ages now. "You put up walls and then let them fall before me and it only makes me want you more, Bennett. I want your past and all your mistakes. I want all your current problems and current joys. I want your future ones too. I want you because I love you."

His chest moves up harshly, and he holds his breath. He closes his eyes and I close mine, too. I hear shifting in his seat before I open them again to see him closer.

"Camilla, don't say things you don't mean."

I shake my head. "I mean it. Never going to stop loving you, Bennett Moore."

His eyes are glassy again and he blinks tears away. I wipe them away from his cheeks with my thumbs. He takes a deep breath before leaning until we're nose to nose.

"I'm scared to lose you, Camilla. I don't want to lose you like I've lost other good things in my life."

I shake my head. "You didn't lose any of the good in your life. They're still here in this town and love you just as much as I do. You just need to see that."

He sucks in another breath and closes his eyes. I take this time to kiss his nose and then his cheeks. I kiss away some more tears that fall to his cheeks.

"I want you in my life forever, Camilla. I love you," He finally whispers.

And just like that, those words leave his lips and it's like the world has come back to a balance. The shift in the air is prominent and I feel almost *dizzy*.

It's like I can *feel* Bennett Moore's scarred and shattered heart start to mend back together piece by piece.

TWENTY-SIX

BENNETT

MY HEART FEELS like it's mending piece by piece as we stare at each other. After talking in my car for over an hour, we're finally back at my place. We started off on my couch, but Bunny insisted we head to the bedroom in case we fell asleep.

But my mind and body were too wired to sleep. We just confessed our love to each other and I couldn't sleep from the excitement.

I needed to have her.

And it definitely got me a little nervous to have her in my place. In my bedroom and this much closer to my tiny bubble. But with the way she kept looking at me tonight on the couch and biting her lip, I knew my worries were just in my head.

Once we make it to the bedroom, she sits on the edge, running her hands through her hair and taking a deep breath. I'm momentarily staring at her from the doorway, leaning on the frame. I can't take my eyes off her, knowing that this beautiful woman before me has the same feelings I've harbored for so long about her.

"You're looking at me again with that face," she speaks up, her voice soft and almost inaudible.

I grin and lift my body off the door frame before walking towards her slowly. I catch her soft, brown eyes watching me as I get closer and reach my hand out to touch her cheek. She closes her eyes briefly, taking a sharp inhale.

Her exhale is shaky and I can't lie because my breathing is the same way. I take this time to kneel on the ground slowly, fitting my legs and torso in between her thighs. The dress she's still wearing from earlier hikes up her legs, and I move my hands to grasp her thighs.

My fingers press deeply into her skin, indentations forming, and a slight moan escapes her lips. I look up at her and we're face to face at this angle.

"Please," she whispers so softly I have to lean in and almost don't catch it.

"Please what?" I ask, wanting to hear it from her lips.

Her brown eyes run along my body until they reach my eyes. Her lips pull into a small smile.

"Love me," she finally says.

I take no time as the words fall from her lips. I brush my hands along her thighs, hiking her dress even further up. She lifts her hands to touch my shoulders before wrapping her fingers around my neck, attempting to pull me closer, and I let her.

Our lips touch and the world flips upside down. My troubles and worries collide with her hope and light. It's like nothing can touch me. Nothing can hurt me anymore.

One of her hands moves from my neck to grasp my jaw and then runs through my hair. She grasps the strands of hair and tugs, causing a moan to slip out of my mouth, and pain shoots through my scalp.

"You can get up and on the bed," she says breathlessly through another series of kisses and moans.

I shake my head. "I was kneeling, ready to worship you tonight."

She giggles and shakes her head as well. "Bennett Moore, you have forever for that. I want you right now."

I pull back to see her brown eyes shine with golden embers, and I'm hypnotized. I'd do anything for these eyes and the owner.

"Yes, ma'am," I whisper before pushing myself off my knees and standing up, lifting my hands to my shirt.

"No," She stops me. I stare down at her and she's already beckoning me closer. I take a big breath before I close our distance. She has to crane her neck to look at me, but her hands find mine at the top of my shirt. I drop my hands and let her unbutton my shirt, letting the shirt fall from my arms and body. It falls carelessly to the floor.

Her eyes study my chest for a moment, lingering on the big scar that drags along my collarbone. And then traveling between each pec, my ribs, and then my stomach, studying the various tattoos and scars that litter my body. But her eyes don't stay too long. They move back towards my face and a small smile fills her face.

I exhale sharply, wondering what she's thinking. If she thinks I'm still damaged and wants to rewind time. Take back all the words she said earlier tonight.

But she doesn't say or do anything. She continues to watch me before she waits for me to continue. So, I do. I lean down, trapping her within my bubble, and she leans back, wrapping her arms around my neck. I grab her from under her thighs and lift her up further onto the bed. She giggles before she drops her head on the mattress. Now, I'm hovering over her and watching her eyes dance all over me.

My hands linger from her thighs and slowly move up towards the dress and underneath it. My fingers hook under the waistband of the thong and she nods her head, giving me permission.

I slowly drag my fingers down, taking the thong with me as I reach her knees. I finally slip it over her ankles and let it join my shirt on the floor.

She exhales loudly and I chuckle, moving my hands back towards her thighs and closer to her core. Her body moves strongly with each breath she takes. It's a magnificent sight to see.

I shift my body enough to face her bottom half and she immediately runs both hands to my head. She grasps firmly, anticipating what I'll do next. I lean down, littering kisses along her inner thighs. She attempts to squeeze them together, but I put more pressure on them, keeping them separated.

"*Oh*," she exclaims from above. I continue to kiss her thighs before I lift my chin along her hips and then her core. Her knees are hitting my sides as she attempts to squeeze them again.

I drag my tongue along her pussy finally, letting my tongue do the work along her folds and clit. She arches her back and squeals before I laugh and lick her folds again. She's wet already and I suck on her clit, causing her to shift in her spot again.

My hands press firmly on her thighs, and she exhales loudly.

Before she can do or say anything, I move my right hand and glide a finger through her wet folds.

"Oh, God," she whimpers. There's silence and then another moan as I insert a thick finger into her.

I take no time to attach my tongue to her clit again as I pump my finger in and out of her. She's getting more wet and with the way her body keeps jolting, I know she's close to her orgasm.

Her walls beg to clench around my finger just as much as she's begging to clench her knees closed. Her fingers along my scalp are tight and I'm positive she's about to tear out a few strands.

Before she can come, I pull my finger out of her. She yelps from the movement and I lift my head just enough to see her face lift from the mattress. Her brows are knitted together, and I can see some beads of sweat along her forehead. She's still beautiful, and she's staring daggers at me.

"Bennett, that's no—"

"Relax, Bunny," I tease, inserting my finger again and watching her eyes roll to the back of her head. I pump my finger again into her before adding a second finger. Her hands move to the side of the mattress, grasping around the sheets tightly.

I move my head back down, licking her clit again, and her back arches again. Her moaning fills my ears, and it causes me to rub my boner against the mattress. My fingers are pumping faster into her and she finally snaps, screaming, before I feel the rush of her orgasms along my fingers. I pull them out and lick them, making sure she's watching as she looks up.

Her eyes are dazed and I can tell she's almost back to the state of ecstasy where all she sees is me and all she feels is pleasure.

That's all I want from her. I don't care about myself. Just seeing her like this is worth it.

But she doesn't let me stay in this moment. She smiles before reaching her hands out.

"Please, come over here," she whispers.

I nod before lifting myself up and moving my hands to the belt around my jeans. I unbuckle it slowly, watching her lick her lips. My heart thuds harshly against my chest as I pull the belt out of the loops of the jeans and drop it to the floor. I then push myself off the bed, unbuttoning my jeans and pulling them down. I step out of them before lifting my head to see her watching.

This is the part where usually insecurity and self-consciousness floods my vision, but for some reason it doesn't come. Her eyes glaze over me and she bites her lip. She's still wearing the dress on the top half of her body.

"Take your dress off," I tell her. She nods before shifting her body enough to grab the fabric of her dress and pulling it over her head.

I take this time to hook my own fingers on the waistband of my boxers and pull them down. My cock springs out, and it's strained and throbbing with wanting release.

I spit in my hand and wrap it around my cock as I watch her throw the dress to the floor on the other side of the bed. My hand pumps around my cock slowly, pre-cum dripping off my fingers. I close my eyes for a moment, relishing in this moment of us in my bedroom.

"Bennett," she says softly, breaking me out of my thoughts. She waits patiently, wiggling her fingers for me to join her on the bed.

I take a deep breath before my knees are back on the bed and one hand moves to keep myself hovered over her. She moves her legs to wrap around my thighs and she bites her lip, looking down at me, still pumping my cock slowly.

I let my eyes roam her body, leaning down and kissing her stomach and then her breasts. My tongue swirls along one nipple before I move onto the next. She moans again, wrapping her arms around my neck to bring me closer up. I let my cock go to steady both hands near her shoulders.

My cock rubs against her inner thigh and we both pause, taking a deep breath.

"Camilla," I breathe out, watching her arch her back from the contact.

"Yes, Bennett, yes," she mutters out before I can even ask her if she's fine with this. "I'm on birth control, so *please* have your way with me. We're safe."

I nod my head and let one hand travel down back to my cock and I guide my tip to her core. She shudders from the contact and I do too as my tip glides along her folds.

"Fuck," she whispers before I push into her. Inch by inch, I enter her slowly. I know I won't last long with how amazing she feels.

"Fuck, you feel so good," I breathe out, leaning down and pressing my forehead against the crevice of her neck. Her legs wrap tighter around my waist and I moan out an animalistic sound as I continue to seat myself inside her.

She whimpers from the feeling as I stretch her more and *more*. I finally lifted my head to catch her eyes. But they're closed.

I kiss her lips softly and she flutters her eyes open.

"Am I hurting you?"

She shakes her head and laughs. "No, it's just been a while. It feels amazing though."

I shift my hips to pull my cock out of her slowly and she shivers, closing her eyes again. I smile as she opens them and then I take this moment to watch her as I *slam* my hips back, causing my cock to thrust fully into her once again.

"Oh!" She yelps, clenching her eyes tightly as I do the motion again.

I chuckle before she wraps her arms around my neck tightly and moves closer to my scalp, pulling on my hair.

"You like it?" I whisper in her ear, and she nods her head quickly.

"Yea-" She starts, but I thrust again forcibly into her and her moans take over any words that were left in her mouth.

One of her hands moves from my hair and glide slowly along my neck and then to my shoulders. Her nails scrape along my skin and it stings, but it's a pleasurable feeling.

"More," she whimpers, and I take no time to pull myself out of her completely. She yelps again from the sudden loss before I slam my cock back into her.

The bed shakes from the movements, and our moans are loud, filling the room. Filling the house.

No one can hear us for miles and I fucking love it. We

continue to kiss and our tongues fight one another as I continue to thrust into her. Our hands are all over each other, never lingering on one part for too long.

We're not just exploring each other sexually, but physically, too.

There's a point where her fingers graze over the healed skin from my long scar and I shudder, but she lifts her lips to litter kisses along the length of it.

And with just that touch, those kisses, I feel like I am completely bare. She really holds the key to my past, present, and now future.

"Camilla," I breathe out, pulling myself out of her for a moment. She lifts her brown eyes to watch as she keeps her hand over my chest, right over the scar.

"Is everything okay?" She whispers, her eyes widening. But I shake my head and move a hand to caress her jaw and then her chin, letting my thumb rub her lip.

"I love you," I say.

She smiles before moving her other hand to caress my jaw as well. "I love you, Bennett Moore."

I smile and we're both naked on my bed looking like complete idiots in love, but I don't care. Because, for once in my life, everything seems to be okay, and it's all because of her.

I lean down and kiss her, letting myself fall into her atmosphere. She glides her tongue alongside mine and we both moan into each other's mouths. I insert myself back into her and let my cock pump in and out of her.

I increase my speed and she whimpers, holding tighter to my chest. Her fingers dig into my pec and I hold on to her hips tighter.

Her back arches once more as her knees squeeze against my hips and she momentarily pulls from the kiss to moan loudly. I take this time to thrust even faster into her, feeling my release on the border.

"Come for me, Camilla," I murmur and she nods, clenching her eyes tightly as her body shakes and she comes all over my cock.

"Where do you want me?" I whisper, knowing I'm too close and will need to release somewhere.

She finally looks at me with satiation in her eyes and smiles. "I'm safe."

That's all I need to know before I keep thrusting, finally feeling my release spill into her and we hold on to each other as our bodies fall onto the mattress. I keep one arm lifted on the mattress to keep myself from crushing her, but she pulls me and lets me rest my head on her chest.

I finally pull myself out of her and she moans again, squeezing me from the feeling.

Her arms are on my back, caressing me softly. My arms go to her side and it's like we can't stop touching each other. I still want to be closer to her. It's never enough.

"That was amazing," she breathes out finally.

I lift my head and kiss her chin before kissing her lips as she looks at me.

"I wasn't too bad?" I joke, watching her brows furrow and a smile spreading across her face.

"You were perfect," She says.

And I feel perfect. I always do with her.

TWENTY-SEVEN

CAMILLA

I FLUTTER MY EYES OPEN, taking in the soft sunlight, attempting to filter through the dark, drawn curtains to my right. My body is warm and there's another heat source that's not from the sheets draped over me.

I groan and move my arms, flipping over to my left to see Bennett sleeping soundly. I can't help but smile at the sight. He's so handsome and his chest moves slowly through his breathing.

My arm drapes over his chest, my palm smoothing over his abs before moving up to his chest and then over towards his collarbone. The healed scar is thick and even more detailed the closer I am to it. I don't dare to touch the actual scar while he's sleeping. I don't know how comfortable he'd be with it. He seemed to be really self-conscious of it last night.

It took everything in me not to ask how he got it, but it's not my business and if he wants to tell me, then he will. If he never does, then that's his choice. I don't know the specific things he's been through while in the Marines or during contract missions. It's up to him to tell me what happened, if he ever does so. I let myself continue to stare at it before averting my eyes to his face.

I let my palm reach over to his chin and let my fingers caress his jaw.

His lips quiver from the touch and I continue to drag my fingers along his chin and jaw, letting my thumb run over his bottom lip.

His eyes flutter open and he looks up at the ceiling before reaching his hand over and grasping my wrist, but not tightly. He turns his head to find me staring, and a small smile forms at his lips.

"How long have you been staring at me?" He mutters, his voice deep and husky from just waking up.

I bite my lip and keep my eyes on him.

"A whole hour," I joke.

He moves my wrist towards his chest, holding it there with his hand. I can feel his heartbeat through his chest and it's beating fast. He blinks a few times and takes a few breaths before laughing.

"I'm surprised I didn't talk in my sleep," he whispers.

He's no longer looking at me, but at the ceiling while he finishes his sentence. I furrow my brows and watch his forehead scrunch in thought. He then turns his head to stare at me again.

"You didn't," I whisper. He smiles, dimples showing, before leaning closer and kissing my nose.

I move my hand that's held by his and wrap it around his neck to pull him closer. He cranes his neck before his lips meet my neck and then my jaw and then the corners of my mouth.

My chest moves rapidly as I feel my core tighten and flutter. He wraps his hand that was once on my wrist around my waist that's covered with the sheets. His fingers trace the outline of my waist and then hips before they reach the outside of my thighs. I close my eyes briefly, letting his fingers do the talking as they caress the outline of my body.

His palm reaches the curve of my ass before he squeezes his fingers around it, causing me to open my eyes and widen them.

He squeezes again and I giggle, pushing him away by his shoulder. He doesn't budge and moves himself closer until we're a breath away.

My eyes meet his chin, so I have to crane my neck to look at him. That's when he moves his hips and I feel his boner hit my hip underneath the sheets. I gasp before lifting my eyes towards him. He has a mischievous smile plastered on his face and it brings even more flutters to my stomach.

"What?" He asks in a low voice.

I shake my head and move my hip to rub against his boner and he intakes a sharp breath. He bites his lip before he moves his palm from my ass to the top of the sheets and moves his hand underneath it as his bare hand caresses my shoulder and travels down the valley of my breasts. I intake a sharp breath as his fingers follow an imaginary line from my chest to my stomach.

"Bennett," I murmured, my breath catching. He chuckles before letting his hand continue to glide lower and lower.

"May I?" He whispers and I nod my head before saying yes.

But I have another idea. He's yet to let me pleasure *him*.

"May I?" I ask him this time and his brow raises before he nods his head.

I smile. "I need your words, Bennett."

"Y-yes," he stutters out, eyes widening. I laugh as I adjust my hand underneath the sheets to touch his shoulders before gliding them down his own chest.

That's until I reach his core, and he closes his eyes. His breathing quickens at the slightest touch. I let my hand continue to glide farther down until I can wrap my hand around his cock. It's hard and the moment I let my hand move up and down in one motion, he bucks his hips forward and a groan slips from his lips.

He opens his eyes and bites his lip. "Please, Camilla."

I nod before flicking my thumb over the tip of his cock, feeling the slickness of his pre-cum. I don't want to hurt him while I give him a handjob, so I lift my other hand to push his chest.

"Get on your back," I tell him.

"Yes, ma'am," he laughs before adjusting his position so he's on his back. I shift until I'm on my knees and the sheets fall off our bodies, laying in a bundle near his legs. I move myself and lean my head to face his throbbing cock.

I keep my hand wrapped around his length before moving my lips down and licking his tip. He moans before moving his hand to grip my hair.

"Is this fine?" He asks, rushed.

"Of course," I tell him before I lick his tip again and then wrap my lips around it. I move my mouth and tongue until they're mostly around his cock. My hand pumps up and down before I add in my tongue's motions.

His thighs go tense from the movement and I grab one with my free hand. His grip tightens on my scalp and pushes me slowly and deeper onto his cock, causing my hand to move away.

His cock pulses in my mouth and I drag my tongue underneath, over the plump vein. He moans at this and I feel my heart quicken at the sounds of his pleasure. He continues to move my head at his pace and I let him, moving my tongue all over his cock, all over the tip, and continually letting him push himself deeper into my throat.

He hits the back of my throat and I halt, adjusting my breathing.

"S-Sorry," he murmurs. "You just feel so fucking good."

I can't respond to him, but I squeeze my fingers on his thighs for him to continue, and he takes this as a hint. He moves my head again and I take the time to hold my breath before I'm able to come up for air again.

I continue this for a few seconds before he moans louder and I know he's closer to his orgasm. I allow myself enough time to take a deep breath before I move my mouth faster around him. His grip tightens even more on my scalp, bringing tears to my eyes. But it's a pain that I'm getting accustomed to and ultimately loving.

"Fuck, I'm going to come," he breathes out before I pick up my speed.

He lifts his hips with my movements before he moans and a grunt leaves his lips before I feel warm liquid shoot at the back of my throat.

It's unexpected, so I attempt to swallow it as best as I can before I lift my lips off of him. His grip on my scalp loosens and eventually moves off my head.

"Fuck, Camilla," he whispers as I lick my lips and he lifts his hands to his eyes, rubbing them.

I move myself to straddle his waist just above his cock. He moves his hands and smiles, looking at me from below.

"It's my turn," I tell him, moving my hips over his waist. He clasps my hips tightly, his fingers making imprints on my skin.

"Do you want me to help prepare you?" He asks, raising a brow, but I shake my head.

"I think I'm pretty prepared for you. That kind of turned me on. I won't lie," I say sheepishly. I bite my lip and he smiles even wider, nodding his head.

I lift my legs, balancing on my knees just enough to back up and align myself with his still hard cock. I grab it to position it perfectly, allowing myself to take a deep breath before I push myself onto him slowly.

He hisses under his breath, and he clenches my thighs tightly. I continue to lower myself until he's stretched me out and is fully seated in me.

I take a deep breath and let my body get used to the feeling of him filling me up in ways I've never felt before. Last night was incredible, but this angle is hitting *all* the right spots.

I move my hips slowly in circular motions, and we both gasp

at the feeling. Moving my hips makes my clit rub against him and it shoots sparks through my body. I can already feel myself closer to coming with just that contact.

"Fuck, do it slowly," he whispers as he grips my thighs even harder. I moan before moving my hips again in a slower motion, causing pleasure to fill us both. He breathes deeply and I can see beads of sweat at the top of his forehead. The nape of my neck is sweaty too and I'm sure it'll just dribble down the length of my back. But I don't care.

I move my hips again, letting myself circle around his cock and letting him hit all the spots again that causes moans to come out of my mouth. He's biting his lips before he leans his head back, shutting his eyes closed.

I move a little faster and this causes a ripple of moans to leave both of us and we're left breathless.

"Please," he begs, moving his hands from my hips to slide down the length of my legs before I lean closer, resting my palms on his chest. This angle puts even more pressure on my clit and I shake from the feeling. A shiver runs down the length of my spine as well.

He moves his hands to grab my wrists tightly, keeping me at this angle.

"Move," he demands through gritted teeth and I obey, moving my hips again at a quicker pace. I feel myself drip all over him.

"I'm so close," I whine before he lifts his hips to match my movements and I squeal, feeling his cock hit an even deeper spot I didn't know was possible.

He bites his lips before moving his hands from my wrists to grip my ass and moving my body with his in a quicker motion. I collapse onto him from the movement and let him take over, moving my hips right where he's making me with his hands.

He continues to lift his hips in just the right time before I feel my core tighten, my eyes shut tightly, my moans filling the room before the coil snaps.

I come all over his cock as he continues to move my ass and then hips over his cock.

"Fuck, I'm going to come," he breathes out.

"Please," I whisper, lifting my head just enough to press my lips against his. We melt into the kiss before I feel his hips and mine clash even quicker, and then I feel another load of his orgasm fill me. It's warm, and he keeps himself inside me as he finishes our kiss.

I clench myself around him and he shudders.

"*Don't* do that. You're going to make me come again."

I giggle and clench myself again before he grips my hips tightly, and I squeal from the pressure. He raises a brow before smiling.

"I always said you were dangerous, Bunny. Didn't think it'd be in this sense, too."

I smile before kissing him again.

IT'S a little after nine in the morning as we eat breakfast in his kitchen. We both showered, and I borrowed some of his clothes as we made our way out of the bedroom. He cooked us eggs and some bacon and I helped set the table with plates and glasses full of water.

I look around the kitchen and smile. It feels homey and feels like *Bennett*. I glance at the fridge and notice a small white board with small text on it. My eyes scan the text and notice it's a board to mark an amount of 'x' days that he's been able to wake up on the right side of the bed. I flutter my eyes towards him and he is chomping on a piece of bacon before noticing my staring.

"What are you looking at, pretty girl?" He smiles.

I nod my head towards the fridge before getting up, abandoning my plate. Bennett is silent as his eyes stay on me. I walk barefoot towards the fridge, lifting my hands towards the white board and grabbing the small marker fastened at the top of it. I uncap it and make a tally.

I turn around and bite my lip, surveying Bennett as he witnesses what I've done. He raises a brow before they pinch together. At first, he looks angry and then he looks confused.

I place the marker back in its spot before making my way towards him. He's wearing a fresh pair of jeans and a dark green shirt. He scoots his chair back enough for me to sit on his lap. I wrap my arm around his neck before nuzzling my head in his clean hair. He wraps his arms around me and he exhales.

"I was witness to that, so you can't tell me the tally is wrong," I tell him before I lift my head and watch his eyes.

They search mine before he smiles softly. I lean down and kiss him, pulling him closer by the neck. He tightens his grip around my waist and we both melt into the kiss like always.

"Don't make me throw you on the table," he whispers, leaning in for another kiss and opening my mouth with his tongue. I moan and close my eyes, moving my hands to his scalp and threading my fingers through his hair. He groans before moving one of his hands to run along my waist before dropping to my thighs. I'm wearing one of his shirts and boxers, so he runs his hand underneath the fabric of his boxers.

I shiver and already feel my body responding so well to his touch.

"Please," I whisper, biting my lip and moving my hips to slowly grind on his lap.

His jaw clenches as his blue eyes search my face.

"Stand up," he says softly. I nod and get off his lap, but he keeps his hands lingering on my waist as I face him.

"Turn around," he adds. So I turn around, finding myself facing the kitchen table now.

"Bend over the table," he says as I hear his chair scrape back. I gulp and lift my hands to push his plate and my plate away and bend down, letting my upper body lean against the table. I steady myself with my elbows.

I hear his belt unbuckling and then the sound of a zipper being undone.

His hands finally reach my waist and I jump from the sudden contact. He chuckles under his breath as he wraps his fingers around the waistband of the boxers I'm wearing and pulls them down. I shimmy my hips so they fall down to my ankles on the floor.

His hands run over my back and then the curve of my ass. He slaps it and I squeal, jutting forward on the table. I turn and crane my neck to look back at him and he's spitting in his hand before wrapping his hand over his already hardened cock. I take a deep breath and turn my head back as I hear him step closer.

I jump again as I feel his cock tease between my folds and then my clit. He continues to rub it up and down and I moan, leaning my head down further until my forehead is touching the table.

"Please, Bennett," I whine, feeling his cock run over me again and I shiver more from the feeling. I'm getting more and more wet for him and then I feel his tip push against my entrance.

We both suck in a breath and I lift my head as he sinks himself into me. His grip tightens on my waist as he guides himself more and more into me. He stretches me again once more and I moan at the feeling.

"Always so *tight*," he mutters before thrusting into me fully. My whole body gets jolted forward and my hips painfully push against the table's edges. I cry out a moan and he pulls himself out just enough before he *slams* himself into me again.

"Fuck," he moans out before he continues the thrusting and I continue to moan and feel myself get closer to my climax.

My hands move to grab the table as best as I can, but then I feel his hands move from my waist to my hands and pull them behind my body, enclosing them together.

"Bennett!" I whine, forming my hands into fists as he continues to hold my wrists tightly and thrusting into me even faster. He pulls my wrists, causing my back to arch and the new angle differs from where he's pushing into me.

I cry out another moan and I feel tears spring to my eyes, but it feels so *good*.

"Don't stop," I moan and he grunts back a response as he thrusts into me more and more before we're both shaking uncontrollably.

It's not too long until I feel my climax come and my legs shake and I clench around his cock tightly and then feel my orgasm make its way. He moans before thrusting a few more times through my orgasm and then I feel the warm feeling of his release in me.

He leans over, breathing heavily and letting my wrists go. I lean against the kitchen table, defeated, and he kisses my back before moving up and kissing my neck. He moves my hair and I crane my head to the side and he kisses my cheek. He's still inside of me and I clench around him.

He groans. "I told you not to do that or else."

"Hmm," I laugh.

He shifts his hand to my ass and slaps it again and I squeal underneath him, moving my hips, but it causes his cock to grow hard again inside me. I groan and I shake my head.

"We're never going to leave this house," I say before he groans as well and rests his head on my back.

"If you have any plans today, you might as well cancel them," he says before he lifts his head and grips my waist, pulling out of me and then thrusting into me again.

I cry out and bite down hard on my lip. I'm overstimulated, but my body is craving him like no other. My body wants another orgasm and I can't deny him one.

Bennett's grip tightens on me before he thrusts into me again, and I let out a sharp breath before arching my back and letting him hit that spot again.

We go at it for a few more thrusts before we're both a sweaty puddle and satiated.

We'll definitely need another shower before we leave his house. But I don't care.

WE'RE MAKING our way towards Oliver's office while Bennett's got his hand resting on my thigh. As we reach the street, we try to find a parking spot.

I was able to finally get home and change into more comfortable clothes. We couldn't keep our hands off each other though and might've had sex again on *my* bed this time.

We couldn't help ourselves. It's like we're horny rabbits and need as many orgasms as we can now that we've felt how great they are. And I don't mind.

He shuts off the truck, and I slip off my seat belt. Before I can reach my hands to the door handle, he's unbuckling his own seat belt, hopping out of the truck, and running towards my side after shutting his door.

He opens it swiftly for me and I smile, taking his outstretched hand and hopping out of the truck. We walk hand in hand towards the office before we're inside.

Oliver comes walking into the lobby and smiles at us as we sit and wait in the nice chairs I remember sitting on when I first moved here.

I momentarily take a breath, remembering that day and how much my life has changed since.

"Bennett! Camilla! So glad to see you guys! You can follow me to my office," he beckons us over and we both stand, keeping our hands laced together as we follow him towards his office.

Bennett squeezes my hand as we sit on the two chairs in front of Oliver's desk. He takes his own seat at the desk as he flips through a folder.

"I gave her a brief rundown of what you told me," Bennett starts, turning his head towards me and I nod my head as Oliver watches us.

He smiles and nods. "Yeah, I wanted to give the people of this town the chance to take the land before the investor made a fantastic deal. It's a good one, by the way. I met with him a few days ago."

Bennett and I look at each other before looking back at Oliver.

Bennett let me know on the ride here that Oliver wanted one of us to take the land in between us before the investor either used the land to build a mansion or a couple, or even a strip of developed houses like the Westland Homes nearby.

I didn't mind what happened to it, but I knew it was important to Bennett and why he wanted me to know what was going on before meeting up with Oliver. It seemed important to him, so I want to do whatever I can to help him.

Whatever was important to Bennett felt important to me too, and I wanted him to have the final say on it. I'd support him whether he ultimately decided he wanted the investor to take the land.

Money wasn't an issue, we already discussed the possibility. I still have funds saved, as well as the profit from the vineyard that's been doing way better than I projected. Bennett also said he's got some savings that he'd pool together if needed and if we took the land together.

My chest tightens at the thought that we'd purchase the land *together*. It felt like we were moving fast, but it's already July and I've been here since the end of April. It feels longer.

"I'm here for whatever Bennett wants," I finally speak up. Oliver nods and smiles before averting his gaze towards his friend. Bennett adjusts himself in his seat before sighing and leaning back. He lifts his hand to rub his jaw and then his chin.

He looks over to me before turning back towards Oliver. "I think I want us to take it. Find something else to do with it. Or eventually sell it to another local."

"Maybe Parker and Mabel will want it when they finish college," I joke. Bennett laughs and nods his head.

"Yeah, that'll be my worst nightmare, having that Parker kid in between us."

"And Mabel," Oliver and I say in unison. We look at each other before we laugh.

Bennett rolls his eyes and chuckles. "And Mabel," he chimes in.

Oliver claps his hand before lifting some papers out of the folder and waves them towards us.

"Well, I got the papers to sign off on the property and then I can get with a lender or your bank to finalize the payment."

Bennett and I nod, standing up from our seats. We head to Oliver's desk and he pulls out a pen from a small cup on his desk and hands it to me. I bite my lip and look up at Bennett, who seems nervous.

"You don't have to do this, it's asking a lot of you," Bennett breathes out.

I shake my head and grasp the pen in my hand. "I want to. Plus, if Parker doesn't want it then we'll just have more land for your animals or my vineyard."

Bennett smiles and nods before I turn my attention towards the papers and sign where Oliver points me towards. We flip through a few more pages before Oliver shifts the papers towards Bennett and I hand him the pen. He takes it slowly and signs the same places I did.

Oliver flips the papers over and then puts them in the folder and stands straight. He reaches his hand over for a handshake. I give him a shake and so does Bennett.

"Proud to know the new owners of the land," Oliver says with a smile. "I'm kind of relieved I didn't have to sell it to the investors."

Bennett laughs next to me before wrapping one arm around my waist and pulling towards his side. He kisses the top of my head, and I smile, nuzzling my head into his shoulder.

"Guess it's time to show Lushie her new land," he says.

"Lushie?" I ask, craning my head up towards Bennett.

Oliver laughs and I turn my gaze towards him. "Lushie is his cow. And it's not that fast of processing the payment. Remember, Bennett, I gotta get the payment."

"I know, I know, Ollie," he laughs.

Oliver waves us off as we turn and make our way out of his office. Once we're back outside onto the street, we face each other and Bennett's grinning. Like full on *grinning*.

"What?" I ask, laughing.

He wraps his arms around me and lifts me up. I squeal and wrap my arms around his neck quickly to steady myself. He leans in closer and presses his lips to mine.

"I love you," he whispers.

I kiss him again and smile. "I love you more, Bennett Moore."

TWENTY-EIGHT

BENNETT

I FEEL like I'm on cloud nine.

It's been two weeks since the Fourth weekend and I can't keep a smile off my face. It's shocking not only to Steve and Oliver, but to *myself*. That tally on the whiteboard? Yeah, it's in the double digits now.

Never happened before in my life. It's all thanks to Bunny.

It's nearing August and business has been booming for her. We got the money approved for the land between us and for now we're planning to upkeep it until we can think of something.

I'd love for either someone in town to take it off our hands, merge our lands with it, or even wait it out and build a house for Morgan to have. I'd love for her to live here in Alpine with me, but I know Peyton is nowhere near ready for that.

As much as I know Morgan would stay here for the upcoming summers, I'd love for her to have a place to actually live whenever she comes of age. A house to call her own right by her Uncle BenBen.

I even talked about it with Bunny and she said that was the best idea for the land and actually started looking up contractors to set up the foundation and start building within the next year or two.

Right when she said she'd love for us to build something for Morgan, I felt like I couldn't breathe. Like all the air escaped from my lungs and I didn't know how to breathe properly.

I've never had someone put this much effort into me *willingly*.

There's no more secrets, walls, or worries between us now that we've been able to talk about it all the past few weeks. We're finally able to enjoy the time together.

And I won't lie. Hearing her agree with the whole idea of Morgan and the land made me want to run into town, find the next best thing to a diamond ring and give it to her.

But I had to calm myself down and know that we're still getting to know each other. I like us being able to go at our own pace. Morgan is a huge part of my life, and Bunny having no issues with it makes me love her even more.

It's early Saturday morning and I've got my bags packed for an overnight trip to Nashville. It was spontaneous, but Bunny wanted to plan an entire weekend since we had tickets to the baseball game that I won at the fair. I just thought we could do a day trip to the game and then come back really late.

Bunny wanted to stay overnight since she's never been to Nashville and I couldn't say no to her. I could never say no to my girl.

We rented a cute house, and I couldn't wait to get there.

I made sure I locked all of my doors in the house and checked one last time in the pasture to make sure all the animals were good before I left. Steve let me know he'd take care of them while I was gone.

Even though they could perfectly graze the grass in the pasture, I always make sure the water in their troughs is cold and clean every other day, as well as making sure they get the needed nutrients for dinner that they can't get with grass.

It felt like I was leaving my children behind as I stumbled into my truck and drove away. I can see a few of the horses amble towards the perimeter of the pasture, following the sight of my truck as I drive off the property.

There are still things I need to patch up with Birdy and Steve, but I'm not looking forward to it. I've only reached out to Steve this week, and it's been surface level talk and he agreed to watch over my land without hesitation.

I plan to talk to him when I get back from the trip and think it'll help me think of what to say while away from this town.

I've gotten so used to running away from people or problems when it inconveniences me and right now, it feels like I'm doing that. But I'm just not ready to reach out to them to talk about it all, so I'm grateful Steve offered to watch my land with no added pressure of talking about the Fourth weekend.

Birdy hasn't reached out to me and I've barely gone around town near her shop to bump into her. Living in a small town means that we'd bump into each other eventually... but it's yet to happen. It's like we're both purposely avoiding each other.

And I know it's for a good reason. We said nasty things to each other. I hope that she and Steve could talk about what happened and patch things up. They've been through thick and thin and although it was my fault it happened, I'm glad they had each other for it and got close because of it.

They're perfect for each other and I hope they see it.

Once I'm on Misty Creek Road, I turn right and make my way to the vineyard. It hasn't opened yet, so I used the pin pad at Bunny's personal gate and it opened, allowing me to enter. I drive up towards her place and I see her closing her own door and locking it, a small cream-colored duffle bag strapped over her shoulder as she turns around and runs down the steps.

A big smile is on her face as she reaches the truck while I put it in park and unbuckle my seat belt and jump out, walking towards her side of the truck. She shifts on the balls of her feet and then her heels as she watches me get closer.

She's wearing cute bell-bottom jeans and a simple black crop top with some sequins running along the collarbone of the fabric. Her hair is even more curly than I remember and it's falling down her shoulders. Her brown eyes are bright under the sun that's already burning us this early.

"Hi," she giggles as I get closer and wrap my arms around her, breathing in her scent and nuzzling my head into her neck and hair.

"Hi," I breathe out, squeezing her with my hands. She squeals and giggles again as she tries to escape my bear hug, but I'm stronger.

"Bennett! You're crushing me!" She laughs until I finally let her pull away to see her face. Her cheeks are slowly growing with rosiness and I kiss her nose before kissing her lips.

She relaxes into it, and we stay like this for a little before we pull apart.

"You ready?" I ask, pulling on the strap of the duffle bag that's over her shoulder.

She nods before letting me take the bag and heading to the back of the truck and opening the door, throwing it on the seat. I shut the door and open the passenger one for her.

"Thank you, sir," she giggles as she hops into the truck. I wait for her to get settled into her seat before I shut the door and make my way back into the truck.

She's running her hands through her hair by the time I strap myself in and we're ready to go.

"Excited?" I ask her, watching her slowly. A smile spreads across her face and it's contagious because I'm smiling from ear to ear as well.

She nods. "So ready. I've never been!"

"You've been to a baseball game, though, right?" I ask, raising a brow.

She rolls her eyes and laughs. "Yes! Chicago Cubs, baby! I almost brought my ball cap."

I shake my head and laugh. "They would kick you out."

She widens her eyes and bites her lip. "Really?"

"No, I'm just messing with you," I say with a wink.

Her cheeks reddened, and she nodded before settling back into her seat. I backed the truck up and finally headed out of her property.

It's not a long drive before we're out of Alpine. We stopped shortly for some gas and some snacks. She gets a bag of peach rings and some Slim Jims. I asked her if she wanted to get some proper breakfast somewhere fast, but she was too excited to get to the city.

I definitely stole a Slim Jim from her.

The drive to Nashville is about three or four hours depending on traffic, but since we left really early, we miss all the traffic in any of the passing cities.

We talk about everything. Our favorite music, food, places to travel, and guilty pleasures. We even played 'I spy' when we hit hour two and couldn't think of anything else to talk about. That's when we passed by a sign on hour three that said we were 30 miles from Nashville.

Bunny's face was glued to the window as we neared the city. We could see the skyline from the highway entering Nashville.

"Woah, it's smaller than Chicago, but I love it," she says as we continue on with the drive.

The Cumberland River is long and I follow it on the highway, making our way just outside of downtown.

"We'll go there tonight after the game. That's where the game is anyway," I promise her.

Bunny turns back to look at me and I avert my gaze for a moment to look at her before going back to the road. Although I'm a pretty good driver, the drivers in a big city are a completely different playing field. People are driving as if they have places to go, even though it's not even noon yet.

"Really? Where are we staying again?"

I turn my signal on and nod my head towards the exit. "Still in the city, but a different part. It's a quieter neighborhood, but with tons of places to walk to and sightsee."

"I can't wait," she says before we finish the drive and make our way towards the driveway of the small rental property I could find on a whim.

The house is a gorgeous white, one-story with its own porch. It has a nice front yard with a black iron fence wrapping around it. The door is a nice mahogany and by the time I park and we get to the door; we see that there's a lock box attached to the doorknob for the keys.

I have to check my email for check-in directions before we finally get the key out and stumble into the home. It's pretty inside too, and Bunny checks every room as I grab our things from the truck. I see other people walking around the neighborhood and it partially reminds me of Alpine, but bigger.

There aren't any homes here that have more than an acre of land unless it's a mansion. You'd have to go into the next city over if you wanted more than an acre. I didn't know a lot of people from Alpine that wanted the big, city life and moved to Nashville. A lot of us loved the open space and small-town feel.

"You coming?" Bunny asks from the porch and I smile, pulling myself back into the moment and heading her way.

"Just checking the area out," I tell her.

She smiles as she lifts a hand and reaches for her duffle that's strapped to my shoulder, but I step back.

"What? That's my bag! I'm not making you do all the work."

"Get used to it, Bunny," I tell her, watching her eyes sparkle and her smile grow.

"Okay," she says before stepping aside and letting me in. I

wait for Bunny to get inside before I shut and lock the door. I head to the main bedroom and she follows me in, watching as I place the duffle bags onto the bed.

"It's a nice place," she speaks up behind me.

I look around the room. It's a king-size bed with a nice wooden bed frame and matching headboard. The side tables are the same wooden color as the dresser in front of the bed. The home definitely has a theme going on with the same wood. A lot of the appliances are white with gold fixtures.

"It's fancy," I tell her, chewing on my lip.

"I love it!" She exclaims, getting closer and reaching for my hands. I let her grab them and she squeezed them tightly.

"It's a few steps above my place. Not up to par with your place though... Those Stones had the best interior designer in Tennessee help them with it."

She rolls her eyes and laughs. "This place is nice for where we are, Bennett! Don't worry too much about it."

"I just want everything to be perfect for you."

She furrows her brows before releasing my hands and lifting hers to grasp my jaw on both sides. Her thumb caresses my cheek and I lean into the touch.

"Anything with you is automatically perfect."

"You're just saying that," I say.

She shakes her head. "Nope. I'm telling the truth. And even if you don't want to believe it, I'm never gonna stop saying it."

I take a deep breath and exhale loudly, finally nodding.

"Okay, fine," I say.

She smiles and shifts on her tiptoes and kisses me. "Now, let's go explore the area. What time is the game?"

I wait for her to step back before I pull out my wallet and take out the tickets she gave me this morning to keep. They have indents from the fold in the wallet, but they still look good. I read the time.

"Six is when doors open. Seven: the game starts. Should be done by eight-thirty or nine."

She nods and spins on her heel, heading for the door. "Then we got tons of time to be tourists. Your worst nightmare."

I can't help but laugh and follow her, attempting to grab her, but she's fast and yelps as she runs through the hallway in the house.

"Tourists aren't that bad!" I yell before snatching her waist as we get to the living room.

She's laughing and I pull her back close to my chest. I lift one of my hands to tickle her and she screams.

"No! Bennett, don't you dare!"

I try to tickle her some more, but she bends down and tries to push me back with her hips. I finally let her go and she steps away, her chest moving rapidly as she catches her breath.

"No more tickling. That's not fair," she giggles.

"I would say that you can try to tickle me back as payback, but I'm pretty good at dodging your small moves."

She pinches her brows together and scrunches her nose before shaking her head. "I know I wouldn't even be able to tickle you before you grabbed my wrists. You're too strong for me."

I laugh before closing our distance, pushing her back onto the couch. She looks up from underneath her lashes and I lift my hand to brush her chin.

"I'd let you win one day," I tell her, giving her a wink.

"Oh, wow. So nice, Bennett Moore," she teases.

I lean down and kiss her again. "Just one time," I joke.

She pulls me with her arms wrapped around my neck to deepen the kiss. I can feel my body fire up for her and I moan into the kiss. She giggles before moving her hand to my chest and pushing me away.

"*That* was payback."

I crane my head back and groan. "Don't deny me that, please."

"I will if I have to. So, no more tickling and then you'll be fine," she points her finger at me, her face attempting to turn serious. I raise a brow and she finally cracks, laughing. I join her and grab her hand and pull her to my chest.

"No more, I promise."

She examines my face before smiling. "Something tells me you're just saying that now, but I'll need to watch my back."

I shrug. "I keep my promises, don't I?"

She looks at me again before nodding. "You do. Now, let's get some actual food."

"Yes, ma'am."

THE NEIGHBORHOOD we're staying in for the night is called 12th South since that's the street where a ton of the shops and restaurants are. There's even a celebrity's clothing shop. Bunny and I walked in just to check it out, but the moment we saw a white shirt for $75, we walked right out.

We even passed by the alleyway that has a mural of the Nashville flag and the lettering of "I believe in Nashville". I asked a stranger to take a picture of us. We then passed another mural full of flowers and took a pic of Bunny in front of it and immediately made it my phone's wallpaper.

There's a taco restaurant on that same strip, so we stopped by for lunch. It was crowded, but it was so good. We got a handful of tacos to try and tons of appetizers. Bunny enjoyed it so much she said we should get it for brunch tomorrow before we left Nashville. I told her I'd do whatever she wanted to do this weekend.

By the time we're done with lunch, we're walking down the rest of the strip of 12th south and we pass by the familiar truck we once saw weeks ago in Alpine. Bunny and I turn to each other and we speed walk towards the truck.

"Hi! Welcome to Amelia's Flower Truck!" A woman in front calls to us as we get closer. There aren't any other customers here, so we take our time.

"Should we get another bouquet?" Bunny asks, as we look at the choices. They're a different selection of flowers from last time.

"We have tons of sunflowers that were picked this morning!" The woman says, pointing towards the metal container that holds the sunflowers. I look at Bunny, who is nibbling on her lip in deep thought.

I look at the woman and pull out my wallet. "We'll take a bouquet of that."

Bunny turns to me with widened eyes. "Are you sure?"

I nod. "Of course. I love sunflowers. We have tons of 'em at the farm."

"Oh, sweet! You guys live on a farm? Where at?" The woman asks as she makes the bouquet and pulls sunflowers from the tin.

I'm about to correct her that *I'm* the one who lives on a farm and Bunny lives on a vineyard, but Bunny beats me to it and doesn't correct her.

"Yeah, we do. In Alpine Ridge! It's a few hours south of here."

The woman nods as she ties the bouquet up around the brown paper with some twine. "I think we started going there this summer! It's a beautiful town."

We nod and Bunny answers her with a laugh. "That's where I first found you guys." She then turns to me and smiles. "It was one of our first official dates."

The woman smiles and looks at us both. "That's the sweetest thing to hear! I'm so happy for y'all."

"Thanks," I laugh as Bunny nods.

The woman finishes up the bouquet and hands it to Bunny, and I pay for it. She gives us her card in case she's the one to go to Alpine Ridge next. We head towards the rest of the strip, hand in hand, while Bunny is smelling the sunflowers.

"They smell so good. Thank you," she says as we get closer to other shops.

"Of course," I tell her, squeezing her hand that's in mine.

We're nearing what looks like a sweets place. Not a bakery, but an ice cream shop. We look up at the sign and it reads:

Pear's Paletas

"Ooh! A paleta shop!" Bunny squeals as we get closer.

"You might have to remind me what that means…"

She looks at me before pointing at one picture plastered on the window that shows a popsicle. "Basically a popsicle. Some make it with water as the base and others make it with milk! My favorite is the fresas con crema, which is just creamy strawberries—like a milkshake."

"Sounds delicious. Wanna go in?" I ask. She nods and we make our way to the golden glass door and open it, chimes sounding above us.

It's bright inside with white walls and pink detailing. There's even a wall in the back that's painted completely pink. Tons of pictures of the menu items litter the walls and some awards that are framed, including a feature in a Nashville Magazine. It's a very feminine take on a paleta shop, albeit never having one in Alpine Ridge to go to, but I think it makes it stand out even more. Bunny looks like she loves it.

A young girl is at the counter waiting for us and waves us over as we continue to walk in. There's a small walkway next to a line of tables and chairs and then to our right are all the glass cases of ice creams and paletas to choose from.

"Hi! Welcome to Pear's. How can I help you today?" The young girl watches us with bright brown eyes. I turn to Bunny to let her take over.

She smiles and waves. "I've never seen such a pretty paleta store before."

The young girl smiles. "Thanks! It's my sister's. This is our second location. I just graduated from college down here and got my business degree and thought, why not help her expand? People love it so far!"

I point to the framed magazine article feature. "Yeah, that's amazing that you guys got featured."

She nods and smiles. "Pear cried for a week after she finished that interview. She even has a frame up in her house."

"Well, you must be a proud sister," Bunny says as we scan the choices.

"I am. She's great. Have you guys heard of Mason Pointe? That's where she started the first shop and where I'm from."

Bunny and I look at each other and smile. We both nod at the girl. I'm the one to speak up this time. "Yeah, I'm from Alpine Ridge. Camilla, my girlfriend, moved down there a couple of months ago. She had her first taste of the Fourth of July weekend with Mason Pointe."

The girl widens her eyes and looks at Bunny. She leans over the glass case with her elbows. "Wow! Small world!! How do you like it? Wasn't it great? I miss that weekend and just being with so many people!"

Bunny laughs. "Yeah, it was pretty great! Got to see the rodeo and everything."

The girl's eyes widen even more and a smile plasters over her face.

"Please tell me you got to see our very own Courtland Hayes." She swoons and closes her eyes for a moment.

We both laugh and Bunny shrugs.

"Yeah, he's okay, I guess. I got my own country man right here." She reaches for my arm and loops hers around it.

My heart thuds against my chest quickly, and I look down at

her. She cranes her neck up and gets on her tiptoes to kiss my cheek.

"Aww! You guys are so adorable," the girl says, looking at me.

I give her a smile. "He was great, as always. I barely get out to Mason Pointe anymore. I didn't know he still did that."

She nods. "Always will. It's like his life. My sister gives me all the deets whenever I call her. If you're ever in town, tell her you met me here. My name's Nina!"

"Nice to meet you. We'll definitely go there now that we know the sister of the owner!" Bunny tells her enthusiastically.

Nina gives us a smile before walking us down the glass cases and giving us recommendations on what to try based on what we're craving. By the end of the small tour, Bunny settled for her favorite, fresa con crema, and I settled for a mango paleta with some spiced seasoning called Tajin. I did not know what it was until Bunny and Nina explained to me it's mainly used on fruits with lime.

Once we pay, we thank Nina for the tour and the time to walk us around the shop and then head back outside. We spend the next two hours finishing our paletas while walking and making a loop around the shops and restaurants. We even found one where they sell custom made cowboy boots.

Bunny insisted on stopping by and getting one. I let her know that we have a place much cheaper back home, but she wanted it to be custom made.

Once she was done talking with the owner of the boot shop, they were able to find her the perfect one and even add on some details. It ended up being a brown based boot with caramel and golden stitching details all over with some stars stitched out. There was one star on each boot that was dazzled in red fake diamonds—Bunny's request.

It reminded me of those jeans she wore with the red stars patched on the back pockets. I loved them and I love these boots.

I'm hoping the next time she wears those jeans, she can wear these cowboy boots with them.

We headed back to the rental property an hour before the gates to the baseball game opened, so we took our time to rest and change into different outfits. Since it was the middle of July, the sun has been boiling and even just walking the streets and shopping made us a sweaty puddle. It was nice to get back to an air-conditioned house before venturing out again tonight.

By the time we're ready, I have a car already pulled up waiting for us through a rideshare app I never heard of. Alpine is too small and everyone has a car there to need this kind of taxi service, but apparently it's a big thing in cities like Nashville.

Plus, I wanted to enjoy the night with Bunny and not drive if I was drinking some beer at the game and then wherever we ended up tonight.

We get into the car and it's a simple fifteen minute drive from the house to the stadium. There are tons of people already milling around, ready for the game to start. The gates are open and we can hear the chatter of all the people getting to the stadium.

"Woah, so many people," Bunny says next to me as we get out and head to the gates.

I grab her hand and pull out our tickets from my back pocket, handing it to the employee working the ticket gates. They scan it and we enter, looking around the stadium. It's not as huge as some stadiums like the Major League Baseball ones, since Nashville just has a Minor League Baseball team. We can see the field from where we enter the gates and there's a guitar-shaped scoreboard.

Bunny pulls on my hand and I turn to see her point towards a concession stand and a cocktail bar. I smile and nod, letting her guide me towards them. We buy some hotdogs and then some beer for me and a Frosé for her at the bar. Once we get into our seats, people are surrounding us and they're all chatting.

It seems more like a hangout spot for people as a lot aren't paying attention once the game starts. Tons are roaming about the stadium and even more are still at the bar watching the game from there.

Once the players take the field and we all clap and root for them, they start the first inning and Bunny and I get to eating our food. The game is fast, as the Nashville team gets a ton of runs and even a few home runs from their best player.

For the seventh inning stretch, they play the well-known song, '*Take Me Out to the Ballgame*'. We use this time to get some more snacks. Bunny ends up showing me she sneaked in the rest of her peach rings from this morning's drive, so we munch on that too.

We're back at our seats with more Frosé and beer when the anthem ends and they start playing more advertisements and even promotions on the scoreboards all around. That's when they show some stats of the baseball players.

"Oh! That's the one that did all those runs!" Bunny screams, slapping my shoulder to get my attention.

I turn to look at the screen and sure enough, it's the player. I haven't done my research to know everyone on this team since Nashville is pretty new to the baseball world.

"He's probably gonna win them tonight," I tell her as I steal another peach ring from the bag on her lap. She turns to look at me right when I pop it in my mouth.

Her eyes widen, and she laughs, leaning closer. "Bennett! You already ate half the bag today. Leave some for me!"

I shake my head and reach for another one and she lets me, all the while giggling. Her brown eyes are bright and the setting summer sun is beautiful against her face and skin. Her body is literally glowing under the sun, and I can't help but keep staring.

"What? Do I have something in my teeth?" She asks, running her tongue over the top of her teeth.

"No," I shake my head. "You're just beautiful tonight. Well, you're always beautiful, but tonight you're glowing under the sunset."

Her cheeks grow red as she takes in my words. "Thanks, Bennett."

I nod and lean in for a kiss and she closes the distance. Once we separate, the scoreboards are going on with more stats about the baseball players before the game continues.

We settle back into our seats as the team continues to get runs and plays defense really well against the other team.

By the ninth inning, the other team gets super close in score to the Nashville team and we're all at the edge of our seats. But once our team is up next to bat, we know we've got it in the bag.

"Is he gonna hit next?" Bunny asks me a couple minutes later, wrapping her fingers around my elbow in anticipation. I nod my head as we watch our outstanding player pull up to the diamond with his bat.

His name is Warren Holt, and he's been on the team since they started here in Nashville. That's at least what I can remember from the promos earlier.

He's swinging his bat, getting ready for the pitch as the crowd goes wild. They've got two strikes already and have bases fully loaded.

If he makes a hit, he'll make a home run… no, a *grand slam*. And the spokesperson over the speaker is explaining how it's yet to be done with the Nashville team. Not only would it bring him more recognition, it'd bring so much recognition for the Nash-ville team.

Bunny grasps my elbow tighter and we all wait as the pitcher throws the curveball and Warren misses just by a shy inch. We all *aww* in unison before he gets ready for the next throw.

His team players on the other bases are getting antsy and looking like they want to make a run for it to home plate, but Warren keeps shaking his head 'no' at them. The pitcher throws another fastball, and it almost hits Warren and he has to dodge just in time.

We all scream at the pitcher, and Bunny is standing in her seat, yelling at the pitcher. I have to pull her back down to her seat as the rest of the crowd follows suit. She smiles and looks at me, and I can't help but beam at her enthusiasm.

Finally, the pitcher is throwing the last ball. If Warren doesn't make this, then the other team gets to make redemption hits to win and we won't get another chance until our defense is superb.

The pitcher throws the ball and we all hold our breath as it inches towards Warren. He slowly takes position and swings his bat.

The whole stadium is quiet, waiting for that sound and, *boy,* do we hear it. The bat hitting the ball makes a cracking sound that echoes throughout the stadium, and we're all standing now to watch the ball fly.

At first we're unsure if it'll just go to left field and fall, but it goes further and *further.* The other players in third and second base are running home while the first base player and Warren are running their fastest. But it's no use. Because the ball flies out of the park and Warren Holt just hit their very first grand slam.

The crowd is cheering and Bunny is jumping up and down screaming while I whistle with my fingers and then clap.

There are fireworks as Warren Holt runs on home base and the team all rushes to crowd him and celebrate. The other team walks back to their bleachers while the rest of us keep screaming in the stands.

"That was amazing!" Bunny screams, grabbing my arms and continuing to jump.

I laugh as I watch her spin around and the girls behind us are cheering as well and lift their hands for a high five. We all high five each other.

The crowd doesn't settle, and the team is out on the field,

taking pictures and still celebrating. It finally dies down after a few minutes and people stand to leave.

We're grabbing all of our things and heading out of the stands and into the main area of the stadium before we leave the gates.

"You have fun?" I ask her as we pass a trash can and I throw away our wrappers and plastic cups. She nods and skips in her steps.

"I had the best time. I didn't know Nashville got down like that! It's nothing like Chicago. We have a complete song to sing when we win, but it's close enough!"

I bring her close and wrap her in my arms and kiss the top of her head. She giggles before I let her go, but keeps my arm wrapped around her shoulder. She wraps her own arm around my back as we walk towards the parking lot where the ride share cars wait. I pull out my phone and open the app to request one.

"We need to come back for another game."

I nod. "Whatever you want, I'm fine with."

"Okay, but did you have fun?" She asks, looking up. I look down at her and smile.

"Yeah, I actually did. It's been a while since I really enjoyed a time out like that."

"It's nothing like Alpine Ridge and Nicky's bar, huh?"

I shake my head.

"Not even close. Even though I prefer the smaller settings, this was really fun to experience."

She hugs me tighter and we make it to the waiting area and my phone chimes to let me know our car is here.

"Wanna go downtown?" I ask her.

She nods her head. Her eyes cast down at her outfit. She's wearing a cute, frilly white tank top with denim shorts and wore her cowboy boots. They fit her perfectly and I made sure she wore some bandaids on her heels and thick socks to break them in comfortably while we're out.

"I'm so down. That game gave me a ton of energy. I think I need to dance it out."

I laugh and grab her hand, pulling her close for a kiss. The driver beeps at us and we laugh as we walk to it and get inside. I tell the driver where we want to go and he plugs in the address for a random bar downtown and we're off.

TWENTY-NINE

CAMILLA

DOWNTOWN NASHVILLE IS MUCH MORE crowded than I expected. The streets are full of people walking around in done up outfits. We've already passed by five bachelorette parties walking down the main street called Broadway. There are tons of rooftop bars as well as clubs lining the street and it's loud and chaotic.

I'm pulling Bennett by the hand as we march our way through the crowds on the streets and finding a bar to get into. Even with the many people out, we're able to move swiftly in the line and get in once we get our IDs checked.

"I didn't know this many country artists have their own bars!" I scream to Bennett as we get into one by an artist I've heard on the radio a few times.

Bennett nods and pulls me through the front entrance of the bar and deeper towards the counter to order. It's packed like sardines and I'm already feeling hot and sweaty. There's a live band playing on a stage—that's something I'm not used to in Chicago. We don't have a strip of bars and clubs with live music at *every* one. It's chaotic on the streets while you pass by them hearing rock music and then the next is country.

Country music is playing and we make it to the bar counter where Bennett orders for us, leaning over the counter and yelling into the bartender's ear. I watch from my place, admiring the way his jaw moves with his words and how his eyes furrow with his expressions. I then let my eyes roam his features.

His arm is resting on the rounded countertop edge and his muscles are flexing not just in his biceps, but his forearm as well. He moves his eyes for a moment to catch me looking and gives me a wink before returning to the bartender.

My stomach flutters with the wink and I lean against the countertop as well. Once he's done with the bartender who starts working on our drinks, Bennett inches closer to me and lands his eyes on me.

"Hey, pretty girl," he smiles brightly.

My cheeks are hot as I smile. "Hey, yourself. I'm glad we're here."

He raises a brow. "Really? Thought you'd get bored. It's not Chicago for sure."

I shake my head and laugh. "No, but it's different. I like it."

We have to get closer to talk to hear each other over the live band across the bar. Bennett's arm brushes against mine and I have to steady my breathing from the contact. It's silly how much his touch still affects me even now.

It feels like we've known each other forever and he's still able to make my body react this way.

"All right, here are your drinks!" The bartender breaks my thoughts as he sets a seltzer for me and a beer bottle for Bennett. He hands the bartender cash and tells him to keep the change. The bartender smiles brightly and nods before moving onto the next customer.

"Ready?" Bennett asks, motioning his head towards the staircase at the end of the bar. I turn to look and see that more and more people are flooding the place as the night gets closer and they're all headed to the stairs. I presume it's what takes them to the rooftops.

I nod my head at Bennett, and he leads the way until we reach the staircase. He lets me go first and keeps a hand on my waist as we walk up the steps. We have to dodge a few drunk people stumbling down the steps from the rooftop, but we make it in one piece in a few minutes.

What was once country music from a live band turns into club music once we reach the top of the staircase. We are met with the open space that connects the huge rooftop to the club.

I turn to Bennett and he nods towards the rooftop and I nod, grabbing his hand that was on my waist and bringing us towards the rooftop. The music is still loud, but it's not as sticky and humid as it is in the club.

There are tons of patio chairs, couches, and tables out here where people are mingling. We walk and hang out by the railing near a table. Just a block away is the huge skyscraper they call the 'Batman' since there's two gigantic structures pointing up at the top to resemble Batman's mask.

"It's so busy out there," Bennett murmurs as we both lean on the railing and admire the city. It's loud and we can see people walking towards other bars from here. We can even see the line getting longer at this current bar we're at.

"I can't believe all these bars have rooftops," I notice, nodding towards the other bars on this street where we can see all the other people on rooftops drinking and partying.

"That's Nashville for you," Bennett says as he takes a swig of his beer. He watches me and gives me a wink. I smile before taking a long sip of my seltzer. It's mango and super yummy.

"Have you been here a lot?" I ask him.

He shakes his head. "Not much. Few years ago when I was with Katherine. But we didn't go out and party like the people here do all the time."

"I can't imagine. I'm such a lightweight I hate wasting my Sundays hungover."

He laughs. "Yeah, you've got to have a ton of energy and not be a lightweight to be here all the time."

"Maybe you're just old," I joke.

He raises a brow before nudging his elbow with mine. "You like me even if I am."

I roll my eyes and giggle. "Oh? Is that so, grandpa?"

We both stare at each other and then laugh.

"Nope, that doesn't sound attractive," Bennett chuckles.

I shake my head as well. "Nope. I regretted it the moment it left my mouth."

We continue sipping our drinks and making casual conversation as the city parties all around us. It's nice to just be here out in the open with the sultry summer air and a cold drink. Being in a city like this is so nice. It's alive and I've kind of missed it since moving out of Chicago.

I haven't gone back home since moving and I haven't really checked up on people there. Viola hasn't been as responsive as I'd like and I know she's been busy, but it's still disheartening.

My parents have always been supportive and we communicate through texts every so often, but I know they'd rather see me in person than stick to communication on the phone. I'm really hoping they can visit me soon or I can make a trip back home before the summer ends.

This gives me an idea and I peer my eyes at Bennett, who is staring out into the sea of people walking the streets of Broadway.

"Would you want to come home with me sometime?" I blurt out.

Bennett blinks a few times before turning his head towards me. I watch him for a moment, nervous at his poker face, but before I can say anything, his lips break out into a smile. His eyebrows raise.

"You want to bring me home?"

I nod my head. "You can meet my parents. My best friends. The whole shebang."

"I'd love to, Bunny. I've never been."

I smile harder. "You'd love it. It might be a little overwhelming at first, but we're not always going to be downtown. My parents live just far enough to be away from the tourist stuff downtown, but close to the lake and whatnot."

"Just tell me when and I'll drive us."

I widen my eyes. "You don't want to fly there?"

He shakes his head. "We've got a truck that drives well. Plus, I kind of like road-trips with you—you let me steal your snacks."

I lean my head back and laugh. "*Okay*, fine, we're driving. But only if I can pick the playlists."

"Deal," he says with a smile before bringing his glass bottle to his lips and taking another swig.

We finish our drinks, and he takes my can.

"Want another?" He asks and I nod.

"I'll save our spot," I tell him and he agrees before making his way towards the inside of the floor where there's a bar. I can barely see him from where I'm standing.

After taking a few deep breaths, I pull out my phone and look at my texts. I don't have many and there's a long paragraph from Parker about the vineyard, but it's mostly about what he did before closing. I send a thumbs up emoji before closing out of the text thread.

I open up the text thread with Birdy and decide to take a selfie with the Batman building behind me. Lifting the phone and turning on the camera, I snap a cute selfie and then send it to her with the text '*Wish you were here!*'. I hit send and then put my phone away. I look around the rooftop and see tons of people my age chatting it up with others and even some people relaxing on the patio furniture.

There's a guy who's dressed in skinny jeans and a button

down long sleeve with the sleeves rolled up and front buttons undone to show off his chest. He's making his way towards me and I widen my eyes.

He's got bright green eyes and unruly blonde hair that falls in front of his eyes. He looks too cocky for his own good. Once he closes the distance, he gives me a big smile.

"You look lonely," he says.

I shake my head. "Not that lonely."

He licks his lips before leaning against the railing. I peer up at him and try to back up to keep the distance. He smells like he's been drinking all day and there are beads of sweat along his forehead.

He's attempting to be flirty, but it's just appearing cocky and drunk. He gives me a smirk before leaning close.

"You're pretty too. Want to go dance with me?"

My brows pinch together, and I press my lips together before folding my arms over my chest.

"You're drunk."

"And you're fucking gorgeous—"

He doesn't finish his sentence as his eyes glance away from me and I turn to watch where he's looking. I smile and see Bennett striding over with another beer bottle and a seltzer can. He's furrowing his brows at the sight, and his jaw clenches.

I want to tell him that everything is okay, but then the blonde leans closer and reaches for my wrist. I pull away fast.

"Woah, I didn't say you could—" I say.

"I'd advise you to listen to her, buddy," Bennett says sternly as he finally reaches us. He's standing tall, and he's definitely more muscular than the blonde who tries to push himself from the railing to stand tall.

He's a lot shorter than Bennett, by maybe four or five inches. Bennett peers down at him and the guy still doesn't budge. The blonde looks at me before smirking again.

"Well, if you need me, baby, I'll be on the dance floor. I

promise to give you a better time than *this*," he points his hand towards Bennett before stalking off.

I'm trying to reach for my seltzer that's in Bennett's hand, but his grip on it is strong. Suddenly, it cracks and the can sprays everywhere.

I jump back and yelp from the cold liquid all over me. It's all over Bennett's shirt, but he doesn't care.

"What did you say?" He calls off after the blonde.

The blonde turns around and laughs, but before he can say a snarky comment back to Bennett, Bennett is reaching for the fabric of the guy's button down and pulling him close.

Bennett's wide shoulders are all I see from here, and I can't tell if Bennett is talking to him or not. He's still got his beer bottle in his other hand, and I'm afraid he'll bash the guy's head with it.

But he doesn't. I reach for his arm with the beer bottle and turn to see Bennett staring daggers into the guy.

"Bro, chill out. I was joking," the blonde says, attempting to get out of Bennett's grip. But Bennett doesn't budge.

"Bennett, he's drunk," I speak up.

"Doesn't make what he said okay. Or what he was doing with you, okay," Bennett says through gritted teeth. His jaw keeps clenching and his fist around the guy's top is tightening.

The blonde widens his eyes and shakes his head. "Fuck, I'm sorry. Okay? Let me go."

I pull Bennett's arm again and he looks at me with hesitation before sighing and letting the guy's top go.

"I'll be watching you," Bennett warns.

The blonde nods quickly before running back into the club portion of the bar. There's a few people milling around us watching, and then they return to their own conversations.

They looked like they wanted to see a fight. I've had my fair share of witnessing fights in clubs and they didn't end well. I didn't want to have Bennett be in one because of someone who was drunk and stupid.

"What a fucking—" Bennett says, but I yell at him.

"Hey! He's drunk!" I cut him off.

I pull him back towards the railing, but Bennett pulls his arm out of my grasp. I gasp and widen my eyes. He sighs and closes his eyes before opening them and looking up at the darkened sky.

"Someone's drunk behavior shouldn't get excused when it involves harassing a woman."

"I was fine and handling it," I spit out. The anger in me is boiling. It started with the blonde, but now I feel like it's getting directed at Bennett.

I don't want our night to be ruined, but Bennett sighs again and clenches his fists. I grab the beer bottle in his hand before he breaks that, too.

"I know you can handle that fucker. What I don't want to see happen is when he doesn't take no for an answer, Camilla."

I stiffen at the use of my name in that clipped tone. Like I'm being lectured. I press my lips into a thin line and I cast my eyes towards what's around us instead of him. The anger is getting to a point where I want to scream at him and leave, but there's no reason to make a scene.

I take a deep breath and try to compose myself. Bennett is breathing faster as I step closer.

"Bennett, I know you want to protect me. Trust me when I say I can handle things. I have for a while. I know how city boys get. Hell, I know how drunk guys get."

He shakes his head and sighs. "If I'm here, I will not let those kinds of things slide when I see it happen. You should know this by now."

I clench his shoulder with my free hand and I bite my lip to keep my composure from breaking down. From tears welling up in my eyes.

"Yeah, I know. I just—I handled that. I *was* handling that."

We're silent for a moment and all we can hear around us is the club music and chatter. I'm no longer in the dancing mood and I just want to go back to our place and cuddle on the couch and pass out.

I've forgotten how different it can be when you go out with your significant other than with your friend group. We all take care of each other, but we're still having fun. With Bennett, he's making it like it's his job to take care of me at all hours of the time when we're out.

I appreciate it, but I want to have fun with him as well. But it's not what's wired in his brain. He *loves* to protect the ones he loves, and I can't stop him from doing that.

I'm still learning a lot about him as each day goes by and vice versa. I can't stay mad at him for something that's so ingrained into his system.

And trying to see it from his side of things, we really don't know if the blonde guy would've taken it too far. If it got to a point where I wasn't able to handle the situation.

I sigh again and close our distance, leaning my forehead against his chest.

He's still stiffened, but slowly relaxes and I can feel his racing heart slowing. He wraps his arms around my waist and I breathe in his scent. I finally look up and he smiles softly, leaning to kiss my nose.

"Sorry, Bunny."

"It's okay," I breathe out. I look at him and smile. "Want to head back? I'm kind of over this place."

"Yes, please," he chuckles before we let each other go and we toss his beer out before heading out of the bar.

Once we get back to our place, it's quiet and we both shower and get into cozy pajamas before getting into the bed and cuddling close.

Although I had high energy earlier from the drinking and the ball game, all I want is Bennett's strong arms around me and his hand caressing my back as I ease into a sleepy state.

It's times like these where I appreciate him always waiting for me and never pressuring me into anything until I'm ready. Tonight took a turn, but I still want him by my side and who I sleep next to. Who I want to wake up to.

I never want to let him go and his soft touches and kisses are all I feel and remember before I drift off into a deep sleep.

THIRTY

BENNETT

THE MORNING IS slow and nice. We both wake up to the sound of birds chirping, but also the sound of cars driving on the road and some even honking.

It reminds me why I enjoy living on my farm and near no one else. Well, except for Bunny living next to me.

Speaking of Bunny, she's shifting in the bed and wrapping her arm around my naked torso under the bed sheets as we both wake up. I run my hands over her dark curls and then down her covered back. Her body shivers under the touch and she groans before she lifts her head from my chest.

Her brown eyes are tired, but she smiles and I can't help but smile back at her.

"Hey," I whisper to her and she smiles brighter.

"Morning, baby," she whispers back as she pushes herself off me and holds herself up by her arms.

The nickname makes me smile even harder to where my cheeks are hurting. I've never felt this in my cheeks, ever.

"What?" She giggles as she keeps her eyes on me.

I shrug. "I like it when you call me that."

She scrunches her nose before she laughs. "I'll say it more then."

Her body moves to get away from me to get up, but I'm not done being in the bed. And I can think of a few things we can do to prolong that wish of mine.

I quickly grab her wrist and pull her to me swiftly, causing her to yelp and giggle as she falls back onto my chest. I hold her close to me, wrapping my arms around her waist. She nuzzles her nose and face into my chest before looking up. She smiles and bites her lip.

"What are you looking at, pretty girl?" I ask her.

There's some rosy shade flowing through her cheeks and she giggles.

"I love you," she whispers.

My heart skips a bit as I hear her say that. It does that anytime she says that. Like my mind and body doesn't want to believe it and it's shocking that she's saying it to me and *meaning* it.

"I love you too," I tell her before pulling her up and closer to kiss her. She moans into the kiss, her curls falling over my face. She adjusts her body, so she's not haphazardly lying on the bed with her chest leaning on me.

She moves enough to straddle her legs over me and right by my belly button. She smiles through the kiss and rolls her hips back, pressing her ass into my growing boner. I hiss under my breath and kiss her even harder.

"Fuck," I breathe out and she giggles.

"Wanna?" She asks, rolling her hips back again and pressing her ass again against my boner. I'm thankfully wearing my boxers, but I want them off. Now.

I nod my head and she smiles before kissing me once more and then moving her hands down my chest, torso, and then to the waistband of my boxers. She has to move her body down in order to pull them down. I breathe out deeply as she pulls the boxers down to my knees and my cock springs free.

It's throbbing and I groan as she leans down, pressing her lips to my tip. I buck my hips up, breathing out loudly as she wraps her mouth around my tip and licking it *slowly*.

"Fuck, please," I beg her softly as she continues to lick the tip and then finally drags her tongue along my hardened length. I move my hands to hold her hair gingerly, but the moment she puts my entire length in her mouth I accidentally grip her hair.

She moans though and I apologize quickly. She doesn't stop to tell me I've hurt her—she continues to go down on me and I move my hips with her movement.

I can feel her other hand trace circles on my thighs before getting closer to my cock to caress my balls, but I know I won't be able to last that long. I pull her head up and she yelps from the immediate pull from her hair, but I need her on me *now*.

"Get on top of me, *now*," I tell her through gritted teeth, and she nods before wiping her mouth with the back of her hand and lifting her hands to the waistband of her pajamas, pulling them down, throwing them off the bed along with her panties. I removed the boxers that were still hanging near my knees.

She climbs back onto my waist and aligns herself to my tip. She presses herself down, both of us holding our breath and moaning once she's pushing herself onto me. I'm stretching her out, but it feels like fucking heaven the way she's still so tight for me.

I close my eyes and try to calm my breathing and my racing heart.

"You feel so good, baby," she moans as she clutches her shirt and I grab the fabric, pulling her close to me. I lift the fabric over her chest and she helps me remove it as she circles her hips.

I latch my lips onto her breasts and focus my mind there as she continues to moan and ride me. I'm getting closer and closer to coming, but I don't want to until she's ready to as well.

But with the way her moans are getting louder and more high pitched, more incomprehensible, I know she's close too.

Once I finish sucking on her other breast, I grab her hips and plant my heels on the bed to lift myself a bit and fuck her faster at a better pace. As much as I loved her slow motions, I need to fuck her harder than that.

She screams my name, and I drive my hips up into the air as she leans down and plants her palms on my chest. We're both breathing fast and moaning through the thrusts before she clutching my chest and closes her eyes.

I thrust into her a few more times before she screams that she's going to come and then I feel my release heighten and we're both coming while we slow our thrusts.

She shakes as I drive my hips one more time into her and she smiles before laying her entire body weight on me and nuzzling her head into the crook of my neck.

My hands are all over her bare skin, relishing on how warm she is. I draw circles and random objects on her arm before she lifts her head and kisses my nose before my lips. I smile and she does, too.

"Now, I'm ready to go back home."

My ears perk from the word she uses. *Home.*

"Me too," I say softly and she smiles widely.

BY THE TIME we get back to Alpine, it's past the afternoon and Bunny gets back to her vineyard after I drop her off. I offered to help unpack her things as she went to the vineyard to check in on what happened while she was gone, but she didn't want to burden me and made me go on with my day.

I took my time unpacking my own things and cleaning up the place before checking on the animals. Steve wasn't on the property when I got there, but he left a note on the white board next to the tally mark.

Fed the animals this morning and at noon. Come by the shop tonight, if you'd like.
Also, that tally mark is getting high. I'm proud of you.

My chest tightens as I read the last line on his note. I look at the tally that Bunny has been keeping up for me. I take the marker and use the eraser on the end to erase what she wrote before we left for our trip. I write the new number and set the marker back on top of the board.

I take a step back and cross my arms over my chest before nodding at the tallied up number so far. It's more than I ever thought I'd get. To be honest, I was ready to throw the white board out and not care what Oliver or Steve said with their bull-shit idea of marking happy days.

But now, I'm grateful they had this idea. It's nice to see how much I'm able to progress with just my morning moods. It's all because of Bunny and being able to really put myself out there.

A lingering feeling in my body makes my smile fade as I remember what else I have to do today. Because if I really want to be my honest self, I have to talk to Birdy and then Steve. It won't be easy, but it's needed.

Birdy and I said some harsh things that were way out of line. They were harbored feelings and thoughts that should've been resolved long ago. And with Steve, those were things I should've told him about. I wasn't honest with him and wanted to save him from the pain of the truth.

Birdy has a hard shell and can take my pain and my thoughts. Steve is softer and would've worried about me incessantly. I didn't want to burden him with that when I could resort to telling

Birdy the whole truth about everything. Giving Steve bits and pieces of the truth worked out perfectly until the night of the Fourth.

The way he looked so hurt once he found out that I kept a ton of things from him… I don't ever want to see that expression on his face again. I know talking to him will be the hardest. Birdy and I seem to patch things up pretty well whenever we clash.

And that's what I'm more worried about. That I've gone past his limit and he no longer wants to know me and casts me out as a friend. As a brother.

I try to distract myself as I get my things and make my way over to Birdy's. I made sure to take a detour when Bunny and I were driving back into town and drove past Birdy's shop to see if she was there. She wasn't, which meant she took today off and was home.

At least that's what I'm hoping as I get into my truck and find my way to her property. It's quiet as I park my truck on her driveway and make my way to her door. I knock a few times and wait. It's even more quiet as I wait, waiting to see if I can hear any movement.

At first, I think she's not home. But her car is in the driveway. Then I hear some footsteps and then the door opening. She's smiling, and then it fades as she takes in my presence.

"What are you doing here?"

I give her a half smile before stuffing my hands in my pant pockets. "Just wanted to come by and talk."

She breathes heavily before looking out around me and then shrugging. "I guess you can. Don't know what we have to talk about."

Her haughty demeanor isn't uncalled for as I nod and make my way into her home. There's soft music drifting through the kitchen as we get closer, and I take a seat at the kitchen table. She goes back to working on a cake that she's mixing icing for in an enormous glass bowl. She's got an apron on and her short hair is clipped back, but some of her bangs are escaping the hold and falling to her face.

"Talk," she says as she wraps her hand around the metal whisk handle and starts turning it into the bowl. She keeps her green eyes on me.

It feels intimidating, and I want to walk out and get out of here. But I stay in my seat and lean back into it and lift my leg to drape over my knee. She watches me slowly.

"I wanted to come and apologize about that night."

She huffs out, and a laugh follows. "You wanted to apologize?"

I nod.

"Wow, never thought Bennett Moore had the guts and the *respect* to apologize first."

Her words are sharp and cut like a knife.

"That's understandable," I tell her through gritted teeth. I want to say more, but I want to maintain a civil conversation. She knows I can just storm out of here, but I'm determined to stay.

She watches me again and shakes her head, laughing. "And you want to apologize *for what*?"

I cross my arms over my chest and stare her down as she stares me down. I'm not about to have her win a staring contest, if that's what she's fucking doing right now. Bennett Moore never loses a competition.

Her brows furrow as she continues her stare.

"I wanted to apologize for being an ass. I shouldn't have gotten between you and Steve that night." My mouth stays open as I want to say more, but I don't want to push her.

Because we were both wrong that night. I shouldn't have involved myself in their shit, but she shouldn't have said what she did to piss me off.

Not in that way, at least. There could've been an easier and more respectable way we could've had that conversation. The three of us.

She watches me before she finally breaks and blinks. She stares down at the glass bowl of white frosting before picking up a small vial of food coloring and squeezing a few drops in. The frosting becomes jade green when she mixes it.

"I'm sorry, too, for making it known that Steve didn't know as much as I did. But you hurt me. You made me feel like you just forgot about our history. You knew me first and then the way you called it out, made it seem like Steve was the one that meant the most to you. Just flushed our history down the drain."

I nod. "I get that. I knew you first, and that's why you know more than Steve. You always did and always will. I just can't go that deep with Steve, you know that."

She finally looks up and smiles. "Yeah, he'd probably seek therapy not just for you, but for himself as well. I had nightmares the first few times you told me things that happened while you were deployed or on a contract mission. You went through a lot of shit that no one knows about."

I laugh at her comment about Steve and lean my head back and stare at her ceiling before looking back at her. "I fucked up, Birdy. I hope you know how sorry I am. I didn't mean for that shit to happen and I shouldn't have told you to fuck off."

She shrugs and stops mixing and rubs her hands against her apron before making her way to the table and pulling out the chair diagonal from me. Her elbows plant on top of the table and she leans an arm down, palm flat against the table.

I undo my crossed arm and lean over, wrapping a hand around hers. They're cold and have dried frosting over some of her fingers. She most likely has been stress baking for days now. Weeks, even.

She does that when big things happen. And this was a big event that happened to the both of us.

"You're such a dick, Bennett Moore," she breathes out, with tears brimming her eyes.

I gulp and nod my head, squeezing her hand in mine. "You don't know how sorry I am for that. I promise you, I'm trying."

She lifts her eyes to look at me before she sniffles and then nods slowly. "I know you are and I can see it. Believe me, I can see it. We all can."

I give her a half smile before releasing her hand and leaning back into my chair. She clenches her hand into a fist and takes a few deep breaths before wiping her eyes.

"I talked to Steve," she blurts out. I look at her and wait for her to continue. She sighs. "Told him that if he doesn't want to be together, then I'm done."

My brows raise. "And what did he say?"

She rolls her eyes and laughs. "He got scared and asked me a million questions and wondered what he was doing wrong."

"That's Steve for you," I tell her.

She nods. "That's when I told him if he didn't answer me by being official and being my boyfriend, that he had to leave... Guess what he did?"

"Fall to his knees and beg you to let him stay?" I joke.

She laughs and nods her head. "Something like that. Anyway, now we're official and I guess there's that."

I watch her for a moment as I see her eyes scan the table and then her hands. She's thinking and I can't tell what she might be thinking about. Doubts? About Steve?

"What's up, Bee?" I ask.

She looks up and shrugs. "It just doesn't feel... any different?"

"How so?"

"Like we're still best friends and we're still continuing to do what we've been doing forever."

I nod. "I'll talk to him. He's Steve—he's a clueless puppy and really just goes with the flow. He doesn't really care about much, but he cares about you. Just doesn't know how to express it sometimes. He'd rather you make the moves, so he knows you feel the same way. It's his own worries and doubts that make him that way."

She nods and sighs again. "I think I'm just worried I'll have to do that forever, ya know?"

"I do," I tell her. "But you need to tell him this. I'll try to talk to him about it as well."

She nods and scrapes her chair back as she stands up. I follow suit and stand up as well, and I pull her into a hug. She gasps from the random action.

"She really changed you, huh?" Birdy whispers as I hug her tighter.

I nod and breathe out loudly. "Yeah, she's amazing. I'm glad I met her."

We pull away and Birdy smiles widely. "I can't believe I'm saying this, but you no longer look like the grump we all got used to. You're becoming the Bennett *I* knew all those years ago. Before Katherine."

I smile at her words and nod. "I'm just relieved that Bunny was okay hearing everything about *that*."

"You've got to give her more credit than you do," Birdy says. "She's very understanding and just wants the best for everyone."

I nod and take a step back, ready to leave.

"Talk to Steve and I'll see you later?" Birdy asks as she heads back to the kitchen counter and grabs the whisk.

I nod and give her a small wave. "Definitely."

I make my way out of her house and back into my truck, immediately driving off towards my other best friend. Steve's shop is closing and I see a few of his workers leave.

I make my way into the lobby of his place and down the hall towards his office. He's not in there, so I make my way back to the front where the shop is. I find him in a small crevice of the shop where no other workers are.

He's sitting on a stool and leaning over his motorcycle and his hands are dirty with oil as he wipes them on a dirty rag. He looks up as I clear my throat.

His blue eyes find mine before he huffs out a breath and then goes back to working on his bike. I linger there for a moment before I search around me and find another stool and move it towards him and plop down.

"You finally came," he says in a monotone voice.

I raise a brow and chuckle. "You left me a love note on my kitchen fridge telling me to come today."

There's a hint of a smile that spreads over his lips as he finishes wiping the rag over a portion of his bike and then looks at me. His brow has a grease stain on it and he looks tanner than the last time I saw him. He must be working in the shop all day and bringing the cars out into the sun.

He tends to do that when he's got a lot to think about and needs the peace and quiet from the workers in the shop.

"It wasn't a love note, but I'm glad it made you feel special."

I laugh. "Yeah, it did. I missed you, Steve. I just saw Birdy."

His brows perk up and he smirks. "Yeah? Did she yell at you?"

"Actually, no," I mutter. Steve then smiles and laughs.

"That's surprising. You were a dick."

"I know, I know. But we hashed it out. I wanted to talk to you and apologize."

Steve is quiet for a moment before he wipes his hands again on the rag and places it across his lap. His shirt is dirty too as he pulls the fabric at the collar and starts fanning himself with it. The shop isn't hot, but I can't imagine how hot it can get with all the shop doors open on a sunny day.

"Go on," he breathes out.

I nod and take a deep breath. "I shouldn't have involved myself in what happened with you and Birdy. I didn't mean for it to go that way. I didn't think my words were going to be taken that way and I shouldn't have said those things to her."

Steve is silent, so I continue. "And I definitely shouldn't have kept those kinds of secrets from you. I just didn't want to hurt you."

Steve looks at me with confusion plastered on his face. "You didn't want to hurt me, yet you told her about everything. You just told me what you wanted me to hear."

I shake my head. "I know you, Steve. You're a fun guy and don't need to know the shit I really went through. I spared you the gory and depressing details."

"Then how would I have known to be a better friend for you?"

He's even more confused now and I can see his breathing pick up and I can already tell he's getting pissed. I scoot my stool closer and I place my hand on his shoulder.

"Steve, believe me. You've been my best friend this whole time. I told Birdy the details of those kinds of things in my life because she can take it. She knew the right words to say. She's not soft-spoken. She'd tell me what I did wrong in an instant and knew that *she* could handle what I told her. You're not like that Steve. And I'm not trying to insult you. You're the *best* friend I could have and in your own way. I don't want to ruin your life by telling you the things I've had to do and what I went through just for you to be included in that. It's not fair."

He's still quiet, but he nods slowly.

"Please know, Steve... I didn't mean harm by any of it. I still have nightmares about a lot of the shit that happened. That whole whiteboard joke? It was real for me. There was really *no way* for my mind to settle, to wake up happy. To wake up on the right side of the bed. I still have my days and I still can't bear to look in the mirror and face the real me. And I couldn't face you and Oliver and tell you the truth about it, so I went along with it. You guys thought most of my grumpy personality came from the divorce, but it was much more than that."

Steve finally looks at me and his eyes avert to my collarbone where my scar is hidden by my shirt. His gaze sits there for a while and I know he's thinking about the real reason how I got it. Birdy is the only one who knows what really happened. She cried in my arms when I told her about it. But then she could be strong—not just for herself, but for me as well.

Us veterans need those kinds of people in our lives that we can bare our souls and hearts to about those things that make us feel less human. She made me feel an ounce more human that night by telling me it wasn't my fault and I had to do what I had to do to survive. But she also *understood* my own thoughts about it. About everything.

Steve wouldn't have been able to say any of that. He would've probably thrown up and then left to wallow in his emotions. I needed someone strong to hold me up and Birdy was that person for me.

"I guess it bothered me finally realizing that she was getting way more information than me. It made me feel left out," Steve breathes out.

I shake my head and squeeze his shoulder. "You'll never be left out, Steve. Trust me. We love you so much and I've just known Birdy long enough that she was the only one I could confide in about those kinds of things."

"I get it, I do," Steve murmurs. "I'd just like to at least know a little more."

"Without the puke-worthy details though," I joke.

"Yes, please," Steve laughs.

My heart thuds against my chest as I watch my best friend smile warmly at me. I've missed him and I'm glad we're able to talk about it.

"Want to go bother Birdy later tonight? I saw her making a

cake. We can sneak a bite in and she won't notice until she needs it tomorrow."

Steve barks out a laugh and nods. "She'll kill us, but she's been baking every day. She'll just make another cake in record time."

I laugh along with him. "She also told me how she made it official with you? Congrats, man."

Steve smiles sheepishly and shrugs. "Thanks, man. She makes me nervous. I thought she'd really end things. I just don't know how to work relationships and I really like her. I don't want to mess things up."

"Just be honest with her. She'll understand, trust me."

Steve smiles and nods. "You're right. Thanks, bud."

I nod and give him a smile.

It feels like a weight has been lifted off my chest. It's still surprising to me that I was able to patch things up with my two best friends. I was worried that they'd never forgive me and leave me in the dirt. Rightfully so, but I didn't want that to happen. I wanted to fix it and I did.

What I thought was impossible became possible and I'm more shocked than Birdy and Steve. I really am changing for the better.

And I like this Bennett. I really do.

EPILOGUE

CAMILLA

IT'S the middle of August and Bennett is dancing in the kitchen with Goose wrapped up in his arms.

She's purring loudly and blinking her eyes slowly at him. I laugh and smile at the sight. I'm in love with them and I can't contain it.

I lift myself off from the stool and head to him where he's dancing, and I wrap my arms around his back. He chuckles and continues his dance and even hums along with the music that's playing on the speakers in the house.

"I love you," I tell him, rubbing my face against his strong back. My arms go to caress Goose and she chirps before continuing her purring in Bennett's arms.

"I love you more," Bennett says in front of me. We continue to dance like this until the song is over and then he sets Goose down. She runs off into the living room and Bennett turns around and wraps his arms around me, picking me up and spinning us around.

I squeal and giggle as he spins faster before stopping. I kiss him and he moans into it.

"I could kiss you forever."

"Oh?" I whisper as we plant ourselves on our heels and he leans his head to touch foreheads together. I breathe in his scent as I close my eyes.

"Mhm," he murmurs.

"Me too," I tell him, adjusting my hands to find his at his side and linking our fingers together.

"Want to get wings?" He says randomly as I open my eyes.

I laugh. "Sure, I could use some fried pickles."

"And wings," he reminds me.

"And wings," I repeat after him and he smiles before leaning back to separate our bodies.

He watches me before biting his lip. I shake my head. "Don't you dare look at me like that or we won't ever leave."

His brow raises. "Is that a dare?"

I shake my head. "No! I want fried pickles now, and you can't go back on your word."

He groans as he hangs his head back. "*Fiinnneeeeee*, we'll go to Nicky's. But I'm going to have my way with you tonight."

I giggle and step back, heading towards the counter where my purse is. "Fine by me, Bennett."

He smiles and claps his hands before he waits for me to make my way back to him and he grabs my hands and we walk out of the house.

The land next to us is looking really nice and we've started cleaning up the area before we decided when we wanted to hire the builders I found for the foundation of the home. We finally settled on the idea that we'd like it to be a home for Morgan when she stays when she's older. Then if she wants to live in Alpine Ridge permanently, then she can stay there.

We haven't told her yet and we plan to do it next weekend when we go to visit them. Peyton insisted on me joining Bennett's trip to them, and I couldn't help but jump in place while Bennett was on the phone. I'm excited that Morgan is letting me into her life—I know how important she is to

Bennett and now she's become that much more important to me as well.

"Ready?" Bennett asks as we get into his truck and buckle in. I nod my head and bite my lip as he leans his hand over and places it over my bare thigh. He starts the truck and heads off my property.

Once we're in the main part of town and find a parking spot, I completely forget that it's karaoke night at Nicky's and we're a little early as they're still setting up while we enter.

We see Izzy serving a table and she waves at us. We make our way into the bar and find a big round table. I raise a brow at Bennett, who's leading us, and he grins enthusiastically.

"I texted Birdy and Steve to come over for karaoke night."

"So this wasn't as spontaneous as I thought?" I laugh.

He shakes his head and pulls out a chair for me. I thank him before he slides me closer to the table. He takes a seat next to me and places his arm over the back of my chair.

"And Mabel and Parker," he adds.

I gasp and that's when I turn towards the door and see a few people walk in. Birdy and Steve are holding hands as they enter and I smile widely, jumping out of my chair. I push past the other vacant chairs in my way and hug Birdy. She laughs and hugs me back tightly.

"I couldn't miss karaoke night!"

"You didn't miss me?" I laugh. She nods and hugs me tighter.

Steve gives me a small hug once Birdy and I separate, and then I look behind him. Mabel and Parker are walking inside as well, and Parker is taking her jacket off and draping it over his arm. They find my gaze and Mabel's smile widens across her face.

"Hi!" I wave to them and let Steve and Birdy make their way to the table as I find my way to Parker and Mabel.

"Hi, Miss Camilla, I hope this was okay for us to join?"

Parker asks with a raised brow. I dismiss him with a wave of my hand and nod.

"Of course! I missed everyone being together. We've all been so busy. I'm glad we can have tonight."

"I'm going to pick the best song," Mabel tells Parker before kissing his cheek and then waving us bye as she makes her way to the machine near the stage.

Parker's cheeks are pink as he watches his girlfriend from a distance.

"Parker, you guys are my favorite," I gush.

He smiles brightly. "Thanks, Miss Camilla. She's great. I'll miss her when she leaves for college next week."

His eyes go sad and I pull him for a hug. "You'll see her soon enough! Just try to cherish this time with her, okay?"

He nods and then we break off. We head to the table and we take our seat as Mabel finds her way back to the table as well.

"The crew is back!" Izzy screams as she nears our table and hands out menus.

We all laugh and greet her as she takes our drink orders. When she reaches me, she wraps her arms around me from behind and kisses the top of my head.

"And I've missed you the most, Camilla."

I wrap my hands over her arms and squeeze hard. "I've missed you too! We need to hang out more."

She leans her head over to the right side of my face, and I turn to see her eyes flicker with delight. "I would love that. You better text me!"

I nod at her, and she releases her hold on me and finishes taking our orders. I look around the table and Bennett goes back to wrapping his arm around the back of my chair. I scoot my chair closer to him and lean my head on his shoulder.

I look across the table and observe Birdy and Steve. They seem better since I saw them after Bennett and I were back from Nashville. She told me how she could patch things up with Steve and with Bennett. But Bennett told me about that the moment he got home that night.

We've been spending way more nights together and started picking out who's house to stay at a couple of nights at a time. There isn't a singular *home* for us. It's just wherever we are together.

Birdy is watching Steve and leaning against his body as well, lifting her hand to brush through his growing hair. He's growing out his beard too, and he's looking even more handsome than he normally does.

They make such a cute couple and I continue to beam at them before Birdy catches my gaze and gives me a huge grin.

"All right, we need to know…" Parker speaks up. We all look at him, waiting.

He raises a brow. "Is Bennett going to finally sing a song?"

We all turn to look at Bennett, and he chuckles nervously before looking down at me.

"What do you say, partner?"

I smile and nod. "Of course. Always."

He leans his head to kiss my forehead and Parker claps his hands before we all go back into other topics to discuss. A lot of it is about how the summer has been for us. We're nearing the end of it and we all want to make the best of it.

Birdy is planning another cookout to end the summer and to have a get together before Mabel leaves Alpine for college. She almost teared up at that announcement and thanked all of us for being so supportive of her dreams, and even Parker got a little teary.

I constantly looked around the table and couldn't help but smile with glee. My chest is tight from the feeling of knowing I found my place here in this town. I've found someone who really loves me. I've been able to open my heart to him and be there for him when he needed it the most.

I found a town that really feels like family. I never want to leave and I know this is my forever. Alpine Ridge is my home and I've never felt prouder to think and say that.

I look at Bennett again and I kiss his jaw before he looks down and gives me a soft smile.

"I love you," I whisper to him. He watches my eyes for a moment before kissing me and moving his lips to my ear.

"I love you more, Camilla Morales."

We kiss again as Izzy comes back with our drinks and then gets our dinner orders. The karaoke starts once we get our food and we stay there until closing time.

It's perfect, like everything else about my life once I opened the map on my phone and pointed my finger at this small town months ago.

THE END

COMING SOON TO ALPINE RIDGE

Untitled

Birdy and Steve

ALSO BY GRACE ELENA

Snowed Inn

(Co-written with Jenni Brady)

THANK YOU

I have to begin my list of thanking people with you, the reader. Thank you for giving my debut a chance. I've loved to write ever since I was a little girl and to *finally* publish a debut novel brings an insurmountable feeling to my soul.

To my promotional team, thank you for supporting every post on social media. An author can only do so much, but it's *your* excitement for my book that helped gain traction. I can't do this without you.

To my beta readers, thank you for helping me get this rough draft of a novel into better shape. Your feedback has only shaped me into a better writer.

To my editor Kayla, thank you for taking on my debut novel. It's a scary thing to give someone something so special, but you've helped so much and I can't wait to continue working with you!

To my dear friends Emily and Shelby who were here since the beginning of this novel's creation... thank you times a million. Your feedback on ideas, plot points, and even offering suggestions has made this novel be as great as it is. You guys are the reason I was able to continue writing this novel when I wanted to give up. You guys were here since the beginning and I can't thank you enough for sticking by me.

To Jenni, my first author friend. You gave my writing a chance and I'm so glad we're close friends now and even co-authors. I wouldn't want to do this author thing with anyone else. I hope you know how invaluable you have been in my life and I can't wait for the day we're able to finally meet in person instead of FaceTime and voice messages.

To Bianca, mi reina. You've supported my writing for what feels like forever. You've become a great friend and I can't thank you enough for being that person that I can bounce ideas off of to know if it's worth writing. You've even helped me create this universe name as well as other novel titles. Your creative mind doesn't go unnoticed and I'm thankful for you.

To Lindsey, thank you for your never-ending support and excitement for this world I created. To have someone visit a place in Nashville, TN just because I mentioned it in my novel is something I can't wrap my head around. You've become a great friend, but you've also been a supportive reader and I will always be grateful.

To Emily and Kelsey, thank you for just being here. Telling friends I've made in my adult life that I like to write cheesy romance novels isn't always easy. You guys had no hesitation and have been supportive since. Can't wait for our next movie night.

To my parents, thank you for the constant support even if this was such a far-fetched idea. Thank you for financially supporting my book addiction as a kid. I wouldn't be here without all those books I was able to devour from Barnes & Noble. Thank you for believing in my passion for writing. For even helping me write that story in 3rd grade that won a contest. That is a memory I will never forget. Y gracias mamá por todo lo que has hecho por mí. Tu fuerza es inspiradora. Todo sobre ti es inspirador. Te amo.

To my childhood friends Adna, Jed, Karla, Nedim, and Sandy. Most of you know about my Tumblr days and even wrote with me. Thank you for just being there and supporting me. We might not live in the same state anymore, but I can't thank you guys enough for being there for me now and especially being there for younger Grace. She needed it.

To Milo, I hope you're proud of me. I think about you

everyday and I wish you were here to celebrate this moment with me.

To my Wattpad community, thank you for supporting my writing. I was a scared writer who didn't believe in my works. We all start somewhere and I'm glad I was able to truly grow as a writer within Wattpad. I'll always cherish those times and friendships I've gained from it.

And finally, I have to thank my other half, P. I've said it once and I'll say it again, you are the blueprint. You've given me the love that I've dreamt of as a little girl who stuffed her nose in romance novels. Your love has given me the ability to write it on paper and actually believe it. I'm a hopeless romantic and you've exceeded all expectations.

ABOUT THE AUTHOR

Grace Elena is a Mexican American author who loves to write slow burn romances with strong Latinx leads. She's been writing since she could remember and even dabbled in some songwriting during her college years. When Grace isn't writing, she's spending time with her partner and cat in Nashville, Tennessee.

Visit her website at graceelenaauthor.com or you can keep up with her on Instagram @graceelenaauthor.

If you'd like to have more insight to her books before anyone else, join her Private Facebook Group "Grace Elena's Vineyard".

Made in United States
Orlando, FL
06 August 2023

35776229R00243